# CHAMBERED

## Six stories revolving around a single revolver.

Edited by Wofford Lee Jones

Novellas written by

Wofford Lee Jones
D.A. Schneider
N.J. Gallegos
Marie Matter
Evan Bond
Elaine Pascale

CHAMBERED

# TABLE OF CONTENTS

# BEHIND THE GLASS

## WOFFORD LEE JONES

*Wofford's Dedication:*

*For Laurie…*
*always for Laurie*

# CHAPTER ONE

**JILL DANFORTH AWOKE** to an unfamiliar sound in the house. She lay there in the stillness of the darkened bedroom, listening intently, sleep zapped from her body. Something had roused her, but she couldn't pinpoint what it was exactly.

All was silent now. Figuring it was merely her imagination, she relaxed, letting her mind drift off. She was close to sleep again when the barely audible sound reached her ears.

Whispering.

Her eyes popped wide again, more startled than outright afraid. She lay frozen under the light sheet, fearful anything other than merely opening her eyes would cause whoever was whispering in the room to turn and focus on her.

The whispering grew a little louder, and she realized it was coming from her husband, Craig, lying on his back next to her.

*Is he talking to me?*

Some of the panic dissipated from her body, seeing that there was no intruder in their room, so she quietly turned her head and whispered back, "What?"

He said nothing. He didn't even turn her way.

Her brows creased in concern. From the hint of blue-tinged light coming from the neon numerals of the bedside clock, she saw his eyes were still closed. She leaned in closer, waiting for him to whisper again.

She smiled. *Oh, man, I am going to give him hell about this tomorrow morning.*

"Where the fu… ya think… you're goin'?" Craig whispered in a sleep slur. It was still soft but a little louder than before; Jill heard his words clearly. The comment wiped the smile from her face. The tone, even in that whisper, wasn't Craig.

"Don'tcha *ever*… run from me… again." It was a slight monotone, and even though it was sleep-induced, it was a threat to whomever he was speaking to.

Wide-eyed now, Jill slowly slid back to her original position. *What the hell is Craig talking about? Who is he talking to? What kind of dream is he having?*

Still looking at him, watching his lips speak phantom words, she thought for a second. She turned away from Craig, careful not to make too much movement and bring him further into wakefulness.

She eyed the distance to her cell phone sitting next to her on the nightstand. It was always within arm's reach. All she had to do was stretch and pick it up. Moving her hand out from under the sheets, she found that it was only fingertips away.

*Fuck,* she mouthed to herself.

She inched closer to it with minimal movement of the bed. Her fingernails grasped the edge of the cover, and she pulled it closer to her. Pinching the top part of the phone between her thumb and her forefinger, she pulled it toward herself. She almost dropped it when the phone went taut in her hand, the cord still plugged into the bottom of it to charge while she slept.

Jill closed her eyes in relief, thankful she hadn't dropped her phone to the bedroom floor. No doubt the loud *thump* would've been enough to rouse Craig from his slumber. She pulled it again, and the cord slid free, dropping softly to the carpet.

She glanced at her husband again, still asleep beside her, his head facing the ceiling and his hands crossed over his upper torso.

Craig whispered again, "Did I not say you'd pay… the consequences… if you ran from me?" A slight chuckle that turned into the light rattle of a snore.

Jill turned back to her phone, which she'd covered with the sheets. She pulled it up to her face and scrolled to the Voice Memos app. She tapped it, and it opened. She immediately hit the red button, desperate to catch everything Craig said.

It started recording. She held the microphone end toward Craig but made sure the phone's glare didn't hit him in the face. She didn't want it to wake him and have him discover she was recording him. Not with what she was trying to capture.

"Pick one, Anna," Craig instructed. "Either Mommy or Daddy. Which one will it be?"

*Anna? Who's Anna?*

The panic of the moment was making her nervous. Her heartbeat had ramped up. She wanted to shake her husband's shoulder and wake him up, tell him he was snoring, anything to stop this nonsense, but she stayed frozen where she lay.

"Oh... wow! You chose *Mommy*? I don't see how... you could choose between the two. Daddy it is." Craig's arm rose slowly above the covers, his finger turning into a gun.

"Blam!" Craig said in an elevated whisper. His hand lowered back to his chest and lay still.

Jill lay there mortified. *What the hell is he dreaming about? Is it possible... no, I won't go there.*

"Oh, shit! Did I just shoot... Mommy?" Craig whispered again. "I couldn't see who was who in this darkness... guess Daddy's gonna have to go bye-bye, too, now, huh?"

Craig's hand returned to the air again, turning once more into a finger gun. There was a moment when his arm was just held there limply, pointed to the ceiling. Then, his wrist bucked as though from the recoil of a real handgun. On that action, Craig whispered, "Blam!" His hand collapsed to his chest again as though holding a heavy dumbbell.

Jill even felt the weight of it as it shook the bed slightly.

Craig turned over in the bed toward Jill, and as he did so, he whispered, "You're not going to need them... where you're going."

Jill glanced at Craig again. She was wide-eyed with terror. That was some dream he was having. She looked at her phone screen to make sure she was still recording.

*Was it a dream?* she wondered. *Maybe dreaming he was telling someone a story? Was he—reliving something? No, surely not. There is no way. Had to be a crazy dream.*

"What are you doing?" Craig asked in a low, sleepy voice.

Jill was about to turn the phone his way to get more of his continuous rambling, but something about his voice rang differently now. She turned to look at him.

Craig was staring directly at her, squinting a little in the light coming from her phone. He was now awake.

"Oh, hey, honey," she said as her body filled with a sudden, dreaded panic.

"What time is it? Why are you looking at your phone?"

She punched the red button again to stop the recording and exited the app. Seeing the time, she told him, "I couldn't sleep, so I'm just doom-scrolling social media until I get sleepy again."

"Oh." He was quiet for a moment, but that simple word was filled with something more than a satisfied answer.

*Is he thinking about something? Did he go back to sleep?* She didn't dare look.

"Well, put that phone out. It's kinda bright. It woke me up."

"Okay," she said, but didn't obey. *It wasn't me scrolling on my phone that woke you,* she thought as she dimmed the brightness a touch more.

He was quiet again.

Jill tapped the Facebook app and began scrolling through posts to make it look like she'd been doing this all along.

"Hey, babe?" Craig asked.

Jill's hair stood on end as gooseflesh prickled her scalp. "Yeah." She didn't look away from her screen. She didn't want him to see the fear in her eyes.

"Was I... talking in my sleep?"

"What?" It came out more as a surprise that she was being asked that question than a reaction to a question that she didn't fully hear.

"I feel like I was talking to myself. Or talking in my sleep. I wasn't saying anything, was I?"

Jill decided to play it off. She chuckled as best she could at his comment. "Uh, no. No talking, but you were sawing some damn heavy logs." That phrase came from her mother, who passed seven years ago; she'd said it often.

"Oh. Okay. That's weird."

"*You're* talking weird. Go back to sleep, dear."

"Okay." He turned away from her in the bed—something she was secretly grateful for—and pulled the sheet over his face. "I'm turning this way, so your damn cell phone won't keep me awake."

"Yeah, you rest. I'll be along shortly as soon as sleep comes to me."

Craig was already snoring lightly as he drifted away to dreamland again.

It was much longer into the night before sleep came for Jill Danforth.

# CHAPTER TWO

**THE NEXT MORNING,** Jill awoke to an empty bed. Craig was already up.

She was relieved and thankful for a few moments to herself as the odd reality of last night possessed her mind again. She sat up in bed, sleep instantly gone from her body.

*Has he already left for work? He does have that major job they're working on.*

Then the distant sound of a utensil scraping across a pan hit her ears as the slight smell of bacon drifted by her nose.

"Damn it," Jill whispered to herself. She didn't know why she was so keyed up. Something was wrong with what she recorded him saying last night. He had never talked in his sleep, much less said anything like that.

It was disturbing imagery; there had to be a logical explanation for it, but deep down, Jill had a feeling there wasn't. Right now, the less time she spent around Craig, the better. At least until she figured out what was going on.

*I need some time to think about this. What better time than on a run?*

She slid out of bed, anxious to be out of the house in the morning air, where she could clear her mind. She quietly moved to the bureau and opened the bottom drawer, then snagged out one of her sports bras and matching leggings. They had been tucked away for a long time. She grabbed her running shoes from the back of the closet and slipped them on. She'd missed those runs, but with what had happened, she had just stopped cold turkey.

*Maybe it's time to start back.*

She grabbed her phone and earbuds case, then moved to the hallway and down the stairs as quietly as possible. At the bottom step, Jill swiped at her face and took a few deep breaths to psych herself up for the acting debut she would have to do when facing Craig. And maybe this wasn't as big a deal as she was making it out to be. She struggled to anticipate Craig's reaction, but she was about to find out.

She stepped from the carpet of the living room onto the hardwoods of the kitchen. "Morning, hon," she said in a cheery voice.

"Hey, babe. Oh, wow, look at you. Always loved that outfit."

She turned and smiled at him as she struck an athletic pose.

"You going for a run?"

"Yeah, I thought about it."

"Hey, that's great! It's been a long time since you've run."

"And because it's been so long, it will be more of a walk with intermittent bouts of jogging. Gotta get back accustomed to it. I just miss it, you know. I think the sunshine will do me some good."

"Oh, sure-sure. What brought this on?"

"I don't know. I was missing Haley this morning and thought I'd take a walk up to the cemetery and sit with her for a while."

"Honey." A caring chastisement.

"I'm okay," Jill lied, putting her hands up to stop any judgmental lectures. "This is just the way I'm still dealing with it. You know me and my alone time."

"I know. I just want to fix what's broken inside."

She shook her head. "You can't." Straight to the point. "It's just something that will heal in time if she comes home." She thought momentarily, then corrected her comment. "*When* she comes home."

"Yeah, I know," Craig said. He moved toward her. "Come here." He held his hands wide and ushered her to him.

She hesitated, not wanting to be that close to him. Not now, not after what she'd witnessed last night. But she knew if she didn't go to him, it would cause friction between them, so she moved into his caring bear hug.

Craig's hugs were always so all-encompassing. They were a huge comfort for her—they always felt like home. They did nothing for her this morning. She needed to get away from him.

"Has Medlin called you… about Haley's case?"

"No," she said, shaking her head against his chest. "I would've told you if he had."

"I know. I was just checking. If he had, it could've just slipped your mind. Thought that might be why you're headed to the cemetery."

"No. I just need to be near some semblance of her." Jill hugged him tight, then wiggled free of his arms. "Craig, if I don't go now, I'll start crying, and I don't want to cry today."

"I don't want that either." He grabbed her shoulders and looked her in the eyes. "I just want to help you heal."

"I know. I'm going to be okay. I just need to spend some time with her today before work."

"Why don't you take the day off? Rest here at the house. Take your mind off things. Don't do anything. That would make you feel good. It would make me feel better if you did."

"I may do that. But idle time could make it worse. I need to keep busy, or I'll dwell on her all day. I'll keep it in mind. Depends on how the run up to see Haley goes."

"Sure. Will you give her my best when you get there?"

"Of course. I always do, you know. She loved you so much. *Loves* you so much."

A pained look crossed his face. Haley's disappearance had been harrowing for them both and still was. "I know she does. I'm crazy about her, too. Stay safe, okay?"

"I will. Don't work too hard on your big project today out at the site."

"I won't. Or at least try not to, anyway."

They shared a courtesy laugh, and then Jill turned and moved out the side door and up the drive. She forced herself not to bolt away from the house, which was what her body was screaming for her to do. It was all she could do not to, with her body being on edge. That would've looked strangely suspicious if Craig were looking out the window, watching her leave.

Once their house was no longer in view, she bolted and ran wild and free.

# CHAPTER THREE

**FOR A TIME,** Jill just ran. There was nothing threatening on her heels, yet she ran as if there were.

She fell into the familiar rhythm she had adopted over her years of running. She kept her body in the most upright position, with her shoulders back, chest up, open, and expanded for new oxygen, allowing her arms to pump in a natural movement with her body. She took air in on an even four-count, matching each step, exhaling evenly on a four-count, and repeating: breathe in on four, breathe out on four.

There were many times when she'd been driving around town and seen runners with incorrect form. They would run with their upper body too far forward, where they were working too hard to keep up with their upper half. Others would force their bodies to run when it was clear they needed a breather. That caused them to run with their feet slapping down on the pavement, making them work extra hard to do the exercise.

When Jill saw these atrocious sights, she always wanted to yell out the window as she passed. "You're doing it wrong, fucker!"

She got lost in the natural rhythm again; that was when her thoughts started piling in on her.

*What am I going to do? What the hell was that all about last night? Did I really witness what I witnessed?* She had a sickening gut feeling that Craig had done something bad. That led to the question: *Who am I married to?*

Her conversation sidekick answered her. *You're married to Craig. You know him, Jill. You. Know. Him—*

*Do I really? What the hell was that? That wasn't normal. Nobody does that. Nobody acts out an executioner-style killing in their sleep if it didn't happen. Why was he doing that? Did that really happen at some time in his past? Was it recent? Or did it happen before we were married? If that was real, and I pray to God that it wasn't, who was on the receiving end of that muzzle flash? Who the hell is this Anna? Who did Craig kill in his dreams?*

*You mean, "in real life," don'tcha, Jill? And were those Anna's parents?*

Her mind drifted back to a few weeks ago—

*Or was that only days ago?*

—when Craig was cleaning his Smith and Wesson. Could that be the gun he used in his dream?

*In real life, Jill. He was reenacting a scene that had already happened. In. Real. Life.*

*No. I won't accept that. Can't accept that. That is not Craig. Sure, he loves guns. He has plenty of them. But he only has those things for our protection.*

*You know I'm right, Jill. You know it. Admit it.*

This thought abruptly stopped her. It was too much of a mental mess for her to continue dwelling on it.

Coming out of her headspace, she realized where she was. She wasn't too far from the cemetery. She'd burned a long trail across town, and now she was breathing big breaths of air.

Thinking back to the poor saps who had never learned to run correctly, breathing heavy from not breathing properly, she wondered if she had fallen into this bad form she'd seen in so many of them and mentally chastised herself for it.

She walked the rest of the way to the cemetery. She pushed all her tormented thoughts to the back of her mind to give it a break from the mental strain. She tried to enjoy the morning.

The day was sunny but not too hot. The air was cool. Occasional gusts of mid-September wind blew through the graveyard, scattering the few fallen leaves that had already touched down. The brisk gust felt good on her skin, chilling her slightly and cooling the sweat she'd worked up from her run.

She cut across the graveyard, reverently touching the taller tombstones as she made her way to Haley's site.

Jill stopped at the foot of Haley's grave, saying nothing at first. She took a moment in silent prayer, asking God to guide Haley back to them. It was the same prayer and constant plea she'd prayed for the last two years. And if Haley was no longer with them, she prayed that God would lead them to her body. If she were dead, Jill wanted Haley to be at rest, so they could finally have some semblance of peace in their life. It was hell not knowing what had happened to her.

Moving from the foot of the grave, Jill stepped to her right—the gravestone's left—and sat near Haley's tombstone. She placed a hand on the granite marker and said, "Hey Haley. It's Mom again. I still miss you. I wish you'd come back to us. Pleasepleaseplease… come back to me. And if you can't, I hope you soon find a way. We haven't stopped looking for you, beautiful."

Jill dropped her hand from the marker and let it move to a few of the leaves that had dropped to the grass there. It didn't really bother her that fallen leaves were on her daughter's grave; it was merely something to do as she figured out how to talk with her daughter about what had happened.

"So, something weird happened last night. Something so odd, I don't know how to explain it. Has Craig ever done something so…" She came up short, not knowing the correct word to use. "So… *unnatural* that you wonder if you really know that person at all?

She let the question sit. She glanced around the cemetery, suddenly fearful that Craig might've driven there to comfort her and was standing behind her now.

There was nothing but another cool breeze of wind that moved through the cemetery.

She turned back to the lettering on the grave marker. "What would you do if you saw your dad reenacting something from some other time in his life? It seemed like a reenactment to me, anyway."

She paused, glancing around the lot again, not so much in fear, but taking in the beauty and the comfort of this place. "It was so out of character for Craig, you know, from what *we* know him to be. It scared me."

A light bulb went on inside her mind.

"Oh, wait! I have it. I can play it for you."

She pulled her phone and rearranged herself to sit cross-legged. She silently prayed that the recording was there. She had a sinister feeling that it was all a crazy dream, or at least she'd heard it but had never hit the record button to capture the one-sided dialogue.

She breathed a sigh of relief. It was there, her phone automatically giving it the name of the street where they lived—Albercourt Lane.

Jill tapped the play button and turned the volume up, glancing around again to make sure no one was in earshot.

The message played, and a few more chills took turns pushing up gooseflesh on different parts of her body.

When it finished, she scrolled back to the home screen and said, "See what I mean? What would you do if you heard him say that? It was all complete with finger guns and everything."

She left it at that. She whispered a reverent prayer to God and to Haley for guidance on this issue.

"And who is this Anna woman he was talking to? *Anna*. A girl with no parents now, probably. If that was even real. Sometimes I wonder if he has another family besides you and me. You know that whole polygamy thing. God, wouldn't that be awful?" She gave a grim chuckle at her crazy wonderings. "It's just so much to take in."

The wind blew over the graveyard again, and between the traffic on the nearby streets, the birds chittering in the trees above, and the groundskeeper's lawn mower the next hill over, the breeze seemed to say, *Follow him.*

"I have a feeling that maybe I should follow Craig and see what—" Jill stopped short, realizing the premonition that had just happened. *Did I really hear that in the wind? Or was that my overactive imagination running wild? Was that God speaking to me? Or even Haley from beyond the grave?*

*No, she is not dead.*

"You're not dead," she said and placed her hand on Haley's gravestone again. "You're still out there somewhere, all alone." This last part came out as a choked whisper.

She let that phrase lie, then shook her head at what she thought she'd heard in the wind. "No. That simply can't be. I'm imagining things. No way."

There was no way it could've been Haley. They'd never found her body. Jill had forced the issue to have a funeral, bury a coffin, and erect a headstone, just as a way of moving on. Jill knew Haley wasn't there in the ground. It was only a way for her to cope.

*I'm going to follow him. I don't know how soon I will know something, but I just need to observe him for a little while.*

She pushed the supernatural feeling of someone speaking to her from her mind.

She stayed with Haley for a good part of the morning. It had been a while since she'd been here to visit. There were moments when she didn't know what to say. Since the body was not there, it was hard to communicate naturally.

She took some time to stretch her legs. Running all-out like that without stretching was never good. She knew she would eventually have to get back. It was going to be more of a walk this time, unless whatever she began to think about pissed her off, then it would be another anger run. When that happened, she could travel far.

# CHAPTER FOUR

**ARRIVING BACK AT** the house, Jill's whole body bloomed with relief when she saw Craig's tan Ford F-250 missing from the driveway. She couldn't help but think she would have run around the block a few more times to purposely avoid contact with him. She needed time alone to contemplate her next moves on how to handle this odd situation and Craig's recent behavior.

She moved through the front door and bounded up the stairs two and three at a time, her body still keyed up with the choice she'd made and being advised supernaturally at the grave to play detective.

She moved into the bathroom, stripping out of her sweaty gear as she did so. She turned the shower knob to hot. She didn't know how long she would be spying on Craig. She didn't want to have a stakeout in her current sweaty state.

The water refreshed her. She felt clean and had a little more positive energy on this decision to follow Craig today, though it all felt a little unnatural to her. What would he do if he found out she was following him?

*He's not going to find out. I'm going to be careful.*

*What am I going to do if I find out he really killed someone?*

*I don't know, but I'll think of something.*

She killed the water and the thought. Grabbing her towel, she dried off as much as she could in the tub, then stepped out and moved to the bedroom.

She quickly pulled out the pieces of the outfit she'd chosen. She quickly dressed in underwear, another sports bra, jeans, a T-shirt, a ball cap, worn tennis shoes, and a jacket—all low-key colors, nothing like the brighter colors of her sportswear from the run.

She grabbed her backpack near the desk in their bedroom and moved back downstairs.

She stuffed some snacks and a few bottles of water into her pack. If following Craig happened to be days in the making, she dreaded coming home tonight. She grabbed her purse, keys, and her phone and made her way to the side door again.

She was just stepping out of the house when a still small voice that argued with her from time to time talked directly to her. *Don't you think you need to consider taking some kind of protection with you in case things get… hairy?* She paused, thinking of the suggestion and that phrase: "In case things get hairy." That was a phrase Craig used often.

*I guess I should.*

*Damn right, you should.*

She glanced out the door toward the front again. No one was out there in the driveway. She stepped back in and closed the door. She moved into the living room and surveyed it, pulling up a mental map of where Craig hid his guns.

Craig Danforth didn't keep his guns in a gun safe in his closet or somewhere away from the main living areas. He always hid his guns in plain sight. Well, not exactly plain sight, but close enough to get your hands on in case there was ever a home invasion. It was something Craig always feared, and he said he'd always wanted to protect his family. His whole thought process wasn't out of the realm of possibility, but the way he approached it with a solution was humorous to her. She never let on how silly she thought it was. Craig always seemed serious that it could happen one day.

She knew the shotgun attached to the underside of the couch was out of the question for her protection. She didn't need that much firepower. She'd always felt a shotgun was crazy overkill anyway, and it was almost laughable that he'd gone to so much trouble.

She could go for the Glock that was underneath the coffee table. The way the coffee table was made, with a raised shelf that was eight or nine inches off the ground, it concealed the Glock that was hidden beneath nicely. Whoever sat in front of the center of the table would have time to lean forward, pull the gun from the holster attached to the bottommost shelf, and come up firing. The threat that was there would no longer be a threat.

Jill could get the 9mm that was in the pocket of the recliner Craig always sat in. If a home invasion ever happened, they would have to make sure one of them sat in the recliner if forced to be seated in the living room. When the invaders were distracted, all anyone would have to do was snake his hand down inside the pocket of the recliner, extract the 9mm hidden there, and unload on said invader, and that would be all he or she wrote.

There were others throughout the house. Jill didn't need to mentally go through the whole list. She put them all out of her head except one that she thought was beautiful and special to her.

She moved to the entertainment center and pulled a decorative box from the chest-high shelf. She knelt beside the coffee table and placed the box in front of her with reverence. It was the way she always approached guns: with a huge amount of respect.

Flipping the latch, she opened the box and let the lid touch down, leaving the revolver fully exposed. She took a moment just to stare at it and take it in.

It was a Smith and Wesson, Model 66, snub-nose revolver with a 2.5-inch barrel. It was polished steel with thick wooden hand grips. She liked this gun. It had a presence but not like a Clint Eastwood hand cannon—enough to be a hard threat in her mind but not so powerful that she wouldn't be able to control its kick should she need to pull the trigger. She knew how to control it; she'd shot it many times at the gun range whenever they went.

She wasn't afraid of this revolver or any of Craig's other guns. Before Haley disappeared, she, Craig, and even Haley had gone to the range quite often, and that "being scared of guns" feeling had long since disappeared from them all. Jill knew her way around guns.

She flipped the lock, snapped it to the side, and let the cylinder fall open. She saw it was fully loaded. All the guns in the house were loaded as a precaution. She jerked her wrist to the right; it snapped shut and she shoved it into the front pocket of her backpack. She pulled the two boxes of bullets and added them to the same pocket, but they were placed in a smaller compartment within, so they would be out of the way.

Closing the lid and fastening it again, she returned the box to the exact place on the shelf from where she'd taken it. Jill turned, grabbed her backpack and jacket. Turning again, her eyes landed on the end table closest to the windows that looked out on their wooded backyard. A pair of binoculars stood on end.

Backtracking, Jill snagged them quickly—*Could be useful in spying on Craig,* she thought—and stuffed them into her backpack, then moved to the side door again and locked it as she left.

As she reached her car and was sliding into the seat, a memory from a few days ago surfaced in her mind. It was of Craig sitting at the kitchen table, cleaning the very revolver she now had in her backpack.

Another flash memory: Craig's hand rising in the darkness, and then a flinch of his hand like real recoil had moved it as though he had taken someone's life in his dream.

*Was the revolver I took… part of an earlier crime?*

The thought stopped her cold, and she looked over her steering wheel back at the house she called home.

*It will be a question I ask him when this inevitable confrontation happens.*

Jill and the house suddenly didn't feel safe anymore.

# CHAPTER FIVE

**JILL CUT ACROSS** town to the construction site where Craig would be. She didn't know immediately what she would do other than maybe find a secluded area away from the site and just watch him from there. If he left, she would just follow him. She shook her head at how stupid and absurd this plan sounded to her.

Arriving at the construction site, she decided to pass the trailer he would be in, spot his truck, and then find a place to watch him. But when she passed by the trailer, there was no tan Ford F-250.

She contemplated the problem. Just because his truck wasn't there didn't mean anything; he could be elsewhere on the premises. He didn't always have to be in the trailer, even though he was the company's owner and main foreman. He could've given a trusty employee his keys to go to another area of the site.

Craig could still be in the trailer discussing the construction plans with other workers. But her gut was telling her that wasn't the case.

She passed the site and turned left when the light turned green. The building being erected was huge, so she surveyed the second side of the site. There was no sign of Craig or his truck. The third and fourth side areas of the site didn't reveal Craig or his truck either. He simply wasn't there.

Jill saw a few of Craig's employees who knew her, but they were so focused on work that they hadn't noticed her driving by in her car.

She did a secondary trip around the site to make sure she hadn't missed him or his truck, but it didn't reveal Craig.

She had seen Gavin Bedford, Craig's second in command. His maroon Dodge was at the trailer, but he was on the other side of the construction site. He was busy throwing hand signals to a crane operator. She pulled into a bank parking lot on the opposite side of the street.

She studied the area around her as she pulled the binoculars from her bag. Looking across the street again, she brought them up and focused on Gavin. He was absorbed in making sure the load the crane was carrying was deposited six stories up for the workers on that level.

Jill watched and scanned the area as she studied the scene. Maybe some intel might help. Surely Gavin would know Craig's whereabouts. But in calling him, she didn't want it to get back to Craig that she was seeking him out.

When Gavin reached a point where the load had been deposited and unhooked and the crane was unmoving and waiting for its next load, Jill grabbed her cell phone and searched her contacts for Gavin's number. Craig had given it to her for major emergencies so that if she couldn't reach him on his phone, she would call Gavin, and he would get word to him to call her back. She punched the connect button and waited for an answer.

Through her binoculars, Jill saw Gavin sign something to the crane operator as he reached for his phone. He glanced at the screen; a big grin spread across his face. He tapped to accept the call. "Jill Danforth. It's my lucky day. To what do I owe this pleasure?"

His voice was boisterous by nature, but he had to half-shout over the construction sounds of heavy machinery moving about in his vicinity.

"Hi, Gavin. I'm just trying to run Craig down."

"Is it that bad at home between you two?" A soft chuckle accompanied his reply.

With what had happened last night and where her mind currently was, Jill didn't grasp his comment. "Excuse me?"

"You trying to *run him down…* like *with your car?*" Another amused chuckle. "How bad is it being married to him? Bad joke. Moving on. What can I do you for?"

Innocent flirting from him; she never reciprocated. She didn't want Gavin to get the wrong idea. Her mind caught up with what she'd said at the start of the phone call.

"Oh," she laughed, even though she wasn't in the laughing mood. "No, I'm just trying to find him. He's not answering his phone." That was a lie. She hadn't even called him. "Is he around?"

"No. He's not here today."

"What?"

"He asked me to cover for him today. Said he had to go up to the cabin. Something about a leak in one of the bathrooms."

There was a silence. Jill's mind was frantic, thinking back to her conversations with Craig. Had he said anything to her about it, and she'd forgotten?

"Hello? Jill?"

"I'm here, Gavin."

"Oh. Good. Thought you'd cut out on me for a second."

"That's right." She played up the surprise of forgetting this detail. "I'd forgotten he was going up there today. He probably has it on airplane mode or something so he can focus."

"Probably. If I hear from him, you want me to tell him you called?"

"No!" she said, a little too quickly and loudly. "No. I'll surprise him a little later. I'll drive up there in a little bit with some food and to see how things are going. See if I can help. It just slipped my mind he was doing that today."

"Sure, I got ya."

"Thanks for refreshing my memory."

"No problem. Talk to you soon. Hey Max! Watch that line! Far side! Far sid—" And Gavin was gone to put out an emergency on the job. She took a brief look through the binoculars again. Gavin was waving his arm, taking back over the direction of construction traffic.

*Good,* Jill thought. *Hopefully, he was half listening to me, so he won't mention to Craig that I was looking for him.* She thought more about what Gavin had said: *up at the cabin. He isn't fixing a leak in the bathroom. He would've told me there was a leak up there.*

"What are you doing up there at the cabin, Craig?" she asked aloud.

Placing the binoculars back in her backpack, she put her Bronco Sport in drive and left the parking lot, answering her own question.

*I'm about to find out.*

# CHAPTER SIX

**THE DRIVE TO** the cabin took just over an hour; she would be there by lunchtime. She only made time to hit Starbucks and grab a coffee and an egg, pesto, and mozzarella sandwich, as she hadn't eaten anything that morning. The run had taken a good bit of her energy. It wasn't that she needed a stimulus to stay awake or give her a kick; coffee was merely a comfort to her, and she needed the biggest comfort with everything that had happened from last night to the present.

With her coffee in the console holder, Jill ate slowly, enjoying the breakfast food as well. She pointed her Sport in the direction of their cabin to spy on and possibly confront Craig at some time in the future. She didn't have an exact plan, but she had a little more than an hour to figure it out.

Why would he lie? The cabin. What about the cabin? She knew of no leak at the cabin, and it sounded so fishy to her because of last night.

When Jill married Craig, his cabin became Jill's and Haley's. But Jill married Craig for love, plain and simple, not for any material possessions. It was a nice bonus, and Haley loved the lake and wanted to go up there way too often. And they did as often as they could.

Sometimes, they went up three or four weekends a month. They stargazed, made bonfires, fished, and went hiking, water skiing, and canoeing. They played board games at the kitchen table or near the living room fireplace long into the night. They watched movies with popcorn, read books, and shared gut-busting bouts of laughter. They were always relaxed and rejuvenated after returning from a long weekend at the lakeside cabin. The place up there was addictive. They could never get enough.

She smiled at the memories, but then Haley appeared in her mind, and Jill's smile faded; sadness poured in again. Those times would never come again unless Haley came back to them. Jill had to believe that James Medlin would find her, or if she'd been kidnapped, she could hopefully escape and find her way back home.

Jill racked her brain for any minute detail that would jump out at her as extraordinary and answer the flood of questions, confusion, and doubt that their marriage was something other than a bunch of secrets.

*When I get there, what should I do? Should I just drive down the road leading to the cabin and park in front of it?*

*No, hell no. I have to watch and observe him to see what he's up to, and depending on what I see, that will be the deciding factor to confront him.*

*And what if you see nothing, find nothing? Then what?*

*I will probably go somewhere for the night. I will straight up lie to Craig and tell him that I need some time to be alone and that I need one of my trips. Visiting Haley's grave was too much for me today, and I need some alone time. For one night, maybe two. I've done it before. I can do it again. He's always been so understanding when I needed to be alone.*

Her plan in action, she drained the last of her coffee and plugged in her phone. She opened her Spotify app and tapped the playlist "Haley and Jill's Feelgood Vibes." It was a playlist of their favorite songs that put her in a great place mentally. She also wanted to push all the questioning thoughts to the back of her mind to give herself a break from the constant barrage that put her on edge.

The music poured out of the speakers, and she turned up the volume and sang along to "Bulletproof Picasso" by Train.

# CHAPTER SEVEN

**FOR OVER HALF** the trip, her feel-good playlist—made solely of songs that reminded her of Haley—gave her a little distance from mental thoughts bombarding her mind. She sang along loud and free to all the songs she'd put together over the past two years. Many of them, she and Haley had sung to as though they were a duet group, and every song was theirs.

But Jill's trepidation mounted with each mile that brought her closer to the cabin.

She had decided in the Starbucks drive-through that she wouldn't go straight to the cabin. That wasn't an option. Instead, she hung a left on Forest Ridge Road, which, for the most part, was an old logging road hardly used anymore. It still had dirt ruts worn by heavy tires, and the middle strip and the sides were thick with overgrown weeds.

The road was difficult to navigate but drivable. There were only a few spots where a heavy dip on one side tested the shocks of her midsize Bronco, but she took it slow and was careful. She didn't want to bust an axle or get stuck in any mud traps made by recent rains and have to call Craig. There would be no easy way to explain why she was up here today or why she had driven down this abandoned road.

She knew this road led to a junction point in a walking trail they had hiked numerous times on their family weekends. The trail came out of the woods, crossed Forest Ridge Road, then picked up on the opposite side and became a more difficult hike after about a half a mile or so deeper into the woods.

She pulled out of the way so she wouldn't be blocking the road. From the looks of the dirt tracks, it seemed as though she had been the only one down it in quite some time. She killed the engine and glanced all around, her guilty conscience getting the best of her because what she was doing was so out of the norm.

But her gut feeling told her that she needed a little time to study Craig. It could be that her overactive imagination had gotten the best of her, and there was a simple explanation for all of this. It could be as simple as Craig reenacting a scene from a movie he'd seen. But her nagging gut feeling wouldn't agree with that; it seemed far more complicated.

Jill reached over and pulled the backpack to her. She put her hand inside the front pocket, felt around, and found the revolver taken from the living room. She felt comfort from touching it. It seemed to tell her that if anything got crazy out of hand, she could use it. It would be a last resort, but it was there for her.

She scoffed at the phrase, *using it.*

She felt a little silly. *I made her feel powerful and protected, but it simultaneously made her feel ridiculous. Maybe even… paranoid?*

*We're talking about Craig here, my husband, the love of my life. How can I possibly use this on him? I have no proof that he's done anything wrong. Just a weird dream that caused him to talk and make some weird hand motions in his sleep. It only looked as though he had done something bad.*

She forced the crazy memory out of her head, withdrew her arm from the backpack, and zipped it up. She stepped out of her Bronco with her backpack and placed it by the back wheel, then closed the driver's door as quietly as possible.

Not that the sound of the closing door would reach the cabin; she was still a good way away. It would be a little hike to get to the edge of their property. But she couldn't be sure that Craig hadn't come up here and gone for a hike to clear his head after the frustrations of dealing with the pipe leak.

She scoffed inwardly. *Yeah, if that's really what happened.*

She put her keys in her backpack, grabbed her jacket from the backseat, and put it on. Sliding into the backpack straps, she hiked it up on her shoulders. As she glanced around the woods again, she said to herself, "I can't believe I'm doing this. But let's go see what my husband is up to."

૭)੦3

**JILL WAS GLAD** she had brought her jacket. The mid-September chill here in the woods was cool as the forest cover didn't allow a lot of sun to penetrate the trees' canopy. Above her, limbs were still full of leaves, most of them green, but some yellows and oranges were just peeking through. In a month or two, there would be a lot more color and hardly any green to speak of. The path that she was on would soon be littered with what she called "October colors."

She was careful as she walked, constantly looking around for anyone who might be out in the woods. She didn't want a stray hiker to see her up here, if they happened to meet in the woods. She didn't want anyone to mention anything to Craig if he happened to be at the diner a few miles up the road from their cabin. The littlest thing could get back to him.

For that matter, as she had thought before, she didn't want to meet Craig out here on the trail. She wasn't ready to talk to him.

Nearing the edge of their property, she could see their cabin through the trees. She made her way to a large oak tree and stooped behind it. She shuffled out of her backpack and pulled it in front of her. Unzipping it, she retrieved the binoculars, then stood again. She stuck as much of her head and the binoculars out around the tree as she dared to survey their property.

She didn't want Craig to see her spying on him at the edge of the woods. They did have a duplicate pair of binoculars inside the living room area of the cabin. That avid bird-watching streak that Craig was always in. She'd seen him numerous times, standing there in their living room at home, and here at the cabin, dutifully searching for all different kinds of birds.

And now, giving that subject more attention, her mind spasmed with another worrisome thought. She ducked back behind the tree as it bloomed in her mind. *Was it* birds *that Craig was looking at? Or was he searching the surroundings for something different? Maybe* someone *or* someones?

She put a pin in that thought. Not fully brushed away, just pushing it to the side for a short while.

She was careful to make sure the sunlight wasn't beaming through the trees and glaring off the binoculars' lens to give a sparkle from the tree line that Craig could notice. She had seen plenty of action movies where the bad guy's sniper lens gave a lens flare of sunlight, or the lit end of a cigarette glowed enough to where they were easily spotted, then were taken out by a bullet through the scope lens, or easily crept upon and snuffed out with a quick, fatal military move.

She wasn't going to get busted because the sun glinted off her binocular lenses, because, she had to face it, he could be in the cabin right now looking out, surveying the woods for those birds or those "someones" he was always looking for.

# CHAPTER EIGHT

**CRAIG'S TRUCK WAS** where he normally parked it. He was either inside working on the questionable bathroom leak, or he had gone for a walk around the lake, maybe even a hike that took him in her direction somewhere in the nearby woods. She checked behind herself again, but all was quiet there.

Jill took turns looking out from behind the large oak tree. She didn't linger too long out in the open. She didn't want to give Craig any chance to glimpse her there.

Minutes rolled by, and nothing happened. Jill began questioning her motives and contemplating her options.

*Am I going to sit here behind this tree all day? What am I hoping to see him doing? Is there a chance he picked up another woman I don't know about and brought her here to the cabin for some afternoon delight? Spend some time in* our *cabin.* She couldn't tell from here if a female was present.

She stooped and looked out again at the cabin.

From what she'd seen him doing and saying in his dream, she almost wished another woman were involved. That was an easy fix. She would leave Craig, plain and simple, and without any questions asked or answered. Jill believed that there was no room for second chances as far as cheating went in a marriage. Because she would never duck out on Craig with another man, she expected the same from him with other women.

With this mystery, she had a gut feeling that something bigger was at stake.

The sound of the cabin screen door slamming brought her out of her thoughts. She was sitting with her head against the tree. She shifted her body weight to peer out around it, but now she was at a lower elevation. She was concealed behind the trunk, looking through some of the wooded vegetation in front of her.

Craig walked down the porch stairs and moved in her direction.

"Fuck," Jill said, chastising herself. She froze behind the tree. Had he seen her? He had to have seen her. But she was so careful. She thought back to any time when she might have revealed herself without thinking, but she couldn't come up with anything that he would have seen.

*Was he that good with those binoculars?*

She kept sneaking careful peeks as he continued across the small field. If he'd seen her, he'd seen her. Why continue to conceal herself? But something within her told her to stay down.

Craig was carrying a coffee cup in one hand. She couldn't fathom why he would just go for a walk or even a hike carrying a cup of coffee. The way he was headed was the way that led to the more difficult hikes around this area, so why he decided to bring a breakable cup along was weird. He had never done that before when they had been up here on their family weekend vacations.

He continued on a straight path in her direction. She was petrified in her position against the tree. She didn't know when the best time would be to reveal herself. Should she just stand up and yell, "SURPRISE!" and scare the shit out of him? Just play it off like she was coming here to the cabin to do that? How would she explain why she'd parked her SUV where it was currently parked? She didn't know if she could give out a yell that was convincing enough to him because her throat was so constricted with fear.

Jill was about to stand and reveal herself as Craig hit the tree line, but he continued walking right past her. He didn't even look in her direction. Jill marveled at this development.

*He hadn't seen me from the cabin. He has no idea I'm up here. But why in the hell is he going for a walk? And with a cup of coffee? That isn't normal. Maybe a thermos with coffee and you hike to a specific spot, sit down, pour your coffee, and enjoy a cup or two looking out at whatever spectacular view you find. You don't just go around a walking trail holding a coffee cup. It's so odd.*

She didn't dare move from her place close to the ground. Rising slightly, she watched him, careful not to make a noise. She breathed with slow, even, and steady breaths. She wasn't going to be one of those victims in the woods in all those dumbass horror movies who were being chased by a killer…

*Killer. Listen to me.*

… and making all sorts of breathing sounds that the bad guy hears and turns on them, starts chasing them, and finally catches them. Or they slip because their footing is in a weird position, or the sound of a breaking stick snags their attention.

Those were always eye-roll moments in a movie for her. Loathsome moments. She understood why they happened. It was only a plot device to move the story along to make it more dramatic. The killer had to give chase to the person who was fleeing from him or her.

*But, come on; it was ridiculous.* The number of times the person hiding gave themselves away. It always pissed her off. Fuck no, she wasn't going to be one of those people.

Lifting herself ever so slightly, she saw above the bushes that had been to her six o'clock. Peering above them, she saw Craig continue walking a little down the trail away from her. About twenty yards or so past her, he stopped. There, he glanced around suspiciously, then took two steps to a place just off the trail and stooped. He felt around on the ground…

*What was he looking for?*

…and then lifted…

*A lid?* Jill could think of nothing else. Her mouth dropped open.

Yeah, it was a lid, alright, a behemoth-sized opening that was seven to eight feet wide. It rose to a height slightly taller than Craig. He moved down into the darkness by what Jill believed was a set of stairs, then disappeared as the hatchway lowered behind him, closing smoothly.

Jill sat there by the oak tree, too stunned to even move. She had no clue what was under the ground or how long it had been there. For all she knew, it had been there before she and Haley had met Craig. The woods around this area had always been tall and green. She never knew this to have been cleared of any trees or any new trees being planted since they had been together. No doubt it had been here for a long time.

She continued to breathe quietly, concentrating on her breath to calm her nerves. She said to herself, "Let's not get ahead of ourselves. There could be a logical explanation for all this."

The other part of her mind answered her own comment: *Nothing logical about this could be explained. If there wasn't anything shady… make that illegal… he would have told you about this when you two were dating. Nothing under that ground is good. There's no getting around that fact, Jill.*

She knew what she had to do, but she was going to give it a few minutes before she did anything. As she contemplated, she reached for her backpack. She placed the binoculars inside and released them just to pull the revolver out instead.

*Thank God I was smart enough to bring this.*

She slid the revolver into the side pocket of her jacket, then stood and slid her backpack on.

She moved to the place where Craig had lifted the lid and looked down at the spot. She couldn't really see anything at a glance. How many times had she and Haley walked these trails with Craig, never suspecting a doorway was hidden in the earth? She couldn't fathom this mystery.

Scrutinizing it closer, she saw the line where the branches met the dirt. It was all so well camouflaged. Craig was in construction, and by that token, he was a master carpenter. It wouldn't be a problem for him to rig this up. She always marveled at the reconstruction projects he did at home and here at the cabin. A master craftsman, good with his tools, and even better with his hands. This, whatever it was, had to be a masterpiece of his creativity.

Jill couldn't wait any longer. To do so would mean that he would be coming up out of this pit at any time. He could be walking up the steps right now; it could open at any moment. She ducked, felt for a lever that would open this doorway. She couldn't find one. She gave up and just lifted the hatchway.

At first, it didn't budge, but then she planted her feet in a deadlift position, placed her hands a little wider than shoulder width apart, and lifted the lid.

The door rose on hydraulic cylinders or hinges, and as it rose, it became easier; the hydraulics did most of the work.

The door was silent, too, which she was thankful for. She was just about to drop lower and place her palms underneath the door as though she were doing a clean and jerk move. But she found that the door held fast in the half-open position.

She quickly slipped inside, having the horrific mental image of the door slamming shut and cutting her body in half, her front torso tumbling forward and bouncing down the stairs, leaving her lower legs hanging out at the top of the doorway. But the door held, and she ducked down a few stairs, found the handle on the underside, and pulled it shut behind her. She was careful not to let it slam down in place and alert Craig that he had company.

Jill immediately reached for her revolver and pulled it from her pocket. Craig had lied to her. She wasn't going to let him slither out of this argument, the one she knew would soon come up. She offered a little prayer of thanks to God for giving her the notion to bring some protection with her.

Thankfully, there were lights on in the underground bunker, though they were subdued. She really wasn't shocked at that fact. Whenever Craig built something, he did it to the best of his ability.

She looked around, surveying every detail.

Handrails appeared further into the underground chamber. And she was thankful for them, as there were stairs, lots of stairs. She was already close to fifteen stairs down. About halfway down now.

She finally touched the flooring at the bottom. She turned quickly, covering her six, and looked back under the stairs. Jill knew that if somebody were there, it was too late and they could've already sliced her Achilles tendon with a razor or grabbed her foot and jerked her off balance, causing her to spill the rest of the way down the stairs.

There was some old stuff under the stairs, nothing she could really make out, but no one was lurking there. She turned forward again but stepped to the far-left side, her body hugging the wall. She dropped her left hand, her non-shooting hand, and placed it against the wall. She felt the wall as she moved forward down the square tunnel. She knew exactly what this underground bunker was made of. She had seen them pulled up and down the highway many times.

*Transfer trailers.*

Whatever this containment bunker was for, it was no good. She quickly pulled her hand back up and cupped the underneath part of her fist to hold the gun steady. Not that she was nervous and her gun was shaky; she was preparing for whatever was at the end of this tunnel. She moved with stealth toward the brighter light that was around the corner to the right at the far end of the chamber.

# CHAPTER NINE

**CRAIG DANFORTH'S MIND** was in the mental storm clouds of thoughts.

He stood in the doomsday prepper room of his underground bunker. He had gathered a nice stash of supplies over the years. Gathered, used, and replaced again as time permitted. If the world went to shit and a zombie apocalypse ever happened—not likely—he would be a king because he always prepared for the worst-case scenario.

But this underground facility wasn't what was bothering him. Jill had been acting strange; she'd been on his mind all morning.

*Running? Why today, of all days, was she starting back running?*

Before they had met, and while they dated, and even a couple of years after they were married, Jill was a vigorous runner. An early riser to get those miles in. The disappearance of Jill's daughter, *their* daughter, Haley, had changed them. It had changed *her*. She had stopped running during the first weeks of the investigation, not completely, but a day here, a day there, then a few days between runs, then finally, she stopped completely.

A grim, concentrated look crossed his face as he thought of Jill and what Haley's disappearance had done to her. He shook his head at their loss. He turned to look behind him. Across the transfer trailer hallway, opposite this doomsday prepper room, there was another doorway. He contemplated going in there but shook his head against the idea. He'd already stepped in there earlier this morning.

*Maybe I'll go in there again before I leave later today.*

He didn't want to think about Haley at present, so he pushed the memories of her to the back of his mind and focused on what was troubling him.

This morning, Jill would've normally sat down and spent some time with him as he ate his breakfast. She would've joined in and eaten a little as well, grabbing stuff off his plate. She didn't do that today. Craig kept having this nagging feeling that she was avoiding him.

*Why would she do that?*

He thought back to when he awoke. He had gotten out of bed and moved to go downstairs, but before he left the room, he'd turned back to look at Jill. She was sleeping peacefully at that point, and he was glad of that fact. Earlier in the night, he'd awoken to her looking at her phone. When questioned, she'd said she was having trouble sleeping.

Who knew what was on her mind? Something about that exchange last night didn't sit right with him, but he couldn't put a finger on the exact troublesome spot in their conversation that was needling him.

He had learned early on that if something was bugging him, it was that his mind was trying to tell him something, and it was imperative that he listened to it. He continued to mull things over, refusing to dismiss it as just his imagination running wild.

Craig replayed the situation. He went back a little further before their conversation.

He had been dreaming of Anna.

God forbid, Jill finds out about Anna and what he had done to her parents. Jesus, that wouldn't go over well at all.

Then, the dim bulb of enlightenment brightened, and he asked himself, "Is it possible… that I did something… or *said* something… in my sleep to give myself away?" He remembered asking Jill if he was talking in his sleep. When he asked the question, he was too sleepy to latch on to her hesitation, but now that he was awake and concentrating on that moment again, it was blazingly obvious.

His body went rigid in sudden fear. He looked up to the far wall, all the way down the center aisle to the other end of this trailer, as the answer bloomed into clarity.

"Jill knew something," he whispered to himself. "That was why she was so distant from me this morning. It had to be."

With a sudden fearful thought, he flipped his hand to his back pocket, retrieved his phone, and pulled it up in front of his face. He couldn't scroll fast enough. Finally, his fumbling fingers found the tracker app he'd installed on his phone a few years ago—the tracker itself was hidden within Jill's Bronco Sport. It was a small thing he'd done back then to ease his mind when he felt Jill might be cheating on him. Craig always called it a "precautionary measure."

Back when Haley had disappeared, with no leads in the investigation and no news of finding her dead or alive, Jill had begun to spiral out of control. There was really nothing he could do about it. She felt like she needed to be alone and would go on two- to three-day trips by herself. Craig's nickname for these getaways was "solo benders." They had knock-down, drag-out arguments over it, but he finally relented, letting her go, and allowed her to deal with Haley's disappearance as she felt she needed.

He would never admit it to Jill, but the alone time helped him out also. To ease his mind that Jill wasn't using their daughter's disappearance as an excuse to meet another man… or other men… or women, for that matter, he installed a tracking device into an area of her car that she would never find.

He watched her on those solo weekend trips, and she was exactly where she said she would be. She was always at the hotel unless she went to an outlying town near the hotel and did some shopping or grabbed food at a restaurant. It wasn't to say that some other guy couldn't have met her at her hotel or at the places she visited. But she was never anywhere suspicious. Never at a residence he didn't know. She always came back refreshed, and honestly, it seemed to be therapeutic for her.

A few times, he'd even followed her at a discreet distance; since there was a tracker in her car, she didn't always have to be in his line of sight. He often waited until she was in the restaurant and ordered drinks before he stepped inside to watch her from across the room. Sometimes, he would step inside a store to ensure she wasn't meeting another guy.

A few times, he had almost been seen by her, and he had gotten the hell out of there. All in all, she had always been completely honest with him, and he loved her for that. And with his mind at ease, he would forget about the tracker. But anytime questions came to his mind about anything that seemed off about her, he could usually check the tracker app and solve what was disturbing him.

In doing so now, and with the thought that she may be on to him about his actions last night, his heart rate went into jackhammer mode. He pulled up the tracker app and adjusted it to where the tracker was blinking. Even though he was nervous about checking, he knew he would see her blinking red dot back at home, her car still in the garage or a nearby store, or at her job, if she had decided to go into work.

But his eyebrows dipped in utter confusion as the screen spiraled down to an area in the vicinity of the cabin. His eyes went wide with sudden fear, and he just stood there, rocked at this news. The blinking red light taunted him.

"No, no, no, no, no, no. This can't be right," he said as he put his thumb and index finger on the screen and blew the map up even more. The red blinking light covering part of the road was labeled Forest Ridge Road.

"Forest Ridge? That's the old logging road no one uses anymore…"

His mind flared with a thought. *That is… until Jill used it today.*

"Fuck!" he half yelled to himself. "Jill shouldn't even be here. Why the fuck is she here?"

He turned quickly and rushed from the doomsday prepper room, and as he went, he began muttering a constant, "No-no-no-no-no-no-no."

# CHAPTER TEN

**JILL HEARD A** movement coming from up ahead and around the corner to her right. She had a gut feeling it must be Craig. Jill had just enough time to stop, plant her feet in a shooter stance, and focus the revolver straight ahead. Then she heard his voice and knew it was him.

Craig barreled around the corner and into Jill's line of fire. He was looking down, focused on his phone's screen and saying, "No-no-no-no-no."

"Stop right there, Craig," Jill commanded. She was shocked at how loud her voice was in this space after trying so hard to keep quiet. Her authoritative voice was like a punch to Craig's system.

Craig stopped abruptly and looked up. He saw the gun, then his wife, and was immediately startled. Guilt bloomed on his face. He threw his hands up as though Jill were a cop and had caught him doing the worst thing imaginable.

"Jill-Jill," he stammered. "What the hell are you doing here? And why do you have… is that my revolver?

Jill ignored his last sentence. "I was going to ask you the same question, Craig. What the fuck are *you* doing down here? What is this place? And why don't I know about it?"

All Craig could do was shake his head. He was at a loss for words. He didn't know where to begin. "I… I… I…" was all he could get out.

While she waited for him to formulate an answer, more questions came to Jill's mind. "What was all that no-no-no-no business? And you said, 'Jill shouldn't even be here. Why the fuck is she here?' How did you know I *was* here, Craig?"

Realizing he had the tracker app still open on his phone, and the phone was in his hand, facing her, and the red dot blinking indicating where her car was, he lowered his phone a little too quickly. Craig tried to slip it into his back pocket.

"Wait! Hold up! Do not move your hands."

Craig froze where he was. "Jill," he began, trying to reason with her. "I'm just putting my phone away."

"And that's why I'm telling you to stop. Pitch your phone over here to me. Don't throw it hard. Pitch it softly. No funny moves, or I'll shoot you in the kneecap. You know I can do it. We've been to the range plenty of times for you to know I'm a damn good shot."

Craig asked, "Is there any way you could lower the gun? You're making me nervous."

She gave him a sarcastic look that told him he'd better comply with her request.

Craig did as he was told and pitched it gently to her at waist height.

Jill dropped her left hand from her gun long enough to palm-snag the phone out of the air. Once she had it in her possession, she moved her hand back up to her weapon and held it steady on Craig again. She backed up a step or two to observe it at a safer distance. She didn't want Craig trying any lunge moves on her now that she was a little distracted by his phone.

"Did you know I was here?" she asked as she looked at the phone. She only took marginal glances at the screen. She kept her primary attention on Craig. Another glance at the screen. "What the hell is this, Craig?"

His only answer was a frustrating breath.

Jill glanced at the phone again and saw the blinking red dot. She glanced again to ensure he wasn't advancing on her. She redirected her aim slightly so she would already be aiming at the middle of his legs should he choose to make the bad decision of trying to be faster than a bullet. She glanced back at the phone and saw the name of the road—Forest Ridge Road—where the red dot was stationary.

"I asked you a fucking question. What the hell is this? Is this a *tracker*? Do you have a tracker on my car? That's how you knew I was here, wasn't it? Why do you have a fucking tracker on my car, Craig?"

"It's been there for a while, Jill. A long time. A couple years ago, I thought you were cheating on me, you know, when Haley went missing. You went off on your solo trips to God-knows-where and left me alone for days at a time."

She shook the phone at him. "Well, it looks like you always knew where I was. Did I ever give you any indication that I was cheating on you?"

Craig was about to answer, but Jill barreled ahead. Pissed now, she answered for him. "The answer is no. I've told you how I feel about cheating in a marriage. I told you from the very start that I would never cheat on you. But I also told you that I expected the same out of you. And if you ever did, there would be no getting me back. You remember that?"

"Yes, I remember that."

"Then why is a fucking tracker on my car?"

"I just wanted to see if you were true to your word. I was worried about those times when you spiraled out of control. I didn't know how to help you."

"I never spiral out of control. I needed that alone time so I *wouldn't* spiral out of control. See the difference?"

Craig nodded. He collected his thoughts and came at her from a different angle. "I haven't used that tracker in a long time."

"Gee, that's so considerate of you. Thank you, Craig, for not spying on me."

"You haven't given me any reason to."

"And what was the reason that you started looking at it again today?"

"You were acting really weird this morning. It was like you didn't want to be around me. I couldn't figure out why you wanted to be out of the house. I thought it was odd that you were suddenly running again after all this time."

"You have to start sometime and somewhere."

"I guess so."

"What is this place, Craig? I asked you earlier, and I'm asking you for the last time, why do you have an underground bunker here at the cabin, and why don't I know about it?"

"Look, it's just a doomsday prepper bunker. I went through a big phase before we were married. I had all the construction equipment and the means to make it. I haven't been down here in years."

"Oh, come off it, Craig. You expect me to believe this is the first time you've been down here in a long time? And it just so happens that these lights still work perfectly? And there's no dust buildup or… or any spiderwebs to be found *anywhere?* It's immaculate down here. You're lying to me. Back up and turn around."

Craig obeyed.

"Walk."

Craig obeyed again.

"I want the complete tour of this place. I want to know exactly what's in here. What's around the corner?"

"Like I said, it's a doomsday prepper area. I've got all sorts of supplies in case *whatever* happens—you name it. I'm prepared."

Jill couldn't help herself. "You weren't *prepared* for me showing up here now, were you?"

Craig said nothing.

Jill took carefully measured steps as she moved back around the corner with Craig to the supply area. The lighting was better in that containment holder. There was a long table that occupied a significant portion of the front space, but walkways on either side of the table provided access to the center aisle, which extended all the way to the back of the bay.

She could see the back wall between the shelves down that center aisle. How long were transfer trailers? The measurement escaped her. The heavy metal gray shelving stood about six to seven feet tall, and they were all filled with supplies.

Jill could tell that the first few shelves behind the table contained nothing but grocery items: canned goods like corn, peas, a variety of beans, and some plastic canisters of nuts.

Jill remembered that on a few of their vacation weekends, they had forgotten to get a certain type of food during their shopping. The very next day, magically, a couple of cans of corn, beans, or other items were there in the cupboard. Craig always said he couldn't sleep on those nights, so he ducked out real quick and drove to the closest 24-hour store that sold canned goods and picked them up. He always said he never wanted anyone's lake vacation ruined because they didn't have the resources they needed.

She realized now that he'd walked out to the woods, stepped into his secret underground bunker, pulled a couple of cans, and walked back while they slept under their comforters in the cabin.

This realization pissed her off even more.

"So, why were you weird this morning? What did I do?"

"Before I answer that, I want you to take the gun you're carrying and slide it across the table to me. Your pocketknife, too. And before you try to play it off that you're not, I know better. You always conceal carry. It's like a Biblical principle with you. Do it now and do it fast. I have an itchy trigger finger, and it's starting to have spasms."

Craig did as he was told. Both the gun and the knife slid across the table to her side. She pocketed the knife and moved the gun farther away to where Craig couldn't reach it before one of her bullets struck him if he lunged for it.

Jill said, "Now, what was your question? What made *me* suspicious of what *you* were doing?"

"Yeah."

"Who's Anna?"

# CHAPTER ELEVEN

CRAIG SHOULD'VE KNOWN a variant of the question—'Who's Anna?'—was going to be asked, but with the realization of Jill being right here in front of him and the big secret of his bunker being found out, that question hadn't even registered in his mind. His mouth dropped open; he was about to say something, thought better of it, and closed it again.

"Craig," Jill's voice crackled with bitterness. "I asked you a question. Who the fuck is Anna?"

Craig shook his head. To Jill, it looked as though he didn't know the answer, but figured it was more of him trying on answers in his mind that would persuade Jill to his way of thinking. Realizing none of his answers would be satisfactory, he stayed silent.

Jill tried again. "Is she down here in this bunker? What's behind that door?" She indicated the one opposite them. "Or that one?" She flicked her hand to the one ninety degrees to where they were standing. "Did you do something to Anna's parents? It looked like you did in whatever reenactment you were doing in your sleep. I guess your guilty conscience is getting the best of you."

Craig spoke, but his answer was to a question Jill had asked earlier. His voice was firm and calculating. "Jill, there are just some things that you don't need to know about."

"Well, this revolver says otherwise, so if you were smart, you might want to start spilling your guts on every question I ask you, or I'll be forced to put a bullet through your kneecap. How's my need-to-know basis now?"

Jill saw the shift from confusion to outright rage. Anger was simmering under the surface of Craig's body. She was on her guard. There was a good enough distance between them that she could get a shot off if he tried anything, but being in close quarters as they were, she wasn't truly comfortable.

"Let's try this again. Who. Is. Anna? What did you do to her parents? And what is behind these other doors? I want a grand tour."

Craig was still seething but remained quiet.

"You have to the count of three or I'm going to start shooting. One."

Craig weighed his options.

Jill lowered the revolver and aimed it at his kneecap again. "Two." She thumbed the hammer back.

She recalculated her aim to make sure it would shatter the kneecap when she fired.

Craig, realizing how serious she was with her threat, rethought his options quickly. "All right," he said, throwing his hands up, settling to do it her way. "Anna is in the next room. Would you like to meet her?"

Now that Craig was consenting to answering her questions, she de-cocked the revolver by lowering the hammer. "You have got to be fucking kidding. You have a woman down here? What maniacal bullshit is this, Craig? What did you do? Take the day off work to come up here and have a rape session or two with her? What sick twisted shit are you doing down here?"

He gave Jill a snide laugh. "I'm not doing anything sick and twisted *with her*. I merely took her. I'm going to sell her for a high profit. Where is she going, you might want to ask? I have no idea, so don't."

"You're using *this bunker* as a way to move humans on the black market?"

"Yes. Now I asked *you* a question. Do you want to meet Anna or not?"

"What the fuck do you think, Craig? Yes, open the fucking door."

He gave a deep sigh of reluctance and a small shake of his head as he moved to the door. He opened the lock and took it off. He pulled the door open, held it, and offered a swinging arm movement as an invitation for Jill to enter first.

Jill gave him a *no chance in hell* look. "You think I'm that stupid, Craig? How about *you* go first? I'm not about to let you trap me in there with her."

"Fine. I'll go first if it makes you feel better." He moved inside but kept to the container's far right side.

Jill moved to the door's entrance. "Move in further."

Craig reluctantly obeyed.

Jill couldn't believe her eyes. The length of this trailer was a complete furnished living quarters, as though in an actual house. There was hardwood flooring over half of it—the kitchen/dining room area. Then it changed to blue carpeting over the last half—the bedroom/bathroom part.

The walls were not corrugated steel like the hallway was. Apparently, Craig had been busy putting up sheet rock and making them look like walls you would see in any house in their neighborhood. The king-sized bed even had end tables with lamps on either side of it that were lit.

There wasn't a closed-off section for the bathroom, just a bedside porta-potty that an elderly person might have nearby. It was all the way in the far-left corner. There were a couple of rolls of toilet paper sitting on the nightstand. Everything was comfortable for whoever was forced to stay here.

Closer to them, there was a table with two chairs. At one end of the table, there was a plate with the remains of some type of food. It looked like breakfast food as though Craig had hurried up here and fixed Anna some sort of nourishment. It could've even been the food he'd made this morning at home to save on time.

But the most surprising thing to witness, even though Craig had told her Anna was in this room, was the figure who rose from the bed and turned to look at them. She wasn't a woman as Jill had expected, not fully. She was an Asian girl, maybe sixteen or seventeen, about the same age as Haley when she went missing.

"Who are you?" the girl asked.

# CHAPTER TWELVE

**JILL STOOD FROZEN** in place, still shocked that Craig had a human being hidden in this underground shelter. She didn't answer the girl's question. Instead, she asked, "Are you, Anna?"

The girl nodded. "Yes. Anna Cheong."

Jill asked, "How long have you been here?"

Anna said, "Three… um… maybe four days. They all seem to have run… together. Who-who are you?"

"I'm Jill. Jill Danforth. And unfortunately, I happen to be this man's wife."

A deeper look of fear possessed the girl.

Jill realized that Anna must've thought that she was in on this elaborate plan. She talked more urgently. "Please don't be scared of me. I'm not going to hurt you. Yes, I am his wife, but not for much longer. I am not associated with what he is doing in any way. I am only now finding out that my husband has been keeping secrets from me. If there was anything to make my love for him dry up, it is this."

"Jill. You can't mean—"

"Shut up!" she snapped. To Anna, she said, "Come on. We're getting out of here." Jill threw out some urgent hand motions. "I want you to stay as close to this wall as you can. Move around behind me. Do not let him get close to you. I'm not going to let him grab you and use you as a shield."

To Craig, she said, "Yeah, I see the wheels moving behind your eyes. You're like a trapped animal, looking for an escape. You've been racking your brain for an escape ever since I got here, but that's not going to happen."

"Jill, you don't understand exactly how bad the guys I'm dealing with can be. So far, nothing has caused them to doubt my services. But this…" He paused, thinking those few sentences would be enough for her to drop the gun and forget all about what he was doing here.

Jill stared at him with loathing. She wasn't going to budge on this issue. She wanted Craig to hang himself.

Craig tried again. "What you're doing is going to throw a huge kink in my plans. I have been a studious seller. I'm dependable. I always deliver."

"Not this time, you're not."

Craig ignored her and pressed on with his soapbox sermon. "That's the reason my business is booming and the reason you and Haley live in such a beautiful house. It's because of what I do here, but if you fuck this up, they're gonna come for us. Why do you think I have all those weapons stashed all over the house? Because I want to protect you and Haley if a hiccup in my plans goes sideways."

Jill was aghast at what he said. She'd never even considered this. "That's the reason? That's why you think we're going to have a home invasion? Because you do *this*? Have you ever thought about living a normal, peaceful life? One that will take that dangerous element of having a possible invasion come to our house out of our lives. You're not protecting us. You've been putting us in harm's way. If I had known you were doing this, I would've ended you a long time ago."

Craig snapped. "Doing *this* is the reason my business is so successful. Putting that money back into the company. Growing the business. Being able to buy bigger machinery to do those monolithic jobs all over town. Sure, I get paid well to do those big jobs and buy some of the equipment I need and use, but I wouldn't be nearly as successful if I didn't do this on the side. The money I rake in doing this is good. Damn good."

"When the fuck is this deal supposed to go down?"

"My buyer, Quinn Stanton, is sending two guys in a few days to pick Anna up. He's got a big party going on in the Hamptons in a few weeks. Shit, for what I do, I should be getting paid more. He's going to sell the women that he gets for much higher prices. Ship them off to God-knows-where. He's going to do a huge auction at this upcoming party."

"And you're just fine to go along with that?"

"As long as I get the money owed to me." He paused, then said, "I've gotten used to it."

Jill couldn't believe the new Hyde version her husband was reluctantly revealing to her. Her mind was blown by his candor about buying and selling humans, like it was nothing more than posting a used piece of furniture on Facebook Marketplace. She couldn't help but stop and stare at him with new hate.

Craig saw her look. "Hey, the world is a bad enough place as it is, and things like this are going to happen whether I do it or not, but if it gives me a better life… and you a better life, then I'm willing to take that chance and roll the dice. That's the terms with Stanton and the agreement that we came up with. I'm going to abide by that promise and allow them to pick her up in a few days."

"No, you're not. Whatever you're doing down here, it ends today. Come on, Anna, we're getting out of here."

"You have no idea what you're getting yourself into," Craig said.

"No, *you* don't know what I'm capable of." To the girl, she said, "Come on, Anna. We need to move quickly. Get out the door."

Anna made her way to the opening, giving Craig as wide a berth as possible. "You're-you're… just going to leave him in here?"

"For now."

"B-but, what if he gets free? He-he could kill us."

"I'm going to let the police deal with him."

"He could kill us! Or someone else just like he did my parents!"

She looked at Craig with a cold, murderous stare. "Is that true?"

It wasn't that she didn't believe Anna; she'd seen the reenactment in their bed last night, and that was real enough. She now wanted to hear Craig admit it. If he was going to go to jail, she wanted to make sure that she had her information correct.

Craig gave a deep sigh, staring straight at Anna as he did so. "I gave *her* an option. She didn't listen to me. *She* got her parents killed. If she'd just gone with me quietly, like I had commanded her to do, then they would still be alive. It's not my fault."

"You're a piece of shit." Jill shook her head and stepped backward out of the room.

Anna said, "I can't believe you're just going to leave him in there."

"We're going to let the cops deal with him. I know someone who's been looking into the disappearance of my daughter. I'm going to call James Medlin. He'll know what to do."

As Jill turned away and closed the door behind her, she glanced behind her to make sure she had her bearings and wasn't going to trip and fall. Her eyes fell on the other door that was diagonal to her. The feeling hit her at the same time her last few sentences were spoken. She hadn't had the full tour of this place. What was so special about that door with a lit red keypad entry?

Then her words came back to her: *my daughter's disappearance.*

"Wait!" Jill stepped back to the entrance of the holding cell and pulled the door open again. "Please tell me I'm wrong. Please tell me that you don't know anything about Haley's disappearance."

Her voice was taking on a heavier intensity. "Please tell me you had nothing to do with our daughter's disappearance. No, *my* daughter's disappearance."

Craig hung his head in shame, then looked back up at her. "Nothing ever really gets by you. I'm surprised it's taken this long. Not that I was playing any sort of game with you."

"What's the combination?"

"Jill, you do not want to go in there."

"You give me the fucking combination right fucking now or I'm going to put a—"

He gave a defeated, reluctant breath. "Why don't you try her birth date?"

"Anna," Jill called. Anna was right there behind her, watching the whole progression of the exchange. "I need you to do me a favor."

"I'll do anything for you if you are truly the one who is going to help me escape."

"Oh, I am. We are going to be getting out of here very soon. I just need to do one thing."

"You need to check to see if your daughter is in that other room. I get that. I can hold the gun on him."

Jill paused and searched the girl's face. "I can't have you shooting him. I still need him."

"Why don't you just lock him in there?"

Jill countered, "And us not see what he is doing? I don't know if he has any secret doors or tunnels in that containment area."

"There isn't, believe me. I have searched the whole room, and there is no way out."

"Well, he's a crafty son of a bitch. There's no telling what kind of weapon he could make with the stuff in there. No, I want eyes on him at all times. Can you promise me you won't empty this gun on him?"

"It'll be the hardest thing I've ever done, but sure, I promise you that."

"If he moves even the slightest bit, you have my permission to blow a kneecap off. Just enough to stop him, but do not kill him."

"I understand."

Reluctantly, Jill gave the gun to Anna. She warned, "Do not let him get close to you." She glanced over at Craig, but her comment was still for Anna. "If he tries any funny business, kneecap that bitch."

"Yes, ma'am."

# CHAPTER THIRTEEN

**JILL MOVED TO** the second locked doorway, trepidation mounting with each step. At the keypad, her fingers hovered over the numbers. After all these years, two long, agonizing years of wondering where her daughter was, she now knew.

Haley was behind this door.

Her mind reeled, imagining the condition in which she would find her daughter. She knew Haley would be dead. That was evident from the look on Craig's ashamed face and what he'd said. She was now mentally preparing herself to look at Haley's remains.

But what had Craig done? Did he just leave her in there without food or water so she would starve to death? If so, what shape would her body be in? Her corpse would be nothing more than withered skin and bone. Just a husk of the beautiful girl that Jill loved so dearly. Had he taken time to dress her or put her in a final resting position?

From behind her, Craig let out a yell. "JILL! I'M BEGGING YOU! DO NOT GO IN THERE!"

Putting all those thoughts out of her mind, she punched Haley's birthdate into the keypad. The red glow around all the numbers switched to green, and the suction enclosure released. It sounded like one of those airlock doors on a spaceship in those deep-space movies. She felt like she was on one of those distant planets from the same films. Jill grasped the handle and pulled it open.

The room was dark at first, but then the lights all along the top corners of the containment unit flickered to life, first near her, then a domino effect of light as they came on in sequence down the line to the end of the container.

Nothing could have prepared Jill for what she saw at the very end of this tomb. Haley was there, still dressed in the same outfit she was wearing to school on the day she went missing.

The tears came first, and Jill's lips and chin began quivering as they fell. Jill was processing what she saw as her mind splintered. A long, heartbreaking wail erupted from her body.

This containment unit was fashioned to look more like a small chapel. It even had a worn red strip of carpeting running the length of it all the way down to the front, where there was a small church pew. It sat in front of what looked like a square, vertical aquarium filled with light green-tinted fluid that was only slightly murky. There were no fish or coral inside; there was only one object: Haley Danforth.

Haley floated there in suspended animation behind the glass, facing outward, eyes open as though wishing to be on the other side of her watery chamber. Her knees were slightly bent, and her left hand floated out away from her body. Her right hand was the only thing touching the glass. Haley's blonde hair spilled out in all directions from her head like a gigantic halo.

In Jill's spiraling, out-of-control mind, she had enough sense to think of one word: *formaldehyde.*

Jill finally made it to the glass coffin on rubbery legs, collapsing in front of the enclosure. Reaching deep within herself, she stood again and placed her hand against the glass, desperately trying to grasp her daughter's hand. Jill had waited so long to touch Haley's hand again, and she couldn't even do that; her fingernails only scrabbled against the glass. More tears of grief poured out of her. Racked sobs shook her body.

What was the thickness of this water chamber? A half inch? One-inch-thick slabs of glass? That small measurement was keeping her from the flesh-on-flesh contact with her daughter.

Jill took a moment to take her daughter in as the grief slowly turned to rage. Haley was dressed in jeans and Converse tennis shoes. She wore a thin zip-up hoodie—one of the many she would always wear because she didn't like even the slightest chill. Her T-shirt was barely distinguishable, but Jill remembered it. She had seen it in her mind every day for two years as she pictured her walking out the door to school repeatedly. It was Haley's woodblock carving design, this cabin and the woods, because she loved it so much that she'd drawn, cut, and printed with her own hands.

*How many countless hours had Haley sequestered herself in her room to cut and carve that design?*

She smiled through her tears at that thought as she placed her hands and forehead against the glass. She wanted to engulf Haley's body with the biggest, warmest hug.

Craig would answer for what he did to Haley. He may have made the sanctuary in honor of her, but to Jill, it was the worst form of sacrilege to Haley's body and her memory.

Jill turned away from the glass, seething rage possessing her body, slowly building like boiler pressure that was redlining and was soon going to spike.

……

**CRAIG WAITED PATIENTLY** for Anna to become distracted, maybe checking the hallway for Jill. It was quiet after the paramount anguished cries of grief that echoed throughout this chambered grave.

Jill was very thorough when covering him with his gun. He remembered how great a shot she was when all three of them were at the range. Those were fun times.

If he was going to get out of this situation, it would be with Anna, not Jill. But if he tried anything, he had to be careful and not damage the merchandise. He wasn't going to have Quinn Stanton and his goons get pissed at him for less-than-average, unmarketable merchandise. An injury would not be good for business.

Anna stepped backward and glanced toward the secret room. Jill was turning and moving back up the trailer. Anna looked past Jill to see just what had brought the wailing grief out of her.

*Now is the time,* Craig thought, and lunged.

From the corner of her eye, Anna saw a blur of movement. She looked back and lowered the gun, just as Craig's arms wrapped around her.

Anna pulled the trigger. The sound of Armageddon detonated inside the transfer trailer.

The scream from Craig was loud in Anna's ear on the tail end of the gun's boom. He immediately released her and grabbed his leg as he hobbled backward, further into Anna's chamber.

# CHAPTER FOURTEEN

**JILL'S HEART DROPPED** when the concussive boom sounded out.

*Fuck,* she thought. *Craig got the best of her.* She ran the rest of the way out of the trailer to where she'd left Anna.

Anna heard Jill coming back toward them. She shifted her body enough at the door and relinquished the gun to Jill as she neared them. She said, "He—he tried to rush me."

Taking the gun, Jill said, "Oh, thank God. I was afraid he'd gotten the gun away and shot you." She stepped into the spot where Anna had been watching over Craig.

"No—no. Not a chance. He was trying his funny business you were talking about, so I kneecapped him as you suggested."

Finding they were still in charge, Jill brought the gun up again.

"Why did you do it?"

"It was an accident," Craig said through gritted teeth.

"Haley didn't just accidentally end up in that glass box floating in formaldehyde. You put her there. I want to know why."

Jill was all business. There was no more playing around. "Why did you keep her body from me all these years? I thought my daughter was still alive *out there somewhere.*" Jill threw her arm in a direction, meaning *out in the world.*

"And me, all these years, I've been feeling guilty that maybe I'd done something to piss her off. To… to make her run away from me. That, or someone kidnapped her. I wasted so many prayers every night praying that she would be safe and that she would come back home. But it was all just wasted energy because you took it upon yourself to keep her *here* in this *boxed grave.* I've been looking for her for two… *long* years."

"I know. And I'm sorry," he said through clenched teeth. "You just don't know how sorry I am."

"You're not *sorry.* There's no way in hell that *you're sorry.*" A seething boiled under the surface of Jill's skin. "Other than sorry you got caught. So, save me all your fucking sob stories. What happened? I want to know why she is in that containment unit. What did she do?"

"She cut class, Jill." The words burst from him like a shotgun blast. "She— she played hooky from school and came up to the cabin on a whim. You know how much she loved being here. She couldn't get enough of this place. She was just gonna spend the day relaxing, sunbathing, and reading a book out on the dock. She was going to leave in time to be home at the normal time, so we wouldn't get suspicious of anything."

"Let me guess. You were already here doing this shit."

"I guess you can say that. Haley was surprised to find my truck here. She went inside but didn't find me. She got a little worried. Thought that maybe I went for a hike and maybe tripped and hurt myself in the woods, so she went looking for me."

"She found the bunker, too, huh?" Jill said, leading him along in his own story. "Just like I did."

"Yeah. She was on the trail heading up to the waterfalls when I came out of the bunker."

"So… what? She got scared and ran from you? You chased her? What, did she fall? Hit her head? How far into the woods did you chase her?"

"It wasn't like that at all. She was interested in what I had built years ago, before you two came into my life. I told her it was a bomb shelter… a… a doomsday prepper room. I told her that I hadn't told anybody because I didn't want the word to get out in case something ever happened, and that we needed to come below ground. She was in awe of the place. She thought it was so cool."

"My daughter. Is in. A glass. Container. I want to know what happened to her. Did you have one of your victims locked up down here?"

"No, I was between business deals. Hadn't yet taken anyone else. The place was empty."

Impatient with the lack of full answers, Jill shook her gun angrily at Craig. "Get to the fucking point! I want to know what happened to my daughter! What happened to my Haley?" Tears were filling her eyes again.

"I showed her the rooms. The one she is currently in. It didn't look like that back then. It was pretty much like this one. I had two holding cells, and I used to do double the amount of trafficking, but Haley put an end to that." He gave a deep sigh in reliving the horrible memory.

"In showing her around, I forgot how open I'd left everything down here. Coming out of the supplies area, she saw the schedule and itinerary of who was coming later in the week mounted on the wall. She questioned me about it, but I played it off as something other than what it was.

"My answer seemed to satisfy her, but I knew Haley… she was such a smart girl. I knew she would keep asking questions about this place. She would eventually figure it out. And I couldn't have any loose ends. I opened the door, let her go in to investigate the room, and as soon as she was across the threshold, I shut it behind her and locked her inside. I couldn't allow Haley to know what I did down here. No one was going to know."

"You just let my daughter waste away in here?"

"No. I was merciful to her. As merciful as I could be, under the circumstances. I turned all the ventilators off in that containment unit, and she expired in a few days with no air coming in or out."

Jill's tears blurred the madman standing in front of her. She swiped her liquid emotion away to see more clearly. "You just let my daughter suffocate?"

"Be thankful I did that. I could've done a lot worse."

"There's something really wrong with you, Craig. How you have been smart enough to keep this from me all these years, I'll never know. But not anymore. I'm going to take *my* daughter now, as soon as some crime lab or CSI people come here to the cabin and down into this hellhole and investigate *everything* you've been doing. And I'm going to bury her where we pretended to bury her a year and a half ago. *You*, on the other hand…" Jill couldn't find the words.

"I really don't give a shit what happens to you. But what *we're* going to do, Anna and I, is we're going to leave you here locked up. I'm going to let the cops figure it all out. My mind is overloaded and exhausted, and I really don't know what to do. I don't have the mental capacity to figure all of *it*… or—or *you* out."

"I know what I would do," Anna said, chiming in. Her voice sounded mousy, dejected, barely audible.

"Oh yeah, what's that, sweetheart?" Jill asked. "What is your grand solution to all *this?*"

"I wouldn't let him leave. If he'd done *that* to my daughter." She let the words hang for a moment as she glanced toward the other chamber. Turning back, she said, "I know I promised you that I wouldn't shoot him, nothing fatal at least. It was the hardest thing I've ever done in my life. I wanted to fucking obliterate him because he killed my parents with no remorse whatsoever. It was all fun and games to him. I would have no problem emptying that gun into him."

Anna held out her hand for the gun. "All you have to do is give it to me without any restrictions, and I'll take care of this problem for us both."

Jill considered her proposal for a moment. Her lips twitched in concentration, weighing her options. Anna's words had hit home. Then, a thought from earlier in the day came to her. She glanced up at Craig. "Is this the gun you used to do it?"

"To do what?"

"Kill her parents?"

"What the fuck does that matter?" His defiance of the question was the same as admitting that it was.

"It is, isn't it? You know, Anna," Jill said. "Your proposal is a very good idea. How about this? There are now five bullets in the gun. Yes, Craig, I checked. It was fully loaded. Anna, since you've already shot him, you can have two more shots. I'll take the other three."

"Really? You're serious. I would be eternally grateful for even one. Two more shots are really all I need. All I really want."

"Two more shots for you, it is, then. The rest are mine. Agreed?" Jill didn't want Anna going off, getting trigger-happy, and emptying all the rounds into him. "Don't cut me out of my revenge. I will not take kindly to that."

"Yes, ma'am."

Jill swung her head back toward Craig with a steely determination on her face.

Craig immediately released his knee and held his bloodied hands up to try and reason with his wife. "Jill, think about this. I know you feel like I took something from you, but it was the only way I knew how to deal with what happened."

Jill moved her aim to numerous parts of Craig's body, trying to figure out where she wanted to place her first bullet. She thumbed the hammer back, lowered her aim, and pulled the trigger. The boom was like another bomb detonating in the confined space. The bullet punched a hole in Craig's abdomen and ripped out somewhere in his back. Jill smiled as Craig's face contorted; he grabbed his stomach and stumbled even further back.

He came to rest against the edge of the king-sized bed. He gritted his teeth, his cheeks puffing out with heavy breaths. "Jill, please. Don't do this!" he pleaded.

"Your turn," Jill said, switching the gun to her left hand and holding it out for Anna to take.

Jill watched as Anna took the revolver. There was nothing timid about Anna's demeanor now. There was an eager confidence. Expecting Anna to place a bullet in Craig's chest or face, Jill's eyebrows lifted as Anna's aim lowered to the center of his legs; then, without hesitation, she pulled the trigger.

A small hole punched into the center of Craig's crotch. A tuft of denim exploded outward along with a spray of blood. Craig's howls filled the room again. Blood began to spread across the front of his jeans as though he were pissing dark liquid. He didn't have enough hands to grab all the places where the bullet holes and the pain had opened him up.

Jill felt she understood why Anna had aimed there. Jill didn't know if Craig had sexually assaulted her, but even if he hadn't, for the past few days Jill had a feeling there must've been a fear that Anna was going to be. Or that she would be after she left this bunker and landed in an unknown place as someone's property.

Over his cries, Anna said, "That one was for me, asshole."

The gun switched back to Jill. She brought the revolver up as she cocked the trigger again, then squeezed the trigger. A rosebud bloomed on Craig's chest. It was a center mass hit. She really didn't even aim because they were in such close quarters. All the trips to the gun range had helped her perfect her shot.

Jill handed the revolver back to Anna nonchalantly, like two women simply sharing a bottle of whiskey.

Anna brought the gun up, this time with a double-handed aim at Craig's neck, and fired. It was slightly to the left, and a chunk of his neck exploded outward. That was a lot of blood. Judging from where the bullet punched a hole in Craig's throat, Jill figured it had severed that main neck artery, and she hoped and prayed it had obliterated it. Seeing all that red brought a smile to her face.

As Anna relinquished the gun back to Jill, she said, "And that one was for my mom and dad."

Jill cocked the hammer again and leveled it at Craig's face. In an even tone, Jill said, "This one is for all those times you lied to me. This is also… for Haley."

Craig couldn't even open his mouth to argue with her. His body was overloaded with pain. Hate was etched into his face. It was red from the buildup of anger he couldn't release; the vein in his forehead was straining against the agony. He could only grit his teeth and growl at her. It was as though he was daring her to pull the trigger one last time.

Jill did.

The bullet punched through the area between his eyebrows and out the back of his head. Craig flopped back on the comforter where Anna had lain during her time down here.

Jill and Anna stepped slowly forward to the bed and looked down at Craig's still corpse. His eyes were open in a shocked stare, looking above him as though observing his craftsmanship of transforming this prison cell into a fake home.

Blood continued to ooze from the numerous bullet wounds in his body, but he was already gone. There was no coming back from that.

"You ready to get the hell out of here?" Jill asked.

"Never more ready."

Anna stepped from the prison room first.

At the door to this holding cell, Jill turned back to take a last look at Craig sprawled on the bed. She pushed the door closed and hooked the lock on it, but she didn't snap it shut as she didn't have the key and she wasn't about to go through Craig's pockets to find it. She didn't have any worries that Craig was going to suddenly rise from the dead, step from this room, and come after them. She knew there was no more life left in him.

They made their way to the steel stairway at the end of the long corridor. This hallway was the length of two tractor-trailers. Jill knew she would have to call James Medlin, the investigator who had been so kind to her and who had followed as many leads as he could before they became cold.

They climbed the staircase holding onto each other for support and comfort. They pushed the hydraulic door up and stepped into the sunlight.

# CHAPTER FIFTEEN

"HEY, JAMES, IT'S JILL."

"Jill. Oh, hey. It's good to hear your voice."

Jill held the phone to her ear as she stared out at the calm lake. She glanced over at Anna, who was now sitting on the porch with her arms hugging her legs and her head on her knees.

James Medlin continued, "I'm sorry I haven't called. I don't have anything new to report on the investigation with Haley. All the leads have gone cold. I can't make any headway on it."

"No, I know you haven't gotten any further with the case. I'm not really calling to check in. I'm calling *you* with information."

"Oh?"

"I was curious if you could come up here to the cabin. You still know the address and the way here, correct?"

"Uh, yeah… I know the way. I could head that way in about five minutes."

"That sounds good. But James, I was going to see if you could do me one special favor."

"Of course. What is it?"

"Could you come alone? I would rather you see what I have to show you and hear what I have to say before involving anyone else. Can you do that for me?"

"Um… I guess. I really don't like the way this all sounds. Not really protocol to do that."

Jill ignored his by-the-book rhetoric. "Once you see it, then I will release you to do whatever police procedures you need to do."

There was a long pause. Jill assumed he was mulling it over, quickly searching out each scenario and if any heat would come down on his head for doing this favor for her. Finally, he asked, "Should I be worried about doing this?"

"No, you shouldn't be worried at all. In fact, I think this information I have will pretty much close Haley's case and maybe a few others that some of your co-worker detectives are working on."

"Okay." The word was said in a long, drawn-out reluctance.

"Good, I'll see you in about an hour. And James?"

"Yeah?

"Thank you for doing me this courtesy."

Jill made sure her phone call had ended, then she turned, moved back to Anna and said, "When James gets here, you never touched this gun. Understood?"

Anna nodded and said, "I understand."

Jill moved to the front porch and put a foot on the bottom stair. "If you're ever questioned without me and they spin their narrative to say anything other than I was the only one who put Craig down, then they are lying. Because I won't change my story. Are we clear?"

Anna nodded emphatically. "Understood."

Jill eyed Anna again, searching her features to make sure she was solid on her promise to her. Satisfied, she moved up the stairs and sat in the chair next to Anna. She stared down at the revolver in her hands. She had a thought and reached into her pocket and extracted Craig's pocketknife. She placed the tip against the wood on the left side and began to scrape lines in the handle.

"I understand what you're saying, but since I joined in with killing that asshole, I feel like I should take my share of whatever punishment is going to come to us."

Jill didn't feel Anna's animosity was aimed toward her in any way; all her hate was focused toward Craig and what he'd done to her.

"It wouldn't be fair. That is, if there is any punishment that comes to us. I may be only a senior, but I'm a big girl. I stepped out on that limb with you knowing the consequences."

Still looking down at the gun, Jill continued to scratch at the handle. "Look, I have no idea what is going to happen in the next few hours, days, weeks, or even months. I don't regret what I did." She glanced over at Anna. "But now, I… maybe, regret having you take part in this. I really didn't have time to consider it. I just went with my gut." She directed her attention back to her handiwork.

"I'm glad you allowed me to participate. *Thankful.*"

"I guess I couldn't take all my rage out on him. I knew you needed a part of that… *rage cleansing* for yourself. That's why I let you take part. But you are a senior, and you have your whole life ahead of you. So let me just take the fall for this and you go live the life you probably wouldn't have been able to live had I not come along." There was no arrogance in her comment; she was just stating facts.

Anna looked over at Jill.

Jill felt Anna's eyes on her; glancing over at her, she gave her a double-take. "Why are you looking at me like that?"

"You are just a godsend." Anna shook her head, not knowing anything else to say about the situation. "I have an extremely odd proposal. It sort of came to me shortly after we locked the door to the room I was in. The one we left your husband in."

"He's not my husband. Not anymore. What's this proposal?"

"I know that no one on this earth could take the place of your daughter. Haley? Was that her name?"

"Yeah. And you're right."

"Just from the way you handled yourself down there and the grief that came out of you when you finally found her…"

Jill didn't say anything but let Anna have her time to present whatever she was going to say in a natural way. It didn't seem like she knew how to voice it. Jill continued to scratch small straight lines in the wooden stock.

"I know I would never even come close to filling your daughter's shoes, and I feel funny even suggesting this. On the other hand, I currently have no parents because that piece of shit…" She looked off into the distance at the spot where they had emerged from the woods. "Murdered them. I don't know if you would even be remotely interested—"

"You want to know if I want to be your mother?"

Anna squinted, shook her head, and gave a grimace. It wasn't the way she was trying to explain it, but it was the most concise way to say it. "Well, now that really sounds stupid when you say it like that. I was thinking that maybe… we could fill the… *voids* in each other's lives. At least be there for each other."

Jill said. "I would never be able to fill your parents' shoes."

"I'm not suggesting you try to."

"You don't even know me. Why would you even want to be associated with me after what my husband did to you… and to your parents? I would think you would never want to see me after all this is over."

"On the contrary. From what you did down there in that room. You saved me. I wasn't just rambling when I said I would pretty much do anything for you because you rescued me." Anna's voice cracked, and the tears started to flow. "When I think of where I may have been in a day or two, and what might have happened to me after I was *bought*. Yes, I would gladly be your daughter or as much of a version of a daughter that I *could* be… that you would *allow* me to be. At least a friend to help you through this grief. I believe you're going to be reliving it all over again now that you have her and know what happened to her."

Anna talked of Haley as though she knew her. "Me too. You don't have to say yes right away. I'm sure there's going to be a lot of shit going on here at the lake very soon. I only ask you to consider it. I would just like to be there for you in some capacity, the way you were there for me. That's all."

The whole time Anna was speaking, Jill was mulling the idea over. True, she would never have Haley back, and Anna would never have her parents back. It was a sweet proposal and one worth considering.

Each of them fell silent, lost in the horrors they had experienced. They each tried suggesting a subject to discuss, but they soon fell silent again. Silence was what they needed to calm their minds. Having each other's company was enough for now, and the serenity of the lake atmosphere helped as well.

Soon, the only sound audible was the continuous scratching of the blade against the wood of the revolver's handle.

# CHAPTER SIXTEEN

**THE UNMARKED POLICE** cruiser pulled slowly down the long, winding driveway to the cabin.

"The cavalry has arrived. I guess this is my cue." Jill stood, dusting off the small wood shavings that dotted her lap. She took the revolver to the head of the stairs and, with an extra flourish of her shirt to the whole gun, she wiped away any trace of Anna's fingerprints. She placed it with the left side of the handle showing. The two boxes of bullets joined the gun, then she closed the pocketknife and set it next to the bullets.

James Medlin pulled beside Craig's Ford F-250. He killed the engine and stepped from behind the wheel. In his hand, he held an Atlanta Braves ball cap, which he flipped on his head. He hitched his pants and surveyed his surroundings, then he moved closer to the porch.

"Hey, Jill," he said. Looking at the Asian girl sitting in the chair beside her, he added, "Ma'am." He gave a nod to Anna.

"Hello," Anna said timidly, still hugging herself in the fetal position she'd adopted since they had come out of the woods.

To Jill, he asked, "Who's this?" He gave another head nod, indicating who he meant.

"This is Anna Cheong. I will tell you more about her in time."

"Okay. You were a little mysterious on the phone earlier. You're being even more mysterious now. I still think I should be worried."

Jill gave him a half-smile. "I know."

"Care to tell me what this is all about?"

"I appreciate you keeping your word to come by yourself. I wanted to talk to you about a few things and walk you through what happened. But first, I have a quick question for you."

"Shoot."

"Do you think I'm a good person?"

There was no hesitation. "Of course. Simply the best. From the time I've talked with you during the investigation of your daughter's disappearance, I have no reason to suspect there is anything bad about you."

"Good. And do you trust me?"

"Sure. For the two years I've known you, you've been nothing but helpful and truthful in anything dealing with your daughter's case. So, yeah, there's a lot of trust there."

"Good. Because I will need you to keep all that in mind as I tell you what happened."

"Okay… sure. But now you're even more mysterious. What's going on, Jill?"

"Before I tell you anything, I feel the need to tell you that I am unarmed." She held up her hands to show him there was nothing in them. "No weapons of any kind. That goes for Anna here, too." Anna slowly showed her hands as well.

"Why are you saying all this?"

"Because you need to bag that revolver, knife, and bullets as evidence. It's the gun that I used to kill Craig Danforth." She pointed to the top porch step. "The revolver is empty, by the way. Well, no live ammo, just spent shells."

James walked closer as he followed her finger's direction and saw what was placed at the top of the stairs. As she had stated, there was a single revolver, two boxes of shells, and a closed pocketknife. He looked back at her with a confused expression on his face.

"You say you killed your husband. Where's Craig's body now?"

Jill pointed. "Out there. In the woods. I'll show you soon enough."

"Why did you do it?"

"Because he was a bad, bad man."

"He always seemed like a nice enough guy to me."

"He had you fooled, too. For as long as I knew him, and was married to him, he wore a chameleon skin. I just found out today the true nature of my husband. And how evil he really was."

James turned and looked back at the woods, then to the items in a row on the porch, then back to Jill. "You said you had info that would close Haley's case and some of the other cases that my coworker detectives are working on? What can you tell me about that?"

"Well, for starters, Anna here… her parents were killed by my husband, and I think it was that same revolver that was used to kill them. You'll have to do a ballistics check on that to make sure. Is that what they call it?"

James raised his eyebrows at the news and terminology Jill was throwing his way. "Uh, yeah. That's the correct term to use."

She pointed at it again. "So, I'm sure there is a case file open for Anna's parents. Craig killed them, kidnapped her, and brought her here. Craig was going to sell Anna for a high price on the black market. Hell, he *was* the black market. One of them at least. Does the name Quinn Stanton ring a bell?"

James considered the question, set his face in a frown, then shook his head. "Not to me, no. But it could be a name that comes up, as you say, in some other detectives' cases. Why?"

"Craig said a Quinn Stanton was sending two men in two days to collect Anna. My thought is that you could probably set up some sort of sting operation here and arrest those guys. If that info is correct, maybe you could get more info out of them. So you may want to keep what I'm telling you and going to show you hush-hush until you capture those men. Maybe stop more human trafficking that is going on. I don't know. God knows too much of that is happening in the world. From how Craig sounded, he was low on the totem pole, but he was part of it. More notes and contacts could be in his underground bunker that's out in the woods."

James shook his head against the information overloading his brain. He held up his hands for Jill to take a breather. "Hold up. There's a lot of info coming at me right now." He paused, seeing how focused she was with her suggestions. "You're serious about this."

"I'm certainly not laughing about it." She paused, wondering where she would go with this crazy conversation. "No. It's no joke. I found out that's where our wealth came from. Most of it anyway, not all. It wasn't from the honest work of Craig grinding his fingers to the bone on the construction site. If another investigator has a case with Anna's parents being murdered, she's your witness, and I'm sure she will help with further details."

Anna and James nodded. James said, "Okay. Yes, that will be helpful."

"But the biggest news of all is that Craig killed my Haley. She's down there in a vat of formaldehyde. In the shrine he built for her."

Jill knew this was a lot for James to take in. Neither of them had ever considered that what happened to Haley was this weird and sadistic. She watched as James's eyes filled with tears and he turned away toward the woods because he didn't want her to see him cry.

She was touched. James had gotten to know Haley through pictures and the conversations he and Jill had about her. She knew his heartfelt commitment and goal were to bring Haley back to her, but that was never going to be fulfilled now. She was sure his heart hurt at not being able to capitalize on the unspoken promise.

He finally turned back. "Jill, I am sincerely sorry for your loss. I always hoped we would find her alive and well… somewhere."

A long silence stretched out between them.

James reached into his jacket pocket and pulled out an evidence bag. He turned it inside out and grabbed the revolver, the pocketknife, and the two boxes of bullets from the porch steps. He inverted the plastic, capturing all the evidence inside. James studied the revolver and noticed two words scratched into the handle.

## FOR HALEY

He looked up at Jill and asked, "You did this?"

"I sure did. I scratched it in with Craig's pocketknife while I waited for you to arrive. No son of a bitch kills my daughter, hides her body under the ground in a vat of formaldehyde, and lives to tell about it. He had no resolve for my daughter's life, so I had none for his. I ended him. It's that simple."

"I see."

"Would you like to see Craig's body? Would you like to see where Haley's been for the duration of this case?"

"Yes, I would."

"Then we need to make a little trek across this field and into the woods. That's where they are."

"Okay. Just let me get this evidence locked up, and we can head that way. This will go into an evidence locker back at the precinct." James moved back to his unmarked car, popped the trunk, and placed the plastic evidence bag in the lockbox inside. He slammed the trunk and waved Jill toward him. "You say their bodies are through the trees there." He pointed.

Jill stood and moved to him. "Yeah," She trundled down the stairs but turned back to Anna. "You coming?"

Anna shook her head quickly. "No, I can't go back down there. I'll wait here on the porch in the sunshine."

"I'm afraid I can't allow that. You're a witness in this case—"

"James," Jill said.

James looked over at her.

"Do you trust me?"

"Yeah."

"Then let her stay. She won't go anywhere. You have my word. We're cooperating. She's been locked up in that bunker for a few days. She's been through a lot. Please."

He took a moment to weigh out his options.

Jill turned to Anna. "You're not going to take off, are you, Anna?"

She shook her head. "No. I have nowhere to go." Anna's voice cracked as tears began building up in her eyes.

Jill turned back to James with a 'problem-solved' look.

"Okay, if she does, that is going to come down on you. Not me."

"Understood. I trust her."

He nodded.

Jill turned to Anna one last time. "If you need to lie down, you can rest on the couch or in any of the bedrooms in the cabin until we finish."

"I don't think I could sleep. It will be a long time before sleep comes to me."

"Me too. We're in the same boat."

"I just want to be in the sunshine."

"We'll be back as soon as we can."

"I'm not going anywhere."

Jill smiled. "That's perfectly fine." She turned and moved toward James.

Anna's voice called to Jill from behind. Jill turned back and was immediately engulfed in the tightest embrace. It took Jill a moment to catch up to this affectionate attack on her. Finally, her arms encircled Anna's body, and they hugged tightly and held each other.

Anna's mouth was pressed into Jill's shoulder; her voice was muffled, but Jill heard every word. "Thank you for saving me."

"You're welcome. I'm so glad I could."

Eventually, they broke their embrace. Anna reluctantly moved back to the porch, and Jill joined James, where he stood watching their exchange.

Together, James and Jill walked toward the tree line in the distance. While walking, she told him everything that happened from the time she recorded Craig talking in his sleep until she called for James to come to the cabin.

As she talked, she couldn't help but think about what she was going to do when this nightmare was over. Would she and Anna be the missing piece in each other's lives? How long would it take her to grieve now that she knew her daughter was dead? Some of those questions were too far in the future to answer.

She knew it would be a long time before she could ever trust or even love again, and that was counting Anna's proposal also. But the more she thought about it, the better the idea sounded to her. It was like a spark of light against all the dismal dreaminess that her life had been for the past two years. She held on to that light and smiled. She knew that, eventually, she and Anna would be all right.

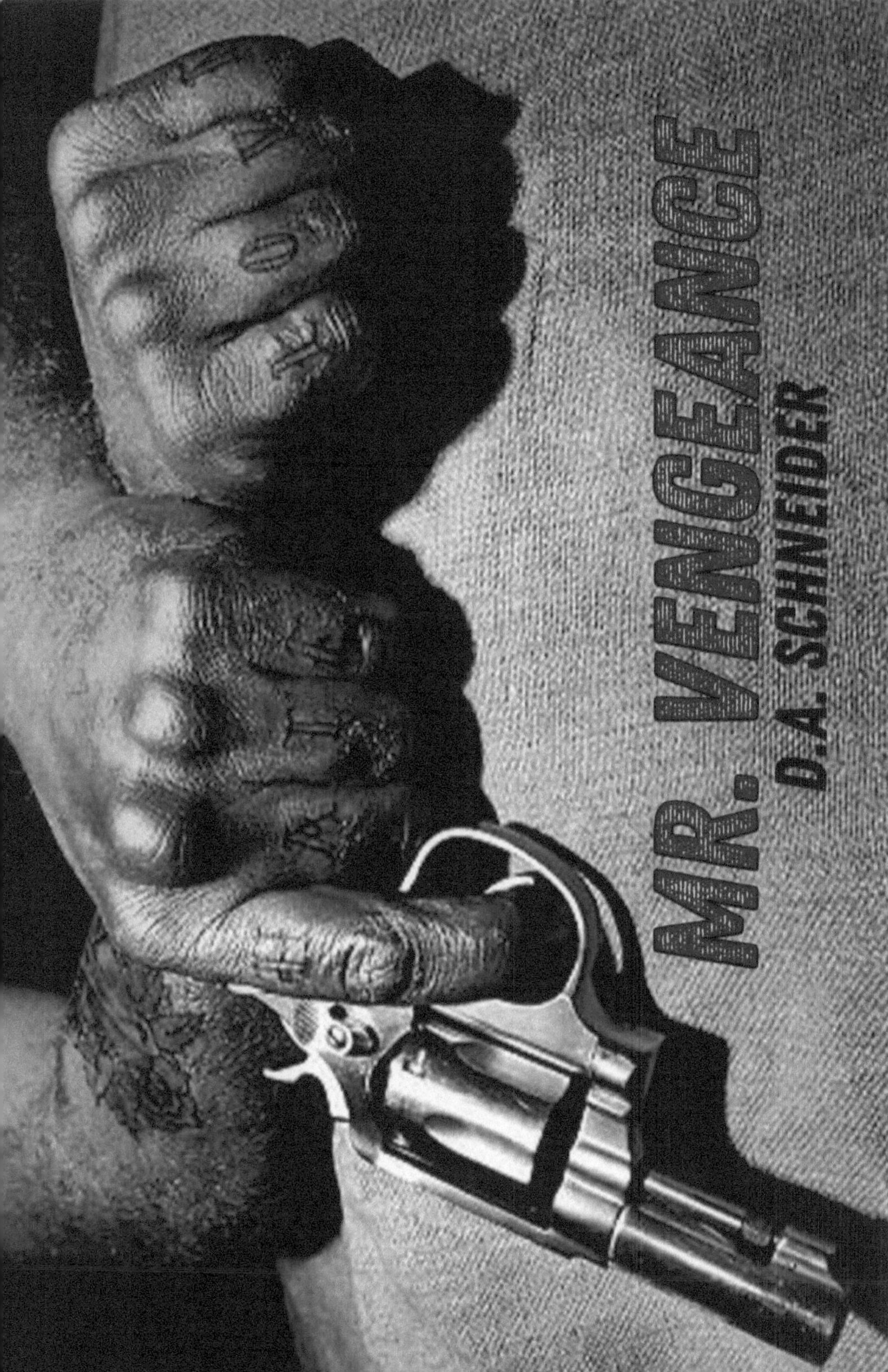
MR. VENGEANCE
D.A. SCHNEIDER

*D.A.'s Dedication:*

*To Tracy*

# CHAPTER ONE

# THREE MONTHS AGO

**"YOU SAID YOU** would come back for me."

Leo looked through the glass divider at the woman he loved. Just three years his wife, Rita, was a Latin beauty with big brown eyes. Now, those eyes threatened rain. Leo couldn't stand it when she cried. It made him melt. Rita was the only woman—hell, the only *person* in the world— who had that effect on him. Besides maybe his mother.

Leo placed one big hand on the divider and spoke in his baritone voice. "I will, sweetness. I just have three more months. When I get out, you and me, we're gonna run away together."

Rita looked from side to side, as if she wanted to be sure someone nearby wouldn't hear what she was about to say. Then, she leaned closer to the partition and spoke quietly into the phone receiver. "Someone is after me."

A blazing fury awoke inside Leo at these words. One that would be familiar to anyone who knew him. One that far too many unfortunate assholes had been on the receiving end of when he was on the outside. And for a time, on the inside. Since he set that example, his fellow inmates left him alone. "Who?" he growled.

"I don't know," she said. "I've noticed them over the past few days. They drive a black SUV with fancy… rims… and…" She was starting to hyperventilate.

"Okay," Leo said, holding one hand up in a calming motion. "It's okay. What kind of SUV?"

She took a few relaxing breaths and spoke in a weak voice. "I don't know what you mean."

"Well, like, is it a big luxury SUV?" Leo inquired. "Or one of those little crossover motherfuckers?"

"Oh." She paused to rub tears from her eyes. "Big. It was very big and fancy. New."

"Did you get a look at the driver?" asked Leo. "Was there more than one person inside?"

"No, the windows were tinted. I couldn't see inside."

"Time's up," called the guard.

"Okay, listen to me," said Leo, his eyes on hers. "Go directly to Higgy. I'm going to give him a call as soon as we're done here. He can find a safe place for you. A place where you can stay hidden until I get out. I'll come for you, okay?"

She nodded nervously. "Okay."

"Be careful," Leo said to Rita. "If you think they're following you when you leave here, lose them before you reach Higgy. Got it?"

"Got it."

"Let's go, Leo," the guard insisted.

Leo stood from his chair and placed his hand against the glass once more. "I love you, Rita."

She placed her hand against his. A tear spilled down her cheek, and her lip quivered as she spoke. "I love you, Leo."

As the guard led Leo away, he kept his eyes on her face. He committed every detail to memory. Her thick brown hair. Her streaming brown eyes. Her full, pouty lips.

As if this would be their last time together. As if he would never see her again.

The guard allowed him one quick call before he was returned to his cell. He got in touch with Higgy, his most trusted friend, and told him what was happening. "When she gets there, Higgy, stash her some place safe."

"You can count on me, Leo," said Higgy.

Leo ended the call. Once he was back in his cell, he sat and worried about the love of his life. He'd call Higgy later to make sure she got to him okay. Until then, all he could do was wait.

The hours seemed to pass at a snail's pace. Leo could think of nothing but Rita, out there on the streets by herself. He should have made her wait. He should have called Higgy and had him come get her here at the prison. What the fuck was he thinking?

Unable to wait any longer, and with lights out only fifteen minutes away, Leo requested a phone call and a guard led him back to the ancient, wall-mounted payphone. He dropped a quarter in and dialed Higgy's number, which was one of the only two numbers he could remember off the top of his head. The other was his grandparents, and the reason for this was the fact that both numbers had been the same for as long as he could remember. His grandparents lived in the same house for over fifty years, and Higgy now lived in the house in which Leo grew up, with the landline still intact. Leo and Higgy's friendship went back to their school days.

"Hello," Higgy answered.

"Did Rita get to your place okay?" Leo asked without pleasantries.

There was a pause on the other end of the line. Leo's first thought was that he'd never heard Higgy stay quiet for so long. "Hig, you there?"

"Yeah, I'm here," his old friend replied. Then, "Leo, buddy, she never showed up."

Leo felt the blood drain from his face. His stomach was suddenly a twisted knot of fear. He realized then that Higgy was talking, but his voice seemed like it was miles away. "Leo, I'm going to go out and look for her, okay? I'm not going to stop until I find her. Maybe she just got held up. I'll keep calling her, I'll—"

Leo hung the phone receiver back on its hook. In a daze, he walked back toward his cell, his brain abuzz with a cornucopia of emotions. They ran the gamut from sadness, to hopelessness, to confusion. By the time he sat down on his bunk and the lights went out, the one emotion that had fought its way to the surface, pounding all others into the fucking ground as it went, was a rage that made his ears ring and his muscles taut.

# CHAPTER TWO

# NOW

**SHAWN HIGGONS HAD** gone by "Higgy" since he was nine years old. It was Leo who started using the nickname, and it just stuck. Back then, they'd both had big dreams. They talked about playing pro football, discovering dinosaur bones, or traveling through space on the first manned mission to Mars. Little did Higgy know, they'd both grow up to take after their fathers and become fucking criminals.

Still, it was better than trying to make an honest living like so many chumps around the country. Those poor, sad fuckers working their hands and backs to the bone and barely scraping by. No, give Higgy the life of crime any day over that shit. And if you knew what you were doing and made some solid contacts, you could get away with just about anything.

It was one of those contacts that brought him to the 99th Precinct police station in Brooklyn, New York. Billy Needler was an old pal of Higgy's. The two went back almost as far as he and Leo. But while Higgy had turned to a life of crime, Billy had taken a very different path and ended up a police officer. However, that didn't mean he didn't have a little criminal in him. Billy got a rush from breaking the law, and since he was in charge of the evidence locker in his particular precinct, he also made some extra cash on the side.

Higgy sat across the street from the station in his utility van. Before long, Billy pulled out in his daily driver after his shift. Higgy started the van and followed. Billy led them to a secluded lot down by the river, with a great view of a couple of condemned warehouses and the Brooklyn Bridge overhead. Parking next to the slightly crooked but never corrupt (as Billy liked to put it) police officer, Higgy got out of his van and rounded it to the trunk of the car.

"Billy Boy," Higgy said, shaking the cop's hand in the secret style they came up with in their youth. "How ya been, man? I bet that little rugrat of yours is getting big."

"Sure as fuck is," said Billy. "He outgrows his clothes so fast, I feel like we buy him a whole new fucking wardrobe every week."

Billy had always been a good-looking kid. He had a round face and a full head of jet-black hair. The Italian was strong with this one.

"What can I do to help relieve this financial burden?" Higgy asked.

Billy popped open the trunk of the car and unzipped a small duffel bag. "This stuff had been sitting in holding for a while. I wasn't able to get much, but what I got is valuable."

"Holy shit!" said Higgy. "Is that heroin?"

The two bricks were wrapped and taped, and it was rare for Higgy to acquire so much.

"Some good shit, apparently," said Billy. "Plus, I snagged this." The police officer hefted a revolver from beneath a towel and handed it over to Higgy. The serial number had already been removed.

"That's a nice fucking gun," Higgy observed.

"Yeah, man," Billy agreed. "I bet you could get about a grand out of it."

Higgy thought he was probably right. "Alright. So, how much do you want for all this? And keep in mind, pawn shop rules apply. I got to turn a profit on this shit."

"I think fifty grand is a fair price," Billy said.

Higgy thought he'd come up with that price pretty fast. "Come on, man, that's pretty fucking steep. I don't even know how good this shit is."

"That's black tar heroin, man. You'll get fifty thousand for *each* of those fucking bricks."

Billy was right. The bad thing about buying shit from cops was that you couldn't bullshit them. They knew exactly what they had going into the deal. Still, Higgy had to try. "I can give you twenty-five."

Billy rolled his eyes. "Oh, fuck you, Higgy. Fifty grand. I'm not budging. You know what kind of chance I'm taking lifting shit from police evidence lockers. How much trouble I can get into. Not to mention the finesse it takes to work around the security system."

"What am I?" asked Higgy. "Do I look like a big-time movie producer? A mover and shaker on fucking Wall Street? I can't just throw around fifty thousand dollars like it's nothing."

Billy took the revolver from Higgy's hand and tossed it on top of the bricks, then closed the trunk. "I know you're small time, Higgy, but damn. If you can't move this and at least double your money, maybe you should get a day job."

The cop moved to his driver's side door and Higgy called him back. "All right, enough with the fucking theatrics. I'll give you the fifty grand."

Billy walked back to the trunk with a satisfied grin. "I knew I could count on you, Higgy."

"Yeah, yeah," Higgy mumbled.

Higgy didn't think he'd have any trouble moving the shit. In fact, he already had a guy in mind. He could make close to a hundred grand off the shit and likely eight hundred to a thousand for the revolver. That would make this a pretty nice little score. He took the duffel bag full of goods from Billy in exchange for an envelope full of cash, then returned to his van to head home.

In a week, Leo would be out, and during his drive home, Higgy wondered what kind of jobs he could line up for his old friend.

# CHAPTER THREE

**LEO STEPPED THROUGH** the open gate as a free man for the first time in two years. He couldn't say the time inside had rehabilitated him. He was a crook when he went in and had no doubt he'd be a crook again. Only now, he might have become something far more dangerous. Rita had been missing for three months. Leo knew that if she was hurt in *any* way, people would die by his hand.

For a time, Leo walked down the dust-blown, cracked road. It was late September and the day had come off unseasonably warm. He didn't try to hitchhike; no one in their right mind would pick up a big man with a shaved head and arms covered in tattoos. He supposed he looked like a skinhead, and the white supremacists had tried to recruit him while he was inside, but he didn't give a fuck about such things. He shaved his head because he was going bald anyway, and it looked better than the patchy bullshit that came in when what was left of his hair grew out.

As for the tattoos, they were all from classic horror movies. Leo was a nut for that shit. Bela Lugosi's Dracula, Boris Karloff's Frankenstein Monster, and Lon Chaney, Jr.'s Wolfman were among the collection on his right arm. Vincent Price and Hammer Film creatures were included among the sleeve on his left. The words "LOVE" across the fingers of his right hand and "HATE" tattooed across the fingers on his left were a tribute to Robert Mitchum's character in his all-time favorite film, *Night of the Hunter.*

Leo was violent as a young man, always willing to rough someone up for money owed to his booky friends or bust a few kneecaps to remind motherfuckers not to snitch to the cops. Nearing thirty-six now, he had worked hard to leave all that behind. He was a thief more than a thug, and he prided himself on being crafty—pulling jobs off with finesse. He didn't like to hurt people. Some just brought it on themselves. One thing he'd *never* been was a killer. He hoped that wouldn't have to change.

Leo made it to the bus stop on the corner, which seemed out of place among the sprawling cornfields, and there he sat and simmered in his anger until a bus came trundling down the road nearly two hours later. He climbed the steps and moved to the back seat of the nearly empty bus. He stared out the window, thinking through his next move, and he didn't stop until they reached the city.

# CHAPTER FOUR

**WHEN HE STEPPED** into the old pawn shop on the west side of town, Leo was struck by the sharp scent of old cigarettes and dust, while his ears were assaulted by the rusty old cowbell that hung over the door. It was a nod to the *SNL* sketch that Higgy thought was about the funniest shit he'd ever seen when it came out.

The shop hadn't changed much in the two years since Leo had been gone. On top of the dusty cigarette smell was a body odor stink that always wafted off the owner/operator of the place.

Looking around, Leo saw a lot of the same old things that were always on display. Ancient stereos and DVD players. Jewelry and CDs. Did anyone even listen to CDs anymore? Then his eyes fell on a faded purple electric guitar that he was sure had been hanging there behind the counter the last time he'd set foot in the shop.

There was movement from the back room, and when the scrawny shop owner came through the curtain that divided the shop floor from the back room, his face lit up with a rot-toothed grin.

"Holy shit!" Higgy cried. He rushed forward and wrapped his thin arms around Leo's large frame. "Fuck, man. You should have told me you were getting out a day early, I would have picked you up."

"It's no big deal," mumbled Leo. "Heard anything about Rita?"

Higgy pulled away and his smile slowly faded. "No, Leo. I'm sorry, I haven't been able to figure that one out."

When Leo only stared at his old friend, Higgy continued. "Well, fuck, man. I'm not a goddamn private detective. Take a look around. I run a shitty pawn shop and sell illegal goods out my back door. Information gathering has never really been my thing. Hey"—now Higgy seemed excited and moved back around the counter—"let me grab you a cold beer. When was the last time you had one of those, huh?"

Higgy disappeared through the back curtain and came out moments later with two open beer bottles. He placed one on the counter and, after a short pause, Leo moved forward and wrapped his hand around the cold glass. He drank as Higgy went on.

"How was it in there? I bet nobody fucked with you. Did you join up with one of the groups in there? Do they even have those? Factions? Gangs? Or is that just something they show on TV? Shit, man, I hope I never have to do time. I don't think I could handle that shit. My skinny ass would be passed around like a fucking joint. Is there a lot of that in there? Ya know, butt-fucking? It doesn't sound appealing. I mean, I suppose I could get used to it. If it's the only kind of fun you can have. Holes is holes, you know what I'm saying. Guy goes that long without female companionship, you got to do what you got to do."

"Higgy," Leo said in his gruff tone.

"Yeah?"

"Shut the fuck up for a minute."

Higgy gave a curt nod. "Sure."

Leo took another tug on the beer bottle before he spoke again. "You know where I can find Draper or Caplin? Or even Stanton?"

"Damn, Leo," said Higgy with a shake of his head. "The old gang split up and went their separate ways after you went up. I haven't talked to any of those guys in almost two years. You thinking about getting the old band back together? I bet I could scrounge up some jobs for you guys. I still have some of the old contacts. It would be fantastic to get back to work on some real shit. I ain't making near as much money as we used to make back in the day."

"Higgy," said Leo. This time, he placed one shushing finger over his lips. Usually, he let the man ramble on as much as he wanted, and most of the time the shit he spouted was fairly amusing, but Leo had business to get to.

"Okay," Higgy said.

"I need to find out what happened to Rita," said Leo. "I would like to start by questioning my old friends. If you got any information at all…" Leo left the rest unsaid.

"I don't know about the other guys," Higgy stated, after a drink from his beer, "but last I heard, Caplin joined the clergy. A priest."

A crooked smile touched Leo's lips. "A priest? Caplin?"

"I guess he saw the error of his ways," said Higgy with a shrug.

Leo doubted this. He had a feeling the old con artist had something else up his sleeve. "He still banging around Brooklyn?"

Higgy leaned a hip on the counter and crossed his arms. "Far as I know. But it's been a while, like I said."

A silence fell between them then, as Leo worked out a few things in his head. There was only one Catholic church in Caplin's old neighborhood. It was a place to start.

"Higgy," Leo said, studying his old friend from beneath a furrowed brow. "I'm going to need a gun."

Higgy's bug eyes went wide. "You hate guns."

Leo said nothing, choosing instead to continue to stare at his friend until the skinny man grew nervous.

"Okay, man," Higgy finally said, holding his hands up in surrender. "It just so happens I recently came across a revolver."

The skinny man entered the back room once more. As he searched for the gun, he spoke to Leo in a loud voice. "You know, speaking of butt-fucking, I recently dated a girl who was really into that. She loved to hold a little vibrator on her clit while I was doing her in the back door. Only thing was, the batteries in the fucking thing were constantly going dead. Then she would pause the action and, while I'm just hanging out with my cock in her ass, she'd go digging around in the fucking nightstand drawer for some new batteries. It's like, maybe if you didn't buy the damn things at *the Dollar Tree* and sprang for some fucking *Energizers,* we wouldn't be going through that shit *every time.* Of course, the pause would help me last a lot longer, so you take the good with the bad, you know."

"Higgy," called Leo, pinching the bridge of his nose with a thumb and forefinger. "What makes you think I want to hear this shit?"

"Right, sorry. Just trying to brighten your mood," said the pawn shop owner. When he returned, he placed a revolver on the glass display case near the cash register. "Found it. Smith & Wesson Model 66, snub-nose .357."

Leo lifted the gun and was surprised by its weight. He liked the silver finish and his hand seemed to fit perfectly around the wooden grip. The serial number was scraped off, making it clear Higgy was ready to sell.

Leo turned the gun over in his hands and noticed two words carved into the wooden grip. "'FOR HALEY'? What's that all about?"

"I don't know, man," Higgy replied. "That's how it came to me."

Leo held it up and stared down its sight. "Got any rounds?"

"Oh, yeah." Higgy reached beneath the counter, dug around a little, then came up with two boxes of .357 Magnum hollow point bullets.

"This should do," said Leo, gathering up the gun and ammo.

Higgy's face went slack. "Wait, Leo, that's like a thousand-dollar revolver."

"Put it on my tab," Leo grumbled as he turned to leave the shop.

"What fucking tab? I need cash for the shit I sell."

Leo turned back to him. "I literally just got out of prison. Why would I have any cash at all? As a matter of fact, loan me some cash."

"Fuck, Leo!" the skinny man exclaimed.

Leo looked at him as he spoke, infusing his voice with just the right amount of pleading, and said, "Come on, Higgy."

The shop owner's shoulders slumped and he let out a long sigh. Leo knew he had him. He'd learned how to play Higgy when they were just kids and that hadn't changed over the years.

"Okay, look, take the gun and the ammo. When you're finished with it, I want it back so I can sell it properly. And I can loan you a few hundred dollars, but I'm going to need you to bring back anything you find along the way that looks even remotely valuable. Got it? This is like me paying you for this fucking job."

"Got it," was all Leo said. He followed Higgy back to the register, where the latter handed the former four crisp one-hundred-dollar bills.

Higgy shook his head. "Ya know, having friends like you is bad for business. I mean, don't get me wrong, I hope you find Rita, and I hope that she's okay. Just take it easy, all right? That gun will be awful hard to sell if you kill a bunch of poor bastards with it." He considered Leo a moment, a crooked grin touching his lips. "Then again, you always were a big softy. Never one to kill anybody, even though you could rough 'em up like no body's business."

"That's true," said Leo. "I guess you got nothing to worry about."

At these words, Higgy's smile faded a little. Leo turned away from the counter and something caught his eye. He turned back. "One more thing. I need that."

"What, that crappy Army jacket?" Higgy said as he rounded the counter and pulled the green jacket off the hanger. "I picked that shit up at a surplus store in the hopes of making a few bucks profit. It's yours."

Leo pulled the jacket on over the faded black tee he'd worn into the prison, then emptied each of the boxes of shells into the pockets.

Higgy watched this with a worried look on his face. Then he shook his head as if clearing it of cobwebs. "Shit. I nearly forgot." He stepped back behind the counter and opened the cash register once more, lifted the cash tray, then pulled a set of keys from inside. He tossed them to Leo, who deftly plucked them out of the air. "I kept it safe for you in a private garage. It's in the alley. Gassed up and ready to go."

Leo smiled. "You're a good friend, Higgy."

"The fucking best," Higgy agreed.

Leo followed the scrawny pawn broker through the back room, which housed a cluttered desk and office chair among the piles of junk that would eventually be rotated onto the shop floor.

"Sorry about the mess. This shit just keeps growing like it's the fucking Blob. I mean, I moved a box of junk aside the other day and a young Steve McQueen crawled out."

This *did* elicit a chuckle from Leo. Higgy seemed pleased.

When they went through the back door, Leo stopped and stared at her. A solid black 1973 Pontiac Ventura that Leo had rebuilt himself nearly six years ago. He rounded the front of his car and touched the hood as he went, just like one would caress the naked shoulder of their lover. He opened the door and stopped when Higgy called his name.

"Leo." A pause. Then, with a sincerity that was foreign on Higgy's face, he said, "Just… be careful. Okay?"

Leo nodded but said nothing. He sat behind the wheel of the Ventura, keyed the ignition and felt the eight-cylinder engine rumble to life. With a determination born of fury, Leo shifted the car into first and drove.

# CHAPTER FIVE

**IT WAS A WEDNESDAY** night and Leo was well aware of the St. Mary's evening services every week. He had a few minutes to kill and stopped for a slice and a cold beer. Of all the things he missed about the real world while he was in the joint, those two were near the top.

By the time he parked just down the street from the church and walked the rest of the block to the entrance, the pews were nearly filled and the organ music was playing. Leo took a seat near the back and waited for the show to begin.

The crowd applauded as Leo's old friend, Bruce Caplin, took the stage. Caplin looked just the same as Leo remembered. He was a black man with skin the color of coffee, heavy on the cream. His bald head gleamed under the light fixtures, and as he approached the pulpit, he flashed that old charming smile that he once said would make a nun's panties drop. Leo wondered if he'd put that to the test now that he wore the collar of a priest.

Leo thought old Caplin must be doing something right. In all his years of being dragged to church by his mother, Leo had never seen such a lively congregation. They clapped and cheered until Caplin motioned for them to calm down. Once they had fallen silent, he began his sermon in earnest.

By the end, Leo had to admit that Caplin was at the top of his game. If he didn't know better, he'd have even been convinced that the old con man had gone straight and actually believed the shit he was shoveling. As the sermon came to a close, a younger man appeared at the front of the aisle. He was dressed in his Sunday best, but Leo recognized muscle when it was presented to him, J.C. Penney suit notwithstanding.

"Mr. Albert is now coming around with the collection plates," Caplin called to the congregation. As you all pass it around, remember that we are in the process of getting approval for the renovation of the church's historical pilasters, and anything you can give would go a long way. God bless you all."

With that, Caplin closed his book and stepped down among the pews for small talk with members of the church. Leo sat patiently as others placed their contributions into the collection plates and moved toward the exit. One of the plates was handed to Leo, who shrugged and deftly plucked two twenties from the top, then slipped them into his pocket, without notice. He passed it on and continued to sit while the church emptied. It was good to know his skills were as sharp as ever, even after all those years in lockup.

Eventually, even Mr. Albert disappeared into the back rooms with the collection plates, leaving Leo and Caplin alone. Leo stood and moved down the center aisle as his old friend gathered his notes from the pulpit and closed them in his Bible. When he looked up, he did a double-take and his eyes widened. Not in fear, but in delight.

"Leo?" he called. He quickly clambered down from the dais and embraced the ex-convict. "Praise the Lord." He gave Leo several hardy pats on his back (while Leo kept his arms awkwardly at his side) before finally releasing him. "I had no idea you were out. How are you?"

"I need your help," said Leo.

"Well, you've come to the right place," said Caplin. "I have been saved from my former life, and I like to think you set me on that path. It was your unselfish act that taught me to embrace Jesus as my Lord and Savior. Now here I am, helping people to find that same love in their lives."

"No," said Leo. "Cap, I need to find my wife. Do you have any idea what happened to Rita?"

Caplin's smile slowly faded and he averted his eyes. "Yeah, I uh… I heard about her disappearance. Leo, why don't you come on back to my office? We can discuss things in a more private setting."

Leo nodded and followed Father Caplin through a door off to the side of the stage.

The office walls were lined with bookcases of a rich oak. Caplin moved to a large desk of matching wood. "Would you like a drink? I have Irish whiskey."

"No sacramental wine?" asked Leo.

Caplin chuckled at this. "No, only the good stuff for you." He poured two fingers' worth into a glass and handed it over. Leo took the glass but didn't drink. "I got to say, it's damn good to see you, Leo. I really hope you'll take me up on my offer. With God in your life, all things are possible."

Leo cocked his head to the side and smirked to let his old friend know he wasn't fooling anybody.

Caplin finally laughed and broke character. "Man, you know this the best con game on the fucking planet. These motherfuckers can't *wait* to give me their money. I don't even know what a damn pilaster is." His laughter had grown nearly hysterical.

"Best part is, it's all legal. Man, I got the idea after I saw a news story about these TV evangelists who spent church money on private jets and shit. That's a whole notha' level right there. I'm a pretty damn good grifter, but these guys are fucking masters."

"Cap," Leo said, forcing a little more urgency in his voice. "We were going to talk about Rita."

He broke eye contact again. "Yeah, man. I'm sorry, Leo, but I have no idea what happened to her."

Leo studied him with scrutinizing eyes. For a con man, Caplin certainly was a bad liar. Or maybe he was just having trouble lying to Leo. "She told me someone in a luxury SUV had been following her last time we talked. Is there anyone new on the scene who drives one?"

"Not that I know of," said Caplin. Another lie. His eyes finally met Leo's and he only stared. As if daring the ex-con to call him out on his bullshit.

Leo narrowed his eyes and saw it. It was only a split second. A flick of Caplin's eyes to the right told Leo he had been lured into a trap.

The attack came from behind. The big man with the donation plates was apparently light on his feet. Leo was quick enough to avoid a fatal stab wound but the knife still sliced through his shoulder. He brought his knee up into Mr. Albert's gut. All the air rushed from the man's lungs and through his mouth. He brought his fist down on the man's face and he dropped, sprawled across the floor unconscious.

Turning back, Leo found Father Caplin fumbling with a case on his desk. Leo pulled the revolver from his pocket just as Caplin brought a small .22-caliber pistol up.

Leo's revolver spoke, a thunderous crash that slammed the fake priest into his desk. He slumped to the floor.

Leo's ears were ringing. Caplin's shoulder was a bloody mess but he was still alive. His breathing was heavy and he gave a low grunt with every exhale. The .22 was out of his reach now. Leo decided it was time to get his answers.

"Tell me what you know," said Leo. "Who took Rita?"

"N-n-no, man," Caplin stuttered. "I-I can't tell you that, Leo. This motherfucker is crazy. He finds out I told you his business, he'll f-fucking kill me."

Leo leveled the barrel of the revolver at Caplin's face and cocked the hammer. "I'll kill you if you *don't*."

To Leo's surprise, Caplin began to laugh. "Leo, man, you are a big bruiser, no doubt. One of the baddest motherfuckers around. You ain't no killer. You don't have it in you."

Leo gave his old friend an incredulous look. Then, he looked down at the unconscious Mr. Albert, still sprawled out on the floor. Without further hesitation, he pointed the gun at the man's face and fired. The top of Mr. Albert's head exploded, spraying blood and brain in a fan-shaped pattern across the hardwood floor.

"Oh fuck!" Caplin screamed. "Shit. Shit. Shit. Shit. Leo, what did you do, man?"

Leo moved closer to Caplin, knelt in front of him, then pressed the barrel of the gun up under the man's chin. He spoke in a low growl. "Now that we understand each other, tell me what happened to my wife."

Caplin's chin was quivering, as if he were on the verge of tears. "It was Stanton."

"Quinn?" said Leo with surprise. Quinn Stanton had been the newest member of their little crew. One of the big reasons Leo took the rap for the last job they'd pulled. He didn't want the kid to go away so young. "He's just a fucking child."

"He's a fucking psychopath," said Caplin. "After you went up, he had all these great ideas. Eventually, me and Henry just went along. We followed him and soon, we were fucking rolling in the dough. Even this fucking priest thing was his idea. He takes like sixty percent of my profits."

"So, he's like your pimp?" Leo asked, adding insult to injury. He went on before Caplin could answer. "What does he have to do with Rita?"

"H-he was obsessed with her, man," said Caplin. "Hell, even before you went away, he was always leering at her. C-c'mon, you remember."

Leo *did* remember, but it wasn't out of the ordinary. Most men leered at Rita. It was something he'd grown used to. "Keep going," he urged.

"It was just a gradual thing, man," said the fake priest. "Over time, he was leading us and when we tried to question it, he went fucking nuts. The kid's out of his mind. He tortured this homeless bastard. Did it right in front of us like he was trying to send a message. I'm talking sadistic shit here, man. Pulled his fingernails out one by one. Nailed his cock to the chair he was sitting in. I still have nightmares. I legitimately pray that I never end up on that guy's bad side."

"Neither of you tried to stop him?" Leo asked, disgusted by their inaction more than Stanton's deeds.

"We're con artists and thieves, man. We ain't got the stomach for that shit."

Leo twirled his finger to hurry Caplin along, then repeated, "Okay, what does all this have to do with Rita?"

Caplin swallowed hard before he answered. "Stanton, he grabbed her. Right off the fucking street. Nobody has seen her since. Draper told me he…" Caplin trailed off.

"What?" Leo growled.

"Draper said Stanton raped her. Then he killed her."

The dull ringing in Leo's ears was replaced by a rush of pumping blood. He could feel his face burning red, flushed with anger. He stood suddenly and paced the room. Images of Rita flashed in his head. Meeting her in Kelly's Pub all those years ago. Their first date, grabbing dinner and seeing a movie. The first time they made love. How drop-dead gorgeous she looked on their wedding day. All the foot rubs. All the laughs. The way she loved it when he ran his fingers through her hair.

He moved back to Caplin, cocked the gun, and pressed it to his temple with a primal scream. Caplin screamed as well but quickly broke into tears. "Please don't," he pleaded. "Don't kill me."

Leo turned away from Caplin. He rubbed one hand over his face. When he looked back, he tried to calm the old grifter down. "All right. Shush now. Listen, I need to find Stanton. Where is he?"

"I don't know," Caplin blubbered. "He set me up here and comes to see me when he wants to collect."

"What about Draper?" asked Leo. "Would Henry Draper know how to find him?"

Caplin nodded. "Maybe, yeah. Draper has a place off 31$^{st}$ and Snyder."

Leo found a pen and a pad of paper on the desk and wrote down the address Caplin gave him. Then he tore off the page and stuffed it into the pocket of his jeans.

"I need an ambulance," Caplin moaned. "Call me an ambulance Leo. I won't mention your name. I won't tell them you shot me or Mr. Albert."

Leo shook his head. "Nah. You're part of this, Cap. You let it happen. You let that cunt kill my wife. He's going to pay. But *you're* gonna pay first."

Caplin started to weep once more but Leo blocked it out, along with the bleeding man's pleas. He raised the gun and fired. The bullet hit Caplin in the mouth and Leo marveled at the sight of his teeth blown through the back of his head. Three of them were embedded in the heavy oak of the desk, while another slipped with a stutter through the blood and down to land on the floor.

Leo channeled his fury through the revolver and continued to fire, emptying the chamber into Caplin's face. He pocketed the gun and moved out of the office through a back door. This led to a hallway with a rear entrance.

Then he paused. In his mind, he was reviewing everything he'd touched since he'd entered the office. The whiskey glass. He re-entered the room, picked the glass up off the floor, and wiped it down with his shirt. Then he took the knife from Mr. Albert and slid it into his pocket. On the way out, he wiped down the knob on the rear door. Then, he used the sleeve of his jacket to open the back door.

He slipped out into the dark, unseasonably warm night, the silence of which had been broken by approaching sirens.

# CHAPTER SIX

**LEO SLUMPED LOW** in his seat, reloading the revolver as police cars flashed by. His shoulder throbbed where the knife had cut him, and it was likely he needed stitches. Once he was sure the coast was clear and that all the flashing lights were occupied down the block, he started the Ventura and pulled away from the curb, moving east and away from the church.

*Fly casual,* he heard Han Solo's voice speak up in his head. It was good advice after you just murdered two men.

He thought about his old crew. Higgy, who supplied them with the jobs and equipment they needed, was more like an outside contractor. He wasn't part of their core group, just a pal who Leo had grown up with that would find them jobs from time to time. It was the reason Leo didn't feel Higgy was a part of all this. Caplin, who could con his way into just about any situation, and Draper, the expert safe cracker who'd never met a lock he couldn't crack, were *his* guys.

Leo was their leader. He made the decisions that got them out of some tough scrapes. He was the muscle, quick to knock the occasional guard or rental cop unconscious. Then came a job where they needed an explosives expert. That was when Draper brought in his pal, Quinn Stanton. He was just a kid then, barely past the legal drinking age, but he really knew his shit.

Leo remembered that for a long time, he couldn't shake the feeling that there was something off about the kid. At first, Leo suspected he was an undercover cop. Apparently, he was way fucking wrong about that. By Caplin's account, the kid was a complete nutcase. And since Draper brought the kid in and did *nothing* to stop him, he was guilty by association in Leo's eyes.

Parking on the street to the north of Draper's building, Leo hit the release on the glove compartment, where he *actually* kept a pair of leather gloves. He hadn't thought he'd need them when he went in to see Caplin. The guy was supposed to be his friend, and he hadn't figured him for setting a trap with his hired muscle. Going in to see Draper, Leo figured he should be prepared.

The apartment building, like most in New York, had a buzzer system that allowed residents to decide who they let in. Leo rang every apartment in the place in the assumption that *somebody* would be expecting a visitor. Sure enough, the door buzzed and Leo was able to pull it open.

It wasn't a bad-looking building. Especially considering where Draper *used* to live. Henry had moved from dimly lit, piss-stained hallways to a bright lobby with flowery décor. Business was good.

Leo called the elevator and waited patiently for it to arrive. Once inside, he pressed the button for the third floor and felt his pulse quicken. The rage that had slowly seeped out of him was returning. A loud ding told him he'd arrived, and the doors opened to reveal a short hallway with purple walls and still-life paintings of flowers in vases hung along its length.

Three doors down and to the left, Leo found the apartment of Henry Draper. For a moment, he only glared at it, as if the door itself had wronged him. Finally, he reached out and knocked three times. From behind the door, he could hear footsteps. He watched the small dot of light that came through the peephole. When it was blocked out by someone on the other side, Leo kicked in the door.

The wood splintered as the door swung inward and Draper fell back on the floor, holding his gushing nose. Leo stepped inside and closed the door on the busted frame.

"Leo?" Draper whined. "What the fuck?"

Draper hadn't changed much since the last time he'd seen him. He was short and broad, with a headful of kinky black hair that had earned him the nickname Pube Head. Leo pulled the revolver from his jacket pocket and held it where Draper could get a good look. The man's watering eyes widened and he began to backpedal away from Leo.

"You know why I'm here?" said Leo, and he could hear the hatred in his voice.

There was a pause as Draper bumped against the sofa. He held out bloodied, shaking hands and nodded. "Rita."

Leo took a step closer. "Rita."

"I had nothing to do with it, man," Draper said. "That shit was all Stanton. He was fucking infatuated."

"You and Caplin were supposed to be my friends," Leo rumbled. "I went to prison for you. Two years of my life gone because I was covering for *all* of you. And all I asked was that you two look out for Rita. You were *supposed* to protect her."

"I'm sorry, man. It's Stanton. You don't know how fucking crazy he is. There was nothing we could do."

"You should have died protecting her!" Leo roared.

"What the fuck did you want us to do?" Draper asked. "Leo, we're fucking lightweights. Me and Caplin, we're just small-time crooks. We're not thugs or killers. *You* were always the muscle."

"Tell me where to find Stanton," said Leo.

"That fucking psycho will kill me if I rat him out," Draper sobbed.

Leo glared at him. "Caplin said the same thing, just before I shot him in the fucking face."

Draper's eyes went wide and his mouth dropped open. "You didn't. Fuck man, please tell me you're joking."

"It's no joke," Leo said, and hated that his voice cracked with emotion. Despite his vengeful anger, these men had still been his friends. They had spent years together not only pulling jobs but also playing cards, drinking, and laughing. Of course, this was all the more reason they should have looked out for the woman he loved. Especially after taking the fall for them on their last job together, which had been botched by miscommunication.

"Tell me," he added, in a stronger tone.

"He's got a big fucking house in the Hamptons," Draper finally said after a pause. "The address is on a piece of paper on my fridge. Under the banana magnet."

It was an open-space living area, and Leo turned and walked to the kitchen while Draper struggled up onto the sofa. He pulled tissue from the box on the end table and held it to his bleeding nose. Leo plucked the slip of paper from the banana-shaped magnet, then returned to the living room. "Was he expecting you up there at some point?"

"Tonight," said Draper. "He's throwing a dinner party. Invited a bunch of his ritzy fucking neighbors from around there. He wanted me to come up and get a feel for some of them. Case some of their houses. Look, man, I can help you out. Take me with you, I can help you get back at this cocksucker."

Leo considered him as he folded the piece of paper and stuck it into his jeans. "Why would I need *your* help?"

"Stanton, man, he's like a fucking Batman villain out there. He's got his own security team. They are armed to the teeth. They're going to be on high alert for this party. Automatic rifles and shit."

"You got a gun?" Leo asked.

"Not here," said Draper.

"Then what the fuck good are you?" asked Leo. "You said it yourself, you aren't a thug or a killer."

The panic was growing in Draper's eyes. "No, I know I said that, but I *can* be, Leo. I *can* help."

Leo dropped to one knee on the couch so that he almost straddled Draper. The bleeding man raised both hands in surrender and looked as if he thought Leo was about to either strangle him or kiss him.

Instead, Leo used his left hand to pick up a nearby sofa pillow, then said, "Thanks anyway, Henry."

Moving too fast for Draper to defend himself, Leo pressed the pillow to Draper's face, pushed the barrel of the revolver against it, and pulled the trigger. The shot was more of a muffled *thud* this time. Henry Draper's body went limp.

Leo stood. His breathing was heavy. His hands shook, not only with adrenaline, but with the anger and grief that continued to spread through his entire body like a fast-moving cancer. Caplin and Draper weren't nearly enough to quench his thirst for vengeance. They had taken his wife from him. The woman he'd somehow known he'd loved long before he'd even met her.

To this day, he still found that feeling hard to explain. It was almost like seeing a movie with your favorite actor and sitting patiently through the opening because you knew it would get so much better when that *one* person came on screen. Without her, there was no reason to sit through the rest of the movie. It was time to walk out of the theater.

It was with these thoughts running through his mind that he entered the bathroom and found a sewing set in one of the drawers. Removing his jacket and shirt, Leo went to work. First, he threaded a needle with a length of black thread. Then, using the bathroom mirror for guidance, he cleaned the area around the knife wound on his shoulder. It had slit the throat of Lon Chaney, Jr.'s Wolf Man. The tattoo had been ruined. Leo didn't much care.

He pulled the needle through the skin around his wound, bringing the flesh together in a little pucker. When he was finished, he broke the thread with his teeth. Then, he found a first aid kit, rummaged through it until he found a large patch-style bandage, and covered the wound.

With that done, he pulled his shirt and jacket back on, then went to the kitchen and found the block on the counter with the set of knives stuck inside. He removed the three largest ones, slipped them into the inside pocket of his old Army surplus jacket, and moved back through the living room and toward the door.

He paused with the door open to look back at Draper one last time. His fingers twitched. The last remnants of a life lost.

Leo exited the building moments later and slid behind the wheel of his car. Pulling into traffic, he drove east. He was bound for the Hamptons. He knew this was a suicide mission. There would be no coming back. The movie was almost over. He was entering the last act and things would soon fade to black. And he was okay with that.

# CHAPTER SEVEN

**LEO KNEW IT** would take around two hours to drive from Brooklyn to the Hamptons, and he was afraid that in that time, he would somehow lose some of his resolve. That didn't happen, though. If anything, the time to think during the long drive only strengthened his desire to see the mission through to the end.

He turned the radio on and found a classic rock station. The Stones were on and "Sympathy for the Devil" came blaring through the speakers. Leo tapped his fingers on the steering wheel to the beat. He thought back to Caplin complaining about pulling real-world jobs.

"Man, long cons are pulled online these days," he had said. "I should be setting up social media profiles posing as a book promoter for indie authors. That's where the money's at."

"I get the feeling your shitty spelling and piss-poor grammar might give you away," Leo had joked.

Caplin had grown defensive. "Well, that was only one example, man."

Draper had expressed similar desires to get away from their usual jobs and engage in more lucrative thefts. Apparently, Stanton had provided this for them. Leo wondered what he was into to be able to afford a house in the Hamptons. Bilking poor fuckers out of their hard-earned money for their religious beliefs and conning others into blowing cash to reach their dreams were one thing.

Stanton had tapped into something else and had made millions. Did this dinner party have something to do with that?

"Sympathy for the Devil" gave way to "A Whiter Shade of Pale" by Procol Harum. The song had always been one of Rita's favorites. Leo cast aside his curiosity about how his former crew had made all their money. He turned his thoughts instead to his late wife. As much as he didn't want to, he wondered how her last moments of life had gone. Had she suffered? Or did Stanton take what he wanted and end it quickly?

Leo's hands tightened on the steering wheel and his knuckles went white. Anger and hatred flooded his brain like the rising waters of a raging river. With a hot, furious flush to his cheeks, Leo gave in to that anger and hate. It would be the fuel for his vengeance.

# CHAPTER EIGHT

**IT WAS THE** biggest goddamned house Leo had seen in his life. Of course, he'd rarely been outside of New York City in all of his thirty-five years.

The front gate was open but that wasn't the way inside. There was a small team of security guards checking invitations and IDs for every car that pulled up. Instead, Leo drove the Pontiac around the corner and looked for the best place to climb over the wall that surrounded the entire property. He parked along the street when he caught sight of a small cluster of trees.

Sticking to the shadows, Leo moved along a narrow path and to the tall wall on the other side, then slipped his gloves on. He jumped to get a handhold on the edge of the brick and heaved himself up to take a look at what awaited him on the other side.

There were security guards around the perimeter, and one who seemed to be doing rounds, as far as he could tell. The trees continued on the other side of the wall and Leo used them for cover as he dropped down to the meticulously manicured lawn. Near the garage, he could see a sleek, black Cadillac Escalade with custom rims.

*They drive a black SUV with fancy…rims,* he heard Rita say in his head. It had to be the SUV she'd mentioned during that last conversation, when she came to visit him and said she was being followed.

So far, he hadn't seen any heavy weaponry. No shotguns or automatic rifles. Not to say the guards weren't armed, but Leo felt his survival rate against a 9mm pistol was higher. He supposed that didn't make much sense. When it came right down to it, a gun was a gun and they were all made for one purpose. Killing. Still, he felt better knowing he wouldn't be the target of some asshole spraying an AR-15 in his direction. They must have packed light for dinner party appearance.

Sticking to the shadows, Leo was able to move in closer to the back door of the house to watch things for a moment. Two young guys in waiter uniforms were standing near a basketball court passing a joint back and forth. Leo was too far away to make out their conversation but was able to hear them laugh from time to time.

One of the men returned to the house and went through the back door, while the other finished off the joint. He knocked the cherry off, then placed the roach in a resealable sandwich bag, before stuffing it in his pants pocket and heading back toward the door.

Leo moved silently through the trees and as the young man neared the door, he made his move. The waiter was slow to react to Leo's large hand closing over his mouth. He pulled the kid down on the ground, lifted the butt of the revolver over his head, and brought it down hard across the kid's nose. He was out cold.

Moving fast, Leo pulled the Army surplus jacket off, then removed the unconscious man's waiter jacket and slipped it on. It was a tight fit. Still, he adjusted his gloves, transferred the shells from the jacket pockets and into the less spacious ones in the uniform, then stuffed the revolver in the waistband of his pants at his back. There was no place to hide the knives, so he settled for stuffing one up his left sleeve and abandoning the other two. He then stepped out of the trees and through the back door.

The kitchen was bustling with cooks and waiters moving about at top speed. Leo went unnoticed as he swiftly moved forward to snatch a tray of hors d'oeuvres from a countertop. He held the tray up near his ear partially because it was how he'd seen it done in movies, but also because it helped hide his face.

Out of the kitchen and into a large room that must have been a sitting room of some sort, where a number of people in expensive dinner party attire mingled and drank champagne from narrow flutes. He seemed to recognize some of the guests. Although he had never been one to keep up with local or national news, Rita had that shit on the TV all the time. He knew some of the faces even if he couldn't recall any of the names.

He was pretty sure one of the guests played for the Jets. He heard another man introduce himself as Jacob Brady and knew the name. He was a notable philanthropist who had his face splashed all over news outlets and social media. Leo was amazed that Stanton was rubbing elbows with the rich and famous just two years after being part of his little crew.

For Leo, it was jarring to step out of prison earlier that morning only to be among the wealthy elite late at night. Weaving through the first floor and its many rooms, he didn't see Stanton, so when he came to a staircase, he placed the tray on a large table in the foyer and moved swiftly up the stairs. The landing wrapped around the foyer and Leo had a better look at the party's guests. Still, no Stanton.

Moving toward the east wing of the second floor, Leo heard a door open and close and decided to investigate. He hid behind a large statue of the Greek Gorgon, Medusa. As a kid, Leo had a brief obsession with Greek mythology after viewing the classic film *Clash of the Titans* with his old man, and he recognized the subject of the sculpture right away. Further down the hall, he caught sight of an old man walking in the opposite direction. Leo followed.

There appeared to be ten rooms along the hallway, with five doors on each side. What Leo found odd about these doors were the numbered keypads affixed to the doorknob on each one. What was it Stanton had going on here?

At the sound of another door opening to his right, Leo slipped into the shadowy doorway of a room across the way in the dimly lit hall. Another older man shuffled out, and Leo was able to glimpse a young woman lying naked in the room beyond.

*Prostitution?* Leo thought. *Was that Stanton's game? Was he a pimp for a high-end prostitution ring?*

That hardly seemed like it would be enough to explain Stanton's fortunes. Of course, that might only be a fraction of what he was involved in. Leo couldn't believe the little bastard had done so much in just a couple of years. The locks on each of the doors, however, suggested something else. It told Leo that these women were perhaps being held against their will.

Leo continued to follow the hall and watched as the older man entered a room around the corner and closed the door behind him. From the other side of the door, Leo could hear jovial voices raised in a cheer. He pulled the revolver from his waistband and prepared to enter. With a deep, steadying breath, Leo turned the knob and pushed through the door.

On the other side, a gun was pressed against the side of his head.

"Hello, Leo," said a familiar voice. Quinn Stanton was as young and good-looking as his name would suggest. He wore his dirty blond hair in a strategically messy fashion that seemed popular amongst men in their early twenties. His chiseled features were even more defined than Leo remembered and it was clear this was because Stanton was bigger than he was the last time they'd seen each other. Even through his tuxedo, Leo could see the cut of his well-sculpted chest and biceps.

Stanton continued. "You've been on a real rampage, haven't you? My guys in Brooklyn found Caplin and Draper, both *brutally* murdered. I knew you'd make your way here."

He grabbed Leo's chin and turned his head, studying him like a Doberman at a dog show. "Leo *fucking* Morrison. Perpetual badass. Mr. Vengeance."

A second security guard appeared at Leo's left and pulled the revolver from his hand. Then he slipped an arm around Leo's. The goon on the right did the same, keeping the 9mm Beretta steady at Leo's temple. Beyond Stanton were several well-dressed, rich men, who watched all this unfold with amused smirks on their faces. Leo looked around at each of them in turn. He said nothing.

"You always were the strong, silent type," Stanton went on with a teasing note in his voice. "Although you look ridiculous in the waiter's jacket. I can't believe you went through all *this* for that filthy Latina whore. I thought we were friends, Leo. What happened to bros before hoes?"

The men surrounding Stanton laughed, while a white-hot fury bloomed in Leo's head. He stiffened. Preparing to make his move.

"Take him out behind the garage," Stanton commanded. "Shoot him in the face, just like he did with my friends."

Each of the guards who had hold of his arms pulled Leo out of the den. Back down the hall and to the stairs, Leo waited for his opening. The timing had to be right. At the bottom of the stairs, they pulled him through the foyer and toward the kitchen. It was here that the guard on his right dropped his gun to his side. They didn't want their guests to get a look at that pistol to a stranger's head.

Leo made his move.

Swinging his left arm, he pulled the goon on that side off balance, and when the one on the right turned his head to see what was going on, Leo launched himself at the man in a fierce headbutt that shattered the guard's nose.

Not wasting any time, Leo turned to the other man and tackled him before he could get his bearings. Partygoers backed away from the two men wrestling on the floor. Leo pulled the knife from his sleeve and drove it into the goon's balls. The man shrieked in pain. Leo pried his fingers off the revolver, turned, and raised the handgun just as Broken Nose worked to aim his 9mm through watering eyes.

The revolver spoke first in a booming crash that sent party guests screaming for the exits. The bullet tore through the man's chest, spraying gore on the same tray of hors d'oeuvres Leo had left on the table before heading upstairs.

He turned back to the guard on the floor, still holding his balls, and cocked the hammer back. Another squeeze of the trigger peeled the top of his head off. It flapped open like the hinged lid of a cookie jar.

A shot from his right caused pain to blossom in Leo's left shoulder. He turned, pulled the hammer back on the revolver, and shot. The goon held a hand to his stomach as blood rushed through his fingers. He fell where he stood.

Another guard entered the room from the front door, and yet another began to fire from the upstairs landing. Leo grabbed the wrist of the man nearest to him and twisted his arm so that the elbow lay across Leo's shoulder. He pulled down and the bone snapped, splitting through the poor fucker's skin as he screamed. His pain didn't last long, however, as Leo ducked beneath him, using him as a human shield from the rain of bullets from above.

Leo thanked whatever deity was looking out for him by seeing to it that Stanton's army of goons carried small-caliber pistols. Otherwise, the slugs may have torn right through the body of the man he hid beneath and killed him anyway.

Once he heard the pistol from the landing above click on an empty chamber, Leo tossed the dead man aside, aimed the revolver at the goon on the landing, and fired. The shot struck the man in the left eye and blew out the back of his head.

Leo was on the move. He took the stairs two at a time. Ducking behind the Medusa statue once more, he reloaded the revolver from the supply of shells in his pocket. As he did so, one of the older gentlemen who had surrounded Stanton exited the den with a shotgun. The statue took the brunt of the scattershot, but Leo felt some of the pellets rip through his left cheek.

The revolver thundered once more, hitting the older man in his thigh. He went down screaming and Leo ended his misery with another shot, this one to the forehead. He reloaded again as he approached the door to the den.

"Leo," Stanton called. "We can work this out. It doesn't have to be this way, man."

Leo pushed the door open with his foot and was greeted by a volley of gunfire that tore through the door frame. He fired the revolver twice blindly into the room. He didn't think he'd hit anyone but it gave him the cover he needed to move through and hide behind the heavy desk to his right.

Stanton opened fire again and Leo thought he, too, had a 9mm Beretta, from the sound of it. He wondered if Stanton had bought the damn things in bulk.

To his left, cowering behind the large desk, was the first old man Leo had seen leaving one of the locked rooms down the hall. He held out his hands and whimpered. "Please, I'm unarmed."

Leo shot him twice in the face, then replaced the spent shells in the chamber.

Maneuvering so that he was down on one knee, Leo flipped the desk over to use the top as his cover, then peeked over the edge to assess his situation. Stanton was at the far end of the room, hiding behind a large bookcase along the wall. The last two friends he'd had in the room with him made a break for the door. Leo shot one and, surprisingly, Stanton dropped the other. "Cowards!" Stanton shouted.

Leo fired twice and the bullets ripped through a leatherbound book at the end of one of the bookshelves. Stanton covered his face, then dove behind the pool table in hopes of finding better protection.

"C'mon, Leo," he called. "This is fucking stupid. Let's be friends. I can make you a very rich man."

Leo ignored him and leaned out from the left side of the desk. Looking beneath the pool table, he could just make out Stanton's foot as he ducked down behind one of the legs. Leo carefully aimed the revolver and fired. The slug tore through Stanton's Italian loafer, surely taking a couple toes along for the ride. The bastard screamed in pain, falling backward as he did so.

Leo stood and came around the other side of the desk where he had a clear view of Stanton. He cocked the hammer on the revolver, aimed again, and pulled the trigger. The slug smashed into Stanton's gun hand, sending the 9mm spinning across the floor along with his pinky and ring fingers.

Stanton wailed in pain now, holding his damaged hand with his good one. Leo slowly walked over to where the man squirmed on the floor and stood over him. For a long time, he just let him writhe and curse. Finally, Leo straddled the man and dropped to his knees. Using the butt of the revolver, he smashed it into Stanton's face so hard that the wooden grip cracked. Staton was dazed from the hit but still conscious. The bridge of his nose was caved in, and Leo could see a white shard of bone there.

He brought the butt down again, shattering Stanton's perfect teeth. Then again, breaking the man's nose and tearing it partially from his face. Then, Leo stood. He opened the chamber on his gun, feeling a little sluggish now that the fight was nearly over, pulled the empty shells, and loaded the gun so that all six chambers were full. Then, he pointed the revolver at Stanton's ruined face, cocked the hammer, and fired. Cocked the hammer and fired. Cocked the hammer and fired. He repeated until the hammer clicked on empty shells. Then repeated a few more times anyway.

When he finally stopped, Leo felt as though he would pass out. Past the quiet of the house, he could hear sirens in the distance. He decided it was time to go. Coming out into the hall, however, the sight of all the locked doors gave him pause. He quickly emptied the chamber of the revolver, pocketing the empty shells once more and reloaded it with fresh rounds.

He went to each door and blew the locks off one by one. The women behind each of the doors cautiously stepped out, then ran around him for the stairs as he went on with his business. After door six, he reloaded again and continued.

At the tenth and final door, he blasted the lock off and the door swung open slowly on its hinges. Leo stopped and stared at the woman inside the room. She was naked and pressed against the headboard, shivering under the sheets. When her eyes met his, her heavy breathing slowed and her eyes went wide. Then she spoke and Leo's cold fury melted away.

"Leo?" she said.

With watering eyes, he said her name in a voice barely above a whisper. "Rita."

She left the bed and rushed into his arms. "I knew you would come for me," she wept, with her head against his chest. "I knew you would."

"I thought you were dead," said Leo, the tears now running down his cheeks. He never wanted to let go. She was alive and he couldn't believe his luck. Then, coming back to reality, he said, "Come on, baby. We have to get out of here."

"But the police will help," she said.

"No," said Leo, an apologetic tone creeping into his voice. "Baby, I killed a bunch of people."

"Oh," she said simply.

Leo could see in her eyes a mixture of emotions at this revelation. He had never been a killer and she seemed devastated that he had lost this part of him. That moral code made him a good man despite leading a life of crime. The tears that filled those eyes, however, said that she was touched by the lengths he would go through to avenge her. She placed a trembling hand on his face before she continued. "Then yes, we should go."

"Do you have clothes?" he asked.

She shook her head. "No, they took my clothes."

Leo yanked the sheet from the bed and wrapped her up. "This will have to do for now."

"Wait," she said in the hallway. Leo paused while she ran down the hall and into the den, then emerged moments later with two briefcases. With a shrug, she said, "We may as well get compensation for this mess. Also, I used a log from the fireplace to set the drapes on fire. We should hurry."

Leo only smiled.

They left the house through the kitchen, with Rita taking note of all the dead bodies along the way. "You did all this?"

"Yes," said Leo.

"For me?" she asked.

He shrugged. "Yeah."

Her eyes gleamed with fresh tears as she looked up at him through her dark hair. "That's so romantic."

He pulled her closer and kissed her as they walked through the yard, only pausing to retrieve his jacket along the way. In the end, they managed to drive away before the police arrived.

# CHAPTER NINE

**IT WAS EARLY** the next morning when Leo pulled up in the alley behind the pawn shop. Higgy was there, hauling in boxes of junk from the back of his van and through the back door. Leo rolled the window down as Higgy approached. He looked in at Rita sleeping in the passenger seat. "I guess everything turned out okay? What happened?"

Leo told his old friend the entire story, then finished by saying, "I think Stanton was involved in human trafficking. From what Rita told me, she had been passed around between a few of his friends. Always in exchange for a large amount of cash. She was all set to be sold again when I got her out."

Higgy looked shaken at this. "Shit, man. I'm sorry. I wish I'd have known."

"I'm sure Stanton figured you were too close to me to bring you in on all this," said Leo.

"He was right about that," Higgy replied. He cocked his head toward Rita. "Is she going to be okay?"

Leo looked at her, gently pushed a strand of hair away from her face, then looked back to Higgy. "Physically, yeah. Mentally, emotionally, only time will tell. But I plan on being there for her from now on."

"What's next for you two?" Higgy asked.

"I'm going to meet up with Doc Sullivan to get this slug out of my shoulder," said Leo, referring to the doctor they paid under the table for all their medical needs. "Then we're leaving town. We need to disappear."

Higgy nodded. "I'm going to miss the hell out of ya, but I get it."

"Listen, about the revolver," Leo said, reaching into the back seat. "You *don't* want that back. There's way too much death connected to it now. However, this should cover the cost."

Higgy took the case, then popped open the locks and looked inside. He closed it quickly and turned his attention back to Leo with eyes wide. "Holy fucking shit! That's a lot of cash."

"Half a million," said Leo. "Don't worry, I'll dump the gun so that it can't come back on any of us."

"Yeah, all right," Higgy stated, still dumbfounded. "You guys… be good to each other. And stay out of trouble."

Leo shook his old friend's hand. "You take it easy, brother. Hopefully, our paths will cross again someday."

With that, Leo drove away.

# CHAPTER TEN

**THE WEATHER HAD** been sunny but cool all day. October was in full swing as Leo strolled through the dog park with Rita on his arm. Their new dog was a one-year-old Siberian Husky named Lily, who pulled on her leash like the untrained puppy she was. Leo had a lot of work to do with her. Today, the park was fairly deserted and the sun was sinking low behind the trees as they wrapped up their long walk on the trail.

As they rounded the path and neared the parking lot, Leo noticed a woman behind the wheel of a tan, soccer-mom minivan staring at him as she waited for a gap in traffic to turn into the parking lot. The look on her face— her scrutinizing eyes and the way she lightly chewed at her bottom lip—said she seemed to recognize him and was trying to place where from.

Leo had to wonder if his mug had turned up on a news report or on a wanted poster at the post office in connection with a fuck-load of dead bodies. It was something he'd been worrying about and he'd tried his best to keep an eye out for anything that pointed to his involvement. He hadn't seen anything but you never knew. He forced a smile and offered the woman a friendly wave, which she returned. Leo and Rita walked on.

When they neared a covered garbage can, Leo pulled a brown paper bag from his beat-up old Army jacket. He glanced back toward the ugly minivan and was pleased to find the woman had made her way into the parking lot and found a handicap space. Her view should be obstructed by the car next to her, and her attention would be on exiting the van.

To any other onlookers, this would appear to be the leftover trash from a fast-food restaurant; however, it really held a revolver that had taken several lives while in possession of the man who wielded it. A tool that had dealt death and vengeance from a man who had been wronged by old friends. Friends who perhaps thought he would roll over and take their mistreatment of the woman he loved with a shrug. *Oh well. What can you do?*

They learned the hard way how wrong they were.

Leo bent and carefully placed the unloaded gun and bag in the trash can. There was a small part of him that would miss the damn thing. For a time, he now realized, it had been more than just a "gun" to him. The revolver had been a companion that he felt shared his unmitigated anger. His unquenchable fury. An extension of his arm that spoke for him in those instances when words were inadequate for getting his point across.

He had kept the remaining ammo and would dispose of it separately or perhaps hang onto it and pick up another gun at some point. He sure as hell didn't want a loaded gun to be found by a kid.

The flap on the trash can closed and the couple walked on. Leo had no doubt the revolver would make its way to the city dump, where no one would ever see it again.

Of course, he could be wrong.

# BACKBONE

## N.J. GALLEGOS

*N.J.'s Dedication:*

*If you've ever been told you can't do something…*
*this is for you*

# CHAPTER ONE

**A CACOPHONY OF** beeps penetrated the darkness, each more irritating than the last. My alarm? Had I overslept? No. That wasn't it. The braying of my phone alarm was familiar and this—was not. Rather than one insistent tone rousing me from slumber, this was an orchestra of instruments, each with a different timbre. A flicker of recognition flashed within me—where had I heard all this before?—then winked from existence. Where… was I?

*Open your eyes, stupid.* Gritty eyelids twitched and rose to half-mast. A murky room materialized, initially composed of fuzzy shapes with no discernible function—a conglomeration of steel and shades of green. Owlish blinking on my part commenced, a chore given the sandpaper blanketing my conjunctiva. A reek of plastic filled my nostrils, and I recoiled, recalling long stints in the dentist's chair. Aseptic gloves and cold instruments against my dry tongue, tiny ice picks stabbing into cavities.

Saliva filled my mouth—the dreaded pre-throw up—and I reflexively swallowed the gorge back down. And couldn't. What? Throat muscles spasmed against a hard tube and I choked. Stark panic flooded my system. Sweat beaded across my forehead and my heart thudded faster and faster—matched *beep* for incessant *beep*.

Another alarm brayed, filling the frigid air with noise lifted straight from a Darude set. *Get it out, get it out!* Driven by instinct, my fingers curled, intent on yanking out whatever-the-fuck-was-shoved-down-my-throat and I thrust my hands to my mouth. Something dug into my wrists, stopping me before I could move an inch. Every arm joint rattled and my world swam. Up became down. Tiny stars blanketed my peripheral vision as I hyperventilated, choking on each breath. Strapped down. Violated.

*BLAT! BLAT! BLAT!*

*Beep beep beep beep beepbeepbeep.*

"What the—" Curtains swished open. "Shit! Get Dr. Hutchinson! And tell her we're gonna need more sedation! She's awake!"

Two firm hands gripped my shoulders and a face swimming with muddy features—a funhouse mirror—filled the rapidly shrinking pinhole of my vision. "Hey, hey, it's okay! You're safe." She squeezed my arm reassuringly. The sheer shock of kind human touch stopped me dead—I'd long associated any physical contact with pain—and I quieted.

She said I was safe? I considered her statement. True—the fabric encircling my wrists was soft yet firm, completely unlike cold stainless-steel bracelets cutting into tender skin, leaving a bevy of bruises no matter how often I repositioned. Sure—I was still shackled but in a far nicer manner than I was accustomed to. I was clothed too, something I learned not to take for granted.

Fright released her talons from my racing heart and my vision sharpened, revealing a slight blonde with eyelids rimmed black, a combination of mussed makeup and thin sleep. My bulging eyes met her gaze, and she offered up a smile, the corners of her blue eyes crinkling into crow's feet.

"There you are. See? Nothing to worry about. Worrying's our job," she said, doling out another calming shoulder squeeze while scanning my panic-stricken expression. My lips twisted around the piece of plastic crammed down my gullet—*choking, choking, choking.* Anxiety flared. "You're probably wondering where you are?"

I nodded—knots at the base of my skull protesting the minute movement—sending a lightning bolt down my spine that spread through my chest. Jaw joints clenched. Hands curled into loose, ineffectual fists at the end of limp noodle arms and I ached like a rotten tooth, a sickly throb deep within the marrow.

My terror ebbed. Damn, everything hurt—not dissimilar to the delayed soreness from my one (and only) marathon. Shoulders throbbed, the sinew between my ribs burned, and I felt like I'd been gut-punched several times. Honestly, the only thing not hurting was—

"You're at the hospital, hon," the woman said, voice infused with honey and comfort.

The hospital? Rather than reassure me, a cold dread overtook me, and I desperately tried to wrench myself free from my prison—a hospital stretcher, if what she said was true. Sturdy restraints thwarted my efforts, and I tossed my head side-to-side violently. I had to get the fuck out of here! The hospital room spun, tilting sickly before me.

"Hey! No! Stop that! You'll dislodge your ET tube!" Firm fingers dug into my cheeks, halting my erratic movements. My neck muscles screamed, and tendrils of fire licked down my knobby spine.

Sneakers squeaked, stopping short of me. "Here—is—the—Versed," they said, panting between each word. Glass clinked and my eyes rolled wildly within my limited view: water-damaged ceiling tiles and a hint of a blue bouffant scrub cap dipping to-and-fro.

"This will help you calm down, okay? Just relax, close your eyes, take a nap."

No! No! No! What about the others? If I'm not there who—who—who—

Liquid heat rolled up my arm. My head grew light and hollow. Consciousness flickered and dimmed as a wave of exhaustion cascaded through me. Eyelids grew heavy, and my twisting mouth slackened. My ribcage's desperate excursions slowed and something within my guts—*tension? Fear?*—uncoiled. A calming gray curtain descended, putting an end to *Act One: Sam Realizes She's in the Hospital and Absolutely Loses Her Shit.*

"Did she move her legs?" came from faraway, distorted and otherworldly. What? What was—

My lights went out and the present bled away. Blessed silence.

# CHAPTER TWO

**I STARED OUT** the window into a deserted courtyard. The only hints of former habitation were deep footprints rapidly filling with snow. Thick flakes pelted down and rendered the earth a frigid Winter Wonderland.

On normal non-frigid days, staff lounged on the benches. Some furtively puffed cigarettes despite their admonishments to patients about the habit. Others sipped coffee, keeping their eyes trained on flickering phone screens. Occasionally, you'd see a patient lugging around an IV pole—accompanied by a nurse, of course; couldn't have people shooting up drugs through their IVs.

The meteorologist—the douchebag with veneers too big for his mouth—forecast three inches. Or maybe two feet. Who really knew? Meteorologists: the biggest hedgers alive.

A sigh escaped my lips, and desperate longing filled me. The dark underside of the heavy clouds to the west promised a corker of a storm, something even we laypeople idiots could tell. Probably would dump layers of powder on nearby slopes to the delight of skiers and snowboarders alike.

I shut my eyes and imagined myself on a chairlift. Cool air prickling my cheeks, wisps of vapor rising from my mouth. The *pffft* of snow swishing under my board as I pushed off the lift, ready to tackle a black diamond. *If only*, I thought ruefully, shaking my head. *If only things were different.*

"Hello, Earth to Sam?" came a vaguely pissy voice, completely interrupting my daydream, jolting me back to the shitty present. Back to four bilious walls plastered with bullshit motivational posters, a legion of exercise machines invented by sadists gleaming sinisterly beneath stark white lighting, faintly scented with the sweat, blood, and tears of those unlucky enough to do time here.

Physical Therapy. Or state-sanctioned physician-prescribed torture. *Tomato. Tomahto.*

I rolled my eyes and turned from the window. "What?"

"We're not here to stare out the window. We're here to work," Dan pointedly reminded me. *Again.* A crisp blue polo accented glacial eyes, framed by thick eyebrows currently drawn into a glower. Dan might be classically handsome—in an Aryan sort of way; Hitler would've loved him if his last name weren't Schwartz—but I'd grown to dislike him intensely, which dulled his good looks significantly. Sure, he was just doing his job—but did he have to be so damned annoying about it? All self-righteous, all oh-look-at-all-my-limbs-functioning-normally douchebag. Dan could be a bit of a prick, truth be told.

"Pretty sure you're the only one getting paid right now," I remarked, tempted to snap the pink bubble gum in my mouth to accentuate my sass, only refraining because Dan threw a shit fit if we chewed gum during our sessions. *Oh no, it'll get all over the carpet!*

He'd make me spit it out immediately; there was the carpet to think about, after all. I could claim ignorance, citing my traumatic brain injury and propensity to forget simple facts. Paint him as the asshole for expecting the girl suffering from amnesia to recall BS rules in the first place. Amnesia wasn't even my real problem, not that they knew that. My problem was: I remembered too much.

*If you ever tell, if you ever say one word, I'll kill you and your entire family. Start with your little sister and slice her stem-to-stern and fuck every hole she's got. Butcher your mom in front of your dad and make him eat her steaming entrails while I lop off his fingers and toes one by one. Punch a few dozen holes in his lungs and listen to the air burst from his body: suffocating on dry land… ain't that a bitch? And as for you… I'd enjoy you one last time; just have a fucking field day with your body before I shove my piece up your filthy twat and unload all the ammo I've got.*

I believed him. Believed the monster's threats. He would absolutely do that. Look at what he'd already done and gotten away with. So, it was safer to forget who I was. *Before.* Or at least—pretend to forget.

Dan shrugged. "You could just fuck around and do nothing if you wanted. I still get paid whether you try or not. You refusing to do something hurts only you. I'm not the one who needs PT."

He had me there. Dan's biceps stretched the limits of his sleeves, and he looked like he could easily run a six-minute mile without breaking much of a sweat. The guy was *in shape*. One of those gym rats who drove women away with cheesy pick-up lines and that weird groaning men do when hefting heavy barbells.

"Fine," I muttered.

With meaty paws on slim hips, Dan directed: "I want you to make three circuits of the room. Then we'll do some grip strength exercises."

"Then what? You'll sign me up for a marathon?" I said peevishly, making no move to fulfill his ludicrous demands. "Then make me pull myself up Mount Everest?"

Dan snarked, "*No, that's next week.*" *Oh, now he had jokes.* "Now get moving."

Letting out an irritated snort, I replied, "This is so fucking stupid." I reached down and touched the rubber tires, fighting the urge to recoil. The material made my hands gross, leaving them in desperate need of a good wash, and my palms were littered with tender blisters that hadn't yet calloused. Even gentle pressure on the raw skin was like grasping hot coals, rendering each session an exercise in agony.

"Go," Dan commanded. His eyes were narrowed and intense, boring into me.

I grasped the hand rims and pushed off evenly using both hands, reminding myself to keep my thumbs pointing forward, wrists as neutral as possible. Overcoming the inertia, the wheels spun and forward I went.

"That's it," Dan said, his voice warming as he cheered me on my pathetic trek.

Despite traveling mere feet, my forearms burned, screaming from lactic acid entrenching itself in each muscle fiber. Beads of sweat rolled down the small of my back and I gritted my teeth, preparing for the fucking turn. And Dan wanted three circuits? Fucking twelve turns? Christ. Was he fucking nuts? *Focus! Ten and three, ten and three,* I reminded myself, urging my upper body to follow my bidding. I started to turn.

"You're doing it, Sam!" Dan said excitedly, as if I'd just executed a slam dunk rather than turning a stupid wheelchair. His positive attitude made me wanna puke most of the time but as I fought for every inch, I appreciated it.

A warmth pervaded my chest and a lump rose in my throat. I was doing it! Fucking doing it! "Oh-oh-look-at-me—" I started.

The left wheel caught—upsetting the delicate display of physics—and the chair tipped, dumping me unceremoniously to the floor. My skull bounced off the ground, cushioned by that ugly brown carpet Dan obsessively worried about. Air gushed out of my lungs and my diaphragm heaved at the insult. My left wrist pulsed in time with my pounding heart; reflexively, I'd thrown my arm out to catch myself. If I broke it…

"Oh shit!" Dan exclaimed, footsteps thudding to my side. "Dude, are you okay?" Thick fingers wrapped around my shoulder and upper arm. "Here, let me help—"

"Don't fucking touch me!" I screamed, tears of rage spilling down my face, yanking my shoulder and arm away from him, my ailing wrist protesting the sudden movement. A lightning-quick anger flashed through me, illuminating every injustice I'd suffered, distorting them, casting flickering shadows on the wall that only hinted at their sinister natures.

A medley of screams rattled against my skull, doubling, growing rapidly in size. Echoes, each louder than the last. Cries I wished I could banish from memory… except—I'd never forget. Couldn't forget. The blood coursing through my veins grew frigid at the thought. I closed my eyes—shut *tight, tight, tight*—hoping to forestall the next bit; praying it passed by without a second glance.

*No such luck.* Flashes of iron bars, cold-to-the-touch in the morning hours. Haunted eyes searching mine, finding me lacking. Cruel fists and harsh words. The copper reek of my spilled blood. The stench of piss and shit and unwashed skin…

*Stop it.* Thankfully, the images dissolved. Still, my hands shook. *That's all it took to take me back,* I thought ruefully, glaring at my overturned chair. *Now look at me.*

Rage deflated and deep exhaustion seized me. Gravity gripped me, doubling, tripling, pulling me down and pinning me to moldy-smelling carpet. Air—and hope—leaked from my lungs. I was nothing. Nothing. Just a gimp.

Tears rolled down my hot cheeks and I surrendered to them, my chest heaving with the strength of my sobs. I gulped up air and my diaphragm hitched, robbed of precious oxygen. My shoulders shook—violently at first—but as my cries petered out, they stilled, leaving me a hollowed-out husk. A nothing. Nothing. Not for the first time, I thought of life with a me-sized hole in it and, rather than terror, felt a sickly sort of comfort.

"Sam? You okay?" Dan asked softly, bringing me back to the present.

Unable to meet his eyes, I pushed myself up with the good arm.

"Fine," I lied.

# CHAPTER THREE

"CAN WE WATCH *Jeopardy*?" Rebecca asked, twining an auburn lock of hair around her index finger.

Rolling my eyes, a Pavlovian response each time her mouth opened, I answered, "I don't give a shit what you do."

Glumly, I examined my tray of dinner, if it could even be called that—slop, more like. My lip curled as I took in the anemic, overcooked chicken breast, mashed potatoes with the same consistency—and flavor—as shower caulk, sad, limp green beans, a roll that could double as a fine doorstop, and the true star of the meal: wiggly green *Jell-O* with mandarin oranges suspended in time.

"Aren't we just a ray of sunshine today? It's called being polite. You should try it sometime," Rebecca quipped, her words cushioned with a mouthful of glue potatoes. She audibly swallowed in cartoonish fashion. "Who peed in your cornflakes?"

Life. Life pissed all over everything. I clenched my fist around the plastic butter knife provided with my subpar meal and—not for the first time—wondered how hard I'd have to press to unzip the skin overlying the bounding arteries in my wrists.

"What's there to be happy about?" I pointed to my tray with the knife. "This shitty food?" To her. "My annoying roommate?" To the window. "The terrible weather? Winter sucks. Or… should I be happy about my fucked up spinal cord?" I said with mock enthusiasm, brandishing the dull blade at my chest. If only it were sharper—I could plunge it deep within my neck and bleed out almost instantly, saving me from Rebecca's Pollyanna bullshit.

With a serene expression. Rebecca fiddled with the amethyst stone dangling around her neck. She claimed the crystal cleared her mind and washed away toxic thoughts. New Age bullshit. "You need to practice gratitude; it'll change your life. You have food whereas others do not—"

"Send it to them then and leave me alone," I interjected, eyeing my fork. I could file the handle into a shiv. That might do the trick. Straight to the carotid. *BAM.*

Ignoring me, Rebecca continued her tirade: "You still have the use of your arms. You could be a quadriplegic. You could be dependent on a trach or a feeding tube—"

"Wait, wait, I've got one!" I exclaimed, snapping my fingers. "I'm grateful I don't have a shit bag like yours. Am I doing this right?" Rebecca gave me a bright smile—twisting the puckered scar snaking across her cheek—and the mean glee capering within me evaporated.

"Exactly! Like that!" She giggled. "I'm just happy the catheter is out."

Me too. I hated looking at the Foley bag slowly filling with human-grade lemonade hanging on the side of her bed. Who could eat when only one layer of material separated me from my roommate's bodily fluids? *Blech.*

"How about you turn on *Jeopardy* and make me grateful you stopped talking? Wouldn't that be fun?" I clapped my hands enthusiastically like a ridiculously perky host on a kids' TV show.

"See? That's another thing to be happy for: *Jeopardy*. And Alex Trebek." She powered up the TV hanging on the wall and buzzed through the channels until she found *NBC.*

I sniffed. "Alex Trebek's dead, you know. Ate a dirt sandwich."

Her eyes widened in shock. "No! Seriously?" Aghast, she put a hand to her chest.

I nodded. "Stage four pancreatic cancer."

Onscreen, the once-alive Alex Trebek schmoozed it up with the guests who were all quite clearly on the spectrum. Who knew so much about World History and Physics?

"That's a bummer," Rebecca said, sniffling. Red blotches bloomed on her cheeks.

I groaned. "You're not seriously crying over Alex Trebek, are you?" I speared two droopy green beans and brought them to my mouth, then thought better of it. Down the fork went. "Get a grip."

One of the contestants laughed at Alex's joke and the silver-haired host shot the camera a mega-watt grin, saying, "And we'll be right back after the commercial break."

Rebecca pulled a tissue from the box next to her bed and gustily blew into it, wet and phlegmy, and quietly said, "I had a crush on him, okay? Ever since I was a little girl. I thought he was so smart and—"

Her words became meaningless—I was Charlie Brown and all I heard was: *Wah Wah Wah*, and I dissociated, allowing my mind to wander. Hmmm…

There was always the window, assuming I could get it open. Three stories down. If I went headfirst—but no, what if my head didn't break open like a piñata and I became a quad? How was I supposed to off myself if I couldn't move at all? No, no, that wouldn't work.

We did have a shower rod in our shared bathroom—a noose. A noose couldn't be too hard to make. I could YouTube it. You could YouTube anything these days. *How to make bombs or poison*, or *how to boil an egg*—but how was I gonna hang myself if I couldn't even do a pullup?

Oooooooh… poison! What was the difference between cure and death? The dose, silly. I could overdose; cheek my pills when the nurses brought them in. What would I OD on, though? The cute little yellow pearl of Vitamin D? Nope. Tylenol? No thanks: I'd just go into liver failure and end up on dialysis or something. Gabapentin? Maybe. I'd investigate… to be sure.

I glanced over at Rebecca, not surprised she was still prattling on, and tuned back into her verbal diarrhea: "I liked to think we'd get married in Canada, since he's from there and all. I even had my dress picked out: this lacy backless—"

She was still on this Trebek shit? Christ. "You should really bring this obsession up in therapy or something, Becs. Wow. Pathologic," I remarked, my gaze floating back to the TV. My stomach plummeted and the world stopped.

It was him. I knew it beyond a shadow of a doubt.

You never forgot the face of the man who abducted you.

# CHAPTER FOUR

**I STARED AT** the ceiling and picked my cuticles, savoring the sharp sting. Rebecca's snores kept me company—a welcome companion for once. Her snorts and snits usually sent my blood boiling. Even the nurses seated down the hall were quiet, probably staring at screens or dozing. Their idle gossip had died down an hour ago, around the time Rebecca started her nighttime impersonations of a lawnmower with a clogged muffler.

Grasping a thin shred of skin near my thumbnail, I tugged, and the flesh gave way. Cool air licked across the wound and sent a shiver down my spine; not wholly unpleasant. Sure, it hurt, but it reminded me I still could fully feel… here at least. Not that my legs were completely devoid of feeling. Oh no, they were a smorgasbord of unpleasant sensations. Sinister flames licking my skin, maddening itching I scoured with ruined fingernails until I drew blood, and sickening pins-and-needles everywhere, if said implements were wielded by Pinhead and Friends.

Tonight, I was restless—and I longed to stretch out: arch my back, tighten my legs, and point my toes until each muscle loosened. Hop from the bed—without a moment's trepidation—bare feet slapping against the floor, sure and sturdy. To stroll leisurely past the nurse's station. Break into a dead run: the easiest thing in the world if you had two legs that functioned appropriately.

Who was I kidding? Where would I even go? I had nowhere. Nothing. No one. But… that wasn't entirely true, was it? The news story… it proved I wasn't alone. Not by a long shot. I knew someone.

And now I knew his name.

Jacob Brady. Jacob Brady was out there wearing a smarmy sneer disguised as a smile, accepting awards for philanthropic efforts in the community, per the fluffy news piece. If only they knew about his basement of horrors and the atrocities committed there.

Instead, he was out in public, surrounded by women and children: his guilty pleasures—masquerading as Citizen of the Year. Clutching his plaque, he gave the mayor's hand a firm shake. A tailored black suit hugged a lean, muscular frame and dirty blond hair tumbled over his broad shoulders. His piercing blue eyes flashed, cold and calculating—the only outward hint of the monster lurking within… if you paid attention.

They said eyes were the window to the soul. He had none. Of that, I was certain. Even through the TV, I felt the frigid heat of his gaze. Familiar fear enveloped me, rendering me nothing more than a prey animal cowering in the ever-enlarging shadow of death.

My guts knotted. Heart kicked into overdrive and blood roared in my ears. I steeled myself for the impending panic attack—an all-body stress response fueled by gulping, shuddering breaths, and realized there was something else simmering below the utter terror, something that gave me pause.

Anger. Deep-seated, hot, and poisonous. It spilled into my blood-stream and whispered in silken, inviting tones, coaxing me. Calming me. My chest loosened. He threatened to kill everyone I loved—then me—but only if I ever went to the authorities. He obviously had money and power, and if life had taught me anything, those men always got away with it. And if they got caught? Big deal. A slap on the wrist. Nothing more. No… seeing Jacob Brady reminded me I had something left to live for.

Revenge. Rebecca was right: I had to be grateful for what I had. I still had my arms and all I needed was a finger to pull the trigger.

# CHAPTER FIVE

**THOUGHTS OF VENGEANCE** cheering me, I fell into a dreamless sleep, black and inviting. A free trial of being dead. I slept a record seven hours and woke to a stray sunbeam shining into my eyes.

"Good morning, sleepyhead," Rebecca chirped. She plunged her spoon into murky gray oatmeal and mechanically shoveled it in her mouth, keeping her eyes trained on the TV screen. *The Price is Right.* Another of her favorites.

I pushed myself up and rubbed my eyes. "What time is it?"

"Eleven a.m., duh. That's when *The Price is Right* comes on. Everyone knows that."

Grabbing the all-purpose remote attached to my bed so I could ring the nurse—eggs, toast, and turkey bacon sounded divine—I answered. "Well, unlike you, I didn't skip class, so I don't have the *TV Guide* memorized. I was an honor student even. Not to brag."

"Wait… I thought you didn't remember your life?" Rebecca asked, hazel eyes narrowing with skepticism.

Frantically, I mashed the call button—*please, please answer!*—and strived for a nonchalant tone. "I mean—I remember—like—random stuff. Here and there. Bits and pieces, you know? Dribs and drabs."

Rebecca nibbled her bottom lip, face clouded with scrutiny. "What else do you remember? Huh? You never tell me anything about yourself and I was okay with that when it was because of 'amnesia'"—she mimed quotation marks with her index and middle fingers—"but I think you've just been holding out on me. On all of us! Why?"

"I—uh—" I started, brain whirling.

"How can I help you?" came the tinny voice from the speaker.

Saved by the bell! "Good morning!" I crowed too enthusiastically, making a show of it to Rebecca, who glowered at me. "I'd like breakfast please."

"The usual?"

I nodded vigorously. "That'd be great! Coffee and orange juice too?"

"You got it, hon," they said, a tell-tale *click* announcing their departure from the speaker.

Feeling the heat of Rebecca's stare on me, I gripped the handle hanging above my bed and maneuvered.

"What are you doing?" Rebecca asked incredulously. A spoonful of oatmeal had stopped halfway to her mouth, frozen in the air.

I gestured to my torso with my left hand. "What's it look like? I've gotta go to the bathroom."

Rebecca held her hand up. "Wait a minute… you're getting yourself up? Not calling the nurses to do it for you?"

"Right," I answered, laboriously yet successfully hefting myself into the wheelchair. Escaping Rebecca's questions: priority number one. Number two: whipping myself into fighting fitness… or my version of it anyway. "Time for me to get my shit together, like you said." I headed toward our shared bathroom, pushing the rubber tires and crossing in front of her bed.

"You were listening to me?" Rebecca asked softly.

I shrugged. "Sometimes. Don't let it go to your head."

Rebecca cocked her head. "Something's gotten into you. You're… different today." She put her chin in her hand and thoughtfully stroked it.

"Just a good night of sleep!" I called out, slamming the bathroom door behind me. Too close.

# CHAPTER SIX

**TIME PASSED, EACH** day blurring into the next, reminding me of a montage in a sports movie. Rocky training his balls off in Russia to classic eighties tunes. I discovered Daft Punk and listened to the *Discovery* album obsessively. "Harder, Better, Faster, Stronger" became my personal anthem. Sweat-stained workout clothes were my uniform, exhausted muscles my reward.

I lifted weights. Completed countless laps in the physical therapy room while snow pelted the ground. Down the hall and back, rinse, repeat. Warmer temperatures found me outside—sometimes accompanied by Dan but mostly alone—exploring the rehab/hospital property while getting my workout on.

When not pushing myself physically, I was researching. Self-defense techniques. Knife fighting, just in case it got up close and personal—not that I was planning on it. Better to be prepared, though.

And my personal favorite study was guns. Now, where to procure such an implement? I couldn't very well roll into the Bad Part of Town and ask if they were packing heat and could I-pretty-pretty-please-with-a-cherry-on-top purchase a gun they kept hidden behind a black trench coat just for idiots like me? No way. They'd think I was a terrible undercover cop or something.

The *Sam of Before* had no interest in such things—buying illegal weapons from the Black Market, which for some reason, I pictured as a shady, creepy stall in an abandoned alley—but *Before Sam* wasn't me. Not anymore.

*Before Sam* loved volleyball, rom-coms, and believed in bullshit like true love. *Before Sam* ran alone on wooded trails, wearing headphones, without a care for her surroundings. The *Before Sam*... she didn't know the bitter truths of the world. The *Sam of Now* did.

I'd put in a hard day of training: three miles in my wheelchair, propelled by my arms, followed by an upper body weight workout. For us paraplegics, every day was arm day. One steamy shower later, I settled into my bed and scrolled on my iPad.

"You gonna watch more weird gun stuff?" Rebecca asked. "Because I was thinking we could watch some *Real Housewives*. If you wanted," she added hopefully.

"I do not want, but thank you for the invitation. As much as I'd like to watch women with too much money and plastic surgery fight with each other, I've got stuff to do."

Rebecca pushed hair out of her eyes. "Oh yeah, like what?"

*Like figure out how to find a gun so I can murder some dickhead.* "Just... stuff."

"Are you looking for an apartment?" Rebecca rummaged in her purse and extracted a small white bag. "We only have like a week left with the program." She plucked a butterscotch out and offered it to me. "Candy?"

I scoffed and shook my head—old people candy, yuck. I didn't want to think about what I was going to do next week, since truthfully, I had no plan. "An apartment? Seriously? With what money?"

"Doesn't the government give you some?" Undressing the yellow disc, she plopped it on her tongue and closed her eyes, savoring it.

"Not enough. Unless I settle for some roach-infested drug den."

Cheeking the candy, she asked, "Why don't you get in touch with your family then? Ask for help? That's why they're there—"

"Even if I could find them... I can't ask them!" I hissed before realizing my blunder. Fuck. I wasn't supposed to remember if I had a family or not. "I mean—I—uh—"

Rebecca fixed me with a stare radiating frank disappointment. "Why won't you tell me the truth about you? You know everything about me."

I put my index finger up. "Not by choice. I want the record to show that it was not by choice."

Ignoring my remark, she continued. "I know something's up with you. You did a complete one-eighty. Started training hard and looking up weird stuff online… all the gun crap. You're not even all that snarky to me anymore—"

"I can be snarky as fuck if you want me to, babe."

"—and you can tell me stuff, you know? We're roommates. And friends," Rebecca said softly, looking down at pink-painted fingernails. "At least, I like to think so."

Something tugged at me then—whether it was the sad cast to her hazel eyes or her heartfelt declaration—and part of me wanted to spill, tell her about the last jog, the abduction, the pain, the suffering, the threats, the escape, everything. But I couldn't. Tears welled up in my eyes and stung. "Becs—I can't—I can't tell you anything."

"Can't? Or won't?"

Both? "I… I don't know," I mumbled, unable to meet her gaze.

Her eyes probed, searching me. Seconds passed. "Fine." Rebecca cleared her throat. "And you're not going to go live in some hovel with bed bugs for roommates. You can come stay with me. Until you find a place of your own or whatever. No rush."

"Wait… what?" Was she serious?

Nodding smugly, she wrinkled her nose. "Unless you want to live in a roach motel. It's up to you."

"Hold on… aren't you married?" I asked, searching my memory. "To that one guy… Chad?"

Although now that I thought about it: he only showed a handful of times, mostly at the beginning when Rebecca wasn't her obnoxiously cheerful self— for good reason. She'd crawled from the car accident sporting two broken ankles, a shattered pelvis, and a bellyful of tattered intestines necessitating radical colon removal and a colostomy bag. A trip through a metal detector would be a noisy affair thanks to the conglomeration of pins and needles embedded in her bones.

That shit would depress anyone, and Becs was no exception. The light in her eyes was near extinguished and anguish clung to her like a funeral shroud back then.

That first time, her husband was completely put out by being at her bedside.

"You know… I postponed a golf game with an important customer to be here." He'd dressed for the links: a white polo that failed to conceal a burgeoning beer belly and khaki pants held up by an ugly beige leather belt.

"I'm so sorry my near-fatal car accident is putting such a crimp in your plans," Rebecca had sniped. Railroads of black sutures—thirty-four stitches in total—ran across the ruined landscape of her face, buttoning together skin shredded by shards of glass from a shattered windshield. The laceration around her mouth puckered at her glum frown.

When the nurse came in and emptied Rebecca's near-to-bursting colostomy bag, Chad loudly retched and gagged. "When does that get fixed? Yikes. Gross."

"Never," Rebecca had answered, sadness lining the statement.

The way Chad's face twisted at Bec's answer as if the in-sickness-and-in health part of the vows didn't apply to this, not to him. Seeing that made my heart break for her—not that I said anything when he left and she turned to her side and faced the wall, shoulders shaking with her silent sobs. What could someone say after seeing that?

Rebecca now held up a bare left ring finger. "Nope. Not married. Not anymore. Separated for now, until the divorce goes through. Chad left me. His version of a trophy wife doesn't have a colostomy and a roadmap of scars." She let out a rueful laugh. "Lucky for me, the house was my grandmother's. It's paid off and in my name. I've got plenty of room."

Anger boiled up and filled my throat. "Fuck Chad!" I spat. "Stupid asshole doesn't deserve you anyway." I snapped my fingers. "That's it, Chad's going on my list." He could join Jacob Brady.

"Your list?" Rebecca asked.

Yeah, my list of shitheads to murder. "Don't worry about it," I said. "All I can say is you're not on it."

Her lip quirked upward. "Maybe you can tell me more about it one day."

"Maybe." My stomach fluttered as I recalled the topic at hand. "Uh… thank you. I'd love to move in but only temporarily, okay? Until I get back on my feet… uh, I mean… until I get situated." Or die in a blaze of glory, blowing Jacob Brady's brains out. "Truthfully, I didn't know what I was going to do so this is a lifesaver. Thank you again."

Rebecca smiled and her cheeks pinked. "It's my pleasure."

"I'm still gonna be snarky," I warned.

She winked at me. "I'm hoping so."

# CHAPTER SEVEN

**KNOWING I HAD** a place to stay assuaged my anxiety and I allowed myself to enjoy the rest of my rehab stay.

The staff held a little party for our group—as was tradition when someone graduated from the unit—which consisted of me, Becs, Jimmy—a guy who ate shit on a motorcycle and had a craniotomy scar and TBI to show for it, and Sylvia—a morose, gray-haired woman on the mend from a debilitating stroke who'd become completely obsessed with death. She'd fancied herself a poet, musing on the mysteries of mortality, happily using her formerly limp right hand to pen diatribes about the human condition. All she needed was a raven perched on her bony shoulder to sell the aesthetic completely.

Party guests included Dan and some of the other physical therapists, Dr. Webb, the techs on the rehab floor, and any patients who felt well enough to attend. We shared a marble cake topped with vanilla icing, a red frosting scrawl proclaiming:

*Happy Graduation! Kick some ass!*

"Dan, how exactly do you expect me to kick some ass?" I wrapped my hands around my wooden, useless leg and hefted it up. "I'm rather offended by that expression."

Eyes twinkling, Dan answered, "Offended, huh? Wasn't it you who suggested it say: *Good Luck Gimps?* Not very PC of you."

I forked a frosting-laden bite of cake into my mouth. "I'm taking back my power, Dan. People want to use gimp as a derogatory term, so I embrace it to piss them off and show 'em their words don't mean shit to me. You see?"

Jimmy brightly added, "It's like how Sam says she's one of them queers."
Rebecca chortled.

"Exactly," I said, giving Jimmy a finger gun and a wink.

Dan cleared his throat and tapped a pen on the protein drink he clutched; his macros didn't allow for punch or cake. "But seriously… I wanted to tell you how proud I am. Of all of you." He pointed to Sylvia. "Sylv… you're able to walk and write again! All because you put in the work. Jimmy, you had to relearn so much: how to read, dress yourself, and your favorite—playing *Mario Kart*."

"Meet me at Rainbow Road… if you dare," Jimmy jeered, flexing his biceps.

Dan tipped the protein shaker to Becs. "Rebecca… you had a rough go of it, and you pulled yourself out of the muck. Your positive attitude is infectious and much welcome here."

"Thank you," she replied. Unspent tears pooled in her eyes.

I put my hand on the small of her back and gave her a reassuring squeeze.

"Last—but certainly not least—we have Sam!" Dan clucked his tongue. "Sam. Sam. Sam. Obstinate would have been a word used to describe you." He shook his head. "Not anymore. Dedicated would be more apt these days. Your gumption impressed the hell out of me." Voices sounded in agreement.

Jimmy slyly added, "Sam did it for the babes. Chicks love muscles." His watery brown eyes flashed behind thick black frames.

"Guilty as charged," I said, putting my hands up. My gaze darted to Becs, and the ghost of a smile twitched her lips.

# CHAPTER EIGHT

**THE HOSPITAL VAN** pulled up to Becs' place and I gasped, throwing open the sliding door. "Becs… you didn't!"

The landscaping was impeccable: neatly trimmed bushes, a lush lawn, freshly cut and tickling my nostrils with its clean scent, and an abundance of flowers—most I recognized from *Alice in Wonderland's* weird garden scene.

Two-story, painted pastel yellow, perfectly matching Becs' sunny disposition. Hummingbirds flitted about sampling nectar. A monarch butterfly fluttered past—adding to the sense of domestic bliss radiating from the place— wheeling about before settling on a wooden railing. Unstained, freshly erected. A hint of sawdust lingered in the air.

My chest tightened and my throat hitched. I tried to keep the emotion from creeping into my voice, afraid if I started blubbering, I'd never stop. "You made this for me?"

"Once you said you were moving in, I called a contractor, and they put it in. Only took a few days." Becs grabbed my hand and squeezed. "Let's go. I'll give you a grand tour. I'll grab the luggage later. Come on."

I swiped at my eyes. "My room better not be in the basement."

"Don't worry. It's not. It's in the attic." The corners of her eyes crinkled mischievously and the red scars crisscrossing her cheeks danced. My stomach clenched, a not wholly unpleasant sensation.

"I should have guessed," I said. Up the newly constructed wheelchair ramp I went. I was home. Tears prickled and my throat tightened.

Becs excitedly showed me to my room—practically wriggling like an over-stimulated puppy.

I looked around and was shocked by what I saw. "Um… Becs… this is the master bedroom. This is where you should sleep, it's your house after all." I spied a picture frame on the dresser and picked it up. Becs had her arms around someone with closely cropped hair, both wearing beaming smiles. "Who's this?"

"Oh, that's Ande. My bestie from childhood." Her eyes grew dreamy with nostalgia. "They were my partner in crime."

A field of corn, frozen in time, colored the background. "Nice corn," I remarked.

"Yeah, they grew up on a farm. Let me tell you, we raised some hell in that place," Becs said, her eyes twinkling.

I wheeled myself to the bathroom and glanced inside. Gasped. "Holy shit! This is huge!" More crisp wood greeted me: handrails mounted at varying intervals so I could maneuver safely. Her contractor had certainly been a busy bee.

She leaned against the bathroom door frame. "Full disclosure. This used to be my room. And Chad's. Not anymore though. Plus," she said, sauntering to the handrails and stroking them with delicate fingers, "the master had more room for you and your ride."

"Well… thanks," I said lamely. How could I repay her for any of this? Truly? "Um… please tell me it's not the same mattress you guys used to bang on in there?" I cocked my head toward the bedroom and arched my eyebrow.

Becs shrugged. "Wouldn't you like to know?"

A kernel of jealousy flared within me at the thought of them together: his brutish, clumsy hands pawing at her. Sloppy kisses. "Ugh, gross," I muttered.

She flapped her hand. "Oh, don't be jealous!"

"I'm not," I lied.

Her slim fingers closed around my right hand and an electric tingle shot down my spine. "You're here and he's not. So… let's celebrate!"

Celebrating for Becs equaled obscene amounts of Chinese takeout paired with glass after glass of Trader Joe's red wine. A store-bought tiramisu for dessert. Followed by an unexpected nightcap.

"Wanna try this?" With the dexterity of a seasoned magician, Becs produced a joint from parts unknown.

"Is that—a… weed? A joint?" I asked. I'd taken a puff or two in high school but felt nothing, no high. The drugs I was familiar with were either sedatives forced upon me or pain medications administered by nurses with exhausted, weary eyes.

Becs nodded. "You don't have to if you don't want to. No peer pressure." A Bic lighter flicked and its flame kissed the tip of the joint perched between her full lips and a red eye flared into being. She inhaled, shut her eyes. Held it. Then let it out with a satisfied sigh. "Ahhhh… I missed that. The only good thing about having a colostomy and chronic pain? A medical marijuana card! Now I get to smoke to my heart's content: doctor's orders!"

"Did Chad like to smoke?" I asked, gingerly taking the joint from her and holding it awkwardly. I mimicked her and drew the dank smoke into my lungs, a small puff to start. A pleasant buzz soon filled my head.

She rolled her eyes. "Oh god no. Chad thought pot smokers were either gangsters or hippies. He preferred shotgunning beer with the boys and going target shooting or playing golf with douchebags."

I exhaled, blowing a plume of smoke into the air. "Chad fucking sucks, dude," I remarked. "How did someone like you end up with a prick like him?"

Becs took another hit and paused. "Well…" she said, releasing her inhalation. "Societal and parental pressure, I guess? It was the next step, you know? You go to college, meet a man, get married, have kids." She stared off, appearing deep in thought. Her forehead wrinkled. "It's funny… I thought I wanted all that but… I think I wanted to be accepted more than anything. I wanted to be—normal, I guess?"

"I get that." And I did. Once, I thought I wanted the same things. With a woman, but yes, the same things. Love. Marriage. Maybe a family. Some dogs and cats. A garden teeming with plump tomatoes and swollen pumpkins. Instead, Jacob Brady happened, and my dreams melted into the ether. Did I dare dream again?

"What about you?" Becs asked, her eyes searching me. The whites tinted red—fed by marijuana—making her irises pop. A wisp of hair hung in her face and she pushed it behind her ear. A warmth bloomed in my stomach and my heart began an aggressive tap dance against my ribs.

Buying time, I grabbed the joint and placed it between my lips. A massive inhale strained my lungs, and letting it out, I dissolved into a coughing fit that brought tears to my eyes.

Becs patted my back as I hacked. "You can tell me. Seriously. You can tell me anything. Anything at all."

How could someone show such kindness, be so wonderful? My mind whirled before I settled on a half-truth. "There was… a bad dude… in my past."

"Yeah?" Her voice was soft, inviting as cashmere.

I leaned forward and grabbed my wine glass and swirled it. Gazed down at the ruby liquid. "I nearly died leaving," I remarked, remembering my legs churning as I ran full out to get away from him, finally free of the restraints: physical, mental, chemical. Sweet freedom lasting only minutes, the cruelest truth. He still got me at the end, one way or another.

My body grew heavy as if gravity hooked talons around my legs and tugged me down, reminding me I'd never feel such exhilaration.

Becs put her hand on my knee. "Did he put you in that wheelchair?"

Raising my fat wine glass to my lips, I drained it. "He did."

"Is he on your list?"

"He is."

Becs cupped my cheek, thumb grazing my cheek, her tender touch making my heart swell and break at the same time. "Good," she said, closing her eyes and leaning in.

She tasted of oak and smoke.

# CHAPTER NINE

**DOMESTIC BLISS WITH** a side of subterfuge ensued.

Becs stayed in the master bedroom. With me. We shared meals again and not of the bland hospital variety. Pizza. Pasta. I made a passable risotto once—painstakingly following each step, wrist throbbing from so much damned stirring—surprising her when she got home from work. Gordon Ramsey would have called me an idiot sandwich but whatever.

Snuggling as true crime documentaries played, afterward talking at length about them: how they fucked up, what we'd do if it were us. Trips to the grocery store together, a special occasion as I got to pilot Bessie—my motorized wheelchair, my hog, all blacked-out with a bright orange frame—through the aisles. Strolls through the local dog park on the weekends, oohing and aahing over the adorable doggos.

Inside jokes. Experiencing the absurdity of reality together. Talking about anything and everything: sharing long-kept secrets, telling her what I could. But not everything.

I didn't tell her how some days I waited until she pulled out of the driveway, watching the clock until ten minutes drained away. Then, into the van I went, operating the gas pedal and brake with my hands until I arrived at Jacob Brady's job—it was easy enough to find with the help of Google.

Casing the joint was my new hobby, sitting inconspicuously in a tan soccer-mom van with tinted windows. I learned his patterns. He frequently took meetings at a local hipster coffee shop—using his silver tongue to spin a line of bullshit. I'd arrive before him and position myself in the corner, making sure his favorite table was well within my line of sight.

He never gave me a second glance, his eyes skipping over me as if I were merely part of the background. Practically furniture. Not surprising since I looked different. Instead of keeping my long hair—all the better to thread his cruel fingers through, yanking and wrenching my head for his sick whims—I kept it buzzed, usually covered by a plain black beanie. My cheekbones were padded with a healthy layer of fat, no longer gaunt and starved, and I never removed my sunglasses lest he look into my eyes and see something familiar there.

Jacob Brady hadn't shown this afternoon, maybe electing to take a private meeting where he could use and abuse. After spending an hour in my designated corner, half-reading a secondhand dog-eared paperback of Stephen King's *Firestarter*, wishing for my latent pyrokinesis to manifest, I took my half-drank matcha tea latte and untouched cranberry scone and drove to the dog park we frequented on days off. Traffic sucked and I patiently waited to turn into the parking lot, intermittently sipping on my lukewarm drink.

A couple with a Siberian Husky walked by on the sidewalk and the man caught my attention. Armed against the crisp, cool air, he was outfitted in a scruffy Army jacket, well worn. Something about him... seemed familiar. Scrutinizing him, trying to remember if we'd seen each other before or if he reminded me of someone, our eyes met. He gave me a neighborly wave and I returned it, feeling oddly friendly. Everyday kindness was underrated.

As he walked, his gaze darted everywhere, taking everything in. Head on a permanent swivel. His body seemed to thrum, crackling with nervous energy. I wondered if he suffered from PTSD, maybe he'd served overseas and simple life overwhelmed him. Maybe they'd just gotten into an argument. Maybe I was massively reading into things and he was just hyped up on caffeine.

A horn yanked me out of my musings on a perfect stranger's life and I turned into the parking lot. Darkness already encroached on the daylight—as it did this time of year—by the time I parked and unloaded myself and Bessie.

A small white paper bag containing my scone rode on my lap and I clutched the drink in a gloved hand, driving Bessie until I reached my favorite spot: a dog obstacle course of sorts.

Settling under the molting maple tree, I pulled the scone out and watched a small terrier mix navigate the course under the watchful eye of his owner. He went through the green tunnel, up the ramp, and across circular discs of varying heights with sure footing. Luxuriating in the crumbly sugary goodness, snappy fall air blowing across my cheeks, I considered the last piece of the how-to-kill-Jacob-Brady-puzzle.

The damn gun. Pawn shop? Sure, but even then, I was pretty sure they kept records of such transactions, and I'd rather fly under the radar. Ask around? Who the hell was I gonna ask? Dr. Webb during my next follow-up visit when she asked if I had any questions? *Yes, Dr. Webb, I do have a question: where in the hell can I get a gun? You know a guy?*

I hadn't completely ruled out the hood, fearing it might be my only remaining option. Visiting some fine establishment with bars on the windows, graffiti of competing gangs tagged on the walls, and asking the man with the most face tattoos *if he could, you know, get me a gun?* Totally not suicidal and stupid. Or maybe, just maybe, a legion of singing angels would appear, bestowing me a crystal-encrusted gun with pearl bullets. Yeah, right.

I tossed the rest of the scone down my gullet and swallowed, my throat stuttering against a sturdy piece of dried cranberry which tickled my epiglottis, threatening to go down my windpipe. A staccato of harsh coughing ensued and I fought to catch my breath.

"Shit," I rasped; tears rolled, and I lunged for my matcha tea latte. Desperate to stave off certain death, I chugged my now-cold tea and the perilous cranberry fragment dislodged and made its way into my stomach. Unfortunately, my cup lid followed suit and forest-green liquid splashed all down my front.

"Shit!" I repeated. Mouth agape, I stared in horror at my gray sweatshirt. Grabbing the paper bag that housed my scone, I tried to mop up the mess and only succeeded in spreading it around. "Fuck, fuck, fuck."

Patting my pockets, I came up empty of napkins. Frantically, I glanced around and spotted a covered trash can on the other side of the flaming leaf-covered tree. I pushed an image of George Costanza pillaging through garbage out of my mind and made my way over; it was my best chance at napkins or something to help with this disaster.

Edging closer, I pushed open the trash can flap and spied a generic brown paper bag, often favored by fast-food franchises. *Please let there be unsoiled napkins inside I can use.* I snatched the heavier-than-expected bag—praying the terrier's owner wasn't watching me dig through park trash cans like some grubby raccoon—and opened it, peering inside.

No napkins but—no wonder it was so heavy. "Holy shit, no way." Elation and panic rose up in equal measure, vying for dominance. Feeling incredibly guilty, I shut the bag and tucked it between my leg and the chair, completely forgetting about my soiled clothing. I had to get to the van. Had to check this out.

Thumbing Bessie's accelerator, I jolted and nearly plowed into the terrier and his dad. "Crap!" I swerved, missing them by a foot. Jamming on the brake, I jerked to a stop. "Dude, I'm so sorry! I didn't see you there."

The man—not terrible looking, if not a bit dweeby—flapped his hand, his eyes resting on Bessie before flickering up to my face. "No problem!" He couldn't exactly get pissed at a chick in a wheelchair, even if they almost killed him. His thin mustache twitched. "Do you—uh—need a napkin?"

"What?"

"Well—uh, you have a bit of a mess there." He gestured at my front, and I looked down at the ugly stain I'd totally forgotten about after my insane discovery.

A laugh, burbling and sounding completely crazy to my ears, barked out of me. "Oh, that. Um. Yeah. Sure. That'd be great."

Surprising me, he extracted a linen cloth from his pocket and offered it to me.

"You don't have to give me this—this is super nice." Pink thread twined the edges and black lettering—monogrammed initials—lined the side closest to me. Fancy.

"Take it." He thrust the handkerchief toward me. "My mom buys me twelve each year for Christmas. I've got a drawer filled with 'em. You'd be doing me a favor taking one off my hands."

I hesitated, then grabbed the handkerchief. "Well… thanks." I ran my fingers over the stitching: A. F.

"My initials," he offered. "Anthony Finnegan. The ultimate Irish Catholic name. She named me after the patron saint of lost causes and things." He laughed. "I go by Tony, though."

I extended my gloved hand to him, and he took it. We shook. "I'm Sam, nice to meet you. My mom named me after a character from *Bewitched.*"

Tony chuckled.

"Appreciate you helping me out here. What a mess." I said, pointing. "Cute dog, by the way."

He brightened. "He's my little guy. Say hi, Alastor." Alastor gave me a toothy doggy grin and wagged his tail. Tony shivered and looked skyward at the rapidly advancing dusk. "We better get going, getting a bit chilly out here. Try to stay dry from now on, 'kay?"

"Since I have nothing else to spill, can do! Thanks again."

I held my breath the entire trek to the van and didn't peer inside the bag until I was safely inside, doors locked, hidden away from the world.

With a shaky hand, I plucked my unexpected treasure from the bag and stroked its cool side. Wondered if someone upstairs—if there was anybody even there—had answered my unsaid prayers. And how weird to meet someone named after the patron saint of lost causes immediately after finding this. Irony? Was that the word for that?

Whatever it was, surety filled me, utter certainty of my mission. I required. I needed. And here it was provided, almost ordained. If this wasn't a go-ahead message from the universe, a heartfelt go for your dreams, Ace of Base's "The Sign" playing out in real time…

I found my gun.

# CHAPTER TEN

**I TOOK A** swig of ginger beer and racked my brain, careful to keep my face placid and agreeable. Not concerned. Not totally fucking freaking out about Becs' abrupt shift in mood. Like a dutiful fifties housewife—jacked up on adrenaline and good fortune at beating her home by mere minutes instead of the typical amphetamine/tranquilizer combo favored back then—I greeted her at the door with a lingering kiss.

"Hey there, gorgeous," she said, pulling away and tossing her keys on the assorted-shit-table in the front hall.

My heart hammered in my ears. "Hi."

Becs cocked her head and pursed her lips. "You feeling okay?" She put the back of her head on my clammy forehead.

"Oh yeah, yeah, totally fine," I said, the words spilling out faster and higher than intended.

"You sure? You feel sweaty and look flushed; maybe you broke a fever?" Stark concern colored the questions.

Guilt licked through me, and I pushed it—mostly—from my mind. "I just finished a workout. Arm day."

Not a total lie. I'd held the gun up and carefully examined it, admiring it from all angles. The cool silver snub-nosed barrel. Cracked dark wooden handle. How'd that happen? Was it dropped? Did they run out of bullets and chuck the fucker at someone? It still could double as a nice projectile. And it had an engraving: *FOR HALEY* painstakingly etched on the disrupted handle.

I'd rubbed my fingertip across the words and a profound sadness washed through me at their meaning. A dedication. A declaration of one thing—something I intimately understood: revenge. It would certainly explain the crack. I imagined a face contorted with rage, the gun whooshing downward again and again, bludgeoning a skull to a pulp. Blood spattering.

Briefly, I'd thought how exhilarating it might feel to beat Jacob's like that but… I'd rather use the weapon as intended. I just needed to find bullets, a fact that simultaneously irritated me and comforted me. The universe couldn't have thrown me one more bone? Included some bullets? Really? Then I thought of a buck-toothed kid finding the proverbial loaded gun in a park trashcan. The carnage. The heartbreak.

Completely mesmerized by the gun, I'd almost missed the garage door trundling up.

"Shit. Shit. Shit!"

Head on a swivel, I had searched for a place to stash it. There! I'd rushed to my nightstand—wheel banging into the wood—and pulled the drawer open. Inside the gun went and I brushed everything off my nightstand on top of it: the perfect camouflage.

Becs' thinking I was coming down with a cold instead of suspecting me of being a deceitful bitch made me sick, but it also served my purposes. I couldn't exactly come out and say: *Oh no, I was in the bedroom fingering the gun I miraculously found in the park. Yeah, I'm gonna kill someone on my list. You have any bullets I can borrow?*

"Go get a shower and put on comfy clothes. I'll get dinner ready and then—maybe—we could watch a movie?" I asked. I didn't have to be on my Martha Stewart game tonight, dinner was frozen pizza and a store-bought mix of Caesar salad with prepackaged croutons, cheese, and dressing. If I had to do anything requiring any sort of concentration in this state, there was a strong chance I'd start a housefire.

Fifteen minutes later, Becs reappeared in the kitchen with wet hair and a weird attitude.

I helped myself to a third slice of pizza, more out of nerves than hunger. I'd just taken a bite when Becs slammed her glass down aggressively, sloshing root beer on the table, nearly making me choke on a glob of cheese and pepperoni.

She waited for me to stop hacking—the room temperature seemingly dropping ten degrees—before fixing me with a hard look. "Is there anything you want to tell me?" Her fork tines scraped against the plate as she stabbed her salad: a horrendous noise that set my teeth on edge.

"Like what?" I asked, trying for a smile that felt like a grimace. My mind flitted from possibility to possibility: she fell out of love with me, she knows I'm a murderous, stalking psychopath, she's mad because I ate all the Thin Mints, she misses dick, she—

The hard set to her eyes didn't abate. "Like this." The fork clattered from her hand and now unencumbered, her hand slipped under the table.

Inside, I screamed. The seconds stretched, becoming eternal, yet I needed more time. Deadly anticipation rose. Disgust twisting her features, she produced the Smith & Wesson I'd hastily stashed—not well enough, it seemed—and held it up. "Why do you have a gun in your nightstand, Sam?"

"Uh—I—um… I can explain," I started.

Carefully, she placed it on the table, barrel pointing to the side. "Imagine my surprise when I found this while looking for a ChapStick."

My mouth went dry, yet I couldn't find any words.

"Why? Why do you have this? And I want the truth. The honest-to-God truth." Her gaze softened. "You've let me in. Not all the way. Not yet. And I understand. You've gone through some horrible things and I'm okay with you unpacking that on your own time. I'll be here when you're ready." Lips quivered and she pulled at the neck of her sweatshirt. "For the sake of our relationship, for our sake: tell me the truth. Now."

Unable to see any other option; I did. I told her everything. When I finished, I was emotionally, mentally, and physically exhausted after finally coming clean. I simultaneously felt lighter and absolutely terrified of what Becs might do.

She abruptly stood from the table and hurried from the room. Panic mounting, I listened to her heavy tread going up the stairs. Down the hall. A door opened. Rummaging. A door slammed. Retracing her steps, she plopped into her chair and pushed something towards me. "Here."

I gaped and accepted the unexpected. "You're gonna need some bullets," Becs said. "Finally, Chad comes in useful after all these years."

I rasped, "Becs, I—" and fought the painful lump of gratitude in my throat.

"And you're not killing that motherfucker by yourself, let's get that straight, okay?"

"Okay," I agreed, my head spinning. "Okay."

# CHAPTER ELEVEN

**BACK AT THE** coffee shop, except this time, I wasn't alone. Becs ordered a chai tea latte, the miel special for me. I assumed my standard post while Becs lounged on the overstuffed sofa, pretending to thumb through a magazine. For the purposes of today, we didn't know each other, and I wasn't terribly happy about it.

"I could just follow him—" I'd protested during the drive.

Becs had rolled her eyes. "And what? Follow him to his job? His house? Or to one of his charitable events? Roll up in your wheelchair and blow his brains out in front of God and everyone? Great idea, Sam."

"It could work," I'd muttered, crossing my arms in front of me petulantly.

She'd flapped her hand, keeping her eyes on the road. "It could. But at the very least, you'll get life in prison. And need I remind you about all the gun nuts with concealed carry just waiting for an excuse to blow someone away?"

"Fine. We'll do it your way, but I'd like the record to show that I think this is a dumb idea."

Waiting to turn left, Becs had pretended to type on the steering wheel. "Duly noted."

I sipped my miel, barely noticing the honey and cinnamon.

Jacob Brady sauntered in, loosening his bloodred tie as the door shut behind him. Ever the predator, he scanned the shop for suitable prey—a momentary delight flickering across his face on spotting Becs, who pointedly ignored him, appearing completely engrossed in the latest issue of *Us Weekly*.

He strolled up to the counter and gave the barista his order. "Large drip coffee—strongest you've got—with two shots of espresso. Piping hot. And two blueberry muffins." I highly doubted it was a treat for his hardworking secretary back at the office. We were a go.

Steaming coffee in hand, he gripped a white plate with two muffins and ambled over to the Becs' sofa. "Hey there," he said in a rich baritone. "Mind if I join you?"

Becs glanced up, her face passive.

He held up the plate and wriggled it. "I've got an extra muffin to sweeten the deal."

"Well… I mean… if you have a muffin, sure." She shot him a smile that didn't quite touch her eyes and patted the couch cushion next to her.

He sat. "I'm Jacob," he said, offering his right hand.

"Anne." She took his hand, giving it a firm shake. My skin crawled, thinking of that monster touching her—even something as innocuous as a handshake. They exchanged small talk, keeping their heads huddled together. Becs giggled girlishly at the appropriate times and placed her hand on his forearm, receiving a smug smirk each time.

My blood boiled and my right hand shook underneath the table. I eyed my latte. Would more caffeine steel my nerves or make me more anxious? Unsure, but needing something to distract me, I drained the drink.

"Listen," Jacob said. "What do you say we go somewhere… more private?"

Becs shifted, giving me a cursory look. I nodded. "I'd love that." Clutching his arm, she asked, "Wanna come back to my place?" The moment of truth. If he said no… we'd have to devise another plan because there was no way I'd let him have the upper hand. Becs was NOT going to the place of his choosing. We needed home court advantage. This was already a huge gamble.

"Yes, please," he said, standing up and extending his hand to Becs, helping her up.

"Oh!" Becs said. "Let me order a smoothie before we go. For later. They've got a killer kale and pineapple smoothie that's to die for."

A momentary thundercloud darkened his face—a flicker, then gone. To his credit, he recovered quickly. "Sure."

I ordered an *Uber*. Three minutes away. I glanced at their abandoned seats and mourned their untouched muffins. Would it have killed Becs to pack them up for later? Manslaughter was sure to work up the appetite. Gathering my things—mindful of the gun's weight in my leather tote—I rolled my wheelchair to the entrance.

"Let me get that for you." Jacob Brady appeared—playing the part of the perfect gentleman rather than the psychopathic sadist he truly was—and held the door open for me.

"Thanks," I said with as much enthusiasm as I could muster. "Appreciate it."

His eyebrows creased. "Hey… do I know you? You look… familiar."

I barked out a harsh laugh, keeping my eyes trained on my lap—on my tote. "I get that a lot. Got one of those faces, I guess."

"Hmmm," he murmured.

"Have a nice day!" I called out. Heart pounding out of my chest, I made my way down the ramp and posted up on the sidewalk, waiting for the *Uber*. Per the app, Sergei was a few streets away. Behind me, the door opened, and two sets of feet made their way down the concrete steps. I pretended to be absorbed by my phone, keeping my head down.

"I'll drive," Becs said, walking to our van parked a few car lengths away. The keys jingled in her hand and the headlights flared as she unlocked it.

"Cool car," Jacob remarked, his sarcasm evident. He pulled the passenger door open and peered inside. "Wheelchair van, huh?" Continuing to keep my attention on my screen, I felt his grimy gaze on me and suppressed the urge to squirm. *Act cool. Aloof. Totally chill.*

"Yeah," Becs said, climbing into the driver's seat. "My mom had a stroke last year. She can barely walk. I drive her to appointments."

"I see." He clambered inside and slammed the door. Becs shifted into drive, checked the side mirror for traffic, and pulled out. Our eyes met briefly, and I sent up a silent prayer that she'd be okay. Who knew what that sociopath might do?

Sergei's Toyota pulled up and a big, bearded man hopped out. "You Sam?"

"That's me," I replied. The van's taillights flared as Becs stopped at the light just up the street.

He nodded. "Tell me how I can help."

"If you wouldn't mind opening the door for me."

He did, standing back. I clutched the oh-shit-handle and quickly transferred myself to the passenger seat. Belted myself in. "I like strong women," Sergei remarked, eyebrows quirking up. He tapped his bicep.

"Me too," I replied.

He let out a warm laugh and, without being told, folded up my wheelchair and stowed it in the back. Settling into his seat, he said, "And now. We go."

"Awesome," I said, ignoring the uneasy feeling in my gut.

# CHAPTER TWELVE

**I OBSESSIVELY CHECKED** my phone during the *Uber* ride. No texts. Becs made it home okay, per her shared location. "You can drop me off here," I told Sergei. Three houses down from ours. Our neighbors' topiary would obscure any view of me.

"Of course." Moving with lionlike grace, he fetched my wheelchair, popped it open, and then grabbed my door. "Here you go."

Repeating my prior movements, I transferred myself lickety-split to the chair. "Thanks."

"Need any more help?" Sergei asked.

I shook my head. "Good from here, thank you."

Sergei cocked his head and shot me a finger gun. "Stay cool out there, yes?"

"Same to you."

Languidly, I rolled down the sidewalk to our place and, as stealthily as possible, made my way up the ramp. Pushing open the front door silently—we'd *WD-40ed* the hinges and applied a piece of duct tape in a ridiculous hot pink color—over the latch earlier that morning, readying everything.

I'd also wrapped some of the pink duct tape around the cracked handle of the gun, right above the engraving, making it look like a Lisa Frank production. I couldn't obscure *FOR HALEY*, someone who meant something to my savior, but the last thing I needed was for the damn thing to fall apart before I blew Jacob Brady's brains out. That would totally harsh my mellow.

Cruising down the hallway, I held my breath. My wheels weren't totally soundless but the music drifting from the sitting room covered their tread.

Before reaching the entrance, I snaked my hand inside my bag and gripped the duct-taped handle. I let out a shaky exhalation, hoping against all hope our ruse worked. That he wouldn't wonder why there was a tarp spread out on the floor—*for painting*, Becs would explain, *I hate this wall color, don't you?* That she was able to maneuver him as planned, seated on the couch with his back to me, his luscious locks a perfect target.

All I had to do was pull the trigger. Easy peasy.

*Here goes nothing.*

I breached the entrance, holding the gun like the internet told me: index finger perched on the trigger—no pressure, not yet, *FOR HALEY* scratching into the palm of my left hand, reassuring, spurring me on, saying *do it*, and applying front-to-rear pressure with my shooting hand.

I froze.

"Hello, there." Jacob's words dripped with pomposity.

Becs sat stock-still next to him, careful not to make any sudden movements, lest the knife he held at her throat move and end her. To her credit, she looked more pissed off than scared.

Not me. Terror held me firmly.

He grinned and tapped his head. "I knew you seemed familiar. Although… now you look like a mega-dyke. I liked your hair better longer."

Hot venom burbled up my throat. "Let her go, you prick." The gun shook in my hands.

"Hmmm… I think not. In fact, I think I'll have a little fun with her first. Make you watch. I'll fuck every hole she's got, including that bonus hole in her belly. They call that a Philly sidecar, in case you didn't know. That'll be a new one, even for me."

He let out an evil chuckle. His lips drew up in a sickening leer. "Then, I'll take this knife and carve her up like a Thanksgiving turkey while you watch. How about that?"

Silent, stoic tears stood in Becs' eyes, and she mouthed: *Do it.*

Primordial dread threatened to overwhelm me. My mind flitted frantically. Uselessly. Rationality bled away.

Holding the knife still and steady with his right hand, Jacob Brady gestured broadly with his left. "And seriously? The tarps?" He pitched his voice high. "*We're painting.* You think I don't recognize a kill room when I see it? I own *Dexter* on DVD for fuck sakes."

Becs' chin quivered and her lip trembled. Watery snot snaked from her nose. Her pallid face was soaked with sweat and silent tears.

If he fuckin' hurt her…

An intense heat lit my heart aflame, ratcheting up my pulse, sending metastasis of indignant anger elsewhere: my cheeks, ears, and neck broiled, jaw clenched, and my grip tightened on the pink-taped handle. Every cell within me vibrated and tingled, making me comfortably numb and… oddly calm. Monkey mind completely stilled.

Becs mouthed: *Shoot him.*

"Don't you fuckin' touch her," I said evenly. My stomach skipped. Quieted.

"Or what?" he taunted in a mocking tone. "Then the cripple'll shoot me? Please. You don't have the guts. You barely had the guts to run away from me when you did. Now… what are you gonna do? Tick-tock. Tick-tock."

His face softened into a dreamy expression and he *tsked*, tipping his head toward me. "Let's have ourselves one dandy last time together, babe. I'll tenderize this slut right here nice and pretty. Butcher her and prepare a tartare from her meat. Force feed you your little girlfriend. Make you really taste her." He shut his eyes derisively and snorted.

Perfect timing.

With eerie tranquility, I slowly released the breath I'd been holding; my hands steadied and the world slowed to a crawl.

For Becs. For Haley. And for me.

I aimed. Pulled the trigger. Thunder roared in my ears.

Blood. So much blood.

# CHAPTER THIRTEEN

**IMPATIENT KNOCKING AT** the door jarred me from my thoughts.

"They're here!" I called out.

Becs capered past me and stood in front of the door, her fingertips unconsciously stealing to the bandage covering the cut on her neck, only a flesh wound, but I could tell it made her feel self-conscious.

"You look great, Becs, sliced open neck or not. Now let 'em in!"

She giggled. "Right." Becs threw the door open and embraced the waiting figure tightly.

"Becca! Long time no see," Becs' childhood best friend exclaimed. Ande. A little older than the picture Becs kept in the bedroom, with more prominent laugh lines.

Ande looked about how I'd expect a farmer to look. Tan Carhartt overalls over a green and red flannel shirt, shit-kicker boots, and a ruddy complexion from plenty of sunshine.

Releasing the hug, their hazel gaze found me. "And this must be Sam!" Rushing forward, they grabbed my hand and shook merrily, with the excitement of a puppy learning a new trick.

"Hi! I've heard a lot about you," I told Ande.

Ande guffawed. "Only good things I hope!"

"I haven't told Sam… everything," Becs said. "So yes, only good things." Becs and Ande exchanged a loaded look.

"Told me what?" I asked.

Ande clapped their hands on their knees. "Welp! Best get to work. Where's the body?"

Becs pointed. "In there."

"Roger that," Ande replied, clomping into the room, leaving traces of half-dried mud on the floor. My eyelid twitched and I fought a major urge to grab a broom. Ande scanned the room and let out a whistle. "Nice kill room!"

"Uh… thanks," I said. "Hey, Ande, quick question: Why are you so nonchalant about this? Your childhood best friend calls and says: *Are you busy because I need help with a dead body?* and it's no big deal to you." I held my hands up. "Not that I'm judging, mind you. Just curious."

Ande exhaled sharply and thrust their hand toward me. "Go ahead. Tell her, Becca."

Becs nodded. Turning to me, she started. "Ande and I grew up together. I slept over at their house more than I slept at mine. Not to mention, having a friend with a farm was cool as hell too." Becs ticked each item off on her fingers. "Horseback riding, feeding the hogs, fetching eggs from the chickens, running away from the randy rooster—"

"Avoiding my brother," Ande added quietly.

Becs held her finger. "And that. Yeah." She kneeled in front of me and grasped my hands. "Ande's brother… he was like Jacob Brady."

"My older brother, supposed to protect me," Ande said bitterly. "Instead, he stole into my room in the dead of night and did… whatever he wanted. My parents didn't believe me; no one did." They paused and shot Becs a look filled with pure gratitude. "No one except her."

Pain shone on Becs' face, and her lips pursed. She closed her eyes and shook her head. "So…" she started. "We Goodbye, Earl-ed him."

"Come again?" I asked.

Ande's eyes widened. "Please tell me you know that song."

"Of course, I know the song!" It had been popular pre-my kidnapping. "You mean… you killed your brother?"

"Just like the song," Ande exclaimed proudly. "Poisoned him."

Becs giggled. "Ground two of my mom's sedatives up and put them in his drink."

"Smart. How old were you guys?"

Ande's eyes rolled back in thought. "Thirteen?"

"Nah, probably fourteen. Remember? Your parents went to the State Fair to see Sara Evans that year, leaving the house conveniently vacant, miles away from your nearest neighbor," Becs replied.

"You guys planned this out," I said slowly.

Becs smirked. "Duh. Didn't you plan your murder too?"

"Touché," I replied. "What—what did you do with his… body?"

Ande tossed their head back and laughed. "Same thing we're gonna do with his!" They kicked the tightly wrapped tarp holding Jacob Brady's bloody body for emphasis.

"Which is?" I asked quizzically.

Becs squeezed my hands. "Ande's got hogs, babe."

"Hogs?"

"Nature's garbage disposal. They'll eat anything: bones, teeth, you name it!" Ande exclaimed. "Plus, they're cute as hell. My favorite's named Snowball. From *Animal Farm*."

I shook my head. "So… hogs ate your brother?"

"Yep. My parents thought he ran off." Ande pointed their thumb behind them. "Becca, okay if I back my truck up into your garage? We'll have to carry this shitbag there."

"Sure, go for it. I left the door up."

Ande hustled out the front door and a truck engine roared to life.

"It's crazy, isn't it?" I remarked.

Becs snorted. "What part? That we killed a guy? That my best friend from back home is helping us get rid of the body?"

I spread my arms. "Everything! Finding a gun in the park of all places, you supplying ammo after hearing my demented manifesto, me nailing him dead center in the forehead, everything! When they say the stars aligned, this is what they mean!"

"Fate has a funny way of working out," Becs said, planting a kiss on my lips. "Now, if you'll excuse me, I gotta help move a body."

"Hey—" I called out to her retreating back

She stopped. "Yeah?"

"I love you!"

"I bet you say that to all the girls who hide your bodies," she teased.

I put my hands up. "Guilty, guilty."

"I love you, too. I say that to everyone who saves my life."

The truth was:

We saved each other.

# CHAPTER FOURTEEN

**"WHAT ABOUT OVER** there? New Vida Developments." I pointed.

My gaze slid from the sign, upward to the scenery. Swaying treetops, ruffled by the breeze, revealed quick flashes of rickey roller coaster tracks and the husk of a Ferris wheel. I dragged my eyes away from the sight and focused again on the stretch of half-constructed buildings in front of me.

Becs tapped the brake and slowed, peering out the window. "Condos? Or houses?"

"Who cares! I see an abandoned construction site and it's perfect!"

Suppressing a smirk, Becs murmured: "I bet that's what the Animorphs thought too."

"What?" I asked. "Who?"

"It's a book series… middle school kids morph into animals to fight aliens." Seeing my blank look, she soldiered forward. "You know? Jake? Rachel. Andalites?"

I rolled my eyes. "Nerd." Reaching over, I grasped her arm. "Think about it: they haven't poured the concrete yet. Check out the holes they've dug for the foundation. We bury the gun, and the builders take care of the evidence for us."

"Are you sure you don't want to just throw it in the river or something?" Becs wearily eyed the dark, excavated smudges dotting the land.

"No way! First off, that's littering and second, it could wash ashore. We can't have that," I replied, examining the plot more closely. Off to the left and right, barebones wooden structures jutted from the damp dirt, giving tantalizing hints to the structures that would soon arise. Our destination: smackdab down the middle.

She smirked. "Or you could—I dunno… put it in a trash can at the dog park. Seems to be a popular spot."

I groaned. "Stop it. That was serendipity. Fate. The world wanted me to have it." I stroked my chin. "Of course… it was really stupid of someone to put it there. What if a kid found it? Or some criminal?"

"It didn't have any bullets, remember?"

Ignoring that comment, I continued. "I mean, I could have shot my dick off with that thing!"

"You don't have a dick, hon."

I waved my arms to my crotch. "My metaphorical spirit dick. It's an expression. A colloquialism, if you will."

"Mmm-hmm, sure it is," Becs remarked, eyes still trained on the smudged dark dirt. Her left eyebrow twitched and her scars puckered.

"And now," I said, opening the passenger door, "it's time to take care of business."

Once out of the van and settled in my chair, I rolled to the edge of the development, stopping just short of the thick mud leftover from last night's rain. My wheels had no chance of traversing the muck and any attempts would literally turn into a quagmire. I hated having to leave this in Becs' hands.

I turned to Becs. "You okay doing this?"

She wore a determined look that almost masked her anxiety—almost—and nodded. "Yeah. I'll be fine. Don't worry." She plucked at her cuticles; a tell I'd long picked up on. Nerves.

"Okay… just don't think about getting buried alive or anything."

"Real helpful, Sam," Becs said. She hadn't taken her gaze from the nearest hole, and I knew she was reliving her childhood fears. Over a joint one night, she'd told me all about it: *Fell into a hole once and now I'm forever scarred for life.* Given she waited in that hole for hours before anyone discovered her, attempting to jump out and only succeeding in pulling more dirt on top of her… it was a miracle she wasn't running off screaming.

"Sorry, my bad," I said. "But it's not gonna happen. You're gonna be fine. Plus, the trenches dug for houses are way bigger than a grave."

Thrusting her hand out, Becs said, "Just… just… give it to me so we can get this over with. You're buying me Indian food after this. Paneer naan, that cauliflower stuff I like, and whatever I want to sample from the menu."

I pulled the revolver from my sweatshirt pocket and ran my fingers along the engraving: *FOR HALEY*. Turned it over, admiring the hot pink duct-tape, I sent up a silent thanks to whoever had placed it on my path. "Here. And I'll buy you whatever you want. Even the curry that makes your breath smell like death."

"You really know what to say to a girl," Becs quipped as she walked to the nearest hole. Her chin tipped down and she took it all in. "Ugh. So much mud. Gross."

"You got this!" I called out.

With a grimace, she disappeared into the crevice and let out a high-pitched squeal.

"You okay?" I yelled, panic rising within me.

"Just peachy," she shouted, her words slightly muffled by earth. I imagined her eyes darting around, taking in wriggling earthworms and grubs, trying to calm her breathing. Clenched fists, gnashing jaw. I should call it off; tell her we'd do something else. I opened my mouth but before any words could come out, she yelled: "Alright. I'm um… I'm digging!" Hideous sucking noises ensued, displaced earth and muck.

I scanned the street and found it mercifully deserted. No one walking their dog down the sidewalk, gearing up for small talk when they spotted me. No cars. Just us. Perfect. The tops of the trees around me swayed and I watched a crow preen, glossy black feathers rippling in the fading sunlight. He paused, fixing me with a beady eyed stare, lingering far too long. *I know what you're doing*, I imagined him saying. *I know what you did.*

"Ugh!" Becs yelled.

Breaking my staring contest with the crow, I glanced over to the hole. "Everything alright?"

"Okay. Okay. It's done. Buried. I'm getting out." The crow took flight and Becs reappeared; splotches of brown muck decorated her clothing, liberally perfumed with hints of earthworm. A streak of dark dirt whispered across her cheek, giving her the appearance of a disgruntled football player.

"Um… maybe we should go home and order in," I said. "And we should put a towel or something down or the van is gonna smell… weird."

Without warning, she swooped down, grabbed my face, and pulled me in for a kiss, smearing mud all over my shirt. She shot me that devastating smile and said, "Now you can smell weird with me."

"I wouldn't have it any other way."

And I meant it.

Jacob Brady took everything away from me. Left me damaged. Molded me into a hateful, suicidal monster. But… everything he did led me to the next step of my life, where I embraced myself: shattered-spine-and-slacking-spinal-cord and all. I met Becs and as cliché as it sounded—and so lesbian, since we love ourselves some astrology—it's like the saying: the stars aligning.

It's right. It's where I'm meant to be. Doing what I'm meant to do: live my life and be happy. Find my family and reconnect.

Now that revenge was marked off the to-do list.

TAKEN FOR A RIDE
M.S. MATTER

Marie's Dedication:


For Dr. Lee, who went far above and beyond his role as a professor
to help me through the hardest breakup of my life.
Until next time on the road that goes ever on.

*"Evil is a very real concept, dancing in the diner to your upset*
*Sharing drinks and laughing through their teeth*
*Their only success is our defeat."*
— "Without Prejudice" by Protest the Hero

Part One
"And if I lose myself, blessed be
I could survive in these chemicals for you
A lonely fool above, just out of reach
I could survive in these chemicals
Only for you."
— "Blessed Be" by Spiritbox

# PART ONE

**CLAIRE FROWNED AT** the faint suggestion of crow's feet issuing from the outer corners of her eyes, hastily blotting them out with concealer. Her thirty-ninth birthday had come and gone without her permission, and forty approached like a swarm of plague rats.

Her mother had taught her from childhood that beauty was ageless, and aside from that, it was ultimately unimportant. However, in the years since, a new sentiment had slinked its way into Claire's mind.

"We leave in an hour," Claire's husband said, his egg-shaped head appearing over her shoulder in the corner of the Airbnb's vanity mirror.

"Yes, dear," Claire replied promptly.

A man twenty-two years her senior, Marcus Templeton exuded an aura of success like solar heat. Some days, she still couldn't believe her luck that she happened to pick up a shift and wait on his table nineteen years ago; a single night that changed the trajectory of her life forever. She'd hardly worked a day since.

Claire felt a well of gratitude spring up within her at the sight of him.

"I love you," she said, smiling prettily.

Marcus smiled back. "I love you, too."

It was so wonderful when they got along.

Marcus didn't have to remind Claire of today's importance—if all went to plan, his company was set to make an incredible acquisition.

This afternoon, they would participate in a walking tour of the abandoned grounds of Dreamscape. Rebuilding a defunct theme park was no small feat, but Marcus's entertainment company, Radiant Realms, was up to the task.

This wouldn't be the first park to be restored to its former glory under Marcus's watch. Despite the occasional controversy, Radiant Realms was responsible for over a dozen cost-effective theme park renovations across the United States.

These accomplishments were reflected in how Marcus presented himself. Despite being five-foot-two (to Claire's five-foot-seven), he stood tall and proud. His suit was tailored with precision, which effectively hid the rotund curves of his belly. His beard was cut short and chiseled, carving out the illusion of sharp cheekbones that weren't actually there. The man was a CEO, through and through. And he had chosen her.

"Is that the dress I bought you?" Marcus asked, gesturing to Claire's outfit.

She giggled. "Of course! I've been waiting for an opportunity to wear it." It was a white, floral sheath dress which reached her calves, with gold buttons lining the tight turtleneck collar. "I feel so pretty."

"As you should."

"By the way," Claire said, drawing lines of concealer under her eyes. "I've really been enjoying the bits and pieces of your meetings that I've heard. Learning all the business lingo in the background. Like, I know what a depreciation deduction is now. That's kind of neat."

"I love it when you talk dirty to me." Marcus grinned.

"It actually kind of got me thinking…" Claire fidgeted with her fingers. "I think it would be really great to go back to college and finally get a degree."

Marcus's smile froze. "A degree? At your age? Why?"

"I really like learning, just in general. I don't know what I would want to major in yet, but I love reading about how things work, and—"

"Hold on," Marcus said sternly.

Claire's face fell. She'd said something wrong again.

"The *whole* reason I work so hard is so that I can give you a good life. *Everything I do* is to make you happy. Are you saying that's not enough for you? You want to turn your back on my generosity?"

"No, of course not," Claire replied, raising her hands placatingly. "I'm sorry, I just think—"

Marcus's phone chimed. He pulled it out of his pocket, staring at the screen.

"Oh God, it's Jack," Marcus muttered. "All the time with this fucking guy." He answered the call. "Jack Attack, how's my favorite executive assistant?" Claire warily watched him walk out of the room.

Once he was gone, she unzipped her Hermes purse to furtively ensure that she had packed the revolver. She had.

She smiled to herself, zipping it back up. Then, she picked up her makeup brush and got to work erasing her laugh lines.

ℬꝏℭ

THE NATURE PRESERVE was huge. The freeway had given out to a narrow two-lane road, allowing a sprawling ocean of trees to dominate the landscape. On either side of them, impenetrable walls of foliage stood tall.

Claire stared out the window of the rental car, taking in the scenery.

"It's beautiful," she said, turning to Marcus for approval. Marcus snorted.

"A waste is what it is. I could fit two Magic Mountains in this place, easy. Probably more."

"What about Discovery Kingdom?"

"I could probably squeeze that in, yeah."

"So, is there any chance Susan, the lovely CFO, called in sick?" Claire asked wryly.

"Afraid not," Marcus replied, smirking. "If I didn't know better, I'd say you don't want to see her."

"Whatever gave you that idea?" Claire asked, covering her mouth in mock surprise. "Was it the time she called my dress 'whorish,' or when she told her husband off in front of an entire party?"

"Stuart, that poor bastard," Marcus chuckled, taking the next exit. "He's actually going to be there too."

"Oh no, does that mean…"

"Yeah, Audrey too. Susan changed her mind at the last second. She thinks it'll be good for Audrey."

"Dammit," Claire groaned. "That kid gives me the creeps, I swear."

"It's not so bad if you don't look at her or listen to anything she says."

They laughed.

Their conversation about Claire going to college had already been forgotten.

The preserve abruptly gave way to a large lake on their left. Stagnant, blue-grey water filled most of the lakebed's volume, leaving a cracked stretch of land between the water and the former lakeshore. Reeds grew in clumps. Algae thickened the water.

"I'm sure that looked much more impressive back in the day," Claire said.

"So I'm told," Marcus replied. "Man-made. They called it the Dreamscape Dreamlake. Put the park right in the middle. Now that I'm seeing it, I don't know if I like taking on the cost of refilling it."

"What happened to it?"

Marcus shrugged. "Time. Heads up, there it is."

Dreamscape rose out of the anemic lake like a massive stalagmite. It had probably been more picturesque when fully surrounded by water, but the low levels exposed the steep, harsh cliffs that encircled the park. It almost looked lonely.

Marcus turned onto a two-lane bridge connecting Dreamscape to land. Claire stared up at the towering, corroded hulk of an amusement park as they approached, picking out the rust-covered arches of a few aggressive roller coasters.

As they approached, faded signs flashed by featuring the theme park's mascot: a giant photorealistic ant named Andy.

"Yeesh," Claire winced. "I'm starting to see why this place went under."

"That's gonna have to go," Marcus agreed. "I'm pretty sure that gave kids nightmares."

They pulled into the parking lot, finding a few other cars there already. Before they could step out, a young man with short brown hair approached from a few cars down and rapped on the window.

"Mr. Templeton," he called eagerly. Claire watched Marcus's face freeze before he forced on a smile. The young man opened the driver-side door, grinning with unnaturally white teeth.

"Jack Attack," Marcus said, shaking his hand. Marcus attempted to pull his hand away, but Jack didn't pick up the cue. "Early and eager as ever, I see."

Claire moved to open her own door, but Jack somehow beat her to it. "Mrs. Templeton," he said graciously.

"Thank you," Claire said, stepping into the cold, damp afternoon air.

"Do you have any bags I can take?" Jack asked. Jack had never learned that suits always need custom tailoring. He always looked as if he was wearing his father's suit, too large and not quite to his proportions.

"It's a walking tour, Jack," Claire replied. "Why would we have bags?"

"What about your purse? I can take that off your hands if you like."

Claire laughed nervously, feeling the cold weight of the revolver as she shouldered her bag. "I appreciate the enthusiasm, but I'll hold onto it." Her smile faded as she looked past Jack.

"Oh God, here she comes," she muttered, eyeing the tall woman with hawk-like features approaching them. Claire projected, "Susan, how are you?"

Susan's face did not change at the greeting. "Busy, as always," she replied curtly. She looked Claire up and down. "You look great."

"Thank you!" Claire replied brightly.

"It must be the beauty sleep, right? Since you don't do anything."

"Always a pleasure, Susan," Claire said, flashing her a forced smile.

Susan's appearance fit her demeanor—her hair had been slicked back and wrestled into submission in the form of a tight bun, accentuating her sharp, thin cheekbones and hooked nose. Her pantsuit was pure practicality—black on grey without an accessory to be seen. She wore tall black stiletto heels.

Susan was an exceedingly difficult woman to maintain eye contact with. There was something in her muted gaze that seemed like it was missing. Like her eyes didn't reflect light but rather absorbed it into the inky depths of her pitch-black irises.

"Now Susan," Marcus chided. "Claire doesn't have to work. I see to that. We just talked about this earlier today." He wrapped his arm around Claire's waist, surreptitiously squeezing her ass in the process. Claire's muscles tightened ever so slightly. "I give her everything her heart desires."

"Must be nice," Susan replied, unaffected.

Behind Susan, her husband, Stuart and their daughter, Audrey, approached. Stuart's hair, thin and balding, made a wiry halo around his head like the dusty fuzz one would pull from a vacuum cleaner. His tan suit fit him cleanly, but his shoes were slightly oversized, giving him a clown's awkward gait. He gave a wave and a ghost of a smile as a greeting.

Then there was Audrey. While all the others looked their best, Audrey appeared as though she had just rolled out of bed. The high schooler peered at Marcus and Claire through a chaotic curtain of long, unkempt blonde hair, her single acid-green streak glowing in the sunlight. The poofy, juvenile dress Susan had forced her into hung lightly off her slight frame as though attempting to minimize its points of contact with her body.

"Isn't it hard to walk in that thing?" Audrey asked, pointing at Claire's dress with a chewed fingernail.

Claire glanced at Marcus. "No, not at all."

"What a dump," the girl murmured, looking at the abandoned park. She pulled her phone from her purse and took a selfie in front of the looming arch of the Ferris wheel, with a finger gun pointed at her temple. "Can't wait for you guys to make it even worse."

Susan shot her daughter a look that could peel wallpaper. Stuart put his hand on Audrey's shoulder and shook his head solemnly.

A final luxurious rental car found its way into the dilapidated parking lot, turning a tight corner into the space next to Marcus's.

"Ah, there's Janet," Susan said. "Just like her to arrive last."

"Come on, it wouldn't be a party without our senior communications director," Marcus replied.

"Yeah, you have *so much* to brag to the media about," Audrey commented, gesturing toward the crumbling park.

"You have to trust the process," Jack chimed in. "Mr. Templeton is like a wizard with this stuff."

"Yeah," Claire added. "You saw what he did with Elysium Gardens in Texas."

"Elysium Gardens," Marcus reminisced fondly. For the first time since they got there, he gave the group a genuine smile. "Some of my best work, if I do say so myself."

"Except for that roller coaster that collapsed onto like twenty people, right?" Audrey quipped. Susan smacked her upside the back of her head, prompting Audrey to release a gale of giddy laughter. Stuart flinched but said nothing.

"She's still got a mouth on her," Marcus said, laughing weakly.

"We're working on it," Susan replied flatly.

"I'm sorry I'm late," Janet called as she exited her car, holding a fat manila envelope. "I was putting some finishing touches on the press release."

"I'll let you off the hook this time," Marcus said, "seeing as we haven't seen heads nor tails of our tour guide yet."

"Thank you, sir. In that case, maybe I could pitch you the headline?" Janet asked. "I was thinking 'Dreamscape Reimagined: A New Park for a New Age.'"

"Eh. Got a backup?"

Janet blinked. A lock of hair flew loose from her ponytail, joining several others.

"Uh, of course. How about 'The Dreamscape Revival: Where Imagination Meets Innovation'?"

"Hmm, keep thinking about it."

"But I already printed the…"

Marcus pinched his brow. "The first one works, Janet. Thank you. Thank you so much."

"I like that one better, too," Jack added, helping.

"Who's that?" Claire asked, pointing toward the park entrance.

The tall, lanky woman materialized out of nowhere, walking toward the group. She wore a faded pink Dreamscape T-shirt, the letters eroded by too many washes. The backside proclaimed in bold text "I'm part of the dream team!" above an image of Andy the Ant in mid-scuttle. A Bluetooth earbud flashed green in her right ear.

"Hey everybody," she said with over-caffeinated gusto. "Welcome one and all to the amazing Dreamscape!"

"Woo," Claire cheered halfheartedly.

"It's true, it's seen better days. But that's why all of you are here now!"

"So, you must be Kaitlyn, then, our tour guide?" Marcus asked.

"That's right!" Kaitlyn chirped. "I'm also one of the property managers. I'm here to show you the amazing investment you're about to make. You must be Mr. Templeton!"

"Guilty as charged," Marcus said. "And here we have my lovely wife, Claire, Jack, Janet, Susan, her husband Stuart, and their daughter, Audrey."

Kaitlyn went down the line, shaking each of their hands. She hesitated when she reached Audrey.

"I... didn't know a kid was going to be here to see this," Kaitlyn said, her cheerful voice straining.

"I was a last-minute plus one," Audrey replied. "Is that a problem? Having a kid in a theme park?"

"Oh no, it just seems like all this business talk would be boring for you, you know?"

"I don't know what you mean," Audrey said dryly. "I'm ecstatic."

"Well, what are we waiting for?" Marcus asked, stepping forward.

"Ope, just one little thing and then we can get started." Kaitlyn pulled her backpack around. "We don't want the magic spoiled for anybody, so I'm afraid I'm going to have to hold onto your cell phones until the tour is over."

"*What?*" Audrey protested. "So I'm supposed to just spend time with *these people? All day?*"

Susan seized Audrey's forearm with a white-knuckle grip, bringing their faces within inches of each other.

Claire gasped.

"Shut your lopsided mouth and give her the fucking phone," Susan said evenly, barely above a whisper. "And fix your attitude before I fix it for you."

A grin split Audrey's face like a fault line and she let out a throaty chuckle. "I love you, Susan," she said, reaching into her purse and handing her phone to Kaitlyn. Only then did Susan release her.

"Susan has spoken," Marcus said wryly, handing Kaitlyn his phone.

Claire looked at Audrey with concern as she shuffled forward with the others to offer their phones. The girl was still laughing to herself as though remembering a joke, staring into space.

"Well, with that out of the way," Kaitlyn said brightly, "let's begin our tour!"

She led the group toward the park's main entrance. Claire was certain that the grand archway welcoming them had been glorious in its heyday. The faded, pastel-pink plastic of the arch was molded into fluffy mounds resembling clouds, with traces of glitter paint still visible in the muted sunlight.

Claire thought of how satisfying it would be to power-wash the thick layer of dust and grime that covered its surface. As she passed through the turnstile into the park, she realized a power-washer would have their work cut out for them in a place like this.

No matter how many walking tours she had been on, Claire never got used to the uncanny quiet of an abandoned theme park. She was surrounded immediately by sun-bleached storefronts, overgrown food carts, and colorful ride queue entrances—all things meant to catch attention, to be given purpose by the people who came through. But outside of their group, there wasn't a soul in sight.

In the middle of the main square was a ten-foot-tall golden statue of Andy the Ant, towering over them with his pincers parted at an upward trajectory. It gave the impression that the sculptor had been instructed to make Andy smile, despite lacking the anatomy for it. The result was more unsettling than inviting. At the base of his abdomen was a sizable stinger. Mounted to the foundation of the statue was a plastic bin holding crisp, new brochures.

"Well, look what Andy scrounged up for us," Kaitlyn said saccharinely. She picked up the pamphlets and passed them out to everyone, apart from Audrey.

"Sorry," Kaitlyn grinned sheepishly. "We didn't know you'd be here, so we didn't print enough copies."

"I'm going to kill myself and it's your fault."

Kaitlyn's eyes flicked up to Susan and Stuart.

"Don't take it personally," Susan said. "She tells me the same thing almost every day."

"Hey, Kaitlyn? What kind of ant has a stinger?" Claire asked, staring at the statue.

"Bullet ants," Kaitlyn replied with uncharacteristic flatness. "They have the most painful sting in the world." Then, she was back. "Okay, everybody! These brochures were made special for this tour. In addition to the park map, you'll find a map of the maintenance tunnels and lots of park trivia to get the ideas flowing!"

Marcus read aloud, "'Dreamscape is home to the largest underwater animatronic in North America.'"

"If we go ahead with the deal, that's another record for you to collect, Mr. Templeton," Jack pointed out eagerly. "Save some for the rest of us!"

"Ah, Klaus the Kraken," Kaitlyn said with delight. "Don't worry, you'll get to meet him soon enough. Why, there's a bit of him all over the park."

Claire's eyes wandered to a nearby fountain, where she saw a single black tentacle with pink suckers draping out of the water.

"What the…" she muttered. What she first thought were meant to be centipede legs skirting the edge of the tentacle revealed themselves to be a series of sharp, silicone barbs upon closer examination. Claire wasn't sure which would have been worse. The pink suckers were in fact mouths lined with irregular rings of teeth. She shivered.

"Krakens, I get," Claire said, flipping through her pamphlet. "Mythical creatures, dreams, that makes sense. But why *photorealistic ants* as a mascot for a theme park about dreams?"

Kaitlyn shrugged. "Our dear founder, Gideon Wilder, was very passionate about insects. Walt Disney came up with a mouse—so why not an ant?"

"Because it's creepy as hell?" Marcus suggested. Jack guffawed.

"You're talking like he's dead," Audrey commented. "He's not. I checked before we got here. He's been locked up in a mental hospital ever since the park went under."

"It's been decades," Janet gasped. "Did the park's failure take that much of a toll on him?"

"Not exactly," Kaitlyn muttered. "But that's a discussion for another time. Now, if you take a look at your maps, you'll see that our park is divided into four zones: Whimsydream Square, where we are now, The Garden of Potential, The Infinite Horizon, and The World of Nightmares."

Claire looked around at this so-called "Whimsydream Square," feeling anything but childlike wonder. Every color, from the yellows and blues of the brick road to the pinks and reds of the buildings, had faded to a uniform beige by decades of sun exposure.

A carousel appeared to be the centerpiece of this part of the park, but Claire felt it would look best hurled into space. The horses were replaced by giant ants as well as bumblebees, hornets, scorpions, and other arthropods with stingers. All were cracked and worn, many were eyeless, and many others were missing limbs.

Several classic carnival games lined the promenade, from test-your-strength meters to ring tosses. A rusted kiddie coaster snaked around one corner, peaking at about fifteen feet. A large, decrepit Ferris wheel stood tall over the area.

On the sides of the walkways were large sculptures of chimeras, manticores, alicorns, and dragons towering over the paths and looking over the zone. Unlike the bugs on the carousel, however, these sculptures were not photorealistic. They looked like they had been based on a child's drawings: simplistic shapes, scribbled-on colors, and random proportionality.

None of this was what kept Claire's attention, though. More than anything else, she was staring with confusion at the dozens of CRT televisions and security cameras mounted on nearly every structure. There wasn't a single blind spot; every square inch of the area was within a camera's cone of sight. There was nowhere Claire could look where a television wasn't at least in her peripheral vision.

"What is… all of this?" Marcus asked, gesturing to the devices.

"Back in its heyday, Dreamscape was determined to maximize profit by constantly playing a loop of advertisements for the park's many amenities. Mr. Wilder made sure that anywhere you went, you were being offered a new scrumptious food item to buy, or the latest action figure!"

"I do like the sound of that," Marcus said, stroking his beard thoughtfully.

"Me too!" Jack contributed.

"And the cameras?"

"After all those tragic accidents, Mr. Wilder insisted we monitor every corner of the park to keep everyone safe from any bad actors."

"Bad actors?" Audrey snorted. "Did bad actors cause the rides to be built like shit?"

Susan smacked the back of Audrey's head. Stuart winced silently. For a split second before laughter spilled out of Audrey's mouth, Claire watched the girl's eyes disengage.

"There's the Wishing Wall," Kaitlyn said cheerfully, pointing to a giant chalkboard underneath an awning. It was adorned with a frame of swirling clouds and sparkles. "This was one of the first things kids would do when they got here. We always encouraged them to dream big—and inscribe it here to leave their mark on the park!"

"Wouldn't this run out of space really fast?" Janet asked, approaching the board.

Kaitlyn chuckled sheepishly and shrugged. "They used to hose it down every week."

Claire walked toward the board, examining the final collection of dreams that had been written before the park's closure.

"I wish to be an astronaut!" one declared.

"I wish to be a princess" said another.

A barely legible scrawl read "I wish to be a dinosaur."

Claire laughed through her nose, smiling slightly. She hoped that kid at least managed to become a paleontologist in the time since.

*I could be a paleontologist,* came a voice in Claire's mind that had hardly spoken in years. Her smile faltered as she pressed her hand to the chalkboard. What would she have written here as a child? What would she write here now? Claire searched her mind, trying to think of something. Anything. Please.

Next to her hand, a single message stood apart from the others in tiny, white letters: "I wish Mommy and Daddy would stop hitting each other."

Claire pulled her hand back, feeling pity tear at her. That message was nearly forty years old. Whatever environment that child had grown up in, it was far too late for them now. She shivered but soothed herself with the notion that someone had intervened and helped the child. Maybe.

Claire heard a dry chuckle behind her. She turned to see Audrey staring at the same message. "Damn, that kid's dad still fights back? Some people get all the luck."

She walked off without another word, whistling a jaunty tune.

Claire tapped Marcus's shoulder. "Did you hear that?"

"What?" Marcus replied, finishing his own contribution to the wall.

"I wish for a better fucking attraction." Claire read aloud. Marcus snorted at his own wit.

"What's that?" Jack asked, pointing to a colorful train at the edge of the area.

"The Andy Express," Kaitlyn said warmly. "This little train goes around the entire park, including a section stretching over the Dreamscape Dreamlake!"

Claire thought of the malnourished lake and wasn't sure whether to laugh or cry.

"Susan, I wanted to talk to you about that," Marcus interjected. "Refilling the lake... how much is that going to set us back?"

"Normally, potable water is around three dollars per thousand gallons." Susan replied, prompting Marcus to wince and inhale through his teeth. "Relax,

I know somebody. He can get us secondary reclaimed outflow for *fifty cents* per thousand gallons."

"Secondary reclaimed outflow?" Claire joined in, looking between them. "What's that?"

"It's not important," Marcus said. "Please, Claire, I'm talking to Susan."

"Oh, alright," Claire said, slinking away and leaning against the wall.

"Shit-water," Kaitlyn murmured, leaning next to her.

"What?" Claire asked.

"Secondary reclaimed outflow? It's treated shit-water. That's what they're trying to fill the lake with."

"I mean, it sounds more cost-effective, as long as no one swims in it," Claire offered weakly.

Kaitlyn sighed and nodded. Her hands were trembling, and up close, Claire could see how pallid and sweaty her face was.

"Are you alright?" Claire asked.

"Never better," Kaitlyn replied, flashing her a PR grin. "We've just been planning for today for a long time." She cleared her throat. "Alright, if everyone's ready, it's time to move on to the Garden of Potential! Right this way, please."

Claire glanced back at the Wishing Wall as she followed Marcus out of Whimsydream Square.

Kaitlyn led them along the walkway out of the area, toward the massive sculptures of manticores, ants, and chimeras. Why they'd thought children's drawings would translate well to three dimensions was beyond Claire.

As they walked, the sculptures were traded for huge bushes which may have once been topiary. She could make out the faint suggestions of wireframes beneath the overgrowth, but any discernible features were lost in an unmaintained tangle.

They entered a plaza which had been strangled by weeds and ivy. The garden's plants, once tidy and picturesque according to an image in the brochure, had entirely reclaimed the land. Violet, red, blue, and yellow flowers sprawled across the bricks lining the plaza floor. On their left, a dried-out log ride supported by decaying wood stood like a propped-up corpse. Black tentacles hung over the entrance into the queue, disappearing out of sight behind the ride.

Straight ahead was a pyramidal greenhouse. On their right, the entrance to a hands-on science center called "Dreamworks." And still, CRT televisions and cameras were everywhere.

"Are they allowed to do that?" Audrey asked, pointing to the science center's exterior sign.

"The film company wasn't founded until 1994," Kaitlyn replied quickly.

A sun-faded animatronic Andy the Ant bent over a planter, tending to the crops for all eternity. Like the statue by the entrance, this portrayal of Andy featured a large stinger. A ring of dehydrated death plagued the plants surrounding it.

Claire frowned at the flaking, rusted metal exposed in the animatronic's joints. "Did they really build an outdoor animatronic with exposed linkages?" She glanced at the ground, noticing the retracted heads of sprinklers. "Next to a *sprinkler system?* This poor guy never stood a chance."

"And here we are, in our beloved Garden of Potential," Kaitlyn welcomed them. "This is where dreaming turns into *becoming.* In this zone, education meets entertainment as we teach families about innovative dreamers throughout history and the amazing contributions they made. Not to brag, but this zone is kind of a big deal. It even won an award in 1986 for educational family environments!"

"What can you tell me about the Winner's Circle?" Claire asked, staring at her brochure.

"Ahh, the park's greatest mystery," Kaitlyn said with conspiratorial vigor. "The legend goes: Gideon had a secret club somewhere in the park that was only accessible to celebrities and the park's top investors. It's been said that the Garden of Potential hides one of the entrances, but no one has been able to prove that it's real to this very day. However, rumored noteworthy guests of this enigma include Bill Cosby, Roman Polanski, and even Woody Allen."

"Cool, did any good people ever go there?" Audrey asked.

"Maybe," Kaitlyn shrugged. She pointed to the greenhouse. "That's the House of Dreamers, a boat ride through the most prized specimens in our plant collection, chock-full of animatronic visionaries telling visitors their life story. We can head inside if you want, it's still structurally sound."

"That sounds great," Jack said, at precisely the same moment Marcus said, "Pass." They glanced at each other.

"I-I just thought it would be neat to update it and teach kids—" Jack started to say.

"We're gutting this entire zone," Marcus interrupted. "People don't come to theme parks to *learn*. Who would devote an entire quarter of their park to educating their guests?"

"Disney World?" Claire blurted out. "Epcot."

Marcus's smile tightened. "That's one of my favorite things about you, my love," he said. "No education, no experience, but you never let that stop you from giving your input anyway."

Claire stared at her shoes, internally cursing herself for speaking so impulsively. This wouldn't be the last she heard about this; she could feel it.

"Does anyone have any ideas for what this place could be?" Marcus asked, gesturing around him.

Janet and Jack both vocalized excitedly at the same time.

"I have something for this," Janet said, frantically flipping through the contents of her press release. "I prepared in case we needed an alternate. I just need to find it."

"*Cowboy dinosaurs,*" Jack said, too loudly. "Like, they're dinosaurs, and— but they live in the Wild West because… no. That's not anything."

"No, it's really not," Susan replied dryly.

"Well, Jack's idea sucks," Marcus said.

"You know who *else* sucks?" Audrey asked in a deep voice.

"No one engage with that," Susan commanded.

"Janet, what do you have?" Marcus asked.

"Here," Janet offered, crossing in front of Jack to hand Marcus a pitch sheet. "I call it Clout Kingdom. Mr. Templeton, *thirty-seven percent* of Generation Alpha wants to be an influencer when they grow up. You're right— they don't want to learn. They want to *trend*. Picture this—photo op backdrops at every corner. A darkroom ride simulating the kids' rise to fame. An arcade where you can livestream gaming to an AI audience that actually reacts to your gameplay and commentary. We could monetize user generated content and have a popularity leaderboard to keep them creating *and coming back*. Plus, think of the *influencer collaborations*. We could even have a huge AI-enhanced mirror that tells kids how they can change themselves to fit in!"

"Holy shit," Audrey cackled dryly. "What could go wrong?"

"I love it," Marcus grinned. "Good thinking, Janet."

"Yeah." Jack forced a chuckle. His face was beet red. "Good one, *Janet*."

"So, you're tearing down the Garden of Potential," Kaitlyn said in a high register. "That's great. That's so great. Um, I can show you the science center too if you want, it's got two main sections—"

"Why bother? None of this will be here in a few weeks," Marcus rebutted. "Let's move on. This is a waste of time."

"Yeah, kids don't need to know learning can be fun, right?" Audrey said sardonically.

"Exactly," Marcus replied. "What's next?"

Kaitlyn cleared her throat. "Okay, we're moving on to the Infinite Horizon!"

Jack sulked in the back of the group. Claire just barely heard him say, "I love Epcot."

Kaitlyn led them down another walkway out of the area. Claire watched as the misshapen topiary was slowly replaced by abstract sculptures with rods of metal twisting in seemingly random directions.

But as they kept moving, Claire realized the brilliance of these structures—they looked different from different angles. One formed into a perfect three-dimensional cube as she passed it. Another went from meaningless visual noise to a human face, or the other way around, depending on your direction of travel. At the entry point to the next zone, the last coalesced to form an infinity symbol.

Marcus chuckled to himself.

"What's up?" Claire asked.

"It's just funny. All day I've been thinking Audrey looks just like you did when we first met."

Claire let out an offhanded yelp of a laugh. "What?"

"Yeah," Marcus replied. "I mean, she's more…scraggly, but I totally see it, don't you? It was the dress that got me thinking about it."

The smile melted off Claire's face. "*What?*" she repeated flatly.

"And here we are," Kaitlyn announced proudly.

Even in a state of decayed abandon, the Infinite Horizon was undeniably impressive. Unilluminated neon tubes lined every structure, and they could see the arcs of a large roller coaster track behind the entrances to line queues. The brick ground of the Garden of Potential had been replaced by cracked asphalt painted with faded, multicolor arrows leading in all directions, twisting around each other, contradicting one another. Some of the arrows seemed to lead to nowhere. Purples and blues were heavily featured in the buildings, adding to the surrealism.

"This place must have been a sight to behold at night," Jack marveled.

Kaitlyn grinned. "Mr. Wilder liked to say you could see it from space. This was the park's zone for thrill seekers with all the mind-bending roller coasters an adrenaline junkie could ever ask for." She gestured to her left, toward a ride queue with a large, neon sign that read "Hyperspace Halo."

"This ride was one of our most popular back in the day. I only *wish* you all could experience it now. It's a massive, spiraling indoor roller coaster that takes you through the rings of Saturn. It's unpredictable, fast, and aggressive. A daredevil's dream."

"That's Space Mountain," Audrey pointed out.

"*No*," Kaitlyn said, too quickly. "No, because it's Saturn."

She pointed to a Gravitron ride shaped like a UFO. "That's Starlight Centrifuge, it, uh…" Kaitlyn trailed off, her smile slowly fading from her face. For a heartbeat, her eyes flicked toward Stuart, then Audrey. She cleared her throat. "Sorry. It spins *really* fast. I'm sure you've seen rides like this before, but this one has a trick or two up its sleeve."

Next, she gestured to the outdoor coaster. "Over there is Dragon Chaser. It features the highest drop in the park, and enough loops to make your head spin!"

"And possibly pop off," Audrey added. "That was the one with the highest death rate in the whole park. And that's a *high* bar. How many decapitations was it? Six? Seven?"

"Is it still operational?" Susan asked. "It sounds like *somebody* wants to ride it."

Kaitlyn let out a pained squeal of a laugh. She pointed to a yellow and black outdoor coaster.

"This was a stroke of genius on Mr. Wilder's part. The Cognito Fall. I bet you've all been on your share of roller coasters, but have you ever had one that drops *sideways?*" She pointed to a long, horizontal stretch of track. "The cars were on a rotating axis, so not only were you moving at sixty-five miles per hour—you were *spinning* while it was happening. This was our janitorial staff's least favorite ride, as you can imagine."

"All these harnesses will need an update," Susan muttered to Marcus. "But if we swap out any cracked plastic and sand the rust, the rest can be fixed with a fresh coat of paint. No replacement necessary."

"Is that… actually fixing anything?" Kaitlyn asked, her voice dripping with honey.

"It'll pass inspection," Susan replied matter-of-factly.

Claire stared up at the track. "Hey, Kaitlyn?" she said. "Some of the track is missing."

"Huh?" Kaitlyn replied, following Claire's line of sight. It was true. A small segment, about two feet in length, had been removed from the track near the boarding area.

"Oh, gosh-darnit," Kaitlyn muttered. "Sorry, this is embarrassing. You'd be amazed what looters take from places like this."

"Who would steal a *roller coaster track?*" Claire wondered. She squinted, stepping closer. "They didn't even disassemble it—look at the heat distortion. They must have used a cutting torch, maybe even plasma."

Marcus blinked at her. "What?" Claire asked. "I'm not just sitting on my ass while you're at work, you know. I do a lot of reading."

Kaitlyn shrugged. "Beats me. But lastly, for this zone, we have Echo Walk." She pointed at a large, indoor attraction. "A hall of mirrors full of optical illusions. It's less of a thrill ride and more of a slow burn, but guests loved it way back when. As a matter of fact, I can take you through it now so you can see why for yourself!"

Marcus laughed. "A mirror maze? Why would I want to see one of the most common attractions at any chintzy county fair?"

"I can assure you, Mr. Templeton, this attraction is more than a simple mirror maze. Would you like to see?"

Marcus groaned. "Fine."

Kaitlyn clapped once cheerfully. "Then let's go!"

They walked into the attraction and were greeted by illuminated, pulsing pink and purple neon lights lining the entry tunnel.

"There's power," Claire said. "*Why* is there power?"

"Watch your step, the floor is a bit warped," Kaitlyn said, not turning around. "And be careful with the mirrors. There's nothing solid behind them—just plywood, then maintenance tunnels."

As they entered the start of the maze, they were greeted by a series of funhouse mirrors distorting their images. Claire snorted at the sight of one that dramatically widened her midsection.

"I told you to lay off the ice cream, my love," Marcus joked.

"Hey, you don't look any better yourself," Claire quipped back, pointing out Marcus's much wider frame in the reflection. Marcus scowled and walked ahead.

They moved forward slowly with arms outstretched, struggling to distinguish reality from mirror images. Kaitlyn led them around a corner, and Janet screamed.

A huge chimera waited for them, hackles raised, heads snarling and poised to strike. Kaitlyn let out a sharp bark of a laugh.

"I told you this place was more than a mirror maze. Some of these mirrors aren't mirrors at all."

The chimera moved sluggishly, its heads pivoting as it lowered into a pouncing stance. The hydraulics gave muffled shrieks, blunted by the windowpane the animatronic lived behind.

"That got me," Jack laughed, holding a hand to his chest. "That was good."

Around the next corner, Janet's scream replayed with crackling bit-distortion.

"What?" Janet muttered, looking toward the sound.

"Sound design was a big part of what made Echo Walk so unique. It's not called that for nothing," Kaitlyn said proudly. "With that being said, surprise! Everything we're saying in here is being recorded and will be replayed randomly as we walk through."

"God, is that really what I sound like when I scream?" Janet asked, running her fingers through her ponytail.

The scream came again, followed by Claire's voice coming from behind them saying "Hey, you don't look any better yourself."

"Alright, very clever, we get it," Marcus said. "Is that the only thing you wanted to show us, or…?"

"Patience, Mr. Templeton," Kaitlyn replied. "What was it Jack said earlier? You have to trust the process."

As they rounded the next corner, Claire paused. "Are… are these moving?"

The mirrors in front of them were subtly shifting. At first glance, the reflections looked normal, but if she looked closely as she moved, her figure would distort. Just a little. Like her entire reflection was breathing. Drifting into the uncanny valley like an astronaut tumbling uncontrollably through the void of space.

"It's a layering trick," Kaitlyn said. "One of Mr. Wilder's favorites. The glass has etched patterns behind it that only show up with specific colored lighting. The effect changes depending on where you're standing. Sometimes the reflections… twitch. And you *know* something is wrong, but you can't name what."

"Jesus," Janet shuddered. "I *hate* that."

They rounded the next corner and stopped short.

"Wait…" Marcus said slowly.

A large, vertically rectangular screen stood in front of them in place of a mirror. It showed security camera footage of Marcus and Susan standing in an elevator.

"Don't worry, we can get out of this," said the recording of Susan. "It's only the fifth death in two years; that's within the legal limit. For *that* park, anyway. Besides, it's not *technically* a safety violation since the new inspection guidelines aren't ratified yet. Let the press run their little circus until the public gets bored. We'll pick up the pieces afterward."

"Good. Janet can tell them we followed protocol," the recording of Marcus replied. "We won't have to stretch it too much this time around."

The screen flickered, then changed to grainy B-roll footage of guests wandering around Dreamscape.

"Kaitlyn, what the *hell* is this?" Marcus demanded.

"Just a little practical joke, Mr. Templeton," Kaitlyn said in monotone. "We added a few clips to the roll with your likenesses using AI. It's not like you actually had that conversation, right? You'd never be that irresponsible."

Marcus paused, then nodded. "Right," he said. "Of course not."

Susan's eyes were flat and cold, her mouth tight as a vice.

"You'd never be that irresponsible," Kaitlyn's voice repeated over the speakers as they pressed ahead.

Another screen disguised as a mirror. More security camera footage.

Jack sat on the floor in an office hallway, his head in his hands. Janet walked into frame and glanced down at him.

"Rough day?" she asked.

Jack looked up and said in a thick voice, "He *yelled* at me. He said if I can't fix the booking issue, I'm dead weight."

Janet shrugged and sipped her coffee. "He yells at you all the time. How's this different?"

"He didn't just attack my performance. He attacked my character. He said my wife settled for me, and my son's going to grow up to be a... a bitch, just like his pussy of a father."

"Jesus Christ," Janet whistled. "That *is* bad." She paused. "You know, I think he needs you a lot more than he says. I mean, you know who *really* does the legwork around here. Marcus couldn't wipe his ass without someone to do it for him. Which means you probably shouldn't kiss it so much."

"He's under a lot of pressure," Jack said quickly; too quickly. A beat. "But *God.* Sometimes, I think I genuinely hate him. And I just found out about *more* bad news and... I just *know* he's going to treat me like it's my fault. I don't know how to tell him."

Janet smirked. "Then don't."

The screen flickered and changed to more B-roll.

Janet's jaw tightened. "That's not real," she said, looking at Marcus. "It's not. I swear."

"Yeah," Jack joined in. "We would never... we wouldn't, Mr. Templeton. You know me."

"Relax," Kaitlyn said coldly. "It's all AI, remember?"

"For the sake of your jobs, it better be," Marcus grumbled, eyeing Jack and Janet. "You're lucky I don't remember saying that to you, Jack."

"You... don't?" Jack asked, his voice barely audible. He rounded on their tour guide. "This isn't funny, Kaitlyn," Jack seethed. "I don't like this. Let's just get through the rest, I don't want to make any more stops for your weird little sideshow."

"I'm sorry," Kaitlyn replied. "Truly. I think we missed the mark here. We wanted to catch you off guard, but we would never try to hurt you."

"Whatever," Jack said. He took the lead, and the others followed except for Claire. She had barely noticed the video of Jack and Janet. She'd been staring at one of the mirrors. Another windowpane? It had to be.

Because what stood on the other side was not her reflection.

In the low, pink neon light, details were difficult to make out. The silhouette was almost human, but it wasn't quite right. The head was misshapen, with two wiry protrusions sprouting from the forehead. One arm was slightly longer than the other. One leg ended in a single point rather than a foot. She could see the outline of tubes snaking in and out of the torso.

"It's an animatronic," Claire told herself. "Just an animatronic."

She slowly raised her hand and waved. The figure did the same with a slight delay.

Around the corner behind Claire, a loudspeaker crackled sharply to life. A smooth, slow baritone Claire had never heard before whispered something she couldn't quite make out.

"Nope," Claire said, rushing ahead to join the others.

A few poorly received animatronic jump scares later, the group found their way out of Echo Walk.

"Okay, I can sense I lost you there for a minute, but what you see next will more than make up for it," Kaitlyn assured them as they headed out of the zone. The abstract sculptures on the sides of the path came to an end, punctuated by an extremely faded sign.

"Warning: this portion of the park contains frightening imagery and is not intended for children under the age of thirteen," Marcus read.

"Consider me spooked," Claire snorted.

"I'm sure we've all had our share of bad dreams," Kaitlyn said ominously. "But Mr. Wilder was known to have exceptionally vivid and unusual nightmares. Honestly, I don't know how he slept at night at all."

She pointed toward the oncoming zone. "And so, he took the most bizarre of them and put them here. The World of Nightmares."

The tonal shift between this zone and the rest of the park was abrupt and unexpected. In the other zones, rot and decay were an inevitability. Here, they were a *feature*.

The painted asphalt of the Infinite Horizon had been replaced by swollen, rotting logs. The zone's walkways were a network of narrow bridges over a shallow pond.

"From a bird's-eye view, the World of Nightmares' network of bridges makes the shape of a spiderweb," Claire read from the brochure. "Wouldn't this be horrible for crowd control?"

"But it's shaped like a *spiderweb*," Kaitlyn replied. "Isn't that so neat?" Claire couldn't tell if she was joking.

Claire looked over the bridge railing into the water. It was nearly more moss than liquid at this point. But beneath the surface of the murky water, she thought she could see the faces of dead underwater animatronics staring back up at her.

"Ew," she muttered.

All around them, pikes rose out of the water, impaling fake corpses that were bound at the wrists and ankles. In some of the spaces between bridges, freshwater mangroves suspended themselves over the water.

"Bit much, don't you think?" Marcus muttered.

"No kidding."

"Alright, this is our last stop," Kaitlyn said, leading the group into the center of the spiderweb. "On our left, we have the Evisceroller Coaster, an indoor thrill ride where the entire set looks like it's made out of guts. Lots of jump scares, big animatronics, demons, monsters, even a few vignettes into classic bad dreams." She laughed. "There was actually a gag room where you get audited by the IRS. Truly among Mr. Wilder's worst nightmares."

Next, she pointed to a large, dome-shaped building.

"And of course we have Night Terrors, a series of walkthrough horror mazes based on Mr. Wilder's nightmares, which operated year-round," Kaitlyn grinned. "Here you could find everything from a brief journey into Hell, to a forest haunted by wendigo, to a secret, ancient civilization of hostile octopus people. One year, we actually featured an experimental maze meant to simulate a nightmare where you end up at work naked."

"How did that work?" Claire asked hesitantly.

"Well, it was for adults only, and there was a liability waiver involved, but it wasn't very popular."

"What the fuck?" Audrey murmured. Claire snickered.

"Well, even as nightmares go, that one's got to be one of the worst." Kaitlyn shrugged. "You can't blame people for not wanting to relive it. Can you imagine what it would do to your reputation if you showed up to work naked?"

"Why are we talking about—" Marcus waved his hand dismissively. "Okay, scary mazes. I get it. What's this?" He pointed to the large entrance to a darkroom ride, which was shaped like a lobster trap. Black tentacles with pink mouth-suckers laced through the netting.

"Wouldn't *you* like to know," Kaitlyn laughed. "Up Close with Kraus the Kla—dammit—Up Close with Klaus the Kraken. This was an indoor boat ride with a truly ridiculous twist—after a darkroom portion explaining Klaus's lore, the track actually led you down and out of the park and into a clear tube that goes through the Dreamlake! That's where you'd encounter Klaus, who, as you may recall, is the largest underwater animatronic in North America!"

Claire thought of the massive, slumbering octopoid animatronic lying untouched, just under the water of the lake, for decades. She shivered.

"Another fun fact about this ride," Kaitlyn continued. "Gideon based it on a recurring dream he's had ever since he was a boy. Attention to detail was especially important with this ride. So much so that it singlehandedly used up thirty-five percent of the park's original budget."

"*Thirty-five?*" Janet repeated, shocked.

"If you could see inside, you would know why. Now, unfortunately, none of these rides are currently structurally stable, so we can't go in just yet." She rubbed her hands together excitedly. "But with that, we have concluded our tour of the amazing, fantastic Dreamscape! If you come with me right this way, we'll go full circle to Whimsydream Square and talk business. Please do watch your step, the wood is *very* distorted here."

Claire carefully negotiated the boards, acutely aware of the restriction her tight dress imposed on her movement. Then, she heard a voice cry out in surprise behind her.

Susan had caught her stiletto heel between two boards, turning her ankle as she sprawled down onto the bridge. She was already on the ground by the time anyone realized what was happening. Stuart, whom Claire had completely forgotten was there, let out a thin, high-pitched shriek of a laugh.

Claire searched her mind for any other instance where she had seen Susan's meek husband react, speak, or even substantially emote, and came up empty.

Stuart, from the look on his face, was just as shocked. But in his eyes, Claire could see something else: desperate, immediate regret.

Susan pulled herself to her feet; the only hint of emotion on her face was the deep flush in her cheeks and the slight, contemptuous curl of her lip. She turned to face Stuart.

"Oh, that's funny?" Susan said in a low, lethal voice.

And then, Susan whipped around and punched Audrey in the eye.

Claire winced at the sound of the impact, only seeing the way Susan's elbow cocked back, followed by a thin *crack* and the cold, grim comprehension of what she had just done.

Audrey spun completely around and nearly toppled over the railing into the pond. The momentum carried her as she grabbed onto the rail, her head lolling as she struggled to remember which way was up.

Everyone was dead silent as Audrey blinked once, twice, with confusion. She gingerly reached for her eye. She let out a single, half-hearted huff of a laugh before wincing as her fingertips made contact. She huffed again, weaker this time, then fell silent as her sclera filled with blood.

Claire was moving; she didn't remember doing it, but it was happening. Toward Audrey. Toward Susan. *Fucking Susan.* But after a few paces, something held her back. She turned to see Marcus gripping her wrist.

"*Don't*," he hissed through gritted teeth.

"She just *attacked her child*," Claire protested in a harsh whisper.

"Don't you *dare* embarrass me, *that is my CFO*," Marcus threatened, his grip tightening on her wrist.

Susan stared the group down, her hollow eyes narrow and condescending. Stuart looked on silently. His face was etched with soul-crushing guilt. Jack looked to the side uncomfortably. Janet suddenly became enthralled by her press packet.

Claire saw Audrey's inflamed eye socket, already starting to swell. Half of her eye was now red. The girl looked from one face to the next with eyes that didn't quite dare to hope.

Then, Claire looked down at the dress she was wearing. "*Fine,*" she seethed, wrenching her wrist out of Marcus's hand.

"Uh…" Kaitlyn said listlessly. "If we could just finish the p-paperwork, please."

ဆာၢ

**CLAIRE COULDN'T RELAX.** The air had turned thick and viscous since Susan had assaulted Audrey. Claire struggled to balance getting as much oxygen as she needed without crossing over into hyperventilation.

Jack and Janet stood quietly off to the side, exchanging occasional grim eye contact. Audrey had gone off somewhere—Susan insisted no one "indulge her" by searching. Stuart paced Whimsydream Square anxiously, stealing ashamed glances at the others. His wrinkles suggested that the look on his face was very familiar to his skin.

Meanwhile, Marcus, Kaitlyn, and Susan stood huddled, going over details of the deal. If Marcus was shocked by what he had seen, he didn't make that obvious now. Susan showed no evidence of distress or guilt whatsoever. The face she made shortly after giving her only child a black eye was the same face she made while doing business, which was also the same face she made when she told her husband that she loved him.

The way Kaitlyn looked at her was different now, though.

Claire didn't intend to eavesdrop, but they were *right there.*

Marcus said to Kaitlyn, "I know you said before that it would be 226 million total to renovate, but..." He turned to Susan. "Did you finish crunching the numbers, Susan?"

"Done," Susan replied. "We can fix it up for eighty-two million. That's enough to keep OSHA off our asses for a while, at least. I'll have to call in some favors, and maybe use unmarked bills for a few of them, but we can get it done."

"*That's* why you're in charge of the money." Marcus grinned. "Isn't she something?"

"She really is," Kaitlyn said. "So, are you ready to sign?"

Marcus hesitated, putting a hand to his round chin. "I'm going to take a walk and clear my head. I'll have an answer for you once I get back."

The trio disbanded. Marcus headed down a side road of Whimsydream Square, following a path through a cluster of trees. Claire hesitated, shifted her purse on her shoulder, then quietly began to follow him.

She tailed Marcus up a gentle hill through the trees, hanging back to avoid making a sound. Her sheath dress prevented her from crouching stealthily, but she was still keeping up with him. Her heart began to beat faster. She felt the

198

jostling weight of the revolver heavy on her shoulder. This was the best chance she would get.

They emerged on a hill of dead grass and tangled weeds, able to see all of the Garden of Potential from that view. It was the only place she'd seen in the park with no televisions or cameras. Marcus would call the rot and decay before them an "opportunity." Right now, Claire just saw a desiccated, eviscerated corpse that he kept insisting was still alive.

Marcus paused at the peak of the hill. Claire inched the zipper of her purse open, adrenaline coursing through her as her fingers brushed the cold steel of the gun inside. She slowly pulled the gun into view, holding it out in front of her, toward Marcus—handle first.

Claire took a shaky breath, steadied herself, and called, "Marcus?"

Marcus turned around and looked with surprise at the revolver Claire was offering him. She extended the handle to him, pointing the barrel at herself in the process.

"What the—*don't hold it like that*," Marcus chastised her, moving forward and snatching the gun out of her hands. "Jesus, Claire, what *is* this?"

"A-a gift," Claire stammered. "It's a gun for your c-collection. I know you said you like pieces with history, so…"

Marcus held the firearm up for inspection. It was a silver-framed, six-chambered Smith & Wesson with a splintered wood handle held together on the right side by pink tape. Most perplexingly of all, the words "FOR HALEY" had been carved into the left side of the handle.

"Where did you find this?" Marcus asked.

"Yesterday, while I was on a walk in the rain around the Airbnb's neighborhood," Claire said. She began to wring her fingers together. "It was in a *housing development* of all places. The rain came back out of nowhere and I ducked into one of the unfinished condos to wait it out. Of course, it wasn't much better inside with all the mud…but it must have been serendipity, since I found this!"

"You're giving me a random gun that you found… in a housing development… as a *gift?*" Marcus asked. "You know I collect *antiques*, right?"

"You said you collect things with a story," Claire said, somewhat defensively. "Remember? And when I found this revolver, all I could think was: 'who's Haley? How did the handle get cracked? Who taped it up?' I thought maybe we could try and figure it out together. Or come up with our own story of how it got there!"

Marcus held the revolver by the thumb and forefinger. "Claire, I have a genuine Civil War musket. I have the rifle that killed one of the last white rhinos. *That* is history. *This* is junk. I'm surprised it's not in evidence lockup."

Claire felt a sickly bolt of adrenaline seize her guts. She was losing him. Time to go for broke. "I'm sorry, I just wanted to do something nice because I… I feel like you've been distant lately. I know you've been busy with work, but I miss you. I miss *us*. I was hoping we could talk about it—it's really been affecting me. Is that okay?"

Marcus smiled at her sadly. "I don't know why I expected any different."

"What do you mean?"

"It is *just like you* to turn this around when that's *exactly* what you've been doing to me. It's a phenomenon called *projection*. Do you know what that word means? It's a form of gaslighting. It's *abuse*, Claire. You've hardly looked at me, let alone touched me, for *three months*. But *I'm* abandoning *you*?" He gestured to the gun. "And even if I was 'being distant,' *this* is what you get to win me back?"

"But I… *abuse?* Oh God, *have* I been ignoring you?" Claire asked, her stomach prickling. "I just meant… I'm sorry. I didn't know I was hurting you that way. I would never want to do that to you."

Marcus's face didn't change, so she added, "A-and I'm sorry for the Epcot thing, that was stupid. And I'm sorry for trying to confront Susan about Audrey, I know it's really important that you guys have a good relationship."

"What do you mean by that?" Marcus asked shrewdly.

"I-I just mean I understand that it's important that you and Susan stay on good terms, even in light of what happened—"

"You're bringing that up *again?*" Marcus demanded scornfully. "Claire, it was *one* time. Just *one* time since we put the previous times behind us. Just *once!* And it was three fucking months ago—it's in the past! Stuart forgave Susan. You're the only one who still has a problem with it."

"That's not what I was talking about," Claire said feebly. She felt tears well in her eyes. "I'm sorry, I was talking about what just happened with Audrey, not… I don't understand, I'm just trying to give you a gift. I don't want to start a fight."

Marcus shoved the revolver back into Claire's hands.

"I'm trying, Claire. I really am. But things like this aren't making it any easier. You tell me I'm abandoning you as you abandon me, then you beat me over the head with my mistakes as you give me this… this *crap?* Is this all that my collection is worth to you? It's like you don't know me at all."

"I'm sorry," Claire said softly.

Marcus stormed away, back toward the main square.

"Wait, babe, please," Claire called after him. "Come back, I'm sorry!"

Marcus disappeared out of sight.

Claire slumped onto a rusted park bench. "What just *happened?*" she muttered, tucking the gun back into her purse.

"You tried to call him out on his behavior, so he turned it on you instead of owning up," said a young voice emerging out of the bushes behind her. Audrey appeared with a couple of twigs and leaves nestled in her golden hair. Her eye socket was bright red. "It's a phenomenon called *projection.* It's a form of gaslighting. It's *abuse.*"

"Oh, hey," Claire said. "Uh, what were you doing back there, kiddo?"

"Saw a baby rabbit. Wanted to keep it."

"Ah."

"I guess that would have been a *hare-raising* experience."

Claire stared at the girl, perplexed.

"Why do you let him talk to you like that?" Audrey sat on the bench beside Claire.

Claire hesitated. "Like what?" she finally replied. "You don't know. He's probably right; I probably *have* been neglecting him. I mean, who would just throw the word 'abuse' around like that if there wasn't a good reason?"

"You just tried to tell him *he's* neglecting *you,*" Audrey pointed out.

"Maybe *he's* neglecting *me* because *I'm* neglecting *him,*" Claire offered.

"Jesus, you're cooked," Audrey scoffed. "But you know, you're still lucky. I can read all the psychology books I want, but I'm stuck with Susan for the next couple years. But you can leave Marcus whenever you want."

"It's not that simple," Claire said quietly. "And I don't want to leave him. I love him. I was nothing before him."

Audrey squinted. "You were a waiter, right? At some bougie restaurant? Getting through school?"

Claire nodded. "Community college, yeah."

"That's not nothing."

Claire shrugged and shook her head but didn't argue further. Her eyes were drawn inevitably to Audrey's developing bruise. "Are you… okay?" she asked. The question felt larger than what the words conveyed. "I've never seen anything like that before, Susan was—"

"So your husband doinked my mom?" Audrey interrupted.

Claire sighed. "I'm not gonna talk about that with you. I'm sorry you overheard that."

"I knew it. That's why she's so warm and friendly with Marcus." Audrey chuckled. "That's hilarious."

"Is it?" Claire said testily.

"Everything Susan does is hilarious." Audrey flashed Claire an uncanny smile, amplified by her bloody sclera. "It has to be." She began to walk back toward the square, kicking her legs wide out in front of her as she moved as though traversing an invisible balance beam.

Claire sighed deeply, mustered up her best public-facing smile, and followed. They returned to see Kaitlyn standing with Marcus and Susan, holding a clipboard with the Dreamscape logo on it.

"What's the latest? Are we doing it?" Claire asked, craning her neck to see the papers.

"We're doing it," Marcus smiled, raising a fist in victory.

"I've got the papers right here," Kaitlyn said, handing them off to Marcus. "They're identical to the ones your lawyer approved. Once you sign here, Radiant Realms will be the official owner of Dreamscape!"

Marcus took the clipboard, pulling a pen from his pocket. "I feel really good about this one, Kaitlyn," he said grandly. "We'll get this place up and running in no time." With a dramatic flourish, he signed "Marcus Templeton" at the bottom of the sheet.

Kaitlyn's strained smile dropped at last as she took the clipboard back, revealing the expression of pure contempt that had always been just underneath. "You really don't remember me, do you?" she asked coldly.

"What?" Marcus uttered.

Kaitlyn tapped her Bluetooth earpiece twice and said in a shaky, low voice, "Yeah, they signed. Do it."

Before anyone had time to speak, an ear-shattering *BOOM* tore through the park with such sudden force that Claire felt it ripple in her diaphragm before she heard it. The ground shook, causing all of them to stumble as they struggled to remain upright.

"*What's going on?*" Marcus demanded.

Claire looked around for an explanation, for anything that made sense, but she was lost in her disorientation.

The sound of crumbling rock continued long after the blast had faded. The group ran to the park gates to see a cloud of dirt slowly settling over the rubble that was once the bridge connecting Dreamscape to land.

"What the hell was *that?*" Claire exhaled.

"The bridge must have collapsed," Marcus replied. "It must have been the exposure over the decades while it wasn't being maintained. It's better that it happens now, before guest liability gets involved. But I swear, it's always as soon as you sign the papers."

"Sure, but then, how do we get off the island?" Jack asked hesitantly.

"I heard an explosion," Claire pointed out. "I don't think it just collapsed spontaneously. What if someone set charges?"

"Yes, Claire, very good. Bridges tend to be loud when they collapse," Marcus jabbed. "What's the alternative? Do you think this is some kind of setup? Who could possibly have a score to settle with us?"

Claire stared at the chasm where the bridge had once been. "I don't know, but Kaitlyn said—" She turned around to face the group. "Where's Kaitlyn?"

The group looked around Whimsydream Square. It was only then that Claire realized they were missing someone else, too.

"Where's Janet?" Jack said, panic rising in his voice.

"*Shit,*" Marcus hissed.

"They couldn't have gone far," Claire said. "Let's look for them. Once we find Kaitlyn, we can call for help on our phones."

All at once, every TV in the vicinity switched on to static.

"*Now* what?" Marcus groaned. The static stretched and twisted as an image slowly came into focus.

It was a video of old, grainy security footage of the Garden of Potential. The camera was trained on the walkway next to the animatronic Andy, now animated to move his trowel around and tilt his head. The sound of families chattering and children exclaiming with delight flowed through the speakers.

"What is this?" Claire muttered.

Then, gradually at first, before quickly rippling out, the shouts of excitement turned to screams of shock and confusion. People on the tape began to turn against the flow of foot traffic, clamoring to get away from something just off camera. After a few seconds, the reason became clear.

A completely naked man sprinted into frame, leaping over the barrier between the walkway and the planters. With zero hesitation and feverish enthusiasm, the man rubbed his extremely engorged penis on the backside of the animatronic's stooping body, searching phallus-first for something to penetrate. As he did so, he screamed "*I AM GOD*" with the conviction of a man who had met Him personally.

Claire didn't know how to process what she was seeing. Some part of her wanted to laugh, but that was overridden by the sheer confusion of bearing witness to this act.

"Alright. Lots of questions," Audrey said. "But… I remember that face from the article I read. I think that's him. *That's Gideon Wilder.*"

"What?" Marcus scoffed. "That's ridiculous, there's no way. This was just some sick vagrant."

"No, no, I remember that handlebar moustache," Audrey insisted. "Oh my *God.*" She began to laugh—not the disengaged, wheezy chuckle she used to shrug off Susan's cruelty, but a genuine belly laugh. "Is *that* why the theme park mascot was a random-ass ant? *Did bro just want to fuck ants?*"

The group watched the TVs in stunned silence as the clip's audio faded out. And then, a microphone system clicked on with a sharp hiss. After a few seconds of dead air, a smooth, slow baritone began to speak.

"Ladies and gentlemen, your eyes do not deceive you," it said calmly. "And I can assure you, AI had nothing to do with anything you've seen today. Here we see Gideon Wilder, founder of Dreamscape, destroying everything he built over his entire career on one fateful day."

"Who are you?" Marcus demanded. "What's going on?"

"I'm an engineer; that's all you need to know. Now, if you listen to the official press release, Dreamscape would have you believe they went bankrupt due to legal fees after all the accidents which resulted in deaths and mutilations for guests, and employees alike. But that's not the case. You see, Gideon always had *appetites*."

The man spoke like the narrator of a nature documentary, creating an unsettling dissonance between the calming effect of his voice and the dread Claire felt twisting her insides.

"He kept his unusual paraphilia for insects under wraps for his entire career, until he took the wrong combination of cocaine, ecstasy, PCP, and a designer drug cocktail. Gideon ended his career doing the two things he loved most: chasing his dream and chasing the dragon. The cocktail of drugs contained multiple unknown compounds, and Gideon has yet to recover from the consequent psychosis. To this very day, Gideon is still firmly under the impression that he is God."

"Bro *just* wanted to fuck ants," Claire muttered in disbelief. "My God."

"The company bankrupted itself by drafting non-disclosure agreements and paying off every guest and employee in the park to sign them. *This* was what precipitated the downfall of Dreamscape. Not the deaths, not the mutilations, not the reckless cost-cutting, not the worker strikes. *This*."

The feed cut and produced an image of Andy the Ant staring directly into the screen. It took Claire a moment to realize she was looking at someone wearing a face mask.

"There is truly no better symbol for how Dreamscape conducted itself during its tenure. After the incident, this profitable deathtrap lay vacant and dormant for decades. The way it should be. But then, I heard that a certain entertainment company was planning a revival." As the man moved and gesticulated, Claire could hear the quiet hiss of what sounded like hydraulics.

"*No one* should be rebuilding Dreamscape, least of all Radiant Realms. I'm well aware of your reputation, Templeton. So loose with your safety standards, guests might as well be putting their kids in a barrel and pushing them over a rocky waterfall.

"Across sixteen parks and just over three decades, you've managed to accumulate two hundred and seven preventable deaths and four hundred and sixty-eight preventable injuries. As you know very well, this is significantly over the norm, and your company should have been shut down years ago. But you always found a way around the consequences.

"So here we are. The people who came to your parks trusted that you did the work to make sure they were safe. You let them down in the worst, most fundamental way imaginable. And you knew it. But the revenue kept coming in, so what difference did a few dead innocents make?"

"Is this lecture going anywhere?" Marcus asked. "If you're going to force us to listen to you, at least be honest. What do you want? Money?"

The engineer sighed. "You're still not understanding. I don't want money. I want *payment.*"

The man groaned as he stood, picking up the camera recording him as he exited the room. More mechanical hisses as he moved. After a few seconds of darkness, he flipped on a switch.

As the lights came on, Claire saw a hint of something silver and metallic recede from the light switch and out of frame.

Now, with the camera pulled back slightly and better lighting, Claire could see the beginning of a large, gnarled scar twisting across the engineer's shoulder and disappearing out of frame. His torso seemed… bulky. Uneven, somehow.

He set the camera down facing a wall and walked out of frame. "It's time to wake up," he said softly to someone they couldn't see. A few tense, quiet seconds passed before the group heard a sharp, sudden gasp and a scream of fear.

"Relax," the man's voice said calmly. "You just breathed in concentrated ammonia. It can feel like a real kick in the teeth, but I need you awake."

"W-what's going on?" stammered a familiar female voice. "I can't move."

"We're gonna put on a little game show, okay?"

"Wh… oh *GOD! What the fuck happened to you?*"

"What had to happen," the engineer replied with quiet dignity. "Don't worry. The rules of this game are simple. It's *very* easy to win."

The engineer picked the camera back up again and set it in front of the woman.

"Oh, Christ," Claire uttered.

Janet knelt at the base of a test-your-strength meter from Whimsydream Square in a dingy, dusty backroom warehouse. The side of her head had been strapped in place at the strike zone with the harness bolted to the panel. Her head was tilted up, with her jaw pronated outward and her hands tied behind her back. Her eyes looked around wildly as she shifted her knees in an attempt to find a semblance of comfort in the position.

Slow, campy calliope music began to play from speakers in the room, speeding up every few measures. The engineer in the Andy the Ant mask began to speak from off-screen.

"No one has to die today," he said in a pleasant, amicable tone. "In fact, this game is *so* easy to win that I'm *confident* that no one will. But that's up to you."

"What do you want?" Janet shrieked.

"I want to see what happens next," the engineer replied. "Now, Janet Conover, all your colleagues can see and hear you, and if you look in that monitor there, you'll be able to see and hear them, too. And just so you're aware, the video of you currently being recorded will be uploaded to the internet one way or the other. I have a series of facts that I'm going to read off to you here. And all you have to do, if you want to survive, is agree that they are facts, and adequately answer my questions about them. And the best part for you? These are all things you already know."

"What?" Janet asked shrilly. "Th-that's it?"

"That's it. Allow me to speak plainly. The bridge is gone, so you can't drive away. You may be thinking that you can just jump into the Dreamlake and swim to shore. Unfortunately, the water has receded to the point where falling into it from here would be like hitting concrete. So, that means there's now only one way off this island: the Winner's Circle."

Claire opened her brochure and flipped to the trivia section, rereading the segment she'd found earlier. "It's real?" she asked.

"A den of unspeakable depravity and indulgence for those who invested in the park at the top dollar. Drug binges, human trafficking, orgies, the occasional errant bestiality; anything went at the Winner's Circle. But Gideon wasn't just eccentric and perverted. He was also *deeply* paranoid. He had one last contingency in mind in the event of an unforeseeable, catastrophic incident that would keep him and his investors safe.

"In the Winner's Circle there's a door leading into a tunnel that takes you far beneath the Dreamlake. I rigged the electrical system myself, as a matter of fact. The tunnel leads all the way to the border between Dreamscape's property limit and the neighboring nature preserve. If you win, you get to advance to the

Winner's Circle and wait for the game to end for everyone else. Once everyone has finished, you'll be able to leave. However…"

The engineer, still mostly off camera, pushed a mechanism onto a spot on the floor marked with green tape. Janet screamed.

It was a motorized, inverted pendulum with a sledgehammer functioning as the striker. The hammer's heavy steel head was locked in place, poised to strike.

Claire's legs wobbled. Her eyes glazed over and she felt a wave of numbness sweep over her. She struggled to reconcile the fact that something like this could happen in the same world she'd lived in for her entire life. Not even ten minutes prior, she had been fantasizing about the decompressing bath she planned to take when they got back to the Airbnb.

"There are consequences if you fail." The engineer pointed to the side of the machine with the hammer with an unscathed hand. "There are three locks keeping this sledgehammer in place. Once all three are unlocked, the sledgehammer will swing and strike you in the jaw with a force of approximately 1,256 pounds per square inch."

"Okay, *okay*," Janet shouted. "I'll answer the questions, alright? I'll agree with anything you say, please just don't—don't…"

"Excellent," the engineer said. "Let's begin."

"What do we do?" Jack asked desperately. His words were swallowed by a curtain of silent anticipation.

"Alright then, Janet," the engineer said. "What can you tell me about Paradise Junction in Georgia? Specifically the ride Ever-After Falls."

Janet's eyes went wide. "R-R-Radiant Realms takes great pride in the work we have done with Paradise Junction in restoring it to—"

"Stop," the engineer said softly. Janet obeyed immediately. "Tell me about Ever-After Falls."

"Ever-After Falls is a marvel of thrill ride engineering and darkroom storytelling, c-combining the best of both worlds—"

One of the locks on the sledgehammer disengaged. Janet cried out in fear. The calliope music went up by a key.

"Talk to me like you're a human, Janet," the engineer warned.

"He's bluffing, Janet," Marcus called. "Don't tell him anything."

When Claire's drifting, floating mind circled back to reality at the sound of Marcus's voice, she clung to what he said. A bluff. An intimidation tactic. Of course. The engineer even *said* no one had to die today.

"The ride had to close for a little while, though, didn't it? Why was that?" the engineer inquired. Janet's face screwed up in desperation.

"There—" Janet's breath hitched. "There was an unforeseen incident involving one of the spark shower systems."

"The titular fall, right?"

"Yeah." Janet nodded. "W-where you go through a tunnel painted to look like a storybook, a-and it's full of mist machines and spark showers."

"How charming. But what would happen if one of the safety harnesses failed, Janet?"

"*Radiant Realms denies all liability pertaining to this or any similar hypothetical incident which may or may not bear passing resemblance to real-life events,*" Janet babbled desperately.

"The alleged harness allegedly failed because the guest was reportedly having an anxiety attack and was tampering with the system by thrashing in her seat and allegedly pulling on it continuously. W-we alleged—no, we *did* test those harnesses dozens of times, a-and quite frankly, every time we tested the harnesses, it caused a little more wear on them. So, if you think about it, if anything, we tested them *too* much because we take guest safety so seriously! And that's why—"

"Revisions of history abound," the engineer interrupted dismissively. "Her name was Stephanie Rogers, wasn't it, Janet?"

"Yeah," Janet breathed. "Yeah, it was."

"She got herself burned pretty badly, didn't she? Mutilated. It's a miracle she didn't die."

Janet gritted her teeth. "Those reports are *overblown,*" she seethed. "People are getting way too liberal with the use of the word 'mutilation,' haven't you noticed that? A few second-degree burns, a few stitches—the photo that went viral only *looked* bad because her wounds were fresh. She's *fine* now."

At this, the engineer walked in front of the camera, crouching down in front of Janet's face. The blurry image was too washed out for Claire to be able to comprehend what she was seeing, but the man's shape just didn't look *right.*

"She's fine now?" the engineer practically whispered to Janet. "She lost her right eye, her nose, and most of her lips. You don't think she still remembers that day every time she looks in the mirror?"

"Stay away from me," Janet bristled.

The engineer slowly reached up to his Andy the Ant mask, still facing away from the camera. He gently pulled the mask off.

Janet let out a strangled, gurgling cry. "Oh, *God*," she moaned.

"Say it to my face, if you're that certain," the engineer commanded softly.

"Please don't…"

"Say it."

"*She's fine*," Janet wailed. "*She's fine, alright?*"

"She doesn't look anything like me?" the engineer asked, inching his face closer.

"No, God, no, Jesus Christ…"

Another lock disengaged. The music's key shifted up again. The tempo ratcheted up into delirium.

"You probably should have paced those warnings out better," the engineer suggested. He slipped the mask back on and stepped off the camera.

"You've been repeating the same story to the press every time someone brings this incident up," he observed. "As if you think that makes it true. Not just Radiant Realms—*you*. Janet Conover. You lie. You deflect. You scapegoat the families. You blame the victim. You deny families justice or even the closest thing to closure that they can get in the wake of such a tragedy. And you make the public believe you instead of the ones you wronged. You attack them at their lowest point, painting them as hapless idiots, as disruptors, as agitators who had it coming. This ride may have actually ended up in even worse shape after you closed it for repairs, because you hired engineering *students* to fix it. And not gifted ones. Does your opinion align with these facts?"

"Janet, be smart," Susan said, but it sounded like a threat.

"No," Janet spat. "No, my opinion doesn't *fucking* align, alright? I'm just doing my job."

"Janet, we have *twenty-six* more incidents that you were personally involved in to get through, and we're not getting anywhere with this. Can we wrap this up? I'm going to ask you one more time: is Radiant Realms responsible for the mutilation of Stephanie Rogers, and did you personally lie to the press in order to downplay the incident, slander her, and avoid fixing the problem?"

"*NO*," Janet roared. "You're not *listening* to me. I was just following orders. I protected the company because that's what I was hired to do. I… I'm *good* at it. I mean, we're still doing business, aren't we?? That's my fucking *life's work*."

"It is now," the engineer said coolly. The third lock disengaged. The machine clicked to life.

"*I hate you, Marcus, I always fucking ha—*"

The sledgehammer struck in the blink of an eye, instantaneously changing the scene before Claire's eyes in a way she couldn't understand. The hammer slammed into Janet's face with a resounding *crunch*, immediately followed by the morose *ding* of the strength meter's ball hitting the bell.

Janet didn't look like Janet anymore.

The sledgehammer had struck her directly in the jaw, shattering the entire left half of her mandible and taking her cheek with it. Her bloody teeth skittered across the floor like pearly beetles. Blood and thick mounds of tissue and bone sprayed across the machine and spattered the floor. The splintered right half of her jawbone slowly moved up and down while her loose-hanging tongue wriggled and curled as though her body were still figuring out why she couldn't talk anymore.

And then, the sledgehammer reared back up, pivoted slightly, and struck again, caving in Janet's temple. More wet, glistening clumps of Janet splattered the warehouse floor as the machine dinged. It reared back, pivoted, and struck again. It reared back.

It was a simple mechanism, carrying out its singular purpose. So why, then, was there undeniable impish glee in the lightning-quick strikes of the hammer, and the playful intermittent pauses between swings? The hammer even elegantly pirouetted every few strikes before further irreversibly altering Janet's anatomy.

*Ding. Ding.*

*Ding.*

Janet was dead. Janet was *very* dead. But the machine kept striking.

As a final flourish that made everyone jump and cry out, confetti cannons in the warehouse exploded, decorating Janet's headless corpse with glitter and streamers. The hammer kept swinging until the TVs clicked off.

The six remaining guests stared at the blank screens with mute terror. Audrey clung to Stuart, horrorstruck. Stuart's arms were locked rigidly at his sides.

"*Christ,* Janet," Jack finally uttered mournfully. "*Christ.*"

"Is that coming for the rest of us, too?" Marcus said. "*God.*"

"She… she just had to tell him what he wanted to hear. She just had to tell the tru—" Jack shut himself up.

"Janet was a good employee," Susan said emotionlessly. "She did what was right for the company." She fixed her gaze on Jack. "Because she knew that if she had *lied* to make the engineer happy, she would never work in this industry again."

"What do we do?" Claire asked.

"We get out of here," said Susan. "We sue him for emotional distress, we make sure he gets the chair for killing Janet, and we rename a building in the park in her honor: Janet… fuck. I want to say Campbell? Culligan?"

Marcus pinched his brow. "Uh, alright, he said the exit tunnel is in the Winner's Circle, right? Isn't one of the secret entrances supposed to be somewhere in the Garden of Potential?"

"Yeah," Claire nodded. "Yeah, if we can find it and get it open—"

Susan was already moving toward that zone, whether the rest of them were coming or not.

Part Two

*"Name your price for the bodies you have slain*
*There's a price for every stain*
*And the currency is pain."*
— "When All but Force Has Failed" by Avatar

# PART TWO

**IT ENDED UP** being fortunate that Claire had skipped breakfast to look her best in the dress, because there was no way she could keep food down now. The moment of the sledgehammer's impact kept replaying in her mind over and over again. The instantaneous and catastrophic *change* in Janet's face. That was the hardest part for Claire to move past—how *fast* she had become unrecognizable. She'd never seen so much blood in her life.

As they entered the Garden of Potential, Claire pulled out her map.

"They don't give any indication of where it actually is," she said. "Guess that would make it too easy."

"The zone is only so big," Susan reasoned. "It's just a matter of time."

Marcus stared at his own brochure, squinting at the map of the employee tunnels. "Hold on," he said. "Look at this." He pointed to an unlabeled room on the map. "Every other room on this map is identified except this one. And look, there's a second door inside that leads right off the map. Maybe that's the entrance to the Winner's Circle."

"Kaitlyn said the entrance was here," Susan countered.

"But that was *Kaitlyn*," Marcus argued. "We don't know what her involvement is with this. What if she lied?"

"And what if while we chase down a random mystery room, we waste valuable time we should be spending on our only real lead?" Susan retorted. "Go waste your time in the tunnels, Marcus. We'll search up here and try to make up for your slack."

"I'll go with you, Mr. Templeton," Jack volunteered.

"Shocker," Susan muttered.

Marcus looked at Claire expectantly.

"Yeah, it makes sense." Claire shrugged. "Alright. I'll go with you, too."

"Perfect." Marcus grinned with self-contentment at Susan. "There's an entrance to the employee tunnels not too far from here."

Claire glanced at Audrey before following Marcus across the plaza. Marcus led Claire and Jack to a door at the back of the Hall of Dreamers, painted to blend in with the wall.

"What if it's locked?" Claire asked.

"Then we won't open it, will we, Claire?" Marcus snarked. But to her surprise, Marcus creaked the door open. The employee tunnels were plain; painted concrete hallways lined with pipes. They were devoid of all the glitzy, aesthetic charm of the public areas, there only to serve a simple purpose. Yet even here, security cameras were visible on the ceiling.

Their footsteps echoed as they walked quickly toward the room without a name.

"Keep up, Claire," Marcus warned, holding the map out in front of him.

"I'm trying," Claire replied. "It's hard to walk in this dress. Give me a second." She grabbed the edge of her sheath dress and tore a long slit up the side.

"That's much better," Claire muttered, flexing her legs.

She looked up to see Marcus staring at her, aghast.

"You told me to keep up," Claire reminded him.

They continued through the tunnels, passing one closed door that hadn't been opened in nearly half a century after another.

Which was why Claire was surprised when she noticed that one of the doors was ajar.

"What's in here?" she wondered out loud, scrutinizing the metal nameplate. It was thoroughly yet neatly defaced to the point of illegibility. Claire figured a Dremel was the most likely culprit. Beneath the space where the name had been, now scraped almost back to smoothness, were the engraved words "electrical engineer."

Claire stepped inside to find a small dark office. An ancient boxy computer that was likely older than Claire sat on the desk. On a cork board was a wrinkled blueprint for the Cognito Fall. All around it were photos of the same man—

one a graduation portrait, another photo in front of the Eiffel Tower, a third cuddling with a puppy. His face had been scratched out in each photo.

"Claire, what's the hold up?" Marcus demanded. "The sooner we get out, the better."

"Yeah, sorry," Claire said over her shoulder. She turned around and was about to head out of the office when something stopped her: a glimpse of a familiar face on an ID card sitting next to the computer.

She reached down and picked it up, scrutinizing the information on the card.

"What is that?" Jack asked, looking over her shoulder. "Wait… what *is* that?"

It was a Radiant Realms ID. Middle management clearance. So *why*, then, was Kaitlyn's picture displayed next to a name redacted in black marker?

"Marcus?" Claire called. "Can you… explain this?"

Marcus squinted at the ID. A brief flash of recognition. Of dread.

"Oh my God, it's *her*," Marcus muttered. "Of *course*. I remember now."

"*Who*, Marcus?" Claire pressed. "Is that woman's name even Kaitlyn?"

"No," Marcus sighed. "I don't remember what it was, but it wasn't Kaitlyn. She worked in system integration. She had access to every department in Radiant Realms. All she had to do was make sure information flowed from one department to the next smoothly. But *one pregnant woman dies* and all of a sudden, she's playing Nancy Drew with everyone's data. She claimed to just be 'raising concerns.' Well… even the internal chief safety officer knew she was full of it when she filed a report.

"And after I reprimanded her, I was going to let it go. Genuinely. You know I'm a forgiver, *and* an empath. I was going to let her keep her miserable little job as long as nothing else happened. It wasn't until she went nuclear and contacted OSHA that we got in real trouble. Next thing I know, we're constantly being accosted by assholes in suits demanding to audit and micromanage every aspect of our workflow."

Marcus scoffed. "The fines we faced… she was a liability. I had to make an example of her. So, I had no choice—I didn't just fire her. I *blacklisted* her. I made sure she would never work again."

Claire and Jack stared at Marcus in shock.

"So… You ruined her life *for telling the truth?* And you didn't even *recognize her?*" asked Jack incredulously.

"She thought she knew better. She tried to change the system. The system *works.* I had no choice."

"Yeah." Jack nodded slowly. "Of course. The system works."

"She was walking us around this park all day, and it never occurred to you that she looked familiar?" Claire said skeptically.

Marcus scoffed. "Listen, I meet a lot of people. I can't keep track of every little position. *Especially* middle management. But in my experience, if somebody has a problem with how things are run, that probably just means *they're* the problem."

Claire stared at her husband, trying to hide how much Marcus's words disturbed her. "…Okay, can we just keep looking for the entrance?"

They continued their winding path through the tunnels, getting closer and closer to the nameless room. After one final turn, they found the spot on the map. In front of them was a door that looked different from the others. It was made of wood, with vivid light olive-green paint rather than aged, chipped white paint on metal. It also featured a minimalist design of a trophy wrapped in a wreath.

"Oh my God, I think this is it," Claire said excitedly.

"You're a genius, Mr. Templeton," Jack cheered.

Marcus approached and tugged on the knob, only to find it locked. "Figures," he grunted. "Jack, get this open."

"How?" Jack asked.

"The old-fashioned way," Marcus replied, patting his shoulder twice.

"You… want me to ram it down?"

"It's an old door. You can do it. Or do you want to make my wife do it?"

Jack sighed. "Yeah, no, I can do it." He backed up several paces.

Claire squinted at the door. It didn't *look* old. In fact, the paint looked fresh.

"That's weird," Claire muttered. Her stomach turned as the pieces came together.

Jack took a breath to steel himself. "This is gonna hurt like crazy," he whispered, and he charged forward with his shoulder projecting outward.

"Wait—" Claire called out.

The instant before he made impact, the door swung open. Jack stumbled forward, struggling for balance and exclaiming in alarm. And then, the door swung quickly shut and locked. Claire made split-second eye contact with their tour guide, the woman who was not Kaitlyn, emerging on the other side of the door as she shut it.

"*Shit!*" Marcus yelled.

"Jack?" Claire called, beating her fist against the door. "*Jack!*"

"Jack is screwed," Marcus said bluntly. "We're not getting in there, and we don't want to. Let's move."

"Are you serious?" Claire demanded. "He's worked for you for *ten years.*"

"Yeah, and I've fired people who have worked for me longer. You can't save everyone, okay? That's just reality. I'm not sacrificing myself for someone who— I mean, look, if he was smart like me, he wouldn't have gotten himself into this mess. We need to get out of here before they come for us next. Let's regroup."

"What's your problem?" Claire demanded. "Why are you being so…"

"So *what?*" Marcus dared.

"I don't know."

"Well, maybe it's because I'm trapped in an abandoned theme park with a pair of maniacs trying to kill me. That's not exactly *business as usual.*"

"I'm in this situation too, Marcus. And I don't want to abandon Jack."

"Fine. You want to be a hero?" Marcus said. "Stay here. See where it gets you. But I'm leaving."

"Babe," Claire said with a hint of desperation. Marcus turned and walked away. Claire hesitated. She placed her ear on the door. She could hear the muffled sound of a heavy object dragging across the floor.

"*Dammit.* Sorry, Jack," Claire whispered, then she followed after Marcus.

ଽଉଓଔ

**MARCUS AND CLAIRE** emerged from the tunnels back into the main plaza of the Garden of Potential, finding Susan and Audrey waiting for them. Audrey was glancing around anxiously and seemed on the verge of a breakdown. Susan looked like Susan.

"I can only hope your news is better than ours," said Susan.

"I doubt it," Marcus replied. "Jack managed to get himself captured. The entrance was a trap."

"So, I was right?" Susan probed.

Marcus stared her down silently.

"Well, Jack's not the only one," Susan said, pursing her lips. "We didn't manage to find an entrance, either."

"Wait, where's Stuart?" Claire asked.

Audrey muttered something in a venomous tone under her breath.

"What did you say?"

"She *left* him," Audrey accused, her words sharp as daggers.

Marcus and Claire looked from Audrey to Susan.

"Really?" Marcus asked.

"Yes," Susan replied matter-of-factly. "I thought that because Stuart doesn't work for Radiant Realms, he wouldn't be in danger. So, when he got his shoe stuck while we were searching the logger ride, I told him every second I waited was a second I'm left vulnerable. I left and took my daughter with me. He never caught up. So I suppose I was wrong."

Even Marcus seemed shocked by this explanation.

"I walked through that fucking ride… must have been eight times. He's not fucking in there," Audrey huffed, breathing in and out in short bursts. "His fucking shoe is still stuck in the same spot. He's just *gone*."

"We're dropping like flies," Marcus growled. "We need to find the way out *now*."

The park TVs clicked on with a sharp hiss. The static sputtered and then shifted. Some TVs shifted to an image of the engineer's masked face, while others cut to show a close-up shot of Stuart's face against a dark backdrop. At the bottom right corner of each screen was a digital display that read "0 RPM."

"Oh my *God*," Audrey gasped in horror. She reached toward the screen. "*Dad!*"

Susan stared at the screen with narrow eyes but said nothing.

"Stuart Greaves," the engineer's voice said smoothly. His voice filtered over the intercom of the room Stuart was being held in. "You have awoken to find yourself restrained in the Starlight Centrifuge. I'm sure you're familiar with rides like this, Stuart. You spin around in a circle at increasingly feverish, frenzied speeds until you find yourself pinned to the wall, immobilized by your own weight. A chaotic, cyclical, and futile fight against the insurmountable rules that govern how you live."

The ride clicked to life, and the counter at the bottom of the screen went up to 1 RPM.

"Maybe that sounds familiar to you as more than just a ride, Stuart."

"Dad doesn't even work for Radiant Realms," Audrey cried. "He didn't do anything!"

"Which is exactly why he's here," the engineer said. "Stuart, as a reminder, everything you say and do here will be recorded and uploaded to the internet regardless of the outcome. Now, a quick lesson for you on *inertia*—a concept you seem most familiar with. You may have heard that force is equal to mass times acceleration, but once you introduce acceleration occurring in a circular motion, something interesting happens: *centrifugal force.* That same force that pins you to the wall is also acting on the blood in your vessels.

"Now, for a normal ride, that's not a big deal. But when you happen to be on one that's been overclocked like this one, that becomes a problem when the force starts pulling the blood out of your brain and into your limbs. That point will fully and consistently occur at about forty-five revolutions per minute. One minute is enough to ensure death. Once that speed is reached, the ride will be left on for three."

The counter jumped up to 5 RPM.

"And all you have to do if you want to survive is tell the truth."

Stuart looked into the camera with a kind of bovine panic in his eyes, his mouth tightly shut like a crumpled sock puppet.

"Your body and mind bear the scars of vicious abuse," the engineer went on. "And for that, you have my genuine sympathy. You are not responsible for the harm that was inflicted on you. But you are responsible for what you do with it. And what you fail to do."

The counter jumped to 8 RPM. It seemed like Stuart was having trouble staying on his feet.

"How many times? How many times have you seen Susan lay a hand on your own flesh and blood and said nothing? Dozens? Hundreds?"

"How could you know that?" Susan scoffed.

The TVs briefly flashed to security footage from the World of Nightmares—the instant of impact when Susan struck Audrey, then back to the game show from Hell.

"You met my associate, *Kaitlyn*. She's quite gifted with computers," the engineer explained. "She was able to get into your daughter's private school database, and what we found… a school faculty member attempted to report bruises on Audrey's face, but the case was mysteriously dropped after the Greaves family cut a generous check for the new auditorium. And that faculty member wasn't the only one at this school to attempt to report these types of events. No fewer than five faculty have raised concerns about Audrey's home life. And every time, the investigation ends with another plentiful donation from the Greaves family." He regarded Stuart.

"You could have stopped it at any time, Stuart. You could have saved your daughter. But that would mean you also would have had to save yourself, and you were too much of a pathetic coward to do that, weren't you? Even if you took your own daughter down with you. Does your opinion align with these facts?"

"Come on, Dad," Audrey whispered hopefully. She had her palms pressed to one of the TVs, practically nose to nose with her father across the screen.

The counter ticked to 15 RPM. Stuart's face read discomfort, but his mouth was still stubbornly shut. The force began working on his skin, pulling the adipose tissue in his face toward the backboard.

A hand reached into the engineer's camera frame and grabbed the microphone. A different voice came through the speakers. "Think about what she put you through. What she put your *daughter* through. *We all saw what happened,*" the voice said.

Claire gasped. It was their tour guide. The whistleblower.

"This is his choice to make," the engineer said placatingly.

Audrey's fingers curled around the TV unit as she stared at the RPM counter. "Come on," she whispered.

The engineer took the microphone back. "Stuart, you know as well as we do that what we all saw today was nothing compared to what Susan gets away with behind closed doors. After all, the last time you took your poor daughter to the pediatrician years ago, you almost lost custody when the doctor saw the damage to her body. And as far as we could tell? She hasn't seen a doctor since. For anything."

Claire stared at Audrey with renewed pity. At the desperation whitening her knuckles as she clung to the TV. At the small, methodical scars covering her forearms. Claire wondered whether Audrey or Susan had inflicted them.

A pained whine escaped Stuart's lungs as the counter touched 18 RPM.

"I feel obligated to warn you," the engineer said with what seemed like genuine concern, "you're approaching the point of no return. Your brain is starving for oxygen. Within two minutes at this speed, you'll pass out. After three minutes, permanent damage will start to occur. And we're not even halfway there. I understand that you've been conditioned into stagnancy, but you have a *chance* here. Not just to save yourself, but your daughter, too."

Stuart's face was being changed by the inertia, forcing him to make a ghoulish expression that would have been hilarious under any other circumstance. His cheeks were pulled back as though he were wearing a dentist's lip retractor. The skin under his eyebrows rose up, emphasizing how small his squinting, watery eyes were for their sockets.

"We're really not asking for much here," the engineer pointed out. "Less than the bare minimum from a father, really. Did you witness abuse firsthand, did you facilitate an environment where it could take place, and did you fail to report it? Answer those questions correctly, and you can leave right now. We'll even slow the ride down once you start talking."

Stuart looked from the camera to the display, and Claire could tell from the soft, subtle shift in his expression that he was looking at Audrey with her nose pressed to the staticky glass of the TV. Even in that state, Claire clocked something like a nostalgic smile crossing his face. He took a breath to speak.

But then, his gaze shifted to another member of the group. A pregnant pause after the inhale. Then, yes, a flicker of fear. Claire glanced over at Susan and saw the woman-shaped monster ever so slightly shake her head *no*.

And just like that, Stuart clammed back up. His head locked to the backboard as the counter reached 23 RPM. To Claire's utter amazement, Stuart peacefully closed his eyes.

"Your vitals still read as conscious, Stuart," the engineer prodded. "*Very* conscious. Your heart is beating like a jackhammer. You're wasting valuable time."

Claire looked back at Audrey, who loosened her grip on the TV and slowly backed away.

"Are you kidding me?" Audrey scoffed, letting her hands fall at her sides. A tense, silent pause, and then her arm flashed up and struck, dislodging the TV from its decaying scaffold. The TV slammed into the ground at Audrey's feet, its screen shattered and its mechanical guts pouring onto the brick road. Claire started and cried out.

"*Are you fucking kidding me??*" Audrey shrieked, picking the TV up with now bloodied hands and hurling it as hard as her thin arms could. She let a hiss of pain escape her lips as she pulled a large piece of glass from her knuckle.

Audrey turned to the nearest camera and screamed, "All you have to do is stand up for me *one time*, Stuart. *Just once.* I'm your *daughter*, you're supposed to *protect* me. I know that's true, but only because other people fucking *told* me. I've never *seen* it, Stuart."

Stuart didn't move aside from the jostling of his body with the ride's motion. The counter touched 30 RPM.

"Last chance, Stuart," came the whistleblower's voice. She sounded exhausted. Stuart didn't respond.

"You rat bastard," Audrey exhaled lowly. "You absolutely pathetic, chickenshit, unfeeling, *cowardly rat bastard. Speak up for once in your miserable life.*"

"Quiet," Susan commanded.

"You disgust me, do you know that?" Audrey screamed into the camera. "Not because you do whatever the bitch says. You disgust me because sometimes you have the audacity to make me believe in you. That little spark of indignation in your eye? The way your body twitches like you're going to stand up? Like you're going to fucking *do something? So fucking do it.* If there was ever a time in your fucking life, it's now. So *do it. Please*, Stuart."

Nothing. The counter reached 36 RPM.

"Is he still conscious?" Audrey asked, her voice raw but not quite resigned.

"Yes," was the engineer's simple reply.

Audrey came closer to the camera and said in a low, broken whisper that wasn't meant for Claire's ears, "Daddy, please. Don't leave me alone with her. Please."

Claire watched with cold disbelief as Stuart simply refused to speak, react, or emote. She glanced at Susan. The woman was staring at her husband with what appeared to be *satisfaction*. Pride. Thrill, even. The expression of a dog trainer watching the conditioning pay off.

"Fine," Audrey said, soft and final. "Fine. You always *did* choose her. Why would this be any different? So, this is how it ends? Well… the least you can do is open your eyes. I want you to look me in the face as you abandon me. As you leave me with *her*. I want to be the last thing you ever see, you impotent, selfish invertebrate. Open your eyes. Open your *fucking* eyes, you coward."

Stuart did not react.

"He's unconscious," the engineer announced solemnly. "Pity."

The counter quickly jumped the rest of the way to 45 RPM before it was replaced by a clock counting down from one minute.

"*You bastard!*" Audrey shrieked, staring her father down with the kind of hatred that could only originate from a lifetime of quiet, unfulfilled hope. "*You BASTARD!*"

Claire took one last look at Susan, and she couldn't believe what she was seeing. Susan was *smiling*. Fully smiling. It was a face of accomplishment. Like she had just confirmed something she'd quietly wondered about for years. Audrey's cries of rage and anguish didn't warrant a flicker of recognition on her face.

Claire stepped toward Audrey. The girl was still screaming, an unending string of expletives and thrashing, furious limbs.

Claire silently took Audrey by the shoulder and pulled her into a tight hug. Audrey's arms kept flailing, pelting Claire's back a few times before gradually settling. Audrey dug her fingers into Claire's dress, shrieking violent sobs.

"I know," Claire said softly. "I know, sweetheart."

According to the timer, Stuart was half-dead. And he looked like it. His face was turning white from lack of blood. His shut eyes appeared to be sinking into their sockets.

"Don't look, baby. Just close your eyes for me, okay?" Claire soothed, placing her hand on the back of Audrey's head and gently guiding the girl's face into her shoulder.

Audrey complied. Her fingers were sunk into Claire's back like fishhooks, like no one ever taught her how to hold something without hurting it. Claire ignored the pain, gently petting the top of the girl's head while she kept an eye on the timer. Second after agonizing second, Stuart's skin grew more pallid, mottled, and slack until the timer finally reached zero.

"He's dead," the engineer reported after a few moments. "The ride will remain operational for two more minutes."

Audrey wailed into Claire's shoulder louder than ever, equal parts devastation and fury.

"I know, honey. I'm so sorry. I'm sorry he couldn't be better for you." Claire's mouth was on autopilot, dispensing one soft-spoken platitude after another as she desperately tried to staunch this poor child's agony.

Claire looked up to see Susan approach them both, her expression severe and predatory. She forced herself between Claire and Audrey, pulling them apart.

"Don't touch my fucking kid," Susan spat at Claire venomously. She rounded on Audrey.

"*You*," she growled. "What is *wrong* with you?"

"Wh… what?" Audrey stammered, looking up at her mother fearfully. "What did I…"

"You watched your father's final moments. You saw his suffering. And you *scream* at him? Call him a coward? Tell all these lies? List off his failings? How *dare* you treat my husband that way, you *cruel, heartless little girl.*"

"But…" Audrey trailed off, her eyes desperate with pain and confusion. "But he…"

"*Look at him,*" Susan demanded, grabbing a fistful of Audrey's hair and twisting her head toward one of the TVs showing Stuart's dead face. "Look what your father sacrificed to protect this family's reputation from the lies of these disturbed lunatics. He did this *for you.* And this is how you repay him?"

As if in response to Susan's cruelty, the TVs shut off.

"That's *enough,*" Claire roared.

"Claire—" Marcus started.

"Shut up, Marcus." Claire walked toward what remained of the Greaves family.

"*Let go of me, you bitch,*" Audrey yelled at Susan, batting her hand off. Claire saw a dangerous glint flash in Susan's eyes, and she calmly and soberly chose the only logical response.

Claire stepped in front of Audrey, taking Susan's fist to her cheekbone.

The left side of her vision went white as her ear exploded with a brilliant ringing noise. Her face felt compressed before anything else, like the bones of her skull had been pushed too close together. But then a sharp pinpoint of pain claimed her cheekbone and pulsed waves of discomfort across the left side of her face.

Claire managed to stay standing, but only barely. She took a moment as she recovered to register that, however much this hurt for her, that was nothing compared to what it would do to Audrey.

Claire breathed heavily, holding a hand to her cheek and staring at Susan with wild shock. Susan stared back, unaffected. Claire shifted her focus to Marcus, who gazed dumbstruck between them.

Claire glared at Marcus, tilting her head toward Susan expectantly.

"Oh, Claire…" Marcus uttered mournfully. "*Why* did you have to get involved?"

"*What?*" Claire demanded, feeling rage fill up her lungs.

"This… this is between a mother and daughter. She meant to hit the kid. *Her* kid. You know Susan would never do that to you, don't you?" Marcus said. "Susan, this is… *mortifying.* I'm so sorry for my wife's behavior."

In that moment, Claire could have killed him. She wanted to maim him verbally, physically, with anything she could reach. Anything to wipe that insipid, stiff cocktail-party grin that had gotten him through so much of his shallow, frivolous life off his face.

But then, she saw the bewilderment, sorrow, and awe all mingling in Audrey's eyes as she looked at Claire as though for the first time. The girl didn't need to see any more conflict emerge.

"We'll talk about this later," Claire said threateningly, pointing at Marcus.

"Yes, we will," he replied evenly.

"If the door you found was a trap, and we couldn't find an entrance, we need another lead," Susan said as though she had just entered the conversation. "Any ideas?"

"Right." Marcus nodded. "Uh… there was a blueprint for the Cognito Fall in the unlocked office we found in the employee tunnels. Maybe there's some kind of clue there."

"Better than wasting time here," Susan replied. With an icy backward glance at Claire, she grabbed Audrey's wrist and began to drag her toward the Infinite Horizon.

Claire's cheek had gone from a sharp pain to a dull, generalized, throbbing ache, but the hurt in her heart made it easy to ignore.

☙❧

IT WASN'T THE first time Marcus had gone cold on Claire, but it was the first time she wasn't praying for it to end.

The sun had set over Dreamscape, and the group finally saw the Infinite Horizon in its full glory. Nearly every surface was luminescent with neon light rods, painting the buildings and asphalt with a kaleidoscope of color. A sci-fi soundtrack was playing over the loudspeakers, which may have added a sense of wonder and possibility to the ambience if not for the fact that it was being played backward.

"It *is* beautiful at night," Claire observed grimly.

Dragon Chaser's coaster cars ran continuously, feverishly, the roars and shrieks of their aging metal loud enough to pick out even at this distance under the music.

Audrey stared blankly at the Starlight Centrifuge as Susan dragged her along—the only part of the zone that wasn't lit up. Claire wondered if Stuart's corpse was still inside.

"There it is," Marcus said, pointing at the Cognito Fall. The entrance sign's tagline proclaimed *You'll never be the same.* "Let's see what we can find."

They walked through the ride queue entrance and found themselves in a set resembling a laboratory. Microscopes, imaging machines, and laboratory glassware lined the counters, which divided the path, glued in place and covered in a thick layer of dust. Mechanical arms behind glass panes went sluggishly about their business. Brains in jars full of a green fluid lined the walls like pickling thoughts.

"This is actually pretty cool," Claire muttered. She watched one of the mechanical arms' movements, tilting her head. "Wow. This thing is barely holding together," she said to no one in particular.

The arm passed a golden orb to another mechanical arm, which placed it on a conveyor belt. "Even back in the eighties, I don't know how it ever ran. No tension release, no redundancy… this thing stalls once, and the whole system locks up."

"*Claire.* This isn't the time for one of your tangents," Marcus spat. "Focus. Look for anything that might be a clue."

"Pretty hard to search when we have no idea what we're looking for," Claire said under her breath.

They continued through the queue, past more fake laboratories and shoddily designed robotics. Finally, they emerged at the loading platform, fruitless. It was here that Claire noticed the missing section of track again. It was a tiny section just past the platform, maybe two feet. But that wasn't the only thing that caught her eye.

"What's this?" she asked, approaching the ride's control panel. A piece of paper had been pinned in place with a metal rod that had been shoved through the panel. Claire slipped it off the rod as the others gathered. Marcus promptly took the sheet out of her hands.

"Some kind of incident report," Marcus said. "From what I can still read."

The report had been partially redacted with black marker, but most of it was still readable:

### "GO WILD!" AMUSEMENT CORPORATE
### INTERNAL USE ONLY

Employee Incident Report: Final Disposition

Employee ID: ███████

Employee Name: ████████████

Date of Incident: July 12, 1987

Location: Dreamscape Amusement Park, Cognito Fall

**Summary:**

At 11:26 AM, Employee ████████████████ was conduct-ing a routine mechanical inspection when the ride's secondary support arm disengaged during a manual stress test. The collapse trapped the employee beneath debris.

**Injuries sustained:**

- Severe craniofacial trauma

- Left arm amputation (beneath elbow)
- Left leg amputation (at knee)
- Seven rib fractures
- Third-degree burns and lacerations across 39% of the body

The employee was airlifted to St. Enoshima Medical Center. Condition: *Guarded.*

**Findings:**

- Pre-existing, undisclosed shoulder injury found in medical history
- No mechanical failure beyond normal maintenance risk
- Employee conducted maintenance during scheduled lunch break, violating safety protocols

**Disposition:**

Following stabilization, the employee was discharged due to rescinded insurance coverage. No follow-up care was arranged. Rehabilitative/psychiatric services and prosthetics for left arm and left leg were not authorized. When reached for comment, founder Gideon Wilder replied in a memo: "he's all right now [sic]."

**Conclusion:**

The "Go Wild!" Amusement Corporation does not accept liability for this incident.

Employee negligence, including failure to disclose medical history and failure to adhere to mandated operational procedures, constitutes a breach of employment terms.

Accordingly:

- Insurance claim denied.
- Worker's compensation claim denied.
- No additional reparative measures authorized.

This case is closed as of August 2, 1987.

Authorized by:

James C. Wrenfield

Senior VP, Risk Management

"Go Wild!" Amusement Corporation

Claire squinted at the report, trying to make sense of it. "Is this… about the engineer?"

Marcus read over the report again and shrugged. "Could be."

Claire shook her head. "I must be reading this wrong. I *must* be. They didn't just stabilize him and throw him out on the street, did they?"

"That's what I read," Audrey said in a low voice.

"He was missing two limbs, and that wasn't even the worst of it. He'd never be able to afford the bill for full rehabilitation out of pocket. What did they expect him to do?"

In recalling the engineer's appearance, Claire answered her own question. The hissing hydraulics. The snaking wires. The irregular shape of his silhouette. "Oh my God," she whispered.

"The company looked out for itself," Susan said. "Seems like they did a good job."

"This is… *despicable*," Claire said. "What kind of system turns a blind eye to all this suffering just to save a quick buck?"

"It's business," Marcus replied.

"It's America," Audrey said quietly.

The TVs in the corner of the loading zone clicked on with a sharp hiss, immediately twisting Claire's guts.

"Oh no…" she whispered. "Please, no. Not another."

Jack appeared on the screen, restrained to a reinforced metal panel, standing upright on a roller coaster track. Claire struggled to make sense of the environment around him. It looked *organic*, as though the walls were made of the epithelial cells that lined the small intestines. It almost seemed to pulsate.

In the background was an animatronic display depicting Hell rendered in pure gore. The platform itself was made of the same fleshy silicone-like material with torture devices, restraints, and rudimentary structures, all made from tooth and bone. Two demons laughed gleefully as they pushed and pulled a crosscut saw vertically through the body of an unfortunate sinner, starting at the groin. Others drowned in lakes of lava, prodded by demons wielding pitchforks. A particularly disgusting display showed a sinner spinning eternally on a Catherine Wheel with each limb hyperextended in the wrong direction.

"Jack Holloway," came the engineer's voice, calm and smooth as ever. "You awaken to find yourself inside the Evisceroller Coaster, a twisted take on a theme park staple, built from bowels and bile and meat-colored steel. A shrine to blood and gore. A reminder, perhaps."

"Oh God," Jack whispered, looking around wildly. "Look, man, I'm just an assistant, alright? I push papers around for Mr. Templeton, that's it."

"Yes, that *is* it," the engineer replied. "Which leads me to wonder how such a simple, braindead job could directly lead to the deaths of twenty-three men, women, and children in a single incident."

Jack's eyes went wide. "That… that wasn't…"

"Jack," Marcus said sternly. "He wants to take your *pride*. You're a *man*. Don't give him what he wants. Remember the kind of employee you've always been. You've been a loyal assistant for ten years. You've always talked about putting the company first. Don't throw it away now."

Jack nodded feverishly, grounded by Marcus's voice. "Th-the company comes first," he echoed.

The feed on the next screen over cut to a live shot of the roller coaster track in front of Jack, showing it curving off to the right to be obscured by the crimson wall.

"What are you going to do?" Jack asked, trying to sound brave.

"That depends on you," the engineer replied. "As a reminder, everything you say here is being recorded and will be posted to the internet one way or another." Around the corner, a faint rattling sound began to fade in.

"What's that?" Jack demanded, his voice cracking.

"Jack, do you know what a sonicator is?"

"No?"

"It's an instrument often used in cellular biology. A probe that vibrates at an extremely high frequency in order to shred the membranes of cells in a sample. However, due to their small size and other more technical factors, sonicators can't do much to hurt human operators. That's why I had to put my own twist on it."

The rattling grew louder as a roller coaster car appeared around the corner, moving at an agonizingly slow pace. A slightly concave metal plate connected to a piston that had been mounted to the front of the car. Claire wasn't sure exactly what she was seeing through the CRT static— she couldn't tell if it was just the visual fuzz of the old TV or the way it was moving, but it was like the camera refused to get a clear picture of the metal plate.

"I'll admit it. This one got away from me a little," the engineer said with a trace of a chuckle in his tone. "I call it the Localized Harmonic Disruptor. Or, if you want something more marketable, the Gut Puncher."

"What…what *is* it?" said Jack.

"Technically speaking? A lateral oscillator performing twenty thousand two-millimeter microstrokes per second. Simple in theory, but that does nothing to detract from its *impact*."

"Oh my God," Claire gasped, pressing her hands to her mouth as she realized what she was about to witness. "Oh my *God*."

"What? *WHAT??*" Jack screamed.

"I suppose I'll have to put this in layman's terms," the engineer sighed. The roller coaster car inched closer and closer, slowly rounding the corner toward the long stretch leading to Jack.

"Once the device reaches you, it will press forward, pinning you against the backboard. At two seconds of contact, your skin will bruise and blister as your superficial blood vessels are ripped to shreds. At five seconds, your muscle fibers will rupture and trigger renal failure. At twelve, your lungs will collapse, your heart will rupture, and your viscera will liquify into a slurry of blood and tissue. At fifteen, you'll be clinically dead. And then, it gets *messy*."

The track began sparking behind the car as it moved, the grating sound of rattling metal on metal growing ever louder. It vibrated so quickly it looked like a heat mirage.

"The plate will keep pushing. Past bone, past cartilage. Until your ribcage gives out and your body splits open like overripe fruit. You'll rupture from the inside out, Jack. You'll weep your own organs. And all you have to do if you want to survive is tell the truth."

"Th-the company comes first," Jack muttered, prayer-like.

Claire regarded her husband with a look of horrified disbelief. "Marcus, what have you *done* to this man?"

Marcus looked back with genuine confusion. "What do you mean?"

The Gut Puncher inched ever closer, creaking like a death rattle.

"What can you tell me about the Wyrm Coaster in Elysium Gardens?"

"Oh, God," Jack exhaled. "Please, I don't want to do this. Please."

"Add that to the list of things you didn't want to do," the engineer replied callously. "You *do* know how to forward an email, don't you?"

"It wasn't that simple," Jack evaded.

"Then explain it to me," the engineer said, anger leaking into his voice. "Explain to me how this couldn't have been prevented by forwarding a *fucking* email. Twenty-three, dead. *Dead.* You got the maintenance report weeks ahead of the incident. It spelled out in no uncertain terms that the Wyrm Coaster was on the verge of collapse. And it rotted in your inbox. All you had to do was forward it to Marcus. And you *didn't.*"

"Look," Jack said, eyeing the approaching coaster car with increasing terror. "I get a *lot* of reports, and all of them claim to be urgent, alright? I get pulled from all directions all the time. At a certain point, I have to make my own call for what needs immediate attention."

"Then you have shit judgment," the engineer replied. "You didn't have to fix the problem yourself. You just had to click a few buttons. Are you that incompetent?"

The Gut Puncher was rattling the track so intensely that parts of it were coming loose. A light shower of sparks and rusty bolts, then an entire segment of railing behind the car fell to the floor.

"Please don't do this," Jack begged. "*Please.* I have a son."

"*TWELVE CHILDREN DIED, JACK!*"

Jack's face was screwed up in panic, his eyes tightly shut as though that would stop what was coming. As if it would halt the slow-moving catastrophe, the machine mindlessly following orders.

But Claire could see something else beneath the panic. Grief. *Shame.*

The rattling was growing unbearably loud as the Gut Puncher closed the remaining distance. It was just feet away now. Claire couldn't watch what came next. She felt nausea overtake her at the mere thought. She covered her eyes like a child scared of the dark.

"*Alright,*" Jack screamed over the roar. "*Alright, I'll talk!*"

Immediately, the sound of the Gut Puncher died down as the engine was cut. Claire peeked between her fingers.

Marcus stared up at the display with an expression of disbelief congealing into dread.

"You want to know why I didn't forward the fucking email?" Jack said, his voice cracking. "You want to know why?"

"Jack, don't do it," Marcus warned, but Jack talked over him.

"*No,*" Jack hissed. "No. I'm done covering for you, Mr. Te—*Marcus.*" He stared head-on into the camera. "I fucked up, alright? I fucked up. I want to say that first. I should have sent it along. It *would* have been easy, at least on the surface. I didn't, and it was wrong, and… and people died. *A lot* of people died, and that's my fault. And I live with that every night when I drown myself in whiskey. Every single fucking night." Tears began to pour down his face. "I would take it back if I could. I would give anything to take it back."

No one made a sound as Jack struggled to control his breathing. "I… I truly *was* going to send it along. Eventually. Of *course* I wanted our guests to be safe. But…" He gritted his teeth as though in physical pain. "*Fucking Marcus.*"

Claire glanced at her husband's enraged face.

"Ten years of sucking up. Ten years of doing anything he said. Being scapegoated for anything that went wrong. Waiting on him hand and foot. Unpaid overtime. Doing him favors *well* out of my job description. I… I did things that disgusted *myself.* And for what? So he could abandon me as soon as my safety became *inconvenient? You left me to die, Marcus.* So no, I'm done with you.

"The day I got that memo was the same day that security footage was taken. The video we saw in Echo Walk. It wasn't fucking AI. Janet knew that as well as I did. I was going to forward it, but… he was already in a horrible mood, and he hated it when he got bad news. He hated it when *I* brought him bad news. 'Hostile work environment' is putting it mildly. So I told myself I would send it the next day. But the next day, it was a new crisis. A new thing to blame me for. And I knew if I sent that email while he was in that state, he would make my life hell for the next month. So I just… *waited.* I waited for his mood to blow over. And it never did. I'm not even sure if he *could* have treated me worse." Jack began to weep openly.

"What a load of bull." Marcus scowled. "Ask any of my subordinates. They love working for me. They say I'm the best boss they've ever had."

"Because they're *scared of you,* Marcus," Jack retorted. "Because you get rid of anyone who doesn't follow your every whim. Because you blacklisted the only person in the company bold enough to tell the truth. That's the thing—it wasn't just me. Marcus treats everyone like rotting shit. I just happened to usually be the most convenient target. Janet's not the only one who hates you, Marcus. We *all* do. Every single one of us. Even Susan."

Marcus glanced at Susan, who shrugged nonchalantly.

"The day the collapse happened, I had just dropped my son off at school when I got the call. I watched him walk to his first class as I heard that all those parents had just lost their children. And all I could think was, what if that was my boy? And that wasn't even all of it. You're right. Twenty-three people died because of me. There's no excuse for that. I'm going to live with that until the day I die. But the least I can do for them is own up now. So… if any of the families see this, please know… from the bottom of my heart, I'm so sorry. I know that won't fix anything, and I would flay myself alive if it meant even one of them would come back. I hate that this is all I can do. But I'm going to do it. I'm sorry."

A long, silent, tense pause, and then the engineer said, "That took guts, Jack." With a loud *clank,* Jack's restraints were released. He dropped onto the floor, sobbing with simultaneous anguish and relief.

The whistleblower appeared in the frame, offering Jack a hand up. "Congratulations," she said. Jack leaped forward, hugging her. She froze, then gently patted him on the back. "Let's go," she said. "You earned your victory. The Winner's Circle awaits. If you come with me, there's an entrance hidden in the ride."

The TVs switched off.

Claire stared up at the screen, nearly as shocked as she had been at Janet's demise. "He… *did it,*" she said in awe. "He actually did it."

"He certainly did *do it,*" Marcus said, his voice simmering with rage as his face turned an almost magenta shade of red. "He just landed himself a defamation lawsuit."

"Don't you have to lie to catch defamation charges?" Audrey provoked.

"Shut your mouth," Marcus snapped. "*Hostile work environment,* he says. I have people lining up out the door to work for me. It's only hostile to losers like him."

"Jesus, Marcus," Claire scoffed. "The guy lived, can't you be happy for him?"

"He lived, but at what cost to me?"

"If you two are done," Susan interjected, "we need to get to the Evisceroller Coaster as fast as possible. You heard her. There's an entrance to the Winner's Circle inside."

"Good plan," Marcus agreed.

"Oh my *God*," Audrey groaned. The bruising around her eye socket had faded to a deep purple. "Don't you idiots get it? We're not getting out of this without playing by their rules. They control everything. They *see* everything."

To demonstrate her point, she put on an absurdly huge Cheshire grin and waved at a nearby camera. "You think you've been making your own choices, but you've been playing into their hands this whole time. They're listening *right now*. They're watching us *right now*. We all know there's only one way out of this."

Susan seized the front of Audrey's dress. "You are working my last nerve," she said, pulling her face in close. "I *want* you to keep pushing, do you understand? I want you to see what happens next."

Audrey swallowed hard. Her face slowly turned from instigative glee to genuine fear as she realized what her life was going to look like without Stuart splitting the abuse.

"That's what I thought," Susan said, releasing her. "Let's go." She grabbed her daughter's wrist and began dragging her forward once again.

"There's always another way out," Marcus said, more to himself than anyone else. "Always. You just have to know where to look."

Pressure was building in Claire's head. She was *exhausted*, even more emotionally than physically. She was angry that Jack's victory had been undercut by Marcus's ego. She was tired of death. She was tired of tension. She was tired of Susan. And yes, she was becoming tired of Marcus. But now Marcus was moving too, and being alone was a bad idea in this place. She followed.

Back in the World of Nightmares, the Evisceroller Coaster waited. The entrance to the ride queue was the huge, gaping maw of a plaster wendigo with pallid skin and pupilless, milky eyes. Claire shivered as she walked inside, eyeing its huge, bloodstained teeth.

Susan led the group forward, still gripping Audrey's wrist, staring straight ahead. Maybe that was why she didn't notice the tripwire just past the wendigo's uvula.

But Claire did.

A split second of light reflecting off the black cord, and she realized why the whistleblower had revealed the entrance to the Winner's Circle before the feed cut. Another setup.

She had one second to react. She could speak up. She could warn Susan. She could save her life.

Claire reached forward, grabbing Audrey's other hand and ripping her away from the she-demon just as Susan's stiletto heel snapped the tense string. Something inside Claire snapped in tandem.

"Wh—" Susan began, before the double doors sectioning off the wendigo's esophagus slammed behind her.

"Susan?" Marcus shouted, rushing forward and pounding on the door. "*Susan!*" He began fruitlessly ramming his shoulder against the steel.

Claire's heart palpitated as she grappled with the gravity of what she had just done. "Are you okay?" she asked Audrey. The girl didn't respond. She was gripping Claire's hand tight, staring at her with awe that bordered on fear.

"*What have you done?*" Marcus shouted, rounding on his wife. "You could have said something. You could have prevented this."

Claire's mind began racing, a reflex to construct the perfect placation, to roll over and grovel for him and pray he accepted her apology. But then, she stopped herself mid-trajectory.

"Yeah," she said simply. "Yeah, I could have. But I didn't want to." Adrenaline surged through her—not anxiety, *thrill*. The words felt strange and powerful to her tongue, like a witch's incantation.

Marcus stared at her with mute shock. "I don't even know who you are anymore," he said.

"I'm not sure I do either," she replied. "But I know an evil cunt when I see one."

The muscles in Marcus's neck went taut as the tripwire as he struggled to figure out where his submissive fuckdoll had gone.

"So, what's the plan, Marcus?" Claire asked. She had momentum now, even if her heart was pounding so hard that she could feel it behind her eyes. "Walk into another trap? Split up again so we're easier to pick off? What are you in the mood for? You *are* the leader, after all."

Marcus pressed his hands to his face, slowly dragging them down. "I..." he began. He had no follow-up.

"You have no idea, do you?" Claire grinned. "Why don't we just let it happen then, Marcus? Why don't we just tell the truth and go home? The engineer wasn't lying. We can survive. Jack proved that."

"Because he doesn't want us to *tell the truth*, he wants us to *lie and defame ourselves*. I'm not ruining my own reputation. I'm not. There's *always* another way."

"Lead the way then, dear."

Audrey stared at the wrist Susan had been gripping—at the red crescent moons where her fingernails had sunk into Audrey's skin. She looked at her other hand; the gentle but firm grip Claire had on it.

There was a kind of reverent trepidation in her voice when she whispered to Claire, "Thank you."

୫୬ଔ

**CLAIRE AND AUDREY** followed Marcus as he wandered around the park listlessly, walking in and out of attractions, looking for…something. Audrey clung to Claire's arm as they moved.

Claire walked with a light, leisurely gait, sometimes sitting with Audrey on park benches and letting Marcus wear himself out, amusing herself with her husband's increasing disoriented panic. She wondered if it was his cigar smoking, age, nervousness, or more likely a combination of all three that made him look so weak.

They were on their second circuit through Whimsydream Square when the TVs clicked on.

"Audrey," Claire said gently. "Remember the grassy hill where we talked earlier? Why don't we hang out there for a while? You don't need to see this."

"No," Audrey replied. "No. I want to."

Claire hesitated. "Fine, but if this goes how I think it will, we're gonna have to circle back to this."

Susan appeared on the screen, seated inside Echo Walk. She tugged on the chair's restraints, looking around with the same expression of malicious boredom she always wore.

"Susan Greaves," the engineer began. "You awaken to find yourself in Echo Walk. A place where *reflection* is inevitable. A place where you have no choice

239

but to face yourself. And a place where even the most objective realities appear distorted in the glass. Perhaps that—what are you doing?"

Susan was rocking the chair from side to side with increasing momentum, eventually tilting it over. The rotting wooden chair shattered, releasing her wrists.

"You're going to have to do better than this," Susan said wryly, climbing to her feet.

"The doors are locked, Susan. There's nowhere to go. This entire area is slowly filling with carbon monoxide; it's a matter of time before—"

"Whatever," Susan dismissed. "Your little friend said there are employee tunnels behind these mirrors, right?"

She took off her blazer, wrapping it around her fist. She turned to the nearest mirror and struck, cracking the glass.

Audrey flinched.

"I wouldn't recommend that," the engineer warned. "It's in your best interest to see this through, Susan."

Susan scoffed and struck again, further cracking the glass.

"Susan, this is a bad idea," the engineer said. "I can assure you, we've planned for every contingency, and we don't appreciate cheaters."

"There's always another way out," Susan said without a trace of pain in her voice, striking again. Glass shards fell to the ground, exposing plywood underneath. She let out a cry of victory.

"Claire, take the girl to the hill," the engineer said, a trace of urgency in his voice. "*Now.*"

Claire didn't need to be told twice. "Come on, sweetheart," Claire said, gently tugging on Audrey's shoulder. Audrey nodded mutely and followed. Marcus hadn't even noticed that they moved. Claire watched the TV over her shoulder as she walked.

Susan punched the wood like it was her daughter's eye. The dilapidated plywood broke open, and instantly something began pouring out of the hole and onto Susan's arm.

At first, Claire wasn't sure exactly what burst forth. It looked like a black liquid, but it didn't behave like it. It moved with intention, *autonomy* over Susan's blazer and onto the bare skin of her forearm.

"Are those… *ants?*" Claire exhaled. "*Why?*"

And then, the screaming started.

Not disgust.

Not frustration.

Agony.

Agony deeper than Claire had ever heard in her life. It was like the hellish sound carved a singularity around itself, blurring the boundaries between self and non-self, ripping scraps of involuntary, painful empathy from Claire's mirror neurons.

For just a moment, a memory flickered through Claire's mind—a memory from before her world went insane: "*What kind of ant has a stinger?*"

"Come on, let's go," Claire said. The last thing she saw before turning her head to run with Audrey was the mass of bullet ants pouring onto Susan's writhing frame. Claire and Audrey had the luxury of escaping the burgeoning event horizon of suffering. But Susan couldn't. Her anguished screams followed them up the hill as Audrey plugged her ears.

Pity sent nauseating adrenaline through Claire's guts—not for the evil woman drowning in what was quickly becoming a veritable ocean of bullet ants, but for the girl who had no choice but to understand that her mother was enduring an unfathomable amount of pain.

They rushed to the park bench on the hill, where Audrey leaned into Claire with her ears covered and her eyes screwed shut.

There were no words Claire could say to the girl. No words in any language could adequately describe the raw sensation Susan was likely experiencing, much less provide any measure of comfort. Her suffering had crossed the boundary into the ineffable. Maybe that was why Susan wasn't saying any words at all.

Claire settled instead for gently stroking Audrey's hair in complete silence, hoping the girl's fingers were enough to block out the ever-growing, horrible din.

She'd missed the connection previously, but Claire suddenly remembered where else she had heard of bullet ants before. A late-night Wikipedia rabbit hole had once led her to a video of a zoologist who willingly subjected himself to a sting on the arm. He'd kept his composure for mere seconds before the grown man was reduced to a gibbering, convulsing mess, writhing on the ground, barely coherent, screaming like a fodder character in an exploitation film. He spoke of the venom's infernal chemical heat. He spoke of his muscles painfully seizing and locking. He spoke of the venom's hallucinatory properties, and the horrifying visions he bore witness to. He spoke of how the pain didn't taper; it only got worse with time. And eventually, he too stopped speaking and simply produced noise.

A single sting to the forearm.

Susan's voice had taken on a new quality. Her cries grew gagged, strangled, the sound of air passing through an ever-narrowing passage. Claire understood that there were only two explanations: it was either merciful anaphylaxis, or the ants had invaded Susan's insides, sinking their stingers into her soft, sensitive mucous membranes.

Something strange occurred then. Susan's shrieks of pain began to take on a layered quality, like multiple screaming voices overlapping, coalescing, breaking apart. It took Claire a moment to realize that Echo Walk was doing what it did best: replaying what it heard.

The screams no longer came only from the distant TVs, but from Echo Walk itself, issuing out of the Infinite Horizon and into the stagnant air. It seemed impossible that there could be so much pain in all the world. It seemed impossible that Claire could be sitting there, intact and physically fine, while less than a mile away, Hell had opened up to welcome Susan Greaves back home.

Perhaps at some point, Susan lost the ability to create sound. With the endless echoes of sheer agony drowning her out, Claire couldn't be sure.

A thought occurred to Claire then for the second time in her life—a thought which originated from a difficult LSD trip decades ago and hadn't crossed her mind since.

*How much pain can a person endure until there is no self to return to? Until they become pain itself?*

Claire never found an answer, but maybe Susan had.

And still, Susan's screams echoed into the night.

# Part Three

*"There's a place I wanna take you,*
*but I'm not quite there myself yet."*
— "YOUtopia" by Bring me the Horizon

# PART THREE

**TIME PASSED. CLAIRE** experienced seconds like hours, looking at the heartbreakingly brave girl sitting next to her and waiting for the moment when she could tell her it was finally over. There had been no end in sight this entire time. Each moment had equal potential to be Susan's last, but none were. It just kept *going*.

The torment dragged on and on until Claire barely made out the whistleblower's voice saying, "Jesus, will you turn that shit off?"

The engineer's distant, disappointed reply drifted out of the square and up the hill. "I was hoping it wouldn't come to that." Then, silence from the TVs. The power seemed to have been turned off for Echo Walk itself, as the screams were abruptly cut off.

Claire gently touched Audrey's wrist, prompting her to lower her fingers from her ears. "It's done," she said softly.

Audrey nodded silently as tears welled in her eyes.

"You can cry," Claire offered.

Audrey sniffed, leaning into Claire's shoulder and letting small, shuddering sobs leak out of her. The full spectrum of emotion behind the tears seemed to be a mystery even to the girl herself.

"I'm sorry," Claire said. "Even if she was… *Susan*… I know it's not that simple for you."

Audrey looked up at Claire with the first smile she'd seen from the girl that wasn't tinged by sardonic cynicism. Her blackened eye crinkled with relief even as tears poured out of it.

"I'm *free*." She couldn't get the words out without interrupting herself with a torrent of crying fused with exhilarated laughter. "I'm finally free," she sobbed, leaning back into Claire's shoulder.

Marcus trudged up the hill toward them. Claire had no idea what he had just witnessed, but he looked like a dead man walking. Sweat rolled down his pale face, dripping off the unkempt curls of his hair. His body drifted more than it moved, as though if he so much as pricked his finger, all the hot air holding him together would come gushing out.

"Is she dead?" Claire asked.

"What?" Marcus replied, finding his way back to earth.

"Susan. Is she dead?"

"Uh…" Marcus stared at a fixed point in the middle distance, clearly processing much more than the dead shrubbery around him. "Maybe? But she was still twitching when the TVs turned off, so…"

"Huh." Claire nodded thoughtfully. "Well, she brought it on herself."

"You…" Marcus began, slowly grounding himself. "You *left* me."

"I took care of Audrey," Claire replied shortly. She barely glanced at him; she just continuously combed her fingers through Audrey's hair as the girl quietly cried. "And you have a pair of perfectly good legs, for now. I didn't make you stay."

Marcus stared at Claire as though she had been swapped out with a doppelganger. There was confusion. Hurt, even. But before her eyes, she watched the gears turn in his head, grinding pain into anger in real time.

"I have given you *everything* you have," he seethed. "Down to the clothes on your back. And *this* is how you repay me?"

Claire glanced down at her dress and the long tear up the side. Reflexive guilt panged inside of her.

"Real kindness isn't bought and sold," Audrey interjected, surprising Claire. The girl took her head off Claire's shoulder and stared Marcus dead in the eyes. "If you were only generous for the sake of controlling Claire, that's viewing a relationship as a transaction. That's emotional abuse."

Claire blinked. It was true. Marcus was always generous, *so* generous—until she crossed him. Then, he held it over her head like a guillotine blade.

"I'm talking to my wife," Marcus said coldly to Audrey.

"Is she wrong, though?" Claire jabbed.

"Did you even know love is supposed to be given unconditionally?" Audrey asked. "Did anyone ever teach you that? Because I had to teach myself. I read every book I could find about abuse dynamics because I never want to end up like my mother. And I'm *fifteen*. How old are you, Marcus?"

Marcus's face was rapidly changing from pale to fuchsia as he returned to the one emotion that felt safe to him. "Claire, come with me. *Now*."

"So you have a plan, then?" Claire prodded. "Did you come up with a way to get out of here? Or are you starting to realize that there's only one way out of this?"

"We… we outnumber them," Marcus said, claiming a shred of confidence in his fracturing mind.

"What makes you think we'll fight with you?" Claire replied coolly.

Claire looked at Audrey, whose fist was still bloody from when she had struck the TV during Stuart's trial.

"We need to get you some first aid," Claire observed. "Are you ready to go?"

Audrey nodded, standing.

"*Claire*," Marcus roared. "I'm telling you, if you walk away from me right now, we are *done*. You'll lose everything. You signed the prenup; you knew what was in it. You'll have to start over from square one, and you'll *never* find anyone else who will put up with you. You'll be right back to waiting tables."

Claire glanced over her shoulder, staring at the pathetic husk of a man who she once worshipped. "Okay," she said.

Claire and Audrey walked back toward the square, leaving Marcus alone on the hill.

₧₨₧

**AUDREY SAT ON** a small table in the first aid station, waiting for Claire as she searched around the stock room.

"Alright," Claire said, dumping an armful of medical supplies next to the girl. "First thing's first—here's some ice for your eye." She handed Audrey an ice pack wrapped in a towel.

"Thanks," Audrey replied, gingerly pressing it to her face.

Claire selected a pair of tweezers from the supplies, squinting at Audrey's bloody knuckles.

"I'm just gonna take out any small fragments in here, okay?" Claire asked. Audrey nodded, and Claire began examining the wound.

"How are you doing?" Audrey asked. Claire let out a bark of a laugh, much louder than she meant to. "You're asking me how *I'm* doing?"

"You basically just divorced your husband."

Claire's stomach dropped. She felt a brief wave of nausea seize her.

"And you just lost your parents," she replied. "I think you win."

For a brief moment, Audrey's jaw clenched. She chuckled dryly. "Nah. They've been dead to me for years."

Claire pulled a small glass fragment from Audrey's middle knuckle, dropping it into a metal tray. Her hands were trembling, her heart palpitating. The harsh fluorescent lights buzzed and flickered overhead. Everything was too loud. Paradoxically, the more the adrenaline in her system tapered, the less calm control she felt. The last twenty-four hours weighed on her, making every movement and thought exhausting. But it would be her secret. She had to be strong for Audrey.

"He used to crack jokes," Audrey said.

"Huh?"

"Stuart. The lamest dad jokes you've ever heard. He'd embarrass us at restaurants all the time. I never told him, but… I loved them."

Claire giggled. "I didn't think he was the type."

"That's cuz Susan only let him meet you in the last few years."

Claire wasn't sure how to respond. The sentence carried an almost unbearable weight. Another small shard was cast into the metal tray.

Claire braced her tweezing hand with the other as she plucked out a tiny sliver of glass.

"Should I be sadder?" Audrey asked hesitantly.

Claire paused with the tweezers closed around a particularly large shard.

"I don't think there's any wrong way to feel right now," she said.

Audrey sighed. "I guess. It *seems* wrong, though."

Claire removed the shard.

"You know, Marcus used to be funny too," she said. "But I think he stopped cracking jokes for a different reason. These days, I only hear anything close to real humor come out when we're in public. At home, it's all so… *mean.*

He loves ridiculing people. Anyone and everyone. And then he looks at me and expects me to laugh."

"So… bullying?"

"Yeah, bullying."

"I hate bullies."

"I did too… and then, I married one." Claire shook her head. "It's like there's two of him. There's the sweet, charming, doting man I fell in love with, and then there's this… *thing* he becomes when he's stressed, or no one else is around."

"That sounds like the mask," Audrey said. "Every untreated narcissist has one. Even Susan—she just realized eventually that no one says anything to stop her when she lets it drop. It's how he suckered you into being with him to begin with. Of course, Susan's also an idiopathic primary psyc—"

"Hold on, narcissist?" Claire repeated with surprise, looking up from Audrey's hand. The word hit her like a truck. Three syllables which offered a potential explanation for two decades of erratic behavior.

"Yeah, I thought you knew."

Claire shook her head, her gaze disengaging from Audrey. "I've never looked into… I'm gonna put a pin in that," she said. She returned her attention to the wound. She pulled a final glass fragment out of Audrey's hand, then reached for a bottle of rubbing alcohol. She doused some gauze in the disinfectant, accidentally replacing the bottle half off the table. It tipped off the edge, landed on the floor and began to roll across the room. "Whatever," Claire muttered.

"Sorry, this is going to hurt," she said. She counted to three and pressed the gauze to Audrey's hand. Audrey didn't flinch. After a few seconds, Claire picked out some bandages from the pile.

"I don't know," she continued. "I just figured it was my fault he was being so cold with me. I mean, he never ran out of things to blame me for, so…" Claire sighed. "I guess I thought if I just loved him hard enough, the man I fell in love with would come b—" Her voice broke.

Audrey reached a hesitant hand for Claire's blonde hair, combing through it with clumsy, unpracticed motions. "You can cry," she said softly.

The dam gave way. Claire began sobbing through her teeth, feebly trying and failing to hold the tears back, to not show Audrey how terrified and lost she truly felt. It was no use. The choice she had just made began to spiral up and up and up in her mind, instantaneously fabricating hundreds of stories of her living the rest of her life in misery, even if she survived this.

"Where did he go?" Claire sobbed. "Where's the man I loved?"

"I'm sorry," Audrey replied. "But honestly, he was never real."

"But he gave me so much." Claire sniffed. "Oh God, what am I *doing*? I just left the man who gave me my *entire life*. What am I going to do with myself now?"

Audrey shrugged, but not nonchalantly. She retrieved a tissue from the pile of supplies, offering it to Claire. "Do you have a degree?"

"No," Claire replied tearfully. She dabbed her running mascara. "I dropped out when Marcus and I started dating."

"Then maybe you should go back to school, if that's your thing."

"No," Claire laughed sadly. "I'm way too old for that now."

"You want to talk about old? I'm going gray at fifteen."

"Seriously?" Claire said with surprise.

Audrey pulled her hair around, pointing to the acid-green streak. "What do you think this is covering? With how stressful my life has been, I'll probably look forty by the time I'm twenty."

Claire snorted, wiping her tears. "Well, even if you do, I wouldn't worry. Beauty is ageless. And honestly? It's really not all that important, anyway."

Audrey half-smiled. "You're probably right. But you know, folks over thirty going to college really isn't all that strange these days, from what I hear. Don't do it if you don't want to, but don't let your age be what stops you."

Claire sniffed, thinking back to a version of herself that had faded and entropized nearly into nonexistence over the course of the last two decades. Nearly.

"I loved school," she recalled. "I was just doing my general education, but I *loved* it. Especially physics."

"Sounds like a good place to start," Audrey suggested.

"Yeah," Claire replied, wrapping the bandage around Audrey's hand. "Maybe. What about you, do you know what you want to do yet?"

"Survive the next twenty-four hours," Audrey said dryly. "But if that actually happens, then I want to be a family therapist."

"That… definitely checks out." Claire pulled the bandage snug and adhered it to itself.

Audrey nodded. "Known since I was seven. No one should have it like I did. Now, if you'll excuse me," she flexed her fist experimentally and hopped off the table. "I've had to pee for like, the last three hours."

"Hold on," Claire said.

"I don't think you're understanding the situation."

"Just for a second."

Claire walked toward the private restroom, gradually opening the door and scrutinizing the room for anything that looked like a trap. She flushed the toilet and rapidly backed away from it, half expecting it to explode, only to find it functioning normally. "Alright, this should be safe."

Audrey entered the bathroom, leaving Claire sitting back at the table.

"Tough kid," Claire said under her breath. "Wish she didn't have to be." She pulled the revolver out of her purse and loaded the five bullets she had found with it, snapping the cylinder back into place.

Behind her, she heard a tiny *thud*, followed by the rolling of the alcohol bottle she had dropped. She looked to see the whistleblower, standing behind her and looking like a deer in headlights, holding a rag soaked in fluid.

"Uh… hi," the whistleblower said. "Oh man. Okay. So, um, this is chloroform." She pointed at the rag. "I was just gonna sneak up and… you know…" She gestured vaguely, bobbing her head as though asking Claire to fill in the blank.

Claire stood and turned to reveal the gun, pointing it at the whistleblower with shaking hands.

"Oh, *Jesus*," the whistleblower gasped. "Where did you even *get* that?"

"Back up," Claire said, keeping the tremor out of her voice by transferring it to her knees. "I said, back the *fuck* up. I'll tell you right now, I will kill you where you stand before you ever get near Audrey. She's had more than enough."

"Audrey?" the whistleblower asked, sounding genuinely confused. "We never planned a trial for Audrey."

"I don't fucking believe you," Claire hissed, cocking back the hammer.

"Claire," the whistleblower said with barely suppressed panic. She dropped the rag and held her hands up in surrender. "Think about this. We didn't even know Audrey would *be here*. She was a last-minute plus one, remember? Susan never told us. We wouldn't have time to set anything up even if we wanted to."

Claire paused, the barrel of the revolver lowering ever so slightly. "You're right," she said.

"Jesus Claire, she's a *child*. We're not monsters."

Audrey exited the bathroom. "*God*, that needed to hap—whaaat is going on here?"

"Audrey, stay back," Claire instructed.

"I'm here for *you*, Claire," the whistleblower explained. "*Just* you. You know as well as I do, it wouldn't make any sense to make Audrey face trial."

Claire stared the whistleblower down.

"Take us to the Winner's Circle," Claire demanded. "If not me, then at least her."

"It doesn't work that way, Claire," the whistleblower protested. "The electronic locks on the entrances to the Winner's Circle only open once per passed trial. Because again, *we didn't know she would be here*. She can't go until you do."

"Then just bypass the trial. Tell the system we did it. Or…" Claire turned, looking into the nearest camera. "Or I'll shoot her."

A brief pause, then the building's PA system clicked on. "Seven hundred and twenty-four," the engineer said.

"What?" Claire demanded.

"That's how many pipe bombs I've hidden around the park. If you shoot her, you'll find out where all of them are at the same time."

"But you're here too," Claire pointed out.

"Yes, I am," the engineer replied simply.

Claire's jaw set. "You're here for me? Fine. Then you can have me. But Audrey isn't leaving my sight." She tucked the revolver back into her purse.

The whistleblower stared at Claire with utter confusion. "We're walking into your deathtrap. She'd be at much greater risk with you than apart from you."

"No, she wouldn't," Claire replied. "I've got some stuff to get off my chest."

The whistleblower nodded thoughtfully, a hopeful glint appearing in her eye. "Alright then. Follow me."

ΩCR

**CLAIRE AND AUDREY** followed the whistleblower back to the Garden of Potential. Claire's adrenals were so spent at this point that she hardly experienced any anxiety at all. After all she'd seen and done since they got to the park, walking into her deathtrap felt easy.

"Through here," the whistleblower instructed, unlocking and opening a maintenance door leading into the Hall of Dreamers.

"You first," Claire said to the whistleblower, arms crossed.

"Claire, we're not—"

"I have a gun. You first."

The whistleblower sighed. "Fine," she said, walking inside. "See? No punji pits, no flame jets, no landmines, no friggin' quicksand."

Claire poked her head in first, checking every corner of the room before setting foot inside. It fed directly into the backside of one of the sets. A static figure stood in the light, facing away from her. It took her a moment to realize it was an animatronic. Based on the unkempt white hair and tweed suit, Claire hazarded a guess that it was Albert Einstein.

The set was decorated in a mixture of overgrown and withered, dead plants: blue and yellow flowers, ivy wrapping around the walls, and even the odd mushroom growing out of the planters. Nothing jumped out as a threat, so Claire followed the exact same path the whistleblower had taken.

"Come on." Claire beckoned to Audrey. "It should be safe."

Audrey peeked around the corner and caught sight of the animatronic. "Fine, but if that thing goes Freddy Fazbear on me, I'm running," she said.

The whistleblower led them through the backgrounds of multiple sets—first, Nikolai Tesla, then Marie Curie, then Henry Ford.

Finally, the whistleblower opened a door to a set decorated with miniature wooden flying machines hanging from the ceiling and a large, Italian Renaissance-era desk sitting in the center.

Unlike the others, this one didn't have an animatronic, though there was an empty pedestal toward the front, which suggested there had once been one. Decaying roses threaded the trellis in the back of the room.

A large camera stood opposite them, pointed at the desk, accompanied by an AV cart with an old TV on top. An empty wooden chair with luxurious velvet cushions sat behind the desk. Its armrests and front legs featured undone metal cuffs.

On the historical display across from the Renaissance-era study, Joan of Arc stood restrained to a pike with simulated flames licking her feet. A ballista in the set had been moved to point directly at the chair. The prop had been modified to actually function, with a thick, hyper-extended string looped under three hooks at the back. Rather than an arrow, a large, solid iron ball sat nocked and ready to fire.

"This is you," the whistleblower said awkwardly, gesturing to the chair.

"Claire," Audrey spoke up nervously, "are you sure about this? I mean, once you sit down… there's no going back."

She wasn't sure. But she couldn't let Audrey know that. She locked onto the girl's gaze. "I promise, I'm not going to leave you."

Audrey gritted her teeth and nodded.

Claire sat, laying her arms on the rests with her wrists over the cuffs. Her purse remained looped around her arm. As she settled in the seat, she noticed a red dot hovering directly over the center of her chest, projecting from the front of the ballista. From that position, she could see the iron ball staring back at her like a bogeyman peeking out of the closet.

"Alright," the whistleblower said, fastening Claire's wrists and ankles with sharp *clanks*. "Please keep your arms and legs inside the—"

"Too much," Claire said.

"Yup, sorry."

The whistleblower walked behind the camera and started recording. Claire stared straight into the camera. The TV on the cart flickered on, displaying an image of Marcus staring up at the screen.

"Marcus," Claire uttered in a low voice, the word bursting out of her as though she had been punched in the stomach.

As soon as she saw the man, some insidious failsafe planted deep in her mind activated, playing Claire's favorite memories of him in high, nostalgia-tinted definition. Their first date, where Marcus treated her to hibachi sushi and brought her a solid gold bracelet as a gift. The weeks they'd spent in his forest cabin overlooking a never-ending valley, surviving on sex, wine, and marijuana. Their wedding, where for one beautiful day, Claire saw the man she'd been trying to find again since.

"Hey," Audrey said, breaking through the noise in her head. "He ain't shit."

Claire burst out laughing and nodded. "Thanks."

A door opened in Claire's blind spot, on her left. "Claire Templeton," came the voice of the engineer, not through the ride's PA system, but from right behind her. Claire's spine stiffened. "One way or another, I'm afraid this is going to crush your heart."

"Holy *shit*," Audrey gasped.

Claire heard the engineer's limping, clunky gait first. Metal pieces jangled, hydraulics hissed, and every normal footstep was accompanied by a much sharper sound. But beneath that, Claire heard labored, pained breathing that the old microphones hadn't picked up.

The masked engineer came around into Claire's field of vision, and she finally saw the man in his entirety.

Her breathing quickened. She knew what she was looking at, but some primal part of her brain kept insisting on rejecting it, like a corrupted movie skipping through frames. But the longer she looked, the more horrible details emerged, the less sense it all made.

She traced his skin with her eyes, watching it melt into plastic and metal. Something about the improvised way his elbow articulated with its makeshift prosthetic made Claire's vision glaze over with a sort of protective visual miasma. She could see the steel pieces built into his torso slide at their articulation points like plate mail as he breathed. Something mechanical in his body produced an almost insectile clicking, muffled by his scarred skin.

"Wow," Claire exhaled, tilting her head slightly. She picked out the black and yellow of the Cognito Fall's missing track segment protruding from the engineer's left pant leg. That was one of the few things she could fully understand about his appearance. "I... I'm so sorry this happened to you."

The engineer shook his head, hydraulics hissing with effort. "It had to. But this is about you."

"How did you rig the—"

"A lot of pain, and a lot of stolen morphine. That's how."

"Ah. Sorry. Uh, you're usually just on the TV feeds—why are you here now?"

"You've caught my attention," the engineer responded. "I don't think you all realize just how lucky you are. When my associate first brought me information about the plans to renovate the park, I was originally planning to just bomb the place to kingdom come the instant you all set foot inside. It was *her* who convinced me you were worthy of a second chance. And I'll admit when I'm wrong. If I'd blown you all up, for one thing, Audrey and Jack wouldn't have stood a chance, but it would also have deprived us of this fascinating odyssey you've been on. I'm here to see if you stick the landing."

Claire swallowed.

"Now, let's begin. Claire Templeton, you have found yourself in the Hall of Dreamers, a place—"

"Yeah, I knew," Claire said. "I knew all along. Marcus worked from home as often as he could get away with it. I overheard plenty of meetings." Claire tasted bile in her throat. There was a terrifying quality to the newfound freedom she was exercising. She felt like her words should be incompatible with her mouth.

"*Claire*," Marcus warned, his voice sharpened by audio compression. It was like the word was tapping directly on her eardrum. "You need to think *very* clearly about what you're doing."

"Don't worry, I am," Claire replied. "Anyway, there was... a *lot* of discussion about damage control. And yeah, I had to piece things together with minimal context, but... I actually kind of had a knack for it. Between that and the way he talked to me about work, it didn't take a genius."

The engineer nodded, crossing his mismatched arms. "What specifically did you hear?"

Claire smiled ruefully. "There was one that always stuck with me."

"Now, before we get carried away here..." Marcus began. Claire heard a specific bravado slip into his voice that she'd learned to associate with last-minute press conferences and bloody accident reports.

"I'd like it to be known that Claire's had her struggles, like any of us have. And so if she says something alarming here, something that could *destroy a reputation*, I ask that everyone please give her some grace and remember that everyone makes mistakes when they're hurt. This whole ordeal has been very hard on her and unfortunately, she's been acting out against me to cope. I would just hate for anyone to think less of her if she starts saying things that don't actually align with reality. Claire, honey, I love you so much, and I'm so proud of the life we've built together. What was it you wanted to say?"

Claire faltered. Marcus smiled up at her so *gently*, an expression she'd only seen a handful of times. He loved her. He was *worried* about her. Surely, she couldn't just turn around and—

"Oh, *fuck off*," Audrey groaned. "Pre-emptive inoculation and love bombing. Plain as day."

"What?" Claire asked, attempting to look over her shoulder.

"He's trying to make you sound crazy to anyone who sees this, and then distract you by throwing some pretty words around. Talk is cheap. You're smarter than that."

Claire nodded, refocusing her attention on the camera.

"All of this will be posted online, right?" Claire asked the engineer.

"That's correct," he replied.

"Good. Thanks for the platform." Claire took a deep breath in, eyeing the ballista. Marcus began to interject, but Claire plowed over his words.

"I overheard him talking to some of his employees about a ride whose safety sensors kept acting up and getting the ride shut down. Instead of paying to get the problem diagnosed and fixed, without even looking into *why* they were going off, he told them, 'Just disable the ride sensors. No alarm, no problem.'"

The engineer leaned forward. "Go on," he invited.

"Honey, I think you're misremembering some *very important context*," Marcus said quickly. "And that's not your fault. I know the business talk can be hard to keep up with. What I said was, 'Let's just disable the ride *censors*.' In this business, people are always trying to tell you what is and is not within the 'laws of known physics.' I was saying if we stop listening to the people trying to *censor* us, there won't be any *alarm* at the company."

"You see this?" Claire's voice cracked as she regarded the engineer. "You see what I have to deal with? He does this… this *shit* to me all the time, and I know it's wrong but I can't put words to *why*. And then I get into these weeks-long self-doubt spirals where I feel like I'm going insane, making things up that never actually happened. He calls me forgetful, talks down to me, twists details *just* enough—I can *feel* it but I don't know how to *prove* it, even to myself. But now I'm looking back, and… I was *twenty* when we started dating. He was *forty-two*. He could have told me fire is cold, and I probably would have believed him."

"*Wow*," the engineer muttered.

"The *really* sick part is, any time I tried to bring it up, he somehow convinced me that *I* was the one twisting things, when all I was doing was saying what I saw with my own eyes. I know what I saw. This man would just outright refuse to pay vendors and throw his entire legal team at any small distributor who tried to speak up. This man cheated hundreds of employees out of thousands of overtime hours. The way this man speaks to his subordinates sometimes makes *me* want to smack him. This man illegally fired and blacklisted at least one employee for whistleblowing, *bare* minimum. *Just today,* he abandoned his assistant of ten years, refusing to help at all when he was captured.

"And… so did I. I'm sorry, Jack. But we're *barely* scratching the surface here. And if that's how he treats the people he does business with, it should give you a good idea of what he thinks of his *guests*. It makes his record make a lot more sense."

"*Quiet!*" Marcus shouted. "You are destroying… *years* of goodwill I've accumulated for us with these lies, Claire. And why? Just to humiliate me on camera?"

He sighed, appearing heartbroken and defeated. "Everyone, I'm so sorry you all have to witness my wife's clear nervous breakdown. You have to understand; this is what she *does*—she takes the tiniest little kernels of truth and spins these wild stories out of them. Oftentimes, it's something I actually love and admire about her. Her mind is so creative, so *vivid*, but sometimes that means she can't tell fantasy from reality."

"Yikes," Audrey chuckled dryly.

"If there really *was* a problem, though, you should have told me. You had *all this time* to do that. You know I would hear you out. I think this has a lot more to do with you *understandably* cracking under the pressure of this situation than it does my supposed 'mistakes.'"

"Oh, that's DARVO," Audrey identified. "Deny, attack, reverse victim and offender. It's like projection's older, meaner sibling."

"That's a thing?" Claire said with surprise. "I thought that was just something *he* did."

"You need to stop butting in while I'm talking to my wife," Marcus said coldly.

"Oh, your wife? You mean the one you said you're gonna *divorce?*" Audrey grinned.

"God, there's so much I could say," Claire said. "I could talk about his bullshit all night."

Across the ride's track, the ballista clicked once ominously.

"What was that?" Claire asked, her humor immediately overwritten by dread.

"That was one of your two warnings," The engineer replied. "We're not here to vent about your ex. We're finding out if you deserve to live or die."

Audrey leaped forward with a cry of desperate fury, prompting the whistleblower to restrain her before she could get to Claire.

"Try that again, and we end the trial right now," the engineer threatened.

"Audrey, it's alright," Claire said resolutely. "I can do this." She gulped, her eyes fixed on the heavy iron ball lying in wait.

"Okay, here's the thing," she sighed. "There's plenty more I could say. I mean, there *really* is. But you're right, that's not what this is about. Because the fact is, I saw how Marcus ran his business—the hostile environment, the cut corners… and the lives lost and destroyed as a direct consequence. And I could have stopped it or at least gotten the right eyes on it whenever I wanted. Sure, he kept work hidden from me pretty well at first, and I wasn't all that interested in it anyway. But he started getting less careful. And I started getting…*bored.*

"It became clear pretty fast that Marcus wasn't operating above board. I knew that better than most. But he was also the man I loved, and so I told myself he was just a good man who occasionally did necessary evil. That it was just business as usual. And, if I'm being honest… I didn't want to lose the lifestyle his job offered us, either. So I just tried not to think about it. I was a coward. It was disgusting."

"A testimony from the CEO's wife would go a long way in terms of public attention," the engineer said. "It would have attracted a major scandal. It could have saved lives."

Claire nodded guiltily. "Yeah, it could have. That's on me. I told myself over and over again that there must be something I'm not understanding. I thought if the love of my life kept insisting on the same narrative, it must be true. But I should have trusted my instincts. My *memory.*"

"Do you hear how *unstable* this woman is?" Marcus laughed nervously, gesturing toward the screen. "Secretly eavesdropping on my private phone calls—who in their right mind would do that?"

"I just *told* you I was doing it earlier today," Claire countered. "You thought it was cute then. And besides, it's hardly eavesdropping since you started taking your calls in the dining room. Did you just think I was too stupid to put the details together for myself?"

"Even if you put the details together, you never had the balls to speak up until now, when your life is on the line," Marcus attacked.

"Yeah, that's true. That's pretty awful of me. And if I get out of here, I'm gonna spend the rest of my life learning how to make up for that. But now you're saying there *was* something to piece together, Marcus. Because you know what you've gotten up to as well as I do, don't you?"

Marcus watched the stock of his social currency plummet in real time. "I… I have given you *everything* for the last nineteen years."

"This again," Audrey scoffed.

"I asked *nothing* in return but loyalty, and you can't even give me that much? All I'm asking here is that you stick up for me for *once*, Claire."

"No," Claire said. "No. You're not. You're asking me to die for you."

"That was transactional gratitude again," Audrey chimed in. "But I think you're starting to get the hang of this."

"I guess while I'm at it…" Claire hesitated, fidgeting. "The months we spent in Dubai came the same year he deferred maintenance on the Wyrm Coaster and fudged the numbers. The next year, the collapse happened. It was my fault the trip was that expensive. There was…" She sighed at how frivolous the truth sounded. "There was a limited-edition purse that I really wanted."

"Wow." The engineer tilted his head as Marcus started up a volley of screamed protests. "I didn't even—hold on." The engineer clicked a button on the TV's remote control, muting Marcus. "I didn't even know about that one. That's pretty bad, Claire."

"Yeah, it is. But not as bad as when I knowingly repeated lies to the press to protect his image. Like, the image management that had to take place after the drop tower incident in Oklahoma? I played a pretty big role in that one specifically. Also, the swing ride in California, and that disaster in Ohio's Tunnel of Love. I did some DARVO of my own. And if anyone hates me for that, I get it. I have that coming. I'm sorry."

"You're ahead of me," the engineer said with approval. "Well, we've already gone over my main concerns, and then some. Is there anything else you want to add while you have this 'platform,' Claire?"

Claire shifted in her seat, thinking carefully. She had so much dirt on Marcus, she could entomb all of Dreamscape. All of Radiant Realms. There was a terrible thrill in it—like an assassin choosing which tendon to sever to best cripple their target.

But then, she stared at Marcus's face through the CRT fuzz. He was *fuming*, still screaming furiously. Maybe it was the high angle, but Claire could distinctly see the desperate, child-like pain behind his rage. There was a time when seeing that pain would trigger an all-consuming protectiveness in Claire. It was a time that hadn't entirely passed.

She realized that even now, she didn't hate him. She could never hate someone she spent so much of her life loving.

"Marcus," Claire said softly, with a kind of warm finality in her voice. "Marcus." On the live feed, he mutely began to settle down and look at the screen.

"I'm sorry," Claire said. "Not for anything I supposedly did. *Never* for that again. But I'm sorry that this is who you are. I'm sorry you were raised to think life is a zero-sum game, other people are just resources to be used, and acquisition is all there is. I know you better than just about anyone, even if I still feel like I've never quite seen all of you. And I can say, it must be *exhausting* to be Marcus Templeton. Beneath the bravado, I know the ache. I know the paranoia. I know the self-loathing. And I know you treat me so cruelly because you once had to do these things just to survive."

She gritted her teeth. "But it *hurts*, Marcus. You *know* it hurts. You always told me you would change, but you never did. I burned out my friends and family, crying to them over the same problems again and again. And even if you *were* changing, I can't keep getting caught in the collateral. I can't."

Marcus stared daggers at Claire.

"You're going to face trial next, Marcus. So dig deep and find your buried heart. I know it's in there somewhere. If you're really capable of change, then *prove it*. I genuinely hope you make the right choice."

Marcus didn't react, glaring up at the screen and breathing so hard she could see his nostrils flex.

A lump formed in Claire's throat. "And no matter what happens next, Marcus… thank you for the good times. I'll always cherish those. I want you to know that." She sighed. "Alright, I've done what I can."

"Well, aren't you something?" the engineer mused.

Claire's restraints were released. She quickly got to her feet and out of the ballista's line of fire. The whistleblower shut the camera and TV off. Audrey ran up to Claire, gripping the sleeve of her dress like it was a source of sustenance.

"Congratulations," the whistleblower said, approaching them. "If you both come with me, I'll take you to the Winner's Circle."

The three of them walked out of the room together. As she crossed the threshold, Claire looked back at the engineer and awkwardly waved goodbye. The engineer waved back with a slight delay.

The whistleblower parted a curtain of ivy, exposing a small keyhole. She reached into her pocket and produced an overburdened key ring, sliding the first into the lock. She twisted, revealing a secret corridor.

"Oh, *hell* yes," Audrey uttered gleefully.

They walked through the dimly lit hall toward a heavy steel door covered in deadbolt locks. The whistleblower began working through them one by one, slowly exhausting the key ring.

Next, she flipped over a wall panel to expose a keypad. She sighed heavily.

The whistleblower proceeded to spend the next twenty seconds straight inputting a sequence of numbers. "Crap, that was supposed to be a three, hold on," the whistleblower muttered, resetting the keypad.

When she finished inputting the code, the whistleblower opened the door to reveal a small, round room with a white pedestal in the center. On top of the pedestal was an opulent, ivory puzzle box.

"Are we… still going to the Winner's Circle?" Claire asked hesitantly.

"Hold on," the whistleblower repeated, picking up the box and turning it over in her hands. "Okay, first you press, then twist, then… what the fuck?"

"Oh, cool," Audrey said. "No, go ahead. Mess with the creepy puzzle box. It's not like we have enough problems already."

The whistleblower slowly morphed the cube into a shape resembling an ant's bent antenna, then walked back out of the tunnel.

"Wh…" Claire and Audrey glanced at each other, shrugged, and followed.

The whistleblower brought them three rooms over, through a locked door with another long keycode, and toward a wall with a faded poster. On the poster, Andy the Ant stared at them with hollow, insectoid eyes, declaring in bold font "**INTEGRITY** means doing the right thing when no one is watching." His stinger was exceptionally long and girthy in this drawing.

The whistleblower took the poster down, revealing a crack in the wall behind it. She fit the solved puzzle box into the crack up to the antenna's joint and began winding it counterclockwise. A resonant series of creaks echoed through the dusty hallway as the entire wall panel swung open.

Behind the wall, an elevator stood with open doors.

"Huh. I guess an entrance *was* in this zone after all," Claire said. "We just never stood a chance to actually find it."

"Take the elevator," the whistleblower instructed. "It opens directly into the lounge. Congratulations again." She turned to leave.

"Hey," Claire called. "Thanks for sticking up for us."

The whistleblower smiled over her shoulder. "Thanks for making it worthwhile. Go make better choices, alright?"

Claire laughed. "Alright."

Claire and Audrey walked into the elevator, the door sliding shut behind them.

There were only two buttons on the control panel: one was illuminated and read "EARTH," and the other said "HEAVEN." Claire's finger hovered over "HEAVEN," hesitating.

"What?" Audrey asked.

"It could be a trap," Claire replied.

"Got any other ideas?"

Claire pushed "HEAVEN," and the elevator began descending.

The air was heavy in the elevator as the two struggled to process all that had led to this point. The elevator continued its descent, humming quietly. The lights were soft. The walls were covered in mahogany wood. A long mirror spanned one wall on their left. As the elevator continued to descend, Claire finally worked up the nerve to look at it.

"Oh, *man*," she laughed grimly. Her makeup was beyond salvaging. Claire's tears had carved a mascara-blackened path through her foundation and concealer, exposing the pre-wrinkles underneath. Her lipstick had all but eroded. Her eyeshadow blurred into her smudged eyeliner, half-melted off.

She was beautiful.

"I can't wait to get this crap off my face," Claire said dryly.

Audrey laughed for a little too long. It turned from genuine and warm to hollow, like she wasn't really there. The elevator continued its descent.

"Are you okay?" Claire asked.

Audrey shrugged. "Those guys killed my parents." She burst out laughing, a series of razor-thin wheezes like her vocal cords were made of sandpaper.

"I'm sorry," Claire said.

"I looked my parents' killers dead in the fucking eyes, Claire. And you know what I felt? *Nothing.* Cuz they *didn't* kill my parents, did they? Not actually. The only time I was actually mad at them was when they threatened you. Cuz honestly? I kinda get where they're coming from."

Claire tensed as Audrey verbalized the very thought she'd been trying to avoid thinking.

"*All* they had to do was own up," Audrey scoffed. "It's fucked up. It's *so* fucked up because the first adult who ever *really* stood up for me was the fucking engineer. I mean, he *fought* for me during Stuart's trial. And all I could think was 'why do I feel grateful to this guy? Is this the closest I'll ever get to a safe adult in my life? *This?*" Audrey shook her head, staring at the elevator doors. "But then, not ten minutes later, you came along."

Claire shrugged modestly. "I couldn't just stand there and watch it happen."

"Everyone else did."

"Yeah… I guess they did." Claire sighed. "Thanks, kiddo. But look, like I said before, I think the last thing you want to do right now is judge your emotions. Sometimes when things get to be too much, everything just shuts off. It happens to me too—sometimes that's the only way to get through it. But grief is strange. It can creep up on you in waves."

"I'll believe it when I see it," Audrey replied.

As the elevator descended, she began to sniff, then let out small, halting huffs of air. Claire opened her arms, and Audrey leaned against her without a word, crying softly. Claire found herself shedding tears, too. For Audrey, for herself, Jack, Stuart, Janet, the whistleblower, the engineer, and for the decades of trauma that haunted this park and others like it to this very day. Even for Marcus.

For the fact that they were finally done. For the fact that they would never be the same.

"I'm still here, baby," Claire said through her tears, as much to herself as it was to Audrey. "I'm not going anywhere."

At long last, the elevator arrived at its destination, letting out a sharp *ding*.

When the door opened, Claire's heart dropped. The elevator opened into a void—complete and utter darkness. For a heartbeat, she was sure they'd been lured into another trap, that Jack was dead and they were next.

But then, off to the side, she could see the soft glow of light. She peeked around the corner to see a neon sign hanging on a brick wall, pointing toward a single doorway off to the right. It read in angular cursive "*Where Dreams Come True.*"

"Oh my God, we made it," Claire exhaled. "Come on, let's go."

The void that the elevator had opened onto was a complete wall of inky, glassy blackness spanning the entire length of the hall.

"Where *are* we?" Audrey asked.

The stagnant odor was what hit Claire first—time had fossilized the organic, sour, *human* stench left in the recycled air by the lounge's previous occupants.

"Oh, *Jesus*," Claire gasped upon rounding the corner. She instinctively put her nose into the crook of her elbow.

The Winner's Circle seemed to have been abandoned at extremely short notice. The white-marble-and-gold-laced columns of the walls clashed with the blue and pink neon lights, casting a surreal glow onto the bottles of liquor strewn about the floor. Fur carpets were laid out for every kind of wildcat. Glassy tables still had lines of cocaine laid out next to hypodermic needles, glass pipes, and rotten food.

But that was nothing compared to the state of the couches. They lined every wall, circling two dancing poles. For some godforsaken reason, they had been upholstered in white. Consequently, the club's sordid history spoke for itself in a colorful constellation of stains punctuated by the occasional tainted contraceptive.

And then, to put a hat on a hat, the walls were lined with portraits of people wearing anteater face masks and little else, performing acts consistent with the darkest aspects of the club's reputation. And worse. Claire's constricted, empty stomach turned.

There were TVs mounted in the corners of the room, but there wasn't a single security camera to be seen. A neon sign overlooking the debauchery read: "*Go Wild!*"

Another void-like wall wrapped around one side of the lounge.

"Uh, Audrey," Claire uttered as the girl rounded the corner. "Don't look at the walls, okay? Or the couches. Or the tables. Just… just look at the floor. Just not *that* part of the floor. *Oh*, look at the black wall, okay?"

Audrey stared at Claire incredulously. "Alright," she said unconvincingly.

Jack stood at the far end of the lounge, looking exhausted but unharmed.

"Jack," Claire breathed, rushing forward and hugging him tightly.

Jack grinned. "Thank God you're alright, Mrs. Templeton."

"You too," Claire replied. "I can't believe you're still awake."

Jack chuckled nervously. "I've been too scared to lie down anywhere. Or sit. I feel like I'll catch something just by staring too long."

"I think I know the feeling."

"Am I allowed to look at Jack, or…?" Audrey asked dryly.

"Oh m—*yes*, you can look at Jack," Claire groaned.

"Uh, there are some *sealed* bottles of water over there," Jack offered. Claire passed one to Audrey before taking one herself. She drank the whole bottle in one shot, only then realizing how thirsty she'd been.

"This isn't a wall," Audrey said, staring into the darkness. "It's a window."

"I don't like the sound of that, Audrey," Claire replied.

"She's right," Jack said. "I think we're seeing the deepest part of the Dreamlake. And since it's the middle of the night, it just looks like… nothing."

"How could that pathetic lake we saw before be this *deep*?" Claire marveled.

"Creepy," Audrey muttered, tapping the glass.

"Where's this exit tunnel?" Claire asked.

"Over there," Jack said, pointing to a door tucked away in the back of the room marked "EMERGENCY EXIT."

"It's electronically locked, though," he added. "Until Marcus is done."

"Right," Claire muttered.

"Do you want some wine?" Jack offered, gesturing toward a table lined with bottles. "I found a few that were unopened. It's helped me take the edge off."

"No," Claire said.

"Yes," Audrey said at the same time.

"I want to be clear headed for what comes next," Claire explained. "I mean, they're probably… tracking him down right now." Helplessness and resignation tangoed in her mind.

"Fair enough, makes sense," Jack shrugged.

Audrey picked up one of the wine bottles, opened it, and took a long drink.

"*Audrey,*" Claire gasped.

"What?" Audrey asked, taking another swig. "You gonna tell my parents?" Claire let the girl drink.

"How are you holding up, Mrs. Templeton?" asked Jack.

"Just 'Claire' is fine, Jack. I can definitely say I'm ready for this night to be over." Claire's voice sounded horribly weary. "But all things considered, I'm actually feeling… pretty good. Lighter. But also, like I need to run into the woods and reinvent myself from the ground up."

Jack laughed.

"What about you?" She asked.

"Well… once my confession goes live, I'm probably gonna have to go to court. That kind of… negligence can actually be considered criminal. They might go easy on me since I confessed and gave them information, but I'm probably gonna have to spend some time in prison."

"I'm sorry," Claire said.

"Don't be," Jack replied. "Maybe if I pay my dues, I'll finally be able to sleep at night."

Claire managed to find a spot on the floor that didn't seem to be soiled in some way. She sat down, feeling an immense release of tension in her legs.

"Oooh *fuck,* I'm tired," she grunted, working her knuckle into her calf muscles. Now that she could truly rest, her breaths became slow and deep, calming her even if it delivered larger amounts of the rancid air into her lungs.

She had done it. She had survived the engineer's brutal game, and she was leaving a toxic marriage. And now, she had to live out the rest of her life accepting whatever came as a consequence.

It was equal parts terrifying and exhilarating. For the first time in nineteen years, Claire's future was uncertain. She sat, quietly pondering the seismic shift that had taken place in her life over the last twenty-four hours.

Next to her foot, she saw a small metal keychain lying on the floor. It was a tiny, cartoonish figure of Andy the ant in perfect condition other than a layer of dust. Claire picked it up, turning it around in her fingers. "If he were actually this cute, he probably would have grown on me," she laughed to herself. She slipped it into her purse.

Audrey found a clean place to sit near the black window, cradling the wine bottle like a teddy bear, staring out as though she had a chance of seeing anything that might be lurking in the dark. Jack finally gave in, joining them on the floor.

The three sat in silence for what could have been five, twenty, or forty-five minutes. Claire stared blankly at a green handprint on one of the couch cushions, wondering how in God's name it got there. She was brought back to attention when the TVs snapped on.

"Here we go," she said grimly, getting to her feet.

Marcus was in a loading station built like a cave, restrained to a boat floating in a narrow channel of water. Two feeds from the front of the boat were displayed on different TVs—one pointing at Marcus and one pointing at the track.

With no person or voice to orient Marcus, the boat began to slowly drift forward.

"Hey, *let me out!*" Marcus shouted, straining against his cuffs. Double doors opened into a white room turned yellow with age. There were two animatronics: a young, handsome man with a handlebar mustache who was lying on a couch, and an older man holding a clipboard sitting in a chair next to him.

"Now Mr. Wilder, what's got you so upset?" the therapist animatronic asked, his delivery wooden and staccato.

"I… I dreamed about him again," the overly flattering Gideon Wilder animatronic said. It represented an era long before even the downfall of

Dreamscape, back when he had black hair, a skinny physique, and evidently, an actual chin.

"Who did you dream about?"

"*Klaus.*"

"We've been over this, Mr. Wilder. Klaus isn't real."

"But that doesn't do anything about the *dream*," Gideon protested as Marcus's boat crept along the periphery of the set. "I've had it nearly every month since I was a boy."

"Would it help to go through it again?"

"Maybe," Gideon said thoughtfully. "I guess there's no harm in trying."

Marcus turned left onto a purple, starry tube as he was thrust into Gideon's nightmare.

"Oh shit, that's kinda dope," Audrey muttered.

Marcus struggled against his restraints, grunting with anger.

"It always starts like this," said Gideon's echoing, distorting voice. "I'm on a big, industrial fishing boat, on this humongous lake."

Marcus pulled into the next room, which Claire first thought opened to the night sky before realizing it was just that large.

"Wow," she whispered. The boat carrying Marcus was floating through what by all accounts seemed like open water. Seamlessly painted walls blended into the water, heightening the illusion. Fog poured into the room from concealed machines, further obscuring the divide between set and backdrop.

The room's centerpiece was a nearly life-size model of an industrial fishing vessel. Another Gideon animatronic stood on the deck in a perfectly clean three-piece suit, surrounded by waterlogged, grimy sailors. He pointed adventurously out past Marcus, toward the horizon. A net full of fish hung suspended over the water.

"We'd been in the biz long enough to have hit our fair share of natural jackpots. But this lake was *different.*"

"I'm going to sue both of you to hell and back," Marcus threatened. "Don't you know who I am? *You can't do this!*"

No response came. Marcus moved through into the next room. Another boat set—this time the ride track bisected the ship. The sailors could be seen dancing joyfully around a large pile of fish. The fish glowed as embedded light strips sent rainbow ripples across their bodies.

Claire squinted at the background of the set. It seemed like there was a mass floating some distance away, or perhaps a part of something larger beneath the surface. Before she could determine what it was, the shape went out of the camera's frame.

"A new species," Gideon's voiceover said eagerly. "The lake was *infested* with them. And what's more, they were *delicious*."

The mechanical fish flopped about weakly. Their eyes were large, cartoonish and kid-friendly, an uncanny detail which stuck out to Claire as she watched them suffocate.

The next set. Gideon had returned to land, now being shown busily writing paperwork at an office desk in a lavish library.

"I got to work. Distributing this fish anywhere that was buying. And *everyone* was buying. Before I knew it, we were going back out into the lake every day."

"But it wouldn't last, would it?" asked the therapist.

"No."

Marcus leaned toward one of his metal restraints as if to pry it open with his teeth, then thought better of it. "I'm not scared of you," he claimed shrilly.

The next set. Gideon was standing as polished as ever at the lake shore, talking to a blatantly racist, nonspecific caricature of a tribal Native.

"Well, that aged like ground beef," Audrey commented.

"The Natives from the nearby village caught wind of my operation, and they told me to stop. They said that in their village, they take only what they need so both they and the fish can thrive. They said it was the natural way. But they were… unsophisticated. They didn't realize what they had. All I wanted to do was share it with the world. And all the while, the demand was only going higher. I tried to explain to their elder the good that this was doing, but he wouldn't hear about it, even when I offered them a cut. He told me that if I kept taking… then Klaus would come to restore the balance."

Marcus drifted into the next room, which opened into complete blackness. Marcus let out a cry of surprise. The front-facing camera turned to the left, showing two massive, glowing green eyes staring out of the dark, disconcertingly close. Each was larger than Claire's torso. The light affixed to the bow of the boat hardly did a thing to penetrate the dark.

"And who *is* Klaus?" the therapist asked, his voice echoing through the dark, empty room.

"They call him the Equalizer. Some kind of monster they say lives at the bottom of the lake, clinging to how things work in the natural world." Gideon's voiceover sighed. "And sure, maybe that way worked before we were clever enough to invent capitalism, but this is the twentieth century, for God's sake! Everyone has to make sacrifices to get ahead."

A deep rumbling resonated through the room Marcus was trapped in as the glowing eyes lowered down, down, beneath the surface of the water.

"How… how much money do you want?" Marcus uttered. "Name your price. Anything."

No response.

"So, what could I do?" Gideon continued. "I went back out on the water one last time. And every time since I was a boy, I've known *exactly* what will happen next. But I can't control my body."

The next room showed Gideon back on his ship, but the setting had changed. The sky and water were illuminated with red light. Gideon stood off balance, clinging to the side of the ship as massive, black tentacles ascended out of the water, thrashing about with claimed pieces of the vessel.

"He comes out as soon as I get into open water," Gideon said, genuine fear in the actor's voice. It made Claire wonder if the founder had voiced it himself. "He rips my ship to pieces, then finally snaps it in half."

A loud *crack* played as the ship's set split apart. Marcus watched the spectacle unfold uneasily.

"But that's not where it ends, is it?" the therapist asked.

"*No*," was Gideon's whispered reply. "He comes for me next, wraps his tentacles around me, and pulls me under."

Marcus's boat turned a tight corner into another black void. The sound of rushing water faded in.

"I never knew just how *deep* the lake was until he pulled me down."

Marcus screamed as the track gave out under him and he fell down an angled shaft. The drop was long. The drop was *extremely* long. He was gasping for air before it was over. And then, at long last, he made it to the bottom, kicking up a massive wave of water all over himself.

He passed through a section of track where the walls were decorated with scraps of the shipwreck, then found himself in a narrow tunnel lined in black. All was silent aside from his grunts of fury and disorientation.

"Claire," Audrey interjected.

"Huh?" Claire asked distractedly.

"Look." Audrey pointed deep into the abyssal, black window, and off in the distance, Claire could see a small light moving in perfect tandem with the live feed.

"Is that… *Marcus?*" Claire asked. She glanced back up at the black walls lining the tunnel Marcus was in, then realized that they, too, were windows. His boat slowed to a stop.

Gideon's voiceover returned, sharp and haunted. "He doesn't eat me, he just holds me underwater and stares at me until I drown."

A deep, rumbling bass note rippled through the Winner's Circle. It wasn't coming from the TVs. It was coming from *outside.*

"What was that?" Claire asked anxiously, squinting out the window.

Another deep rumble came, the chest-rattling register of a tuba.

And then, a series of red lights came on. There was no need for Claire to check the live feed, because it was *right there.*

"Oh *God,*" Audrey screamed, pinwheeling her arms as she stumbled away from the window.

"*What the fuck is that?*" Jack yelled.

The deepest point of the Dreamlake had been rigged with several extremely powerful lights, illuminating in vivid detail what had always been waiting in the depths.

Klaus was, in his own way, magnificent. The animatronic's head alone was at least forty feet across. The bulbous cranium of an octopus was scarred by the presence of multiple mouths distorting the silhouette. They were lined with jagged, serrated teeth of random shapes and sizes. He had well over eight tentacles, each of them sprawling across the floor of the Dreamlake, some of them connecting to each other in random places to form a pseudo-organic tangle. The sides of each tentacle were equipped with hooked barbs like centipede legs. Each sucker was a circular mouth with a rim of mismatched teeth.

Klaus *breathed.* Claire watched the thin, manufactured skin of his head pulse as air bubbles escaped his massive siphons. Under the thinly stretched skin-like material, Claire could see the slick shine of silicone organs. The low sound was deafening, all but drowning out Marcus's scream of terror.

His *eyes.* Klaus's glaring, green eyes followed Marcus's tiny vessel as it came to a rest near a closed gate at the end of the tunnel, conveying a kind of vicious, primal contempt. It was clear this was the aspect the crew had spent the longest time and highest budget on perfecting. They were the eyes of something older, smarter, stronger, and utterly apathetic.

Another feed appeared on a few of the TVs within the Winner's Circle. The whistleblower, not the engineer, sat in front of a camera with a cold look of disdain on her face.

"Hi, Marcus," she said with vindictive glee. "You've awoken to find yourself aboard Up Close with Klaus the Kraken."

Marcus thrashed in his restraints, staring up in terror at the animatronic looming over him. Two of Klaus's tentacles were pounding on the clear tube he was trapped in.

"Impressive, isn't he?" The whistleblower grinned. Marcus watched through a TV on a cart along the side of the track. "I hope you like him, because we blocked off the exit."

The waterway just ahead of Marcus came to an abrupt stop at a set of metal grate-like gates that had been welded shut.

"So, let me just ask you a few questions now that you two are acquainted," the whistleblower said coyly. "And as a reminder, you are being recorded and this will be posted to the internet one way or another. But don't worry. All you have to do if you want to survive is tell the truth."

Marcus had one foot in reality, at best. He looked exhausted, sallow, pale, like a bloated corpse. He stared up at Klaus with lethargic, petrified fear.

"You're in *deep,* Marcus," the whistleblower said. "Figuratively and literally. Not even *we* have an easy way to get to you right now. The only way out is through a secret tunnel to the Winner's Circle hidden somewhere in the shipwreck section you just passed through. If you confess, we'll tell you where it is and give you the key code."

Marcus's gaze drifted about the tunnel.

"Oh, and just so you're aware," the whistleblower pointed out, "we've also planted a couple of bombs in this tube."

A counter reading five minutes appeared static on the bottom of every screen.

"Once we begin, you'll have five minutes to start talking, or we detonate. Any piece of you unfortunate enough to be connected to a functioning brain afterward will have the lake to reckon with."

"I won't…" Marcus began, his voice already sounding defeated. "I won't slander myself for your amusement."

"That won't work, Marcus," the whistleblower replied coolly. "It's not slander. I saw the evidence firsthand. And then you ruined my career. But Marcus… I kept the *receipts*. Every deleted security tape. Every NDA. Every chatlog."

This got Marcus's attention.

"Two hundred and seven deaths. Four hundred and sixty-eight injuries. All on your watch," the whistleblower said scornfully. "Not because they had to happen, but because your priority was never safety. Because you never wanted to make an entertainment company. You just wanted to make money."

"*That's not true*," Marcus said angrily. "How *dare* you reduce all I've accomplished like this—*no one* cares about integrity more than I do. Ask Ja— uh, ask anyone."

"Then let's begin."

The timer blinked and read 4:59. 4:58.

"Alright, if we're doing this, we're doing it on *my* terms," Marcus blustered.

"What?" the whistleblower replied.

"What?" Claire and Audrey said at the same time.

"I want everyone who's watching to remember who it is we're talking about here," Marcus explained. "I'm *Marcus Templeton*. I'm a Florida success story. I rebuilt these parks, I kept the lights running, and I provided a service. The service of *nostalgia*. Every day out, every holiday weekend and family vacation, the *formative memories of your childhood*—who made that happen? I did. I was working sixteen-hour days before most of you could even walk. I poured every ounce of myself into this company. And sure, mistakes happen, and sometimes people die, which is terrible. But it's also… inevitable? And it's all in service of creating the best experience possible for you and your family. And from the bottom of my heart, I am very sorry if you think that some bad memories may be related to my company."

The whistleblower nodded solemnly. "Cool. If you're done, you now have four minutes and twenty-one seconds to start telling the truth. We can start whenever you're ready."

"Oh my God, he's an idiot," Claire exhaled in disbelief. "Has he *always* been an idiot?"

"Yes," Jack and Audrey replied simultaneously.

The whistleblower picked up a heavy stack of papers and set them in front of her.

"Incident number one of six hundred and twenty-three," the whistleblower began.

"This night is never going to end, is it?" Claire groaned.

"Look at that—opening day of your very first park renovation!" The whistleblower pointed at the sheet. "An entire bloodline was ended when you decided to cheap out on a wooden coaster's up-stop wheels. They hit that hard corner and the whole car went flying. Does your opinion align with these facts?"

"That's not what hap—" Marcus began.

Klaus slammed his tentacles into the tube, accompanied by another loud, droning bass note.

"Alright then, champ, we can circle back to that one," the whistleblower said curtly, flipping over the sheet of paper. "Incident number *two* of six hundred and twenty-three."

What followed was a sort of verbal duel, with the whistleblower pivoting from one incident to the next and Marcus confidently denying culpability in all of them. He managed to waste two minutes and thirty seconds that way.

A pit formed in Claire's stomach as she realized she may be about to watch her husband die. But at the same time...

"I really thought he would get his shit together, just this once," Claire muttered. "I... I wanted to believe he *could*."

"He's living in a maze of his own making," Jack said grimly. "I've seen it. All the lies he has to keep track of. All the different narratives he's living. I don't think he knows what truth *is* anymore."

Marcus's face had finally reached full magenta. "I *never* claimed Ever-After Falls was 'completely safe.' I make a point to never use that phrase in press conferences."

"*Really,*" the whistleblower retorted, putting a video onscreen of Marcus at a press conference claiming Ever-After Falls is completely safe.

"That's AI," Marcus replied.

"He's never going to change, is he?" Claire sighed, stepping away from the window in the Winner's Circle. "He's going to *die* because optics are more important to him than life itself. Does he even understand that?"

"Probably not," Audrey piped up. "I think this is the first time he's ever faced a consequence."

"When she lays it all out like that, though…" Claire sighed. "*Six hundred and twenty-three* preventable incidents. And he hasn't apologized for a single one. Not once. Not to mention everything wrong with our marriage." She clenched her fist so hard, she thought her knuckles would crack and break. "If this is how he's going to play it, maybe he has it coming."

Audrey stared at her with surprise. "Damn, Claire," she said with approval.

"Alright, *fine,*" the whistleblower said with frustration. The timer read 1:16. "I guess it's easy enough to deny when the victims aren't here to tell their side of the story, isn't it? Then let's move on to something a little more personal. The whistleblower incident last year. You took an employee who hardly ever called in sick, worked overtime during company crises, kept the company's communication flowing, and *never even asked for a raise,* and you *ruined her career.* Why did you do that, Marcus? *Why did you do that?*"

"You were a *liability,*" Marcus seethed. "Going over my head to OSHA and getting all these citations slapped on us—What were you *thinking?*"

"I *tried* to go through your channels—it went nowhere. I was sick of how you ran that company. I was sick of *looking* good being more important than *being* good. I was sick of… watching kids die."

"Imagine how *I* feel," Marcus argued. "I had to deal with the legal fallout from all of those incidents *and* I had an employee betray me. As if I didn't have enough on my plate, running the company that paid your bills."

"You have *forty-five seconds* to say something truthful," the whistleblower reported. "I don't know what more I can say to you. You're going to die, and the world will keep turning. I hope it was all worth it."

Marcus eyed the timer nervously and finally broke. "Wait," he said. Claire blinked.

"You want the truth?" Marcus asked. "I'll give you the truth, alright?"

The whistleblower froze the timer. "Start talking."

"Okay, for starters, I'm sorry that some people are under the impression that my team was at times a bit too frugally minded—"

The timer started again and jumped down to twenty seconds. "That's for wasting my time," the whistleblower said.

"*I don't know what you want me to say,*" Marcus screamed.

"You know what, Marcus? As much as I hate your guts, I wanted you to survive this. I wanted you to prove that people can change. I wanted you to give a semblance of justice for the lives lost and ruined. But there is nothing in you to give. Nothing. All you know how to do is take, and take, and *take.*"

The timer ticked down to five seconds as the engineer walked into frame behind the whistleblower. "Wealth is a sick man's game," he said simply. "Goodbye, Marcus." Claire took a deep breath in and prepared for the worst. Marcus's face screwed up in anticipation.

The timer reached zero, and nothing happened.

"What?" the whistleblower uttered.

"What's going on?" the engineer asked, sitting beside her and looking around the control panel in front of them.

"I-I don't know," the whistleblower replied.

"I just checked those bombs myself this morning—there's no reason they should short out," the engineer spoke in a low, urgent voice.

"Watch out for the coffee—" the whistleblower warned, before an offscreen mug tilted over onto the control panel.

"*Shit,*" the whistleblower hissed, blotting the spill with her shirt. In doing so, she accidentally flipped a switch.

At the bottom of the Dreamlake, Marcus's restraints released. Claire heard the emergency exit door let out a high *beep* behind her.

"*No,*" the engineer cried furiously.

Marcus stood, rubbing his wrists with a look of elated surprise on his face.

"Wait, what's Klaus doing?" the whistleblower asked anxiously.

Claire watched one of Klaus's animatronic tentacles slowly rise too high.

"I don't know. He's underwater, I wasn't able to do any maintenance," the engineer replied, panic rising in his voice. "He's not supposed to be active this long without a break, but I didn't think it would…"

Klaus brought his great tentacle down directly over Marcus's head with enough force for the barbs to puncture the old, beleaguered glass. The hole wasn't large—just enough to let a small gushing stream of water in, but the pressure shift was sufficient to trigger the ride's evacuation protocol. A red light began to flash in the flooding tunnel as every door in the ride swung open. Including the secret entrance to the Winner's Circle.

Marcus laughed with giddy disbelief, stepping off the boat and running for the entrance.

"What do we do?" the whistleblower asked desperately.

"I… don't know," the engineer said. "The fucking—since his restraints released, the system thinks his trial is over. The emergency exit lock in the Winner's Circle is disengaged."

"Can you fix it?"

"Not from here. It's locking me out, and we'll never be able to reach him before he escapes. *Shit.*"

Marcus let out an exhilarated laugh as he entered, leaving the camera's line of sight.

"Turn it off," the engineer said, barely suppressing his anger. "Turn the fucking cameras off." The TVs in the Winner's Circle snapped off.

Claire, Audrey, and Jack all stared in shock as the lights illuminating the depths of the Dreamlake flickered off and Klaus was swallowed by darkness once again.

"You're… *joking,* right?" Claire said in a hollow tone.

"What the fuck was *that?*" Audrey demanded.

"He…he never confessed to anything," Jack muttered. "They can't even use the footage they got of him."

A door opened in the back of the club, and Marcus came swaggering in with all his five-foot-two glory. For a moment, he just stood and spread his arms out as though embracing the lounge's depravity. Then, he began to laugh hysterically—a jagged, grating, pompous noise as though every stain in the room had grown a set of vocal cords.

"I win," he said gleefully, stepping toward the trio. "I *win*. Do you see this? Do you see what happens? The mighty *Klaus the Kraken himself* was no match for Marcus Templeton!" He laughed again. Claire felt sick.

"And that's the difference between me and you, Jack. You *whine and moan* about your mistakes—that doesn't get you anywhere in life. All you did was ruin your reputation. You can't fake what I have, you never could, no matter how pathetically hard you've tried. It's called being a *winner*. I make the rules, the laws *and* the luck. I told you all along—there's *always* another way. And by the way, you're fucking fired."

Jack glared at Marcus with wounded rage but said nothing.

"And then there's you," Marcus sneered, turning to Audrey. "Trying to turn my wife against me with your armchair psychology. You're just a self-important child. And the world will *never* care about your hurt feelings."

Audrey was too beaten down and exhausted for snark. She just looked at Marcus in disbelief.

"*And you!*" Marcus roared, rounding on Claire. "You've had quite the little adventure today, haven't you? Well, it ends here. I've got some good news for you—I'm not leaving you after all. I'm going to stay and keep my eye on you to make sure you don't tell any more lies. And if you try to run? I'll just find you."

Claire stared him down with steely eyes. The tectonic plates within her shifted.

"Oh yes, my love," Marcus grinned ruefully, stepping toward Claire. "This attitude of yours stops *now*. We are going home, and you are going to go right back to being a sweet, grateful, submissive, dumb little fuckd—"

Claire pulled the revolver out of her purse and shot Marcus in the face.

The expression of shock only made it to Marcus's features after the bullet had already exited his skull. He dropped like a bag of rocks, dead. It was all over in one stunned, horrifying second.

Claire breathed hard through her teeth, feeling nausea rise in her gut. She turned to see Audrey and Jack's shocked expressions.

"Anyone have a problem with how I handled that?" she asked shakily.

"All good here," Audrey said quickly.

"If anything, you've been patient," Jack added.

Claire nodded. "Good. I don't—" Nausea surged through her and she hunched over to make a fresh contribution to the club's history.

The visual miasma returned, blurring and confusing the image of Marcus's dead body before Claire's eyes. She took a long drink of water, panting heavily. She needed to get out. She needed to get out *now*.

"Let's go," she said, snapping Audrey and Jack out of their stupors. "Come on. I'm so *fucking* sick of theme parks."

They opened the door leading into the emergency exit tunnel, going forward together.

The walk through the featureless brick tunnel was long and quiet. Not tense, but tired. Audrey stared at the bloodstained bandage wrapped around her knuckles as she moved. Her black eye was dark and purple, but it would heal. Claire gingerly touched the cheek where Susan had hit her, wincing. She realized then that she was still wearing her wedding ring, which she ripped off and dropped to the ground as though it had burned her. Jack walked half-slumped toward an uncertain future.

At the end of the passage was another elevator which took them up to ground level. The elevator door opened to a wall slanted toward them featuring a heavy steel hatch. On the hatch, spray-painted stencil letters read: "GO WEST TO FIND ROAD." Six flashlights lay next to the door. Claire picked one up, grabbed the hatch's oversized handle and twisted, opening it outward into a moonlit forest.

"Oh, wow," Claire breathed. "This must be the nature preserve."

"We don't have a compass," Jack said.

"We've got the *first* compass," Claire smiled, pointing skyward. "Let's see… there's the Big Dipper, so *that's* the north star. That means west is this way."

"How do you know that?" Audrey asked.

"I told you; I used to get *really* bored."

She helped Audrey out of the hatch, then let it fall shut. The exterior side of the hatch, built into a small hill, was completely featureless with no way to open it from that side.

As she cast her flashlight beam around the trees, she caught sight of something reflective. A final security camera hidden in the leaves, trained at the exit. Claire approached it and said, "Don't worry. He's not coming." She gave a final wave and led the others west.

As they walked, Claire propped her flashlight in her elbow and slipped the Andy keychain she'd found onto the trigger guard of the revolver. She turned it over in her hands, still wondering who Haley was.

And then she remembered that she had just murdered her husband, and she had to sit down on the forest floor.

"Are you okay?" Audrey asked.

"I just need a minute," Claire groaned. The memory of the gunshot played over and over in her head. Each time, it was accompanied by a fresh memory of their early relationship from deep in her hippocampus. When she never thought someone could make her so happy. And all at once, his most heartfelt gestures came rushing back in rapid fire. The passionate anniversary vacation to the Bahamas. The way he supported her through her father's death. The day he signed away everything to Claire in his will.

"Oh my God," Claire gasped.

"What?" Audrey asked.

"I'm a billionaire."

"Wait, really?"

"Marcus left me everything in his will because he wanted to brag to people about how good of a husband he was," she scoffed. "He kept meaning to revise it when he got bored of telling people, but he never did."

"Everything?" Jack repeated.

"Yeah… even the company. He designated me the acting CEO if he dies while his team finds a new one."

"Not Susan?" Audrey asked.

"He never trusted her not to just drain the company's assets for her own gain," Claire said. "He just thought I was too incapable to do anything during the gap and told me to let upper management handle it all."

"Holy shit," Jack marveled. "What are you gonna do?"

Claire thought for a moment, then said, "It'll probably be a fight, but I'm gonna try to dissolve the company and shut down all the parks. Use the money from assets to give the employees a good severance. I think I'll keep enough of his savings to be comfortable, but the rest… I'll find a way to give it to the victims and their families. Seems like the least I can do. Honestly, I'm kind of *over* money."

Jack nodded grimly. "End of an era."

A deafening series of explosions rang out behind them, causing all of them to scream in surprise. They whipped around to see a massive burst of flame erupt higher than the trees, filling the nearby air with smoke and debris.

It came from the direction of Dreamscape.

"Well… we really blew that opportunity, didn't we?" Audrey quipped.

Claire stood, smirking. "I guess he got to blast the place to kingdom come after all. Good for him."

They walked. The awe that Claire felt toward the revolver gradually soured, replaced by an unease with its presence. It was all too real, too *fresh*.

Just when she started thinking of where to dispose of it, she nearly tripped over a raised root. Claire stumbled forward and flung the revolver out of her hands. It landed in a puddle of mud, half-obscured by dirt and plant life. She walked closer to where it landed, staring down at it.

"You know what? Yeah, that works," Claire muttered. She had the uncanny sense that the gun had landed right where it needed to be.

"What happened?" Audrey asked, approaching. She tripped over the same root, pitching forward.

Claire took wide, unrestrained strides toward Audrey, just quick enough to catch the girl in her arms.

"Whoa there," Claire giggled. "Are you okay?"

"Yeah," Audrey replied breathlessly. "Thanks, Mom." She clapped her hand over her mouth, her ears turning bright red. "Oh my God, I'm so sorry. That's so embarrassing—I didn't mean…"

Claire just smiled and hugged Audrey tight. "No problem, kiddo," she said softly.

As the three of them kept walking, leaving the revolver behind, Claire said, "You know what? I think I finally figured out what I want to major in."

"Oh yeah?" Audrey replied.

"Yeah. Engineering."

Audrey burst out laughing, a pure and uninhibited sound like a bell tower's cascading chimes.

"*Really?*" Jack said. "After *all that,* why would you want to study engineering?"

Claire looked back at the fading fire lighting up the night, consuming what was once a den of greed, abuse, depravity, and neglect. The orange light flickered in her fierce eyes.

"There are a lot of things I want to fix."

EXCALIBER
EVANBOND

*Evan's Dedication:*

*To my Patreon followers,*
*my own knights of the Round Table*

# EXCALIBER

**THE ROAD THROUGH** the nature preserve was always one of Aida Hunter's favorites. Usually, there weren't many other cars on the road, especially at this late hour. The trees and underbrush surrounding the two-lane highway seemed more like a tunnel than a forest, and she liked it that way.

Every few miles, a quick turnoff would indicate the start of a trailhead. Hiking trails that she had traveled many times, though she had yet to conquer them all. They were certainly on her bucket list. She hoped a day would come when she had hiked them all.

Parts of the preserve were fenced off for wildlife conservation areas. Places with certain habitats where animals could roam around in peace, far from the roads and hiking trails to ensure they had little contact with the world around them. Humans had cut through the woods to make their roads and structures, but there were still areas where nature thrived.

During the day, the surrounding preserve was a beautiful backdrop of natural colors and wonder zipping by in a blur outside her car windows. In the darkness, it was more ominous and threatening. Aida wondered what sort of animals stalked the woods at night. She would prefer to never find out.

This stretch of road would be the longest of her journey home. After a weekend-long stay at a work convention, she was ready to go home and relax. Maybe not tonight since she would be getting home around midnight, but tomorrow would be a quiet day. A glass of wine in hand and several chapters of a good book. She had brought one with her on the trip but never opened it.

As the road stretched on through the trees for what seemed an eternity, she spotted the disheartening view of brake lights up ahead. They were distant, but they were there all the same. It wouldn't take long before she caught up with this other driver. The one bad thing about this two-lane highway: it was easy to get stuck behind the slower-moving traffic.

She made a mental plan to overtake the car when she was close enough, knowing that she didn't want to be slowed down. Home was still a way off, and she wasn't going to let anything get in her way. She could almost hear the alluring call of her bed. She wanted nothing more than to go to it and lay her head down on her soft pillows.

There was always something peaceful about sleeping in her own bed after a long trip. It didn't matter how soft the hotel pillows were or how big the bed was, coming home to her own comforter was always better. Her own space. Her own dominion.

Thinking about the hundreds, no thousands, of people that had slept in the hotel bed before was always something she did her best not to think about. If she spent too long on the thought while in the hotel, she would wind up sleeping in one of the armchairs instead. And that would only lead to waking up sore in several places with a kink in her neck that would take days to come out. Damn, it sucked getting older.

When Aida was a young girl, she could sleep almost anywhere. On several road trips with her parents, she would curl up into a small ball in the back seat, a blanket strung up like a pillow fort, and sleep in the strangest angles, all while still wearing her seatbelt. These days, if she slept with her head facing a few degrees the wrong way, she would be stuck looking that way for a week.

The brake lights grew brighter as she neared the car in front of her and she swore under her breath. This was it. Time to try to overtake the car so she could continue speeding off through the preserve toward her destination.

The other vehicle was traveling at least ten miles under the speed limit and even though she was doing almost fifteen over, she wasn't worried about getting pulled over. The police didn't speed trap this road, especially at this hour. A major accident out here would likely result in the person being stranded for hours. No tow truck or emergency service would travel this far into the middle of nowhere in the middle of the night to rescue someone dumb enough to speed and wrap themselves around a tree.

As she approached the other car, Aida sped up in an attempt to pull left and overtake them. She wanted the driver to know she was passing them, almost like she was teaching them a lesson. How dare they drive slower than she wanted to go on an empty road in the middle of the night? The nerve!

Before she could pull the wheel left and sail past her new, annoying friend, the rear lights grew brighter as the person stepped on his brakes, hard. Aida's foot instinctively went for the brake, even though her brain told her to follow through with the maneuver of overtaking him instead.

There was no time to come to a complete stop. At about twenty miles an hour, the front of her hood crumpled into the ass end of the other vehicle. It bent upward toward the dark sky, blocking her view from outside the windshield. She felt the car lurch backward about a foot before grinding to a stop.

At the same time, the airbag deployed, cushioning her face with all the softness of a punch from a professional boxer. Her body flung forward, bouncing off the airbag before snapping back and hitting the headrest behind her.

"Fuck!" she yelled as the airbag deflated like a party balloon at the worst children's party ever. Her senses had dulled for a moment as if protecting her from hearing, seeing, or feeling the accident around her. All at once, they came flooding back. She was painfully aware of a small trickle of blood running from her right nostril and over her lips.

Her head spun as she reached down to unclip her seatbelt, but it wouldn't budge. She jammed her thumb into the button as hard as she could to no avail. Panic set in now as she feared some unknown gas leak might erupt into flames and explode the entire vehicle while she sat helplessly inside. The result of too many action-packed thriller movies.

A noise startled her, causing a scream to erupt from her mouth without warning, scaring even herself. Aida turned toward the sound and peered out the driver's side window to see a man standing there with his knuckles against the glass.

"Are you okay?" his muffled voice came from the other side of the window.

It took Aida longer than it should have to realize this was the man she had just rear-ended. He had come back to check on her likely because she had yet to get out of her car to assess the damage.

She shook her head and pointed to the seatbelt. "It's stuck," she said, giving it a yank as if to prove she wasn't lying.

"I can help. Hold on." The man disappeared around her crumpled hood and she could see nothing. She heard the faint sound of a car door opening and then closing before the man returned to her view again. He held in his hand a small folding knife. When he flicked the lever with his thumb, the blade popped out. He grabbed the door handle, pulling hard, but the door did not open.

"Can you unlock it?" he asked. "Does it work?"

Aida reached out and pressed the button. To her relief, the doors unlocked. Within seconds, the man was leaning over her grabbing at the seatbelt. He slipped the knife under the strap and yanked, cutting it free.

Feeling an intense anxiety well up inside her, Aida pushed past the man and out of the car. Once she was safely removed from the death trap, she could see her fears were unwarranted. The crushed hood of her car was bad, but it wasn't as bad as she had originally thought. Still, it was probably not in any sort of drivable condition.

At that moment, she realized the horrible truth of what this meant. Her car was totaled in the middle of the nature preserve. The tow bill was going to be a damn fortune.

"Hey," the stranger said. In her dismay, Aida had momentarily forgotten about the man. "Are you alright?"

Without realizing she was nodding, Aida stood there staring at the wreckage, only worrying about what grief this was all going to cause her. And to make matters worse, she would be the one at fault. She rear-ended him. This was going to be terrible for her insurance.

"I'm so sorry," he began again. "An animal ran out in front of me. Didn't see how close you were to me. Just glad you're okay. That's the important thing."

She wanted to tell him it would be more important to have a working car in the middle of the woods, that being alone in the middle of nowhere with a stranger whom she had rear-ended wasn't ideal either. Instead, she said, "Yeah, I guess."

He stood for a moment staring at her as if he expected her to say more. When she didn't, he looked down at his feet. "Should we, uh, exchange information or something? This is actually my first time getting hit so I'm not sure what to do."

Aida shrugged. "This is my first time hitting someone, so I guess we have that in common."

The man laughed and it eased Aida's tension. She had heard too many stories of terrible people faking injuries after a car accident in order to sue or make a major claim against the insurance company. She was glad to see this guy might not be one of them. So far, he seemed rather pleasant for someone whose night she had ruined.

"Well, here, let me give you my information. You can take a picture of my ID if you want. I'm not going to file a police report since my car looks fine." He turned to face his bumper, which had miraculously suffered only minor cosmetic damage. His eyes floated back to the damage of Aida's car. "I can't believe how bad that looks. You'd think it would be so much worse."

Aida didn't know what to say to that, though she agreed. It seemed impossible that her hood could crumple like a soda can while his bumper had nothing more than a surface-level scrape. She counted herself lucky. This could have been a lot worse.

"Oh, right, my ID," the man said as he stuffed his hand into his pocket and approached Aida. She held out her hand, ready to receive his identification and not entirely sure what she should do once she got it.

The man's hand pulled free from his pocket and shot up past her outstretched arm like a rocket. A moment later, there was something pressed up against her mouth and nose, hard. She could barely breathe. Her world began to darken almost immediately as a pungent odor assaulted her nostrils.

Then Aida's world went dark.

଼ଠଔ

THE WORLD RETURNED to her in flashes. Her sight was cloudy and dim and all the noise around her seemed muffled and distant. She could feel her body, though it felt more like it was floating through the air.

As her sight dimmed in, she saw trees and patches of dirt before the world faded out again. The distinct smell of pine filled her nostrils. More feeling returned to her body and she realized she was suspended in the air as she moved.

Her head spun as she tried to make sense of her surroundings. As her vision faded in and out one more time, she saw a pair of boots below her and finally realized she was being carried.

Aida felt weak, as if her limbs would not move, no matter how hard she struggled. Despite the fear now coursing through her veins, she found she could not scream. Her body simply would not obey her commands. She felt groggy, like awakening from a dream.

After what seemed an eternity of listening to crunching leaves, she was hoisted up into the air and tossed back down to Earth. Her senses all came rushing back in an instant when she connected with the ground and the air was forced from her lungs. Now, she was able to cry out in pain but only in short gasps as she attempted to catch her breath.

As her lungs burned for oxygen, her vision slowly returned as did the control of her limbs. Every fiber of her being was telling her to scream and run away, but she still did not have the strength. Flashes of the car accident came to her as she remembered the man reaching into his pocket before pressing something against her nose.

At that moment, she finally realized the horrible truth of her situation. She had been taken. For what purpose, she still didn't know. But with her surroundings being somewhere deep in the woods, she could only surmise nothing good.

A dark figure stepped into view, standing over her and blocking out the light from the moonlight streaming through the trees. She couldn't see the man's face, but she didn't need to. It was the same man she had rear-ended on the road. No doubt about it.

He was now wearing a black hoodie and gloves with duct tape around the wrists. Something large glinted in his right hand and Aida's eyes grew wide with fear. Suddenly, her ability to scream flooded back and she let out an ear-piercing cry for help.

The man standing over her laughed and began to scream as loud as he could alongside her. "Yes, please come help!" he yelled. "Hurry!"

Their voices echoed in unison through the trees until they drifted away on the wind.

"There's no help coming, Aida," he said as he held up a plastic card in his left hand. With her vision finally returned, she could see it was her license. "There's no escape and no help out here, Aida. Scream all you want. I encourage it, actually." With that, he let out another yell filled with primal rage. Aida's skin began to crawl.

"I'm s-sorry I rear-ended you," Aida muttered. "I'll p-pay for the damages. Just please…" She let her words trail off, unable to finish the sentence.

The man let out a laugh and crouched lower, looming over her. "I'm not mad about the car. A little paint and she'll be as good as new. Bumper is reinforced anyway, so shouldn't even be much more than a scratch. She's been through this before."

Despite the hot, humid air of summer, Aida felt a winter storm roar up in her veins and travel all throughout her body. This was clearly not the first time this deranged man had done this.

Aida tried to slide her body backward through the dirt to escape the stare of the wild man standing over her. He stood, shook his head, and pressed his boot against her pelvis. She felt intense pressure and feared the bone would crack.

"And just where do you think you're going?" the man said, looking around. "In case you hadn't noticed, there isn't much out here."

She knew pleading with the man would do her no good. He seemed to want nothing other than the satisfaction of hurting her. Crying and begging would only make things worse for her. Control over his helpless victim. Despite her utter fear, she refused to give it to him. He stared at her for a moment as if waiting for the tears and begging to start.

"A quiet one, huh? The others always begged, screamed, and cried at this point. You are a fascinating one, I'll give you that."

Without warning, the man released his foot and bent down in one swooping motion, picking up Aida by her collar. He flung her into the air with ease, pressing her firmly up against the bark of a tree. One hand gripped around her throat while the other held her by the wrist.

Her chest ached and burned for want of air as her windpipe closed. In desperation, her free arm shot up and flailed around like an injured snake before it finally found its fangs and slashed across her attacker's face. He let out a cry, losing his grip as he stepped back and pressed his hand against his left eye. Aida fell to the ground, gasping for air.

"You little bitch!" the man screamed as he pulled his hand free and checked for blood. There was only a trickle, but Aida was proud.

"F… uck…. yo… u," she panted. This only served to enrage her attacker, who delivered a kick to her stomach, sending Aida rolling through the dirt and landing face up. An intense pain stung in her abdomen but quickly dulled as her adrenaline began to flow.

"You're going to beg before the end. I promise you that." The man stepped forward, straddling Aida before dropping on top of her.

The most intense fear Aida had ever felt in her life erupted up and down every nerve ending in her body. There was no knowing what this man would do next. Would he continue to assault her? Would it turn sexual? Was he planning to end her life now? These thoughts all flashed through her mind in an instant, nearly overwhelming her. She felt like she would black out and vomit simultaneously.

Seething anger burned in his eyes as his hands rose toward her throat. He wrapped his fingers around her neck, squeezing as tightly as he could. Aida's hands lashed out, desperately trying to claw and gouge any sensitive area she could reach, but to no avail. He was able to keep his face just out of her reach.

Now, with her vision blurring and lungs burning, her hands probed the forest floor. Her nails dug into the soft Earth, clawing and reaching for anything she could use to defend herself.

Drool hung from the man's bottom lip as he squeezed her throat. His own eyes bulged and his skin turned bright red from anger and exertion.

Despite the gut-wrenching fear of her life ending at that very moment, a strange thought fluttered through Aida's mind. Not giving in or showing fear seemed to have only made him angrier. She wished she had cried and screamed and fought back more to buy herself some time.

As her world began to darken, Aida's hands stretched out, combing the dirt around her for anything she could use in one final attempt to save her life. If she didn't find a way to break free from this man, she would be dead in a matter of seconds. Her left hand probed the ground and found nothing but a fistful of dirt. The fingers on her right hand dug into the earth, looking for anything hard. She would even take a fallen branch. Anything she could use.

Her lungs ached for air as her vision began to fade. Desperately, she tried to inhale but no air could enter. Right before she felt as though she would pass out, her fingers wrapped around something hard buried in the dirt. Without a second thought, she clawed the object free and swung it as hard as she could. It connected with the side of the man's head with a loud crack and he toppled over on the ground, groaning.

Air rushed into her lungs all at once causing her to gasp, coughing as she attempted to stand. The rock she had clawed free was still tightly grasped in her hand. She barely noticed it there as she struggled for air. Despite the fire in her lungs and the cramp forming in her side, Aida raced off into the darkness, panting hard as she ran.

Several times, she stopped for a few seconds to catch her breath, lean against a tree, or search for a spot to hide. Each and every time, the smallest noise would send her back into a blind panic and on a wild run through the trees.

After what seemed like an hour, Aida dropped to her knees behind a tree and wept. Finally, she had caught her breath and felt as though she could move at a faster pace, but she needed to compose herself.

Tears rolled down her face. Aida pressed her forehead against the tree, bracing herself. She listened for any sound in the distance of the man following her but heard nothing. She wished she had smashed his head in with the rock until his brains had splashed out over the forest floor. Everything had happened too fast. There was no time to think, only react.

At that moment, she realized she was still holding the rock. She readied herself to drop it but then thought better of it. Having any sort of weapon could prove useful.

She leaned back and pulled the object up to her eye level, moving it around until she could see it under a thin strip of moonlight, only to realize something amazing. This was no rock. Caked in dirt, grass, and a little bit of mud was something she never could have expected to pull free from the ground at her moment of absolute necessity.

Aida stared at the object in her hand wondering if it had been sent to her from the heavens in her time of need. Like Arthur finding the Lady of the Lake, who offered him Excalibur. This item was her Excalibur.

Lying in her dirt-encrusted palm was a revolver.

₧⁖

**AIDA STARED AT** the hunk of metal in her hand, wondering how something like this had ended up half-buried in the woods where she would eventually stumble across it.

God had provided for her in her time of desperate need. Aida wasn't the most religious person in the world. She had grown up going to Sunday school with her grandparents but had hardly ever gone to church as an adult. After this, she might just start going back. It was a sign.

The whole thing was caked with dirt and had clearly been buried under the soil for an extended period. She quickly began to brush it off with her hand, trying to clear away everything she could. As she worked, a noise off in the distance caught her attention. Somewhere in the trees, a twig snapped.

Her blood ran cold as she craned her neck, looking every which way to find the source of the sound. She tried to calm her nerves by telling herself it was nothing more than a woodland creature stalking through the night, but she feared it was something far worse.

She looked down at the six-shooter in her hand, knowing she now had the tools to defend herself if the man attacked her again, but not feeling much safer. Aida had never fired a gun before, nor did she know anything about them. Guns needed bullets and she had none, nor did she know if there were any inside. Hell, she didn't even know where to look to figure it out.

She turned it over in her hand trying to find a safety switch. Movies spoke about them all the time, but she didn't see anything that looked like one.

As she looked it over, a strange thing caught her eye. An odd bit of plastic shrouded by mud clung to the trigger guard by a couple loops of metal. It looked like a keychain or a phone charm. Perplexed, she swiped a finger over it in an attempt to clear the grime away.

Another crunch pulled her attention away from the revolver and back into the endless void of darkness and trees around her. Only a small stream of moonlight filtered through the trees and to the forest floor below. Whatever was moving through the darkness had grown closer.

Deciding it was best to keep moving, Aida started walking through the woods hoping she would stumble upon a trail or a way back toward the road. Her car was in a bad way so she likely wouldn't be able to drive away and get help. But perhaps she could make it back to the road before her attacker and take his car. Her phone was likely in his vehicle as well. She would be able to call for help. With a plan in mind, she began to move faster.

As she wove through the trees, she heard crunching leaves and twigs behind her. Something was moving. Chasing.

*Shit!* she thought. *He's found me.*

Without thinking, Aida began to run.

The sounds of pursuit grew louder as she snaked through the forest, hoping to find the road but knowing she was likely nowhere near it. The revolver's weight grew heavy in her hand, begging her to turn and wait for her pursuer and pull the trigger. Her nightmare could be over in a matter of minutes. She finally had a way to end it.

Coming to a stop, Aida dropped behind a tree and caught her breath. After a few heart-hammering seconds, she turned and braced herself against the trunk with the pistol out in front of her. Her finger wrapped around the trigger like a little girl desperately holding on to a balloon in a windstorm. Through shaking hands, she waited.

All around her, the woods came alive. She couldn't tell if the wind had stopped blowing and the insects had stopped buzzing or if her mind had just blocked out all the noise in her moments of panic. Now, she was hypersensitive to it all. Every creaking branch stole her attention. Every light crunch on the ground pulled her gaze.

She felt on the verge of a panic attack as tears stung her eyes. More than anything, she wanted this man to step out before her so she could put an end to this nightmare.

Another twig snapped, this time much closer to Aida. She pivoted so that she would face in the direction of the sound. A few agonizing minutes marched by before a figure emerged from behind a tree. It moved slowly and crouched as it weaved from tree to tree.

Her hands shook as she aimed the barrel of the revolver in his direction, following him as he moved. He was oblivious to her as he stalked through the darkness. When he was near enough that she felt she could take the shot and safely hit him, Aida pulled the trigger.

*Click!*

She panicked, pulling the trigger two more times.

*Click! Click!*

The gun refused to fire. She peered down at it for a split second, wondering what was wrong but had no time to investigate. The man had heard the loud clicks and was now turned toward her position. Thankfully, it appeared as though he had not seen her yet.

As he scanned the trees, Aida ducked and fiddled with the gun, hoping to find whatever malfunction had caused it not to fire. She desperately searched again for a safety switch, certain that this was why it had not gone off.

She held back tears as she heard the man creeping closer and closer. Her heart pounded in her chest like a boxing match out of control. Letting out a short breath, she tried to calm her nerves to no avail.

Another crunch indicated the man had stepped even closer. She could almost hear his breath now. If she couldn't get the gun to fire, she would have to run. The decision would need to be made in a matter of seconds. If he came too close and grabbed her, it would be all over. He was too strong to fight off.

Panic took over and Aida began to run. As she did, she heard thundering footfalls behind her as the man gave chase. His feet hammered the ground, crunching over leaves and snapping sticks as he pursued her. Feeling him approach, Aida let out a scream, which only served to wind her more than the run. Through heavy panting breaths, she carried forward.

Like a vicious dog, he ran only a few feet behind her. She could have sworn, though it could have been her imagination, that he had snarled and snapped at her heels a few times.

Aida dashed through the trees, trying her best to lose her attacker but he stuck close behind. She could somehow feel his presence there. It would only be a matter of time before he grabbed her, and ended her life. This damn gun had appeared to be some sort of lifesaving miracle but had been nothing more than a useless hunk of junk.

She kept running until her legs burned and even then, she continued. Aida ran until her lungs felt like exploding and she collapsed into the dirt crying and wheezing. When no one grabbed her from behind, she realized the impossible had happened. She had lost her pursuer. Now, she cried relief-filled tears of joy.

She panted like a dog on a hot summer hike. The air entering her lungs felt like life itself as a cramp formed in her side. She invited the pain. It meant she was alive. For how much longer, she didn't know.

When her breathing finally returned to normal, she decided to take a look at the gun in an attempt to learn why it hadn't fired when she needed it most. From her current position, she could hardly see the weapon in her own hands. Looking around, she spotted a small pillar of moonlight pushing through the trees.

Aida took the chance and shuffled toward it. As the pale light engulfed her, she felt exposed, but she could now see the revolver better as it shone in all its glory. She rolled it over in her hands. There seemed to be no major defect or issue with the gun, except for some small bits of wear and tear she could see through the dirt.

A little piece of metal beside the grip that looked like a button stood out to her, now. She pressed her thumb against it and the cylinder popped open. Aida held it with the barrel pointed toward the sky and waited for the bullets to fall out. Each hole was caked with dirt and pieces of grass, blocking any escape for the loaded rounds.

Aida went about cleaning the dirt from each cylinder. The first two chambers were completely empty. She blew into them to flush out any extra dirt and debris. The third chamber had a round inside which she pulled out and placed carefully on the ground. In the next chamber, she found a second bullet behind a wall of dirt. Pulling it out, she placed it by the first. Behind some crushed blades of grass and mud, she found two more rounds in the final chambers, which she laid on the ground.

Taking the tail of her shirt, Aida wiped the entire revolver clean of any filth. Underneath the layer of dirt was a beautiful gun with a stainless-steel body and an ornate wooden grip. The grip was wrapped with a few straps of hot pink tape. There was a small crack in the wood and some scratches across the barrel. Clearly, this gun had seen some crazy days.

The craziest bit of all hung from the trigger guard. A figure plastered beneath a layer of mud and grime.

Aida took a moment to wipe the thing clean. The charm resembled an ant or maybe some other sort of insect Aida couldn't place. She assumed it was some sort of mascot from a theme park or maybe a children's show. What the hell it was doing attached to this gun, she couldn't even imagine. What sort of events had unfolded to bring these two items together? It boggled her mind.

She turned the piece over in her hands and spotted a message carved into the grip just above the tape. FOR HALEY. She could only wonder who Haley was and why the message had been carved. Was it a gift for someone special? Was this gun used to avenge Haley? Or, like Aida, had this gun come to Haley in a time of great need?

She scoffed at her own thought but still wondered about it all. This was no ordinary gun. It seemed special, somehow. She could almost feel an energy pulsating from it like many souls had been saved by this very tool and it could somehow save hers, too.

Her hands shook once again as she wiped the bullets down with the tail of her shirt before loading the four rounds back into the chamber and sliding it back into place. Now, she knew the gun would fire if she needed it once again.

And she was certain she would. Her ordeal was far from over. That man was still out there somewhere hunting for her, and she had no clue which way led back to the road. But with her new gun in hand, which she had begun to think of as her Excalibur, she felt far less weak.

A smile crept over her face as a funny thought fluttered through her mind. *It's not my Excalibur*, she thought. *It's my Excaliber.* She laughed as she carried forward.

⊱⬥⊰

**IT WASN'T LONG** before the smile fell from Aida's face. When the reality of her situation came flooding back, she realized she was still in a deadly game of cat and mouse with a serial killer deep in the woods. Even with the revolver gripped tightly in her hand, she still felt no better about her odds. Especially knowing she only had four shots. She would have to make them count.

Another realization dawned on her. She had never fired a gun before and she had very limited ammo. If she were to defend herself tonight, she would need her attacker to get in close and personal. It was unlikely she would hit him from a decent range.

The thought of letting that man get near her raised the hair on her arms and sent shivers down her spine. It was a horrid idea. Her only other option would be to escape the woods and run for rescue, but that seemed like an unlikely outcome. He had already admitted to doing this before and likely knew the woods better than she did. Right now, she was lost, turned around, and scared. The advantage was his.

Aida crept on through the woods hoping to find any landmark that looked vaguely familiar. If she could find anything that might lead her back to the road and safety, she would follow it. Unfortunately, everything looked exactly the same. Endless miles of trees and underbrush with no remarkable characteristics at all.

She snaked through the shadows of the trees, making sure to keep out of the moonlight filtering down through the canopy. Even though all her instincts screamed at her to stay in the light so she could see her surroundings better, she knew it would mean she was more visible. What she needed was to be invisible. If the man couldn't see her, he couldn't catch her. It was the only advantage she had.

Something crunched over dry leaves nearby, sending a snow flurry through Aida's veins. She froze before crouching behind a fallen tree. Peeking over, she caught a shadowy figure lurching through the trees ahead of her. Her lungs seized while her heartbeat was like a wild drummer in her chest.

Lucky for her, he seemed not to be heading in her direction. Even still, the revolver in her hands shook wildly. Her instincts told her to pull it up, aim down sight, and pull the trigger until the bastard dropped. But she knew it would be futile. She would miss from this distance. Missing was not an option. Not with extremely limited ammo.

Her hand gripped the handle tighter until her knuckles turned white and her finger hurt. It helped calm her rapidly beating heart.

The shadow turned and stepped in Aida's direction. She froze in horror, not certain if he had seen her or not. Crouching as low behind the tree as she could, she made sure to keep her eyes on the man in case he started to approach.

He walked into a beam of moonlight and stopped. His head rotated from side to side as he scanned his surroundings.

Aida watched in horrified confusion as he seemed to sniff the air like he could catch her scent on the wind. Her hands shook harder and the impulse to raise the gun and fire became almost overwhelming. Still, she fought the urge to move, mostly out of fear of exposing her position.

After several excruciating minutes that felt like an eternity, the man began to move again. He stepped toward Aida's left and out of the column of light. Instinctively, she shifted to her right to keep herself out of his view. As he moved, she moved.

Their one-way game of invisible cat and mouse went on for several minutes. Aida was careful to keep her footing light and only on the dirt. She would not be caught thanks to a snapping twig.

After a few minutes, the man seemed to lose interest in this area and slinked away into the woods. Aida listened to his footsteps carefully. Only when they had faded behind the wind did she feel safe to breathe again.

She started to move only to hear a sound that turned her stomach upside-down. Heavy footfalls stomped through the brush not far from her location, growing louder by the second.

Aida stumbled backward, tripping on an exposed root. She watched as the world spiraled downward until her vision was met with the sky. Her back slammed against the dirt with a loud thud. As quickly as she could, Aida rolled to her stomach and attempted to push herself up on her feet before she felt the driving force of her attacker landing on her back.

He wrapped around her like a blanket, pressing her body into the dirt. She could feel his weight pinning her to the ground, pushing the air from her lungs. Something hard pressed against her sternum and she realized she had landed on her arm still holding the gun. He still didn't know she had one. It was her only saving grace. If she could somehow—

A fist jammed into her rib cage sending a white-hot pain through her entire body. The punches came again and again. She was certain one of her ribs would break. He was yelling something as he wailed on her midsection, but the blood rushing in her ears kept her from hearing much. All her thoughts focused on finding a way to shoot her attacker. This could be her only opportunity.

Her left hand shot out almost as if it were not under her control. She scooped up a handful of dirt and flung it backward as hard as she could. For only a brief second, she felt the weight on her back shift but it was long enough for her to react.

Twisting her body, Aida managed to squirm sideways and push the man off her back. He fell to the side, landing on his hip. She tried to bring the gun up and aim but her body was so contorted she couldn't get the barrel pointed straight at him.

Fear took over as she tried to wiggle free but he pressed his weight down further as he finished clearing the dirt from his eyes. He now spotted the gun in Aida's hand and his eyes grew wide. As he reached toward the barrel, Aida instinctively pulled the trigger.

A thunderous clap echoed through the silent forest. The faint aroma of gunpowder singed her nostrils. Her ears rang for only a moment until a new sound replaced it. Screaming.

Her attacker had fallen back, clutching at his hand. As Aida pulled herself free, she could see torn flesh in the center of his palm where the bullet had passed through. For a brief moment, a beam of moonlight pierced through the wound and almost made Aida sick.

Climbing to her feet, Aida turned to finish the job. One to the forehead would put an end to his screaming and to Aida's nightmare. But as she turned, the man dove for cover in the brush. Her finger squeezed the trigger for a moment before she remembered her limited rounds. She didn't want to waste ammo by blindly firing at the man.

She stuffed the revolver in her waistband like she had seen in the movies, the charm catching on her pants. She tried again, this time tucking the ant-charm inside with the gun. It pressed against her flesh, biting her like an ant, but she ignored the discomfort and ran off.

The goal was to put as much distance between the two of them as she could, hoping to finally stumble upon the road. Maybe the bastard would bleed to death somewhere in the woods. She didn't know if it was possible to die from a gunshot wound to the hand, but she could hope.

She ran until her legs collapsed and she fell face-first into the dirt. Scrambling up to her knees, Aida caught her breath. After a few minutes of deep breathing, the realization of what had happened set in. She had actually shot the man. Sure, it was only the hand, but she had managed to hit him.

With only three remaining shots, she realized she couldn't rely on the revolver alone. She got lucky with the first shot, but what if she missed on the second, third, or fourth? Or maybe those shots would only be wounds the same as the first.

No, she needed more protection than just the gun. She would need something to allow the man to get close enough for a lethal shot but still keep him at arm's length. She looked around the forest floor for anything that could be a weapon. A large branch or sharpened stick would work if she could only find one.

After searching for several minutes, she found one that could do the trick. It was slightly shorter than she would have liked, with a crooked tip, but it was better than nothing. If anything, she would be able to use it as a club. Bash him in the head, bring him to the ground, and pull the trigger. It was a simple plan, but ruthless and effective.

Her attacker may have been wounded, but she doubted it would stop him for long. Ideally, he would have slunk back to his car and retreated to whatever rat's nest he called home but Aida knew it was unlikely.

Something had awoken inside her. Yes, she was scared. Petrified. Now there was something else there. A feeling she hadn't been able to place until that very moment. Call it adrenaline or her fight-or-flight response, but Aida knew what it really was. Survival.

ℰ◌ℛ

**OVER THE NEXT** hour, Aida spent her time navigating through the trees in the hopes that she would find her way out of this forest maze. While she moved forward, still sticking to the shadows, she looked for whatever items she could use as a weapon.

She had found a large stick, bigger and sharper than her first. Discarding the old, she kept the new. It doubled as a walking stick and would help her reach an attacker who was just outside of her arm's reach. She discovered a thick vine hanging down from a tree. After several minutes of tugging, she managed to bring the vine down. It now sat looped through her belt loop, coiled up as if she were Indiana Jones, ready to take on Nazi scum.

Of course, the revolver, her Excaliber, was still safely tucked into her waistband. It helped her feel safer and more powerful, but it was only to be used as a last resort. With only a few bullets remaining, she couldn't rely on it.

A large, disc-shaped rock was stuffed inside her left pocket. It barely fit with most of the rock poking out but it was so wedged it had nowhere to go. The rock fit perfectly in her hand and she figured she could use it as an additional weapon if need be. She could only hope all of her bases were covered.

Now, Aida stood before a calm lake watching as the moonlight bounced across the surface. It was as smooth as glass, reflecting what few stars poked through the forest canopy. Despite the scene bringing her a sense of surreal calm, a new thought emerged. She had not seen this lake before, which meant she was not heading back toward the road. Instead, she found herself deeper in the woods.

On the plus side, she had not seen or heard from her would-be murderer in some time. Perhaps he had made a run for it after the gunshot wound. Somehow, she still doubted it.

Sitting down by the lake, she thought over her next moves. Blindly walking through the woods was getting her nowhere. Even if she survived the night from her assailant, she could easily die from exposure or be mauled by an animal.

She could defeat one predator only to be killed by another. The image of a bear crushing her bones danced through her head and somehow it scared her less than the man wanting to end her life. She supposed death by a bear made more sense than death by a serial killer.

A smile crept over her face as she realized what needed to be done. It filled her with a mixture of dread, excitement, and fear. This was where she would end it all. Right here. Right now.

ଛୌଓଷ

**THAT BITCH HAD** shot him in the hand. Victor had retreated to his car to bandage the wound before heading back off into the woods to find his prey. She would be harder to find now after wandering the woods for several hours, but he would find her. He always found them. Many had tried to escape, but none had ever slipped him for long. Even the biggest man he had hunted had eventually gone down. So too would she.

Victor had retraced his steps to find the location where he had been shot, making sure to bury any traces of blood left on the soil. From there, he had tried his best to follow her tracks but they had quickly disappeared. Now, he found himself wandering in the woods hoping for any sort of sign she was near. He listened intently but hadn't heard a peep in a long while.

He wouldn't let her get away. Couldn't. Not just because she had seen his face and could end his spree, but because it would end his perfect streak. So many bodies were buried in these woods and others like them across the country. He'd lost count of total victims years ago.

Pain in his hand throbbed fiercely, only fueling his anger. She would pay for this. He would kill her slower than any of his other victims before her. After all, she deserved it the most.

For fuck's sake, she didn't even beg or plead for her life. What the fuck was wrong with her? They always begged. They always pleaded. He liked that part the most. Before the end, she would do both and he could finally have his ending. He just had to find her. It was only a matter of time.

After another fifteen minutes of aimless wandering and looking for any tracks, he heard something on the wind. Faint at first, but then louder. His grin grew so wide it touched his temples. His prey was out there, screaming for help.

Maybe she thought she had seen someone else out in the woods who could save her. Impossible. Or perhaps the sly fox thought she could set a trap. It would be inconsequential. She would die one way or another.

He slithered off into the darkness toward the sound like a snake on the hunt for a defenseless baby bird. Finally, this night was back on track and it would end exactly as he wanted.

ℰᏉ૦Ꮕ

**FROM THE UNDERBRUSH,** the man emerged with a knife gripped in his uninjured hand. He paced around before walking closer to the lake. After a minute, he spotted tracks in the soft mud near the bank. His head popped up like a meerkat and swiveled around, no doubt in an attempt to decipher which way his prey had gone.

He approached the edge of the lake and stood for a moment, only staring. As he stared off into the distance, Aida prepared herself to strike. If she mistimed her attack, everything could be for nothing, and her fight might be over quicker than intended.

She braced herself as the man turned on his heel, foot sinking in the slippery mud by the lake for only a moment, and made his way toward the tree she had nested in. Gripping her weapon tightly, she readied herself to pounce.

Everything happened in the blink of an eye for Aida and yet somehow still seemed slower than normal.

She felt weightless as her body dropped toward her target, the sharpened stick in her hand pointed downward. As she landed on top of her pursuer, the tip of her spear pierced the flesh of his shoulder. He screamed out in pain as the pair crumbled to the ground.

Aida rolled herself off the man and sprang back up to her feet as fast as she could. She pulled the vine from her side and pounced downward. She wrapped it around the man's neck and pulled with all her might.

He began to choke and struggle. The more he squirmed, the tighter she pulled. His hands flew up and pulled at the natural cord around his neck as he tried to dig his fingers underneath to no avail. With bulging eyes and blue-tinted skin, his reign of terror was coming to an end.

The man's hand shot up and gripped the spear lodged in his shoulder. A second later, it was yanked free with a sickening crunch of destroyed cartilage. Blood poured from the wound like a river.

He swung the weapon backward toward Aida. Lucky for her, the spear only scraped her skin, leaving behind a thin trail of blood. Unlucky for her, she had loosened her grip on the vine just long enough for the man to pull free.

This was it. The moment when she needed to use her Excaliber. The whole reason it had come to her in the first place. That strange gun with all its little markings, alterations, and strange charm dangling from the trigger guard. It would end this terrible nightmare for her.

The man advanced as Aida pulled the revolver from her waistband. Her arm swung toward her attacker, finger snaking toward the trigger.

To her horror, she watched as the man swung the spear like a club and knocked the gun from her hands. It sailed through the air, landing in the mud by the lake. He stood between Aida and the gun like a gatekeeper to her salvation.

Aida took a large step backward, defenseless. How could this be? Her only means of defense had been taken from her in the final hour, condemning her to a horrible fate. There was nothing left for her to do. Nowhere left to run. The man sneered as if thinking the exact same thing.

"Wow, you sure are feisty," the man hissed. He took a step forward, the spear pointed towards her. "Much more fight in you than all the others, I promise you that." He took another step closer. "You'll certainly be remembered as my biggest challenge. Set the bar really high for the next one." He stepped closer still, wiping sweat from his brow.

She glanced over his shoulder at the revolver half-sunk in the mud, wondering how quickly she could make a dash for it. The man let out a boisterous laugh.

"You think you'd make it there in time before I pinned you to a tree?" He shrugged at her, shaking his head. "You can certainly try!"

There was no chance she would make it there before he lunged. He was bigger with a large reach. One jab and the spear tip could pierce her abdomen. There would be no fighting back then.

Her mind raced as it tried to cope with her mortality until a single thought broke through the noise, almost bringing a smile to her face. There was still a chance of surviving this night. She just needed him closer.

"All this trouble for me?" she said, her voice shaking. "You think you're this grand killer, but you know what I think? I think you've only ever been lucky. You didn't outsmart or overpower your other victims. You got lucky none of them had the chance to fight back. If they had, you'd probably had your ass kicked by now."

The shake slowly left her voice. "I wasn't even a true challenge. Just a girl who managed to slip free and run. You couldn't even handle that."

"Shut up!" he yelled, stepping forward.

"Not the big, strong man you thought you were, huh? I mean, who could have guessed with you picking on small, defenseless women?"

"I said, shut up!" He took another large step forward, the stick white-knuckled in his grip.

Before she could reconsider, Aida lunged forward, throwing her shoulder downward and curling up as tightly as she could. She rolled through the air like a wild soccer ball, crashing against the man's knees. He had no time to react before he was thrust head over heels, landing face-first in the dirt. The spear lay next to him.

Aida was back on her feet, snatching up the makeshift spear. As the man rolled onto his back to face her, Aida drove the spear down with as much force as she could muster. The point pierced through his abdomen. To her surprise, she felt the tip push all the way down, burying itself in the dirt.

He let out a violent scream that shook Aida's eardrums. She stepped back for a moment, surprised by her own force.

As the man yelled, he grabbed at the stick protruding from his body. Each time he tried to pull it free, he screamed louder. The pain kept him pinned, but Aida couldn't know how long that would last.

Her eyes lifted toward the gun resting in the mud and a twisted smile stretched across her face. With a thudding heart beating wildly in her chest, she raced toward the lake and snatched up the revolver. The little ant danced happily beneath the trigger as if in excitement of what would come next.

Aida was careful to clean the mud from inside the trigger guard, barrel, and hammer. This time, when she pulled the trigger, it would surely fire. Sauntering back to the man pinned to the ground, she looked him over. Blood pooled around his midsection, bleeding into the dirt and caking him in maroon-colored mud.

"Thanks for *sticking* around," she said with a laugh and gestured with the gun toward the stick. "Sorry, that was awful, wasn't it? I guess I'm just feeling…" She paused for a moment as she pulled the hammer on the revolver back with a satisfying click. "*Cocky.*"

She lifted the gun and pointed it straight between the man's eyes. His mouth opened as if he were about to speak, but all Aida heard was the thundering roars of the revolver's final three shots echoing through the forest.

₧₨

**AIDA SAT IN** the back of an ambulance on the side of the road watching as her car was lifted onto a flatbed tow truck. The paramedics had checked her over to ensure there were no major injuries. Other than some scrapes from the brush, a gash on her forearm where the man had scraped her with the spear, and some bruised ribs, she was alright. She didn't exactly feel alright, but she was alive and that was most important.

A few police officers paced back and forth in the strobing red and blue lights. She had already given her statement about what had happened that night, but somehow, she felt it wouldn't be the last.

"Good evening, Aida," a soft-spoken, plain-clothes detective said as she approached the ambulance. "I'm Detective Reese. Was hoping to ask you a few questions about your encounter tonight."

Aida hid a roll of her eyes. How many times would she have to repeat her story? Though she knew exactly why they were asking so many times and what they were looking for. "Nice to meet you, Detective Reese," she said, sounding as pleasant as she could. "I can tell you the same thing I told the other officers."

Detective Reese smiled. "I know, I'm sorry. You're probably tired of telling it. I just need to ask them myself so I can record it all. Unfortunately, the other officers don't file the report, so it falls on me. Can you tell me again, in your own words, what happened tonight?"

Aida cleared her throat, which still felt raw from her encounter with the killer. She told her story from start to finish.

Adia told the detective about how the man had caused the collision, only to drug her when they exchanged insurance information. She told her about how she was dragged deep into the woods where the man tried to kill her. What she didn't mention was how she had obtained the revolver in the eleventh hour, exactly when she needed it. That part probably made her sound crazed. Instead, she informed the detective that she had managed to wrestle the firearm away from her attacker.

"That's why I was able to stab him with the sharpened stick," Aida claimed. "He dropped the gun he had pulled from his waistband, so I wasted no time in grabbing it and pulling the trigger. I've never…" She paused for a moment as real tears streamed down her face. "I've never shot someone before. I didn't know what to expect, but it was awful."

The detective stared at Aida as she spoke, nodding along and following the story. If she was suspicious, Aida couldn't tell. "And what happened to the firearm after that?"

There was the million-dollar question. Exactly what she assumed the police wanted to know. Unfortunately for them, they wouldn't be finding it.

"I was so scared and I wasn't thinking. I just wanted that hunk of metal as far away from me as possible, so I threw it as hard as I could toward the lake. If you have a dive team, I suppose…" Aida let herself trail off.

The detective shook her head. "Not necessary. This is a pretty open-and-shut case. If his other victims' bodies are out there, we'll find them. I think with your testimony, we might be able to finally give peace to a lot of families. You're lucky to be alive, Aida. If you ever need anything or think of anything else you want to share, give me a call."

With that, Detective Reese handed Aida a business card with her cell number on it. Then, she turned and disappeared into the flashing lights and out of Aida's vision.

Aida let out a sigh of relief. It seemed the police had believed her lie.

✂

**TWO MONTHS AFTER** the incident, Aida's life had returned to some semblance of normal. She had spoken with reporters about her ordeal and a few more officers letting her know they were finalizing the case, and she'd had her fair share of internet fame. Not all of it good, however. Not that it surprised her. The internet could be a shitty place.

She often pulled up Instagram and surfed through specific hashtags outlining women's struggles, offering her words of encouragement. If she even made a small, tiny fraction of the people she messaged better, she would feel as though something good had come out of her experience.

Aida had thought about starting her own business, perhaps a self-defense studio or something like that. There was no way she felt qualified enough to actually do it. Simply surviving something horrific didn't qualify her to teach others how to overcome their demons. She thought about a firing range, but she didn't know the first thing about guns. The only gun she had experience with was the revolver she had found in the dirt.

By no means had she become a gun nut, but she did have a newfound respect for them. Without one, she would currently be worm food as she rotted in an unmarked grave in the middle of the woods. Part of her wanted to buy a gun safe and start stockpiling weapons and ammo.

As she doom-scrolled through her social media feed, a notification appeared over her direct message inbox. She stared at the little red icon for a moment, uncertain if she should open it. Finally, she clicked the icon and found a new message from someone named Naomi.

The message was short and sweet; Naomi telling Aida she admired her strength. Where most would have seen a woman merely trying to connect, Aida looked deeper and saw someone crying out for help. This Naomi needed something and Aida knew exactly what it was.

They continued their correspondence for a short time, never truly getting to the root of what the woman's problems were. It wouldn't have mattered if they had. The proverbial Lady of the Lake who had once touched Aida's life and handed her the life-saving tool had reached out again.

She walked over to her bookshelf and removed her copy of *Canterbury Tales*. Swinging open the cover, she peered inside at the hollowed-out space housing the revolver she had told police was resting at the bottom of a lake. Across the barrel, she had etched the letters E-X-C-A-L-I-B-E-R.

The gun no longer had the ant mascot hanging from the trigger guard. Instead, Aida had taken the time to carefully install a charm holder to the bottom of the grip. It now hung down where it would never get in the way for anyone trying to use it. Aida had thought about removing it altogether but couldn't bring herself to do so. The gun was special and came to her with all its beauty marks. She didn't feel right removing a single one.

Picking up the revolver, she flipped open the cylinder and counted all six bullets. She'd made sure to buy a whole box of ammo so the firearm could always be loaded. She placed the gun back inside the book and closed the cover with a smile. Once the hollowed out copy of *Canterbury Tales* was firmly placed on the table, Aida sat and began to write a note.

*Naomi*, the message started. *I know you don't know me, but I was once in your shoes and when I needed it most, help came to me. I think I can send it to you now. Please. I can help you.* With that, she folded up the piece of paper which she slipped inside with the revolver. Patting the hardcover book, she readied a box to ship it in. She had a feeling Excaliber had found its next Arthur.

# THREE STORMS

## Elaine Pascale

# CHAPTER ONE



**"DON'T YOU COME** near me." The growl originated from the front of the store and barreled to the middle of the center aisle where Naomi was struggling to read the supply list on her phone as she juggled a small collection of items in her arms. No shopping baskets remained as all islanders were prepping for the worst of the hurricane while also praying for it to pass them over.

"I have a restraining order." The woman's voice climbed a notch, assuring that all within earshot heard her. People stopped listening to the emergency message that had interrupted the generic ballads being broadcast and focused on the interaction between the two women.

"You do not," Naomi called, adding C batteries to her teetering pile. "And I'm here as a customer, not because I want to be anywhere near you."

Veronica leaned closer to the cashier and, in a stage whisper, said, "She assaulted me."

"That part *is* true." Naomi wanted to purchase her items and return home to "batten down the hatches," as the islanders said when one eye was on the weather satellites and the other was on the remaining supplies that dwindled by the hour until there was nothing left to scavenge. She reluctantly approached the cash register, fearing that would send Veronica into a tizzy and cause her to claim she was being stalked and threatened.

"Stay safe," Veronica said sweetly to the cashier as she accepted her receipt. She then turned and said in a low voice, "I would wish the same of you… really."

Naomi watched the woman escape through the automatic doors. If cosmic justice existed, those doors would have slammed shut on Veronica's ample figure, slicing her in two.

Naomi shook off her murderous thoughts, which she had been experiencing with increasing frequency, and headed to the cash register. The young cashier eyed Naomi's supplies before beginning to ring them in.

"Don't listen to her, you'll be just fine. Storm has made her crazy."

The cashier's nametag caught Naomi by surprise. It had been many months since Naomi had last seen Bea, and the young woman had matured greatly. A slicked-back bun and make-up aged Bea, but her body was also curvier than Naomi remembered. Curvy in the right places. Naomi pulled herself up taller, trying to minimize the roll of flesh that slouched over the top of her pants.

"I mean, crazier than usual. Back when my mom worked here, she would give me an earful about that woman." Bea whispered conspiratorially, "Mom's on your side. Given the chance, she probably would've hit her, too."

As the girl leaned into her gossip, the necklace she was wearing swayed in the space between them. It was shaped like half a heart. The pendant had a single butterfly wing etched on it along with the words *Big Sis*. Naomi suspected that the cashier's sister, Anna, had worn the other half.

This show of camaraderie made Naomi feel guilty that she had joined in spreading rumors about poor Anna. Anna had disappeared during the last storm, Hurricane Yara. A note had been found on Anna's empty bed, stating she had run away. At thirteen, it was doubtful that she had gotten very far. Most suspected that she had come across the wrong person while seeking shelter and she was now lost in more ways than one.

"Everyone's so nerved up." Bea rolled her eyes. "It's not even supposed to land here."

"We are well outside of the cone," a man behind Naomi agreed. "People just love the idea of a storm."

Naomi could not agree with this assessment. Not when they were still working on repairs from Yara.

"Hurricane Quincy. If you lived through that, you can live through anything," the man continued, shoving his items closer to the register even though the conveyor belt was working fine.

Naomi shook her head. "I lived through it, but I was just a kid. It's different…"

She wanted to add *when someone is taking care of you*, but she and Brad had ridden out Yara together and they would support each other through this one, too. The difference was that as a child, she had her father to protect her. Her father had always made her feel safe, like he was some kind of superhero who could battle and win against even supernatural elements.

She hadn't been alone in that feeling; the island community had regularly relied on Earl to see them through both physical and emotional turbulence. He had been steadfast and strong and he managed others with an enviable ease. She had never seen him succumb to emotion. She wondered what he would think of her losing control and hitting Veronica.

"I barely remember it," she added as she slid her arms through the plastic handles on the grocery bags.

"You're lucky. Most of us sat on our roofs for days, waiting to be rescued. Those that survived the water died of heat stroke."

She let the door close behind her, assuming the customer would continue his tale of doom even if no one was listening. Naomi considered him Bea's problem, just as getting supplies home and fortifying her house was her problem.

And it was a major problem. They hadn't made the slightest dent in the loans they had cobbled together to rebuild the bedroom that had been squashed by a tree during Yara. If any damage befell them this time, they would not qualify for additional funds for repairs. Hurricane Yara had been devastating, but the old timer had been right; that storm didn't hold a candle to Quincy.

Naomi had lied; she remembered much more of Hurricane Quincy than she had admitted. It had been a terrifying time. She had watched as Earl helped with rescue efforts. He and other men from the island had been appointed to paddle rowboats and steer skiffs from roof to roof. On occasion, they were able to pull grateful people into the boats with them and transport them to shelter. Other times, the men were forced to crawl into attic windows or ax through layers of shingles and insulation to remove waterlogged corpses.

Naomi placed her bags in the backseat and slid into the driver's seat. She paused before turning on the ignition. She tried to remember how many Seres she had taken that day. She took out the bottle she had stashed in the glove compartment and gave it a shake. It was still nearly full, as were the bottles she kept in various places in her home, and the cartons full of bottles she stored in the garage. Seres was the one thing she did not need to stock up on.

She popped a gummy in her mouth and chewed. It was both sweet and sour. It made her tongue tingle and her salivary glands sprinkle the inside of her mouth with moisture. She tested the durability of the gummy by replaying that most recent scene with Veronica. Naomi's murderous rage had definitely lessened.

As she drove, she thought of the man from the store and his monologue. She was surprised that he hadn't mentioned her father, being of the generation that considered Earl a hero. Perhaps she hadn't given him enough time to speak.

She peered at herself in the rearview mirror and considered that her bloated face no longer held the family resemblance. Years ago, her nose had been thinner, her cheekbones more pronounced. Her metabolism now crawled with a sloth-like speed; simply imagining food caused her to gain weight. If the storm weren't approaching, she would force herself to go for a walk or a bike ride, anything to combat the weight that anchored her.

The man had been right about post-storm existence. Once the clouds dissipated, the sun had scorched the rooftop castaways, forcing them to risk climbing through windows to sit in water-logged, mold-infested houses. There had been two to three days of a survival dance: stay on the roof for as long as the heat allowed, then go into the house until the mold caused coughing fits. After day three, the water had receded and supplies had been brought to the island. Despite this reprieve, Earl had been called to a final rescue mission.

Naomi had been angered; she hadn't understood why her father was being pulled away from her once more. The times he had been gone before had been terrifying, but she had consoled herself knowing that he was aiding the community. At this point, he should have been left alone to help his family rebuild. When Naomi had cried from fear and exhaustion, Earl had told her to be resilient. That he and the other men were making sure that this would be the last storm they would see.

꧁꧂

**ONE OF THE** last times Naomi had allowed herself to cry had been when the school reopened two weeks after Quincy. A strange woman sat at the desk at the front of the room, the desk that had been occupied by Naomi's favorite teacher.

Naomi had adored Mrs. Dollinger with her soft voice and her sparkly eye shadow. Mrs. Dollinger always wore the prettiest and softest dresses and she smelled like powder. Naomi had looked forward to being reunited with her beloved teacher who was the antithesis of the decay and devastation left behind by the storm.

At recess, Naomi's best friend Sharon had tried to console her.

"She's on maternity leave, remember? Before the storm, they kept telling us she would have the baby very soon." Sharon slipped her hand into Naomi's and tried to lead her to the jungle gym. "I'm sure she'll be back before we know it. Maybe she'll bring the baby to visit."

A voice from behind them chimed in, "That's not what I heard." It was Kevin, a quiet, lanky boy with a greasy cowlick and a bad habit of creeping up on people.

Sharon turned abruptly to face him. "And what did you hear?"

Kevin shrugged. "She disappeared. Her husband said she went to lie down on the day of the storm. And then she was gone. I mean, who takes a nap during a storm, anyway?"

Sharon did not hide her exasperation with Kevin. "What do you know? C'mon, Naomi. Don't listen to him."

When Mrs. Dollinger and her baby never visited, Naomi began to believe Kevin. He would whisper things across the row from his desk to hers. His father was the fire chief and Kevin had a habit of eavesdropping on his parents when they discussed town misfortunes.

"Six generations of chiefs" was Kevin's family's claim, which would make Earl laugh and question, "Only six?" The islanders took pride in the longevity of their geographic location, and that one extra generation that Earl and a few other families had accumulated was a badge of honor.

During a recess, Kevin showed Naomi a photo. It was of Kevin and a teenaged girl seated on a couch, each holding an ice cream cone with three full scoops. "That's Emily," he said.

"Who's Emily?" Naomi's eyes were drawn to the charm bracelet the girl wore on the wrist of the ice cream-holding hand. She could make out a charm of a ballerina with a pink gemstone for a tutu. She was familiar with the charm as she had seen one in the jewelry store in town. She had wanted to ask for it for her birthday but knew her parents would say no as she was not a dancer, nor did she have a bracelet from which she could dangle the charm.

"My babysitter. She disappeared, too. Just like Mrs. Dollinger."

Naomi remembered hearing something about a girl who had gone missing. "Was she the one who ran away with her boyfriend?"

"What boyfriend?" Kevin scoffed.

"When we were at the rec center, getting food, the grown-ups were talking about it."

Kevin shook his head. "I'm telling you she didn't have a boyfriend."

"Maybe you thought *you* were the boyfriend," Naomi fired back. She knew that was mean, but she had grown tired of Kevin and his acting as if he had an adult's arsenal of knowledge.

Kevin blushed. "I know I'm not her boyfriend and I know what happened to her. The men took her. Just like they took Mrs. Dollinger."

"What? What men?"

Kevin shrugged, as if the answer were obvious. "Ask your dad."

# CHAPTER TWO

*Can you afford not to feel your best?*

**NAOMI GLANCED AT** her phone and deleted the IM that was one of a series of related messages. She returned her attention to the house that she could see from her back window. The house was larger than the others in the neighborhood and there were many conversations among neighbors about how that affected market value. While there were arguments for both sides, Naomi cared more about one of the occupants of the home than the economic effect of its existence.

"Stop looking over there." Brad emerged from the pantry with several flashlights and a small radio.

Naomi thought she had been stealthy. She didn't want to upset Brad, especially with the storm approaching, but she also couldn't stop thinking about Veronica and the incident at the store. Naomi felt that she had played it cool despite being on the precipice of a panic attack.

"You're lucky she didn't make us move or run us out of town."

Naomi turned away from the window. "Does she have that much power?"

Brad stopped dropping batteries into a flashlight and looked at her skeptically. "Are you really asking me that?"

"No. I know the answer. Even the police are afraid of her." Naomi tried to take a seat next to Brad but he immediately stood up and moved to the center of the room. He was nervous and that was unusual for him, even during a storm.

"Besides, we all know nothing comes from the cop energy around here." She pointed to the left, knowing Brad would understand that she meant the neighbor who lived in that direction. "If he's still here…"

"That has nothing to do with cop energy. They had nothing on him; the man's innocent."

Now it was her turn to look incredulous. "Wife disappears during Yara? Wife disappears when she's *nine months pregnant.* That alone is enough to lock him up if you ask me."

"Maybe she left. Believe it or not, this island is not a life sentence."

"Said by a seventh generation-er." She thought for a moment. "So you're saying she just waddled on out of here without being noticed? She got back to the mainland without anyone on the ferry seeing her? A ferry that happens to be running during a hurricane, mind you, and not a single person saw a woman who was as big as a whale?"

"If I'm not allowed to body shame, neither are you."

"No shame. She had a whole human in there."

He shook his head. "I know nothing about it. All I know is they always blame the husband."

"Because ninety-nine percent of the time, he's the guilty party."

Brad shrugged. "No body, no crime."

"Alligators?" She came up behind him and wrapped her arms around his waist. She needed a hug, she needed his warmth, but she only received his stony back as he continued fiddling with a flashlight.

"These all the batteries they had?" he asked as he slipped away from her to root through their junk drawer in the kitchen.

"Yeah. It stays light late, though, so we won't need flashlights for much. Plus, the generator… right?"

"Hmm?  Right," he responded, but she wasn't sure he had heard the question.

Naomi sighed. "This is one of those times I wish we could fast forward to past tomorrow, to a few days from now. When all of this is over."

She noticed that Brad's jaw clenched, not with anger, but as if he were trying to stave off tears. She wondered if men also experienced heightened emotions as they aged and their hormones shifted. She could confess to recently sniffling over television commercials and songs on the radio, which would cause her to pop a Seres to mute those sentiments. Being a tough islander, Brad was not one to get teary-eyed easily, especially not over fears of a storm.

"Brad? What's wrong? Talk to me."

His face became composed again. "Honey, I'm serious. Don't even look over there. Ignoring her is the worst thing you can do to her, worse than hitting her again, even."

"She does love attention," Naomi agreed.

"And I love not having my blood pressure skyrocket."

This hit her. She knew how much stress she had caused him just in this year alone. When she had started feeling strange, she had sought help. She reported her insomnia and weight gain and sudden escalations of anger. Her therapist and her primary care physician had not been sympathetic to those complaints. Both suggested that she was simply not trying hard enough. If she just ate less, exercised more, and counted her blessings, she would see the world through rose-colored glasses.

Then, her thirty-year-old petite gynecologist suggested Naomi "learn to love her new body," and Naomi became despondent. Her old self-soothing tricks were failing her; she could no longer binge on chocolates, alcohol now made her sick, and she couldn't retreat into the world of dreams as sleep escaped her.

Following a panic attack and a hospitalization for pains (listed in her patient notes as "phantom pains"), Naomi was given a prescription for a hormone replacement. That prescription had felt like a winning lottery ticket until she tried to redeem it at the pharmacy and was told how much she would owe after insurance.

That was when she began lurking on social media, virtually eavesdropping on the conversations of women who claimed to be feeling better than they had when they were twenty. Her lurking was detected and she started receiving messages asking her if she could afford not to feel her best. She would not only be healthier, she would also join the countless others who became their own bosses and took control of their lives.

Thousands of dollars later, with a garage full of Seres gummies, and she was not feeling anywhere close to her best.

Thinking about Veronica made her want to take another Seres, but she was afraid to take too many too close together. Much of her time was devoted to thinking about Veronica and it had been that way for most of her life. It was just that now, with the hormones in her body rising and falling like carousel horses, the thoughts led to extreme emotions like rage and depression.

Seres took some of the edge off those emotions. While it was also supposed to help with weight gain, hot flashes, and insomnia, Naomi had not felt any relief from those symptoms. Regardless, she convinced herself that chewing the gummies made life safer for those around her.

Seres was a play on the goddess Ceres and also an allusion to the interconnectedness of women going through "the change of life." The marketing machine behind the gummies encouraged women to view life as episodic; more importantly, each episode, or series, could be an improvement on the prior one. And Naomi desperately needed things to improve.

"Brad?" she called, as he had gone to busy himself in another room. She desperately wanted to be comforted by him in that moment. She wanted him to assure her that all would be fine and if it weren't, he would do everything he could to protect her. "I have a feeling this is going to be bad again. Worse than Yara… more like Quincy."

Brad was not picking up on her needs. He called back, "If I were you, I'd ignore your feelings and rely more on the weather reports. You've been so ramped up; how can you tell if it's—"

"—I know, intuition or hormones."

"Exactly," Brad replied, effectively shutting down further storm speculation.

℁ℂ

**NAOMI HAD BEEN** journaling to keep track of her anxiety, from moderate to crippling episodes. She was also writing down her triggers. There were pages where the name "Veronica" was written over and over. Some of the pages contained ink that was scratched so angrily it didn't even look like her writing. Naomi was ready to consider that she might be harboring an obsession.

She had struck out at Veronica at the worst possible time. They were still making repairs on their home from Yara, and Naomi had also needed to cut back on work due to the symptoms she was experiencing from perimenopause. She and Brad were barely living paycheck to paycheck. Somehow Brad had persuaded Veronica to forego filing charges. He had assured Veronica that he would convince Naomi to see a therapist.

He had only bothered to remind Naomi about therapy once.

Naomi took advantage of the quiet of her bedroom to scrawl her feelings about the storm. This led to her feelings about the island. She wanted to write with nostalgia, with love. She tried to capture fond memories, until she realized she had very few. She loved her family and her husband, but she felt confined by a place where everyone knew each other and cruel rumors were exchanged as often as pleasantries.

Maybe talking about this to a new tele-therapist would be beneficial. Maybe getting it out to someone far removed from the island would prevent another incident, like the one with Veronica, from happening.

She heard Brad's voice from the other room. *"If this is the one… of course I'm ready but I'm not convinced of this storm yet, is all."*

Naomi finished writing her thoughts, hearing muffled speech from the other room. When finished, she tucked the journal beneath her arm and peeked out the bedroom door. "Were you on your phone just now?"

Brad looked startled, then he shook his head. "I don't have my phone, too busy getting ready for tomorrow. It's in there with you, charging."

She slipped back into the room to return the journal to her drawer. After securing it, she checked Brad's side of the bed. The empty charger spoke a confession. His phone was not in that room.

Her heartbeat crescendoed. He was lying to her, but why? She needed him to partner with her during this storm, not hide things from her. She knew he tiptoed around her to avoid emotional outbursts, but his doing so made her feel even more alone.

She began to try to name all that she was grateful for as a way of calming herself down and slowing her heart. Both her grandmother and her father had died from heart attacks and it unnerved her when she experienced cardiac symptoms. The irony: thinking about heart attacks nearly gave her one.

She began reminiscing about her grandmother and the things she had enjoyed about the woman in an attempt to distract her from Brad's fib about his phone.

She knew if she confronted him, he would accuse her of overreacting and that might spark a disagreement that could grow into a fight. She had to be prepared for the likelihood that they would be stuck together for a few days without any outside entertainment or interference. In the past, this type of togetherness had proven challenging. With her increased anxiety, a storm-based quarantine could be detrimental to their relationship.

Naomi shifted her mind from Brad to the cookies she and her grandmother used to bake. Her favorite had been the peanut butter with the Hershey's kiss on top. She would be allowed to eat one straight from the oven, the chocolate and warm dough synthesizing into a soupy delight on her tongue.

In addition to baking, her grandmother had also sewn clothes for Naomi's dolls. While Naomi could no longer remember the individual outfits, she could both imagine and nearly feel the strawberry pin cushion that her grandmother employed. It was hand-sized and soft with a smaller berry that was a needle sharpener attached by a green "vine." The sharpener made a scratching sound when Naomi rubbed it between her fingers and her grandmother would say, "You're waking the mice that live in the strawberry." Naomi wished she had the pincushion now to use as a stress ball.

When she was ready to return to the living room, she found Brad seated on their loveseat, looking up as if counting the minuscule mounds on their popcorn ceiling. She immediately regretted not wanting to be stuck with him following the storm. There was no one else she would rather be with.

It was just difficult, at times, to separate her recent unhappiness with the island from feelings about him. He and his family were so entrenched in island life, just as hers had been. That had been her initial attraction to him—he had been as committed to community life as her father had.

She sat beside him and placed her hand on his knee. "You know, it's weird, there were no storms while I was away."

Brad considered this. "You're right. It was Quincy when we were little. Then not another bad one until… Yara."

"And now two almost back-to-back."

He ran a hand through his hair. "We don't know that, not yet. This could still blow over. It really should."

She wasn't sure what he meant by *should* as he hadn't been looking at any of the weather reports. "This might have to be our last one, honey."

His eyes widened. "What are you suggesting?"

"I don't know… maybe climate change is making things worse." She stroked his leg, but he reached down and removed her hand. "Maybe we should think of moving, leaving the island. We aren't getting any younger and if we're going to be faced with a storm every season—"

"We won't. We won't see a storm every season." His voice caught and he swallowed hard to clear it. "That's not possible."

She sighed. "I was born here, too. Don't act as if you have some secret island sense and can tell what Mother Nature has in store." She put her hand beneath his chin and tried to turn his face toward hers. He resisted at first, seeming angered by her presence. Finally, he looked at her.

His eyes seemed to harbor tears again.

# CHAPTER THREE



**NAOMI DELETED THE** emergency text as she walked outside to anchor and lock the mailbox.

"Naomi? Naomi!"

It was too late; she had been spotted. Her neighbor, Todd, was coming from his garage with a plastic container balanced in one hand and a pair of knee-high rubber boots clasped in the other.

"I was just going through the last of Claire's things." Todd tilted the pair of boots toward her. "You could maybe use these? I hate to throw them out. I think she wore them once. And last storm…"

They both know how he intended to end that sentence.

Naomi chided herself for the awful thoughts she harbored about Todd. Wasn't she the same person who was lamenting the rumor mill on the island? Brad was right, they had no evidence against him and maybe his wife had simply left. Naomi could vouch for the impact hormones had on rational thought.

She smiled sweetly and accepted the boots. "They're very nice, thank you."

He returned her smile, only his was laden with sadness. "I hope… well, you know, I hope you get some wear, *more wear*, out of them."

"I'm sure I will. But probably not this storm. Brad keeps saying it'll pass us by."

"Brad said that?" Todd looked off into the distance as if calculating the storm's trajectory. "He may be right, or he's trying to convince himself…" He looked back at Naomi and smiled a more genuine smile this time. "It *is* projected to pass us over, land much further north."

Naomi sighed. "We keep repeating that, to make ourselves feel better."

"We have to. We have to keep our spirits up since this is the world we live in. The one we chose to live in. Islanders deal with storms; that's just the truth."

Without thinking, Naomi added, "The truth is, after Yara, we're all afraid of getting hurt again." She immediately bit her tongue; Todd's scars from the last storm ran deeper than most.

She nervously tried to cover for her error. "The problem is that none of us really knows where this one will land. None of us ever knows and the experts have been wrong before."

"And you… you and Brad, how are you feeling right now? I mean, about this storm and everything."

She didn't have the type of relationship with her neighbors where they spoke of feelings, so she wasn't sure how to respond. "We're fine. Just doing some last-minute things, you know, to prepare."

Todd looked away again. He seemed troubled, and Naomi could only imagine the painful memories that were resurfacing due to the eerily similar storm warnings. "I just hate to think that… what we've done, the precautions, would be for nothing."

"You mean, lose the renovations?"

He looked back at her, remembering she was there. "I guess." He shrugged, and the box he held moved with him. It was lamentably light, demonstrating how little remained from his marriage.

"This time might not be so bad." Naomi tried to be reassuring. "The rebuilds are strong. With the price we're paying for our roof, it should hold up until judgment day." When Todd did not immediately agree, she added quietly, "I hope."

It became clear that Todd had been referencing losses that could not be replaced. "Claire had never been through a hurricane before. She was naïve about it. I keep thinking about… if she hadn't got mixed up with me, if she hadn't moved here. I just never thought… it would be my turn."

Naomi was unsure how to respond. "No one's heard from her? Not her family or anyone?"

His nervousness dissipated and his eyes cleared. He spoke with purpose. "An aunt. An aunt of hers reached out to let me know she was safe. But I'm not to be in contact. Ever again."

"Todd, I'm so sorry. That's really difficult." She drew a deep breath before asking, "The baby?"

He shook his head, his expression despondent. "Some of us aren't meant for that kind of happiness." He reached into the box with one hand and pulled out a crocheted bootie. "She'd been working on these… before the storm."

Lifting the bootie had caused the container to tilt so that Naomi could see inside. "There's only one," she noted.

"That's all she got done, I guess. Once she set her mind to leaving there was probably no point."

There was something so desperate about the man, holding a solitary bootie in one hand and balancing the few mementoes of happier times he had left. She felt she had to say something. "I lost my grandmother with Quincy. She had a heart attack during clean-up."

"Yeah, I remember hearing that. I'm sorry."

"It really made me hate this place. I blamed the island for what happened to her."

Todd looked toward the bay again. "It's hard to hate a place that's in your blood. We have a responsibility to this place. For better or worse."

His cryptic pronouncements were not quelling her anxiety. She began seeking a polite way to excuse herself from the conversation when he added, "Everyone keeps telling me I have to move on."

"That's not anyone else's decision."

He smiled gratefully. "Claire always liked you. She never listened when Veronica…" He stopped himself. He squinted at something behind their homes and she imagined he was reliving an awkward scene between Veronica and his wife.

"It still didn't make me hate it here. My family has been here for generations, seven if you include me. I can't imagine being anywhere else. So, sometimes we face… sacrifices. You know what I mean?"

She nodded, even though she didn't share the sentiment.

"I was never turned upon, even in the darkest times." He looked at her in a way that made her uncomfortable; the eye contact was that deep. "People understand. Those that have been here so long… we share in this. We have all made sacrifices to be here."

She wondered why having a home required a sacrifice. Did people in other geographic locations suffer devastation and have to rebuild over and over? People said the islanders were lucky because the scenery was so beautiful and the way of life was idyllic. They didn't see the accumulation of loss that constituted the cost of living.

Todd continued, "Sometimes I wish the old timers were still around, like your dad. I would love to know what he went through."

Naomi was taken aback by this. She had not considered her father as having "gone through" much of anything. Until his paranoia set in later in life, he seemed to enjoy his work, his family, and his status. And most on the island were unaware of his mental state during his final years. He was a pillar of the community and when he passed, he went the way he would have wanted: on his beloved boat.

Earl had been found, not long after Naomi had married Brad, enshrined in a tarp that had covered his mother's house when she died. His boat had been in the bay, and based on the gear he had on hand, it had been assumed he had gotten cold while fishing. At some point after wrapping himself in the tarp, Earl had suffered a fatal heart attack.

"My dad would tell us to be resilient," she assured Todd, and he appeared grateful for the encouragement.

Naomi lifted the boots, bringing Todd's gaze back to them. "I should go back in now… help Brad. If you need anything…"

Her neighbor nodded, but he did not meet her eyes as he said, "I just wanted… again, I wanted to express my… I am grateful for all you've done."

She watched as he turned and walked down his driveway and into his house. She wondered what it was she had done for him.

# CHAPTER FOUR

*What is stopping you from taking control of your health, your finances, your body, and your life?*


**NAOMI DELETED THE** comment without posting. She hadn't used her social media for marketing in days, but she lacked the motivation to start a new thread. She knew this could set her back; she feared they might soon be without power and that it could be some time before it was restored. She would lose sales during that period, not that she truly had sales to lose.

"We have enough gas to keep the generator running for at least a day or two, right?" she asked Brad as he filled thermoses and stainless-steel cups with drinkable water. "At least until we can get out."

Brad snorted. "What do you take me for? A newbie?"

She hadn't meant to question his experience, but they had been without power for a week and a half following Yara and had run out of gas by the end of the first day of that week. The island's two gas stations had both been badly damaged and there had been no way to travel off the island to replenish. Yara had still been better than Quincy when the entire grid had needed to be rebuilt.

"We could be offline for quite a while," Naomi reminded him.

"Yep," he agreed, "but birds still sing after a storm."

She chuckled, happy that he was being silly and playful after his earlier sullen mood. "What does that mean?"

He shrugged. "It's an island thing."

*It's an island thing* was always said with a bit of a bite when those words were directed toward Naomi. In those instances, it referred to her going away to private school. Her friends at the time resented her, as if she had chosen to leave them.

The truth was her heart had broken when she had been sent away. And that was exactly how she had seen it: "sent away," banished. Her mother had assured Naomi that it was for the best. The island schools were lacking; they wanted to provide her with more opportunities, and so on.

Her mother's enthusiasm waned slightly as Naomi's departure date grew closer. "A bird is safe in its nest, but that is not what wings are for," the woman had managed, holding back tears as she helped Naomi pack.

"Actually, birds are safer on their wings than in their nests," her father had chimed in. He had the opposite energy from her mother; he seemed impatient for his daughter to leave.

Despite her parents' desire for the contrary, she ended up right back in "the nest" after falling in love with Brad when she returned home following high school.

She had lived with her parents while planning her wedding. Her joyful time had been darkened by a disturbing difference in her father's faculties. He had taken to pacing in the middle of the night and staring out their windows. He had become obsessed with the weather. He made sure he was in front of the television for the morning, noon, and evening news. At other times, he had the weather channel on the television as his "background noise" while he completed his chores. He had a maritime radio that he kept on, at a low volume, even while he slept. He also maintained a weather log, noting any discrepancies between the professional forecasts and the actual weather.

Earl had not taken to Brad with enthusiasm, either. Every so often, he would mention young men from the mainland, encouraging Naomi to "spread her wings" before settling down. Naomi knew that he did not know of any young men off the island and that no one she picked would be good enough in his eyes.

Oddly, Earl seemed most displeased that Brad was seventh generation.

◈

**WHILE SHE HAD** been away, Naomi had remained in touch with Sharon, who kept her abreast of the island gossip. Naomi always fished for dirt on Veronica and, at first, Sharon had been happy to supply it. Over time, Sharon lost patience with Naomi's obsession.

Following an awkward silence during one phone call, Sharon had lamented, "You haven't even asked me about my date with Kevin."

Naomi had inhaled sharply. She hated that she hurt her friend. "I'm sorry. I really am. I guess I still can't believe you went out with him. You hated him when we were kids."

"I didn't hate him… besides, you haven't seen him since he spent all summer on his uncle's fishing boat. I'm talking muscles for miles."

Naomi had pretended to gag, which caused them both to giggle.

"It's not all physical, we actually have stuff in common."

"Like what?"

"Like we both like foreign movies."

"Foreign meaning not made on the island?" Naomi teased.

"Shut it. You know what I mean. Clever films, with subtitles."

"You've always been so sophisticated. I remember you only eating the imported glue at school."

"Yuck it up, have yourself a good laugh," Sharon had said. "I like him and we're spending more time together. We both volunteered for the 'Clean the Bay' project. Kevin's very community-minded."

"I'm sure his mind is on other things besides the community when he's with you." Naomi had realized she was taking her teasing too far; Sharon was very serious about environmental projects. "I think it's cool that you two like each other. I never had a problem with him. And I didn't realize how much you have in common."

"Yep." Naomi could hear the grin in Sharon's voice. "So much. Movies… music, we have so much to talk about. And, we're both seventh generation, isn't that crazy?"

Naomi had laughed. "I got each of you beat by one, then."

"Nope. You left. That wipes the slate clean."

Adult Naomi would often wish the slate could be wiped clean that easily.

When Naomi had finished school, she and Sharon had renewed their friendship easily, but things had changed. While away, Naomi had learned how unique the beliefs of the people on the island were.

The church was not regularly attended; its dilapidated exterior and the parking lot, more potholes than spaces, demonstrated its lack of use. Instead, the community invested in the old ways of the people who were indigenous to their land. Or, at least, they attributed their customs to those native people.

From talking to her classmates who came from other places, Naomi had learned that the island people appeared a bit backwards and superstitious. Their festivals and gatherings were not celebrated anywhere else and their desire to commune with nature was labelled "pagan-like" by Naomi's fellow students. The image Naomi had conjured from the word pagan felt incongruous with the people she grew up with.

Yet, there was something distinctly different about the island's culture and Naomi had always felt set apart from that.

Another difference when Naomi returned to the island for good was that Sharon had become Kevin's wife. While the young women were still strongly committed to each other, Kevin seemed to feel that Naomi was intruding on their time as a couple.

Kevin had followed in his father's footsteps and become a firefighter, so Naomi took to seeing Sharon only when Kevin was at work. At first, he was working just one forty-eight-hour shift a week so Naomi had to tread very carefully. Eventually, construction began on a new station and Kevin was asked to help with moving equipment and supplies. This freed up Sharon's time even more.

Kevin had proudly given a tour of the new station to Sharon and Naomi. Naomi, happy to be included, had gushed with excitement over the construction. Sharon had taken a different tack; she had questioned the move along with the status of the old building.

"The old building's condemned," Kevin had answered her angrily. "What do you care about it anyway?"

"I just don't understand why they can't tear it down, then? Put that land to good use?"

"I'm not the mayor; I have no idea." He'd wagged a finger between his wife and Naomi. "Just promise me the two of you will stay away from it. Don't go snooping around."

"We won't," Naomi had quickly agreed, but Sharon had other ideas.

"They should have one last good party in it, right before the wrecking ball comes. Send it off right."

"There's not going to be a wrecking ball."

"It's a waste then." She'd raised her hand and smiled. "I vote to demolish it."

Her husband shook his head. "Birds don't destroy their old nests, not when new uses make themselves known."

Sharon had rolled her eyes. "Whoa… slow down, Socrates."

Naomi laughed. "What does that even mean?"

Kevin grew serious and said, "It's an island thing."

# CHAPTER FIVE



**THE WIDESPREAD, LONG** list of closures made their breakfast less appetizing on the morning of the storm. Brad shut off the television and Naomi later regretted that he did as the power went out an hour later at approximately 9:30 a.m. She would have preferred those extra moments of feeling connected to the world before that line of communication was cut.

"Power's out," she said, stating the obvious. "Or maybe it just evacuated the island. Like we should have." She went to the nearest window and looked out. "At least we still have daylight. We could read or do a puzzle or something."

"Or nap," Brad offered.

Her stomach sank. Sleep did not come easily to her anymore and she feared being alone in the storm more than she feared the storm itself. She remembered her father leaving during Quincy and how vulnerable she had felt. She remembered Brad relaxing during Yara and how she had envied him. Yara had been before her perimenopausal anxiety; she worried about how she might react this time if she felt he was not supporting her, or worse, abandoning her.

Rain and wind pounded against the windows as Iago inched ever closer. The storm made short work of Naomi's plans of using daylight as cloud coverage sank their home in darkness.

Something from the back window caught her eye. "Hey, Brad? The lights are on. Over there."

"What?" He seemed to have been resting his eyes; they were red once opened.

"Veronica's. Do they have power? Are we the only ones without?"

He shrugged. "Might be a generator."

"Why would they run it now? That makes no sense." She could feel her rage rising irrationally. "We have no idea how long we'll be without power."

"Maybe they have those battery-powered lamps like you use when camping."

She had stashed some Seres in a plastic baggie in her pocket "in case of emergency." This was starting to feel very much like an emergency so she put one in her mouth but did not chew. She let it dissolve on her tongue, numbing the muscle until it felt like she had a small weight inside her mouth. "Veronica doesn't camp, too dirty. Her family never camped."

Brad repeated his shrug, this time accompanying it with a sigh. "If they choose to run their generator, it has no effect on you."

She laughed bitterly, letting him know that it did affect her, at least mentally. "They better not wander over here when they run out of gas."

"Like *Mad Max*?"

"I was thinking more like *The Purge*." Naomi stopped there. Brad had no idea that she had a weapon stashed in the house and she was afraid that if she kept talking, she would mention the fantasies she harbored about protecting her home and herself with the gun.

He scoffed. "People are nothing but helpful during these storms, so don't go getting any ideas. Remember last time? Everyone was more than civil."

"We weren't as desperate last time. No one was this desperate. We've never had two hurricanes nearly back-to-back like this." She walked past him to grab a pair of binoculars from their coat closet.

"Put those down, are you crazy?"

"She can't see me." Naomi pressed the eye cups to her face and peered through the lenses but saw no movement from Veronica's house. She also could not tell if she saw lights or if her eyes were playing tricks on her. Her hormones were wreaking havoc on her eyesight, as well.

Brad came up beside her. "It's a reflection. You're making yourself crazy." He placed a hand on her shoulder. "Why don't you go lie down?"

"When have you known me to lie down in the middle of the day? Especially now?" *Especially now* had more to do with her emotional state than the storm that was raging outside. She leaned against him, just in time for him to pull away.

"Relax, the bay side never gets it as bad as the ocean side."

She knew that was another lie from her husband. She remembered climbing onto the roof as the water rose during Quincy. Their house had been on the bay side and the damage had been devastating.

They had been among those stranded on their roof. Her father had grabbed some downed branches and miraculously started a fire despite the dampness. He provided them with light that first night. While working on the fire, he mumbled some words that she did not recognize, and it seemed he was addressing the flames. It was not unusual for Earl to make up words and speak gibberish in an attempt to amuse her, but this time he did not check to see if she laughed.

The sun rose but the flood remained, so Earl built a shelter from the tarp he had stowed away in their skiff. When assembling the survival kits, Naomi had seen two tarps. One had the outline of a bird on it and she had thought that was pretty. The bird looked like the ibises that she found so funny. She loved to watch them scurry around, digging their long beaks into the ground with a frenetic energy. She asked Earl where that tarp was.

"Gave it to your grandmother," he'd answered. "She needed one, too."

Naomi had crawled from beneath the shelter, feeling abused, as only a child could, by not having the ibis tarp. She refused to return beneath the shelter, no matter how her parents pleaded with her. She stayed on the hot roof until she could no longer feel the sun, until she could no longer feel anything at all.

Her mother had led her back to the tarp as her father climbed into the skiff, the same boat he later died in. And Naomi had continued to sulk about tarps, when the tarp was the last help they had offered her grandmother.

As she thought about genetics and heart attacks and her very real chances of having one, Iago established residence above them. The house groaned and the roads outside were no longer visible beneath the rising water.

Naomi wished she could go on the internet and dive down a comforting rabbit hole for a mental break from this stress. Despite saddling her with more Seres than she could ever sell, TikTok and Instagram had allowed her to feel less *alone*. She was grateful for women who shared similar experiences to hers, who felt ill or out of control. She especially appreciated the stories of women who were "on the other side" of any kind of trouble or conflict. They gave her hope.

While normally a lurker, and nervous of engaging and falling prey to further MLMs and scams, Naomi had been inspired to reach out to one woman named Aida. Aida was a survivor of extreme circumstances. She had almost become the victim of a serial killer but had managed to fight him off.

Naomi had messaged Aida to say how much she admired her strength, knowing Earl would have lauded the woman's resilience. To Naomi's surprise, Aida had replied. The two corresponded a bit, and Naomi found in Aida a kindred spirit. She felt more support from this internet stranger than she had from anyone close to her in a long time.

Instead of asking anything of Naomi, Aida had asked how she could help her. According to Aida's story, she had dumped the gun that had saved her into the water. Naomi was shocked when a box arrived addressed to her with a revolver hidden inside a hollowed book titled *Canterbury Tales* and a note that said, "Naomi, I know you don't know me, but I was once in your shoes and when I needed it most, help came to me. I think I can send it to you now. Please. I can help you."

Naomi was not sure why Aida had lied about the gun or why she would think that Naomi now needed it, but having the revolver in arm's reach was soothing. Naomi's father had taught her to shoot and she and Brad had spent more than a few dates at the shooting range.

The noise the anxiety was making inside her head was now louder than the storm. Naomi knew she had taken more than enough Seres, so she dug into the back of her closet and pulled out an old shoe box. The box was where she hid the gun Aida had given her. She pulled the revolver out and felt her anxiety ebb due to the comfort of its weight in her hands. She traced the silver barrel and pink duct tape wrapped around the wooden handle.

The gun was engraved, but not professionally. On the handle, someone had carved "FOR HALEY." Naomi wondered who Haley was and if Aida had received the gun from her. Across the barrel, someone had etched

"EXCALIBER." It was evident the two dedications were made by two different people as the lettering did not match. She remembered mentioning *The Purge* to Brad, but this gun looked more like it came from her favorite romantic crime film, *True Romance*. That made her value the weapon even more.

There was one aspect of the gun that she did not cherish, as it only added to her misery. There was a keychain with Andy the Ant attached to a charm holder at the bottom of the grip. Naomi felt warmly toward Aida, as the woman seemed to want to help her. But if Aida had been the one to add the keychain, Naomi could not help but to equate her with yet another "loss" to Veronica in her life.

As a child, Naomi had begged her parents to take her to the Dreamscape amusement park. She had seen commercials on television featuring children experiencing enchanting adventures while eating theme park food and collecting souvenirs. She pictured herself stuffed to the brim with hotdogs and cotton candy, laden with trinkets, and riding marvelous rides. Her parents always refused. Their standard vacations were of the camping variety, as was the case with most islanders. Since they already lived in paradise, why did they need to go anywhere?

Veronica and her family were not like most islanders and Naomi could still remember the day when Veronica swanned into class after winter break, cuddling a stuffed Andy the Ant doll and regaling the crowd around her with tales of Dreamscape.

Despite Veronica's showboating, the stuffed ant did not invite snuggling. Its legs were long wire covered with spiky fur that was irritating to the touch. Worse, the face of the toy was an iron-on photorealistic decal of Andy. Andy was not cartoonish or cute, yet children received the mascot affectionately, as they had been trained to be devoted consumers since birth.

The doll was passed around at recess and lunch, each devotee remarking on its value, and thereby adding even more value to Veronica. Naomi had refused to touch the doll, and Veronica had appeared surprised by that. Surprised and a little hurt.

Naomi removed the keychain from the bottom of the grip and put it in her pants pocket. She then slipped the gun into her hoodie pocket, feeling more in control than she had for days. Even though a gun was useless protection against a hurricane, a nagging inner voice told her to keep it close.

ॐ

**ACCORDING TO THE** battery-powered clock on the counter, the water pipes beneath the street burst shortly before noon.

"Did you hear that?" Brad asked. "It's like the pipes screamed."

Naomi wanted to scream along with them. Instead, she offered, "The bathtub is full. We can still wash our hands, brush our teeth… basic hygiene."

They fell silent for another hour, both listening to the storm and watching from the windows. Shortly after one p.m., the palm tree in their front yard fell on their car. The shrieking metal was almost an embarrassment, as if the storm and falling tree had been their fault and the neighbors would be gossiping about it soon.

"Only six payments left," Brad muttered.

"Will insurance—?" The look on his face answered her question.

The house was being battered and Naomi swore she could feel it rocking on its foundation. She had been right: the new roof was holding up and for that she was grateful. Just as the winds seemed to slow, a siren shook the air, causing Naomi to jump.

"That's coming from the firehouse. Kind of a 'last call' for evacuations." Brad looked out the window. "I would say it's too late for that."

She remembered hearing sirens during Quincy, but none from Yara. "I didn't realize we could hear those sirens from here."

"They gotta make them loud. No other way to get the message across with no power."

She reached for a Seres but thought better of it. "Is that coming from the old station? Do they set off alarms on both sides of the island? That station is just down the road so we would hear it clearly."

Brad looked startled. "The old station… it's condemned."

"For years. It's been condemned for years." Naomi did not know what it was with these men and the old station. They imbued so much meaning into that old relic. "With storms like these, it seems unsafe to have 'condemned' buildings. What if pieces of it come loose, fly around and cause all sorts of damage? We've all secured our properties, is anyone looking after that building?"

"Honey, the storm is right above us. Can we not fight about buildings and neighbors?"

"And Seres and finances?" she suggested tentatively.

"And Seres and finances," he agreed.

Naomi's recent jump scare had woken her bladder. "I need to go to the bathroom; I promise I won't flush."

Brad grinned and said, "Unless something comes out that's so big it looks back at you."

"Gross."

As soon as she finished, Naomi peered out the bathroom window, as she had not been keeping tabs on how the storm was affecting that side of her house. She saw lights flicker in Todd's driveway: car lights. She hated to break the agreement she had with her husband only minutes after making it, but she could not remain silent.

"His car lights are on," she announced when she returned to the living room.

"Whose?"

"Todd's. They flashed. His car lights flashed off and on, like you do when you're warning other cars about police presence."

"He was probably testing his car fob. Maybe thinking about making a dash for the car and evacuating."

"On these roads? He might be a wife-killer, but he's not stupid."

Brad grimaced. "You're too invested in the comings and goings of our neighbors."

"No one should be coming and going right now. And the last time—"

"I really want to stop you right there."

"*She* disappeared right after the last one. And that little girl disappeared, too."

"Yep. And old Mrs. McPherson had that stroke, too, brought on by the storm." He shook his head. "Things come in threes, you know."

"Exactly." She felt for the gun she had secured in her waistband while in the bathroom. "And I don't want to be one of the threes this time."

# CHAPTER SIX

*I am so sorry for your [loss, illness, environmental disaster].
Depression is a natural outcome of this type of experience. But it
doesn't have to last. Our ancestors knew of the power of the organic
ingredients found in Seres. Unleash that power.*

**NAOMI TRACED THE** slightly raised, bumpy line on her knee, unsure if
she could truly feel it through her yoga pants or if her fingertips held the
memory of the scar she routinely touched to ground herself. It was barely visible
now, a phantom stroke of white swathing through her tan flesh, but the incident
decades ago that had dug a small channel in her flesh had felt life-changing at
the time.

Kevin had told her that pieces of his babysitter had washed up on the
bayside. *Pieces* was the exact word he had used and it had caused Naomi's
stomach to plummet while her curiosity soared. Had someone dismembered
the girl or had an alligator, or multiple gators, gotten to her? Even at the age of
eight, Naomi knew that alligators did not leave leftovers behind.

She and Sharon had followed Kevin on their bikes. Naomi had not wanted
to go alone with Kevin; she feared he might try to do something gross, like hold
her hand or even kiss her.

The bayside smelled like rotten fish and what Naomi imagined the innards
of dead vegetables to smell like, if vegetables died and had innards. The scent
was as familiar as it was disgusting and it heralded the onslaught of rain. It was
the scent of bacteria seeping in the humidity. By the evening, the sponge-like

clouds would be wrung by invisible hands, drenching the hard ground on which they now stood, converting it to a thickening mud.

The bayside was usually deserted in comparison to the beach and this day was no exception. The scenery was nothing but shells, dirt, and bones. The majority of the bones clearly belonged to fish. There were a few that were difficult to place.

"I don't think that's a person," Sharon had insisted.

"Then explain that." Kevin kicked at a small bone with a curved end. "That's a finger. That's where the knuckle would be. Fish don't have fingers." He pointed to the odorous water. "Nothing's got fingers in there. So, explain that."

"I can explain it," a voice had called. Naomi was disappointed to see Veronica and her friend, Gita, pushing their bikes closer. Veronica and Gita had a way of ruining even the simplest of things. They were nosy tattletales. The last thing she and her friends needed, if they had truly found human remains, was for the loudest kids in their school to know about it.

Kevin had folded his arms across his chest. "You weren't invited."

"We don't need to be," Gita retorted, "you don't own the bay."

Veronica moved past the group to the jetty of sharp rocks. "Was this hers? The babysitter, I mean." She pulled a piece of fabric from a crevice.

Kevin shrugged casually, but his face displayed concern. "How would I know? I didn't go through her things."

Veronica had turned the swatch in her hands. It was brown and thick, like canvas, and was decorated with a white Ibis. Upon closer inspection, it was clear that the Ibis was tearing open its chest with its spear-like beak. Despite this disturbing action, the ibis sat comfortably on an ornate nest which rested on a branch far above turbulent water.

"Have you seen this?" Veronica asked the group, but her eyes rested on Naomi. Naomi immediately thought of the ibis on her grandmother's tarp, but how could that have gotten here?

Sharon took a step back. "Don't touch that. You don't know where it came from." She'd darted a panicked glance at Naomi. "That could have been on a dead body."

"I thought you said the bones didn't belong to a person," Kevin grumbled. It was obvious that this excursion was not going as he had planned.

"Do you know what this is?" Gita whispered to Veronica while pointing to the fabric. Her whispers were louder than intended.

"I guess…" Veronica had stopped herself. "Kevin, you would know."

"Shut the fuck up, Veronica," Kevin snapped and the others gasped. They had never heard one of their peers say that word.

Veronica was not deterred. "Our families have all been here… anyone who has been here this long…" Veronica struggled to find the words. "I mean, the elders from long ago, they—"

"That's a legend, Veronica," Sharon interrupted, "like Santa Claus or something."

Gita paled. Naomi had wondered if the girl still believed that her presents arrived via a sleigh and reindeer.

"Besides, this cloth is here now. What would it have to do with the elders?" Kevin asked.

"I don't know, I just heard."

"We've all heard things." Sharon took on an adult tone, which sounded funny coming from her small body. "But it's over. The storm is over."

"For now," Veronica had conceded. "But the next time… we have to worry about the next time. The men, I mean, the rescuers, they weren't doing that, they weren't rescuing. Not that final trip."

"What are you talking about?" Naomi could feel her face reddening.

"Tell her, Kevin," Veronica's voice was insistent.

"He doesn't need to tell me anything. You're the one with a big mouth." Naomi put her hands on Veronica's shoulders and gave her a shove. To her surprise, Veronica shoved back.

"Hey, guys, let's—" Sharon had tried to intervene but it was too late. The two girls were lost in a melee of slaps, pushes, and hair pulling. It was Naomi's first fight and it looked nothing like the ones she had seen in the movies. Veronica's slaps stung and Naomi wanted to stop fighting, but she knew she would look weak if she put an end to it first.

"Veronica!" Gita yelled. "Don't do this!"

A bolt of lightning danced across the water and that was enough to break the spell. They had all been warned countless times to go inside during a lightning storm. The children grabbed their bikes and began pedaling furiously. Veronica and Gita glided ahead quickly with Kevin and Sharon not far behind.

No matter how rapidly Naomi pumped her legs, she could not seem to close the gap between herself and the group.

A clap of thunder spooked her and she swerved, falling and skidding across the gravel road. Her bicycle fell on top of her leg, pressing it against the hot pavement. For a moment, she could not move, could not breathe. Then, a burst of air entered her throat and she screamed.

Naomi rolled over, kicking the bicycle off. Her knee was skinned. Hot tears burned her eyes but she refused to let them fall. Shadows were growing closer and she feared that Vernonica would think she was crying over the fight.

The kids leapt from their bikes and Kevin bent down beside Naomi, looking at her bloody knee, while Sharon examined Naomi's bike.

"If you put some of the mud from the bay on it, it will protect it until you get home." Veronica started to kneel down to help.

"Get away from me!" Naomi had swatted at the girl but she was just out of reach.

Sharon pointed at one of Naomi's tires. "That's your earring, Veron."

Veronica's hands moved to her ears, verifying that the tiny one embedded in Naomi's tire matched the one penetrating her lobe.

"You did this!" Naomi screeched. "You…" She gestured to her knee. She had wanted to weep, both from pain and from anger, but she had promised her father she would be resilient in times like this.

"I didn't!" Veronica had insisted. "The earring fell out. I would never puncture your tire."

"Yeah." Gita defended her friend. "I've been with her the entire time. She didn't do anything."

When Naomi said nothing, but quietly glared at the girls, Kevin had instructed Veronica and Gita to ride home, leaving Sharon and him to help Naomi. The two girls protested at first, then reluctantly peddled away.

Kevin crouched beside Naomi and carefully pulled her to her feet. "Can you go get help?" he'd asked Sharon. "Like maybe her dad or my dad? They could come with a truck and get our bikes."

Sharon nodded and took off.

"We can't stay here." Naomi sniffled. "The rain."

"We'll start heading home. That way, they'll find us sooner." He'd threaded his arm across her back and placed her arm over his shoulders. They began to move slowly. Kevin kept that pace, so that Naomi did not have to struggle, even when the rain came down in torrents.

"What are you thinking about?" Brad's voice interrupted her thoughts, sounding more concerned than conversational.

"Just thinking about Kevin… and Sharon, I guess."

"You miss her."

Naomi sniffed, suddenly aware that she was moments away from tears, and she didn't want to pull a Seres from her pocket in front of Brad, as he would see the outline of the gun. "When you get to be our age, you've said your fair share of goodbyes." She pulled a pillow over her lap, hiding her weapon.

"I should talk to Kevin more. I kind of avoided him after Sharon's accident. It was too painful. All those years ago, I was only thinking about myself and not about his pain. He lost a wife."

Brad's face paled.

"I'm sorry, I didn't mean to upset you. They're your friends, too."

"No. It's okay. You… you didn't upset me. It's just the storm and everything."

Naomi picked at the pillow. "I don't remember it being this rough… with Yara. Is this PTSD or something?"

"Something like that."

"Brad…" She waited until he looked her in the eyes. "We'll be okay, right?"

He took a deep breath. "I'm going to get you something to drink. You need to stay hydrated."

She was very aware that he did not answer her question. He did not have a great track record for articulating his emotions, and she was afraid if she pushed further, he would shut down completely.

He brought her an opened Gatorade and she seized the opportunity to elevate the energy in the room.

"You roofie this?" Naomi launched into their shared joke, one they repeated often and enjoyed each time.

Brad's lips turned up in a smile, but the mirth missed his eyes. "Of course."

She lifted the bottle as if toasting. "Well, enjoy yourself later."

He wriggled his eyebrows as he always did; he was following the script, faking the humor. His voice dropped an octave as he said his line, "Oh, I plan to."

# CHAPTER SEVEN



**A SIREN SHRIEKED** from Naomi's phone. Her first thought was that she had not been too far off with her comparison of the storm to purge night: the warning sounds of both were identical. Her second thought was that the cell towers must still be standing if she was receiving an alert. And her third thought was one of surprise that she had managed to fall asleep. She had never been a napper and her newly habitual anxiety manifested as insomnia. To drift off during a major storm when her nerves felt like live electrical wires was unbelievable.

A fourth thought, after rubbing her eyes and sitting up straighter on the couch, was that there was a shadow at the front door.

"Brad?" she called. Their bedroom door was shut. She assumed he had gone to lie down and get some rest once she had conked out.

The shadow was large and it was clearly not her imagination. As it shifted, she made out another shadow of similar size. Were there two people at her door? This would not be the time for Jehovah's Witnesses to be about, or the people who were constantly trying to sell solar panels. She slid the revolver from her waistband. Whoever was out there was up to no good as no trustworthy person would be prowling on people's porches during a major hurricane.

"Who's there?" she called. There was no answer, or maybe she couldn't hear it above the wind.

"I have a gun," she warned, ineffectively, as the doorknob began to turn. She and Brad only locked the doors at night, while they slept, so there was nothing to prevent the shadows from opening the door and coming in.

She leveled the revolver in her right hand. She clenched her left hand beneath her right for stability. She pointed it at the door, cocked the hammer, and put her finger on the trigger.

As the door opened, the shadow evolved into the clear image of her husband. "Jeezus, woman! One of the storm shutters looked loose and I was fastening it."

She lowered the gun, her heart pounding so strongly she was sure it was visible. "I thought you were napping."

"I thought you were napping!"

"I never nap. You know that. Besides, you can't be outside now." She was gasping and rambling as her mind tried to convince her that the two shadows she had seen had only been one. There was no way her husband could have cast both.

"Safer out there than in here."

As soon as Brad said this, they heard a horrible crash coming from the house that bordered theirs on their right. They ran to the window to see a boat drifting into the extended porch at the front of the neighbors' home, nosing through the door and leaving a pile of beams and scattered screens in its wake.

"Not safer over there," Brad said, and Naomi was out the front door before he could call her back. She heard him yell something about the gun but she was more concerned with inviting the neighbors to shelter with them as they no longer had a barrier against the water.

Even though their homes were a few yards apart, it required a great deal of energy to press through the wind and call into the blackness around the boat.

"Hello? Sam? Kate?" Naomi could see no movement and no one responded to her calls. She pushed her way in, mostly to grab a break from the pummeling rain and wind before heading back to her home. The house appeared deserted and she remembered that the older couple who lived there were visiting their children. They were not even in the state, let alone in danger of the hurricane.

She cursed her forgetfulness and she cursed Seres, which was supposed to lift the "brain fog" associated with the change of life. As she turned to head back, she saw that the neighbors' grandmother clock had fallen off the wall.

As if to make up for the casualty that was now their front porch and door, Naomi lifted the clock and decided to place it inside the dishwasher to keep it safe from floodwater. It was heavy and as she struggled with it, a piece of folded canvas that had been taped to the bottom came loose. She was able to bend and grab it while maintaining hold of the antique clock.

Naomi placed the clock inside the dishwasher and attempted to re-fasten the canvas to the wood. She had no intention of examining the material, but the fabric unfurled enough to get the best of her. Once she realized it was a map, she could not help but look.

*A treasure map?* The neighbors' family predated both Brad's and Naomi's on the island; they could possibly hail from pirate stock. They might even be able to trace their lineage back to the earliest Spanish explorers.

It did not take long for Naomi to recognize that it was a map of the island. The map was old, but well preserved; it contained marks and a smattering of handwriting. There were swirls and thin lines drawn on the water around the island with arrows pointing in different directions. It looked like a primitive version of the weather tracking systems her father had been so obsessed with.

She traced the lines with her finger, feeling patterns more than seeing them. There was something relaxing about the swirls; she nearly forgot she was in the center of a raging storm. She smoothed the material where the bay was represented, noting that the shoreline had been drawn much broader than it was now.

*This is a pre-Quincy map,* she thought, *who knows how many storms prior? Back before the erosion… before the sea started to swallow us whole…*

Her fingers moved from the bay inland. The topography was detailed enough that Naomi could pick out familiar locations. There were markings and notations made on areas that she knew were now bare. She assumed that there had been buildings or homes there previously.

Several structures were circled with numbers beside them. Naomi searched until she found the neighborhood where she'd lived as a child. Both her parents' and her grandmother's houses had been marked, in different colors and with numbers.

Her grandmother's house had been sold and renovated years ago and Naomi's childhood home had been bought by a family from the mainland after Naomi's mother passed. She wondered if the numbers related to real estate sales and the fluctuating market, a topic even more popular than the storms. 197993 was beside her grandmother's house, perhaps that had been the sale price? But beside her parents' was 1994512 and she knew for a fact that house did not sell for a million.

She decided to take the map with her. She would return it after she had a chance to examine it further. After all, the owners of the map were in no need of it now. She smoothed it again so she could fold it and noticed something curious.

In their neighborhood, both her house and Todd's house were marked.

# CHAPTER EIGHT

*To honor your time, I would like to offer you one of our special gift boxes.*


**MONTHS PRIOR TO** Iago, Naomi had stood nervously on a doorstep a mile or so from her house, fidgeting with cue cards before stuffing them into her purse.

*You don't have to do this,* she told herself. *You can turn around right now.*

Only she hadn't been able to leave. Naomi had promised Brad she would try to sell the Seres, that she would take advantage of opportunities. Unfortunately, this opportunity contained people she knew, some for decades, and shilling her wares was the equivalent of wearing a neon sign that read "I am struggling."

And she would rather die than admit she was struggling, especially in front of one woman in particular.

She had practiced her speech multiple times. The trick was that it wasn't meant to sound scripted; it was to appear organic to the conversation.

Naomi knew that when this group of women congregated, they engaged in competitive misery. They lay all the cards on the table: laborious work schedules, insurmountable household chores, demonic children, and deadweight husbands. She could introduce the idea of Seres as a solution and, conveniently, have some available for purchase in the trunk of her car.

This assurance did nothing to staunch the flow of sweat that ran down her face and onto her blouse, making her appear as if she had just run a marathon.

She pulled a bottle from her purse and popped a Seres into her mouth. Fanning herself with her hands, she managed to clear some of the droplets.

She raised her fist and rapped on the door. She was going to do this. She was going to prove to Brad that she *could* do this.

The door was opened to grant Naomi entrance, and her eyes were immediately drawn to the buffet laid out on the kitchen island of the open floor plan. It was a sumptuous spread. An oasis of delights unattainable due to her sluggish metabolism. Her gaze traveled from end to end of the counter, calculating caloric intake. She could either eat nothing there or eat one item and spend approximately five hours on a treadmill hoping to expend eight times the energy she consumed.

The women were already seated in the living room engaged in conversation. They were chatting about a television show they all watched, and their plates were frustratingly full of delectables.

"He's much more handsome on this show than he was on *Behind the Door*. He's really grown into his face."

"Grown? That's filler, honey. Nothing natural about that," said Rika, who had been a few years ahead of Naomi in school.

Naomi had put carrot shreds and mushrooms she had extracted from a vegetable lasagna on a small paper plate and walked toward the women, only to find that all seats were taken. She'd awkwardly perched on the arm of the couch next to Nia and Amani. They had been inseparable in high school and seemed to have carried that over into adulthood. They also could have slid over and provided her a portion of the cushion.

"No shame in using fillers, they all do it," Nia insisted

"What's so wrong with growing old naturally?" another woman inquired.

Naomi took this opportunity to make her presence known. She gripped her plate so that her shaking hands were not noticeable. "There's nothing *wrong* with growing old, but, at times, it can be unpleasant, right?" She lifted her plate as if making a toast. "I mean, I was really struggling with insomnia and moodiness and…"

She stopped herself before mentioning weight gain. She didn't want to give anyone that ammunition, especially not Veronica. "It was rough for a while, then I started on Seres and—"

"Oh no, " Nia groaned, not bothering to turn her head to look at Naomi, "you're a Wilma."

"Excuse me?"

"A Wilma. A female Willy Loman. You know, *Death of a Salesman*. Weren't you in that piece of shit back in high school?"

Naomi could feel herself blush. "No. Not me."

"No, to which? Being in the play or being a depressing, unwanted"— Veronica looked around the room, finally making eye contact with the hostess—"and probably an uninvited salesman?"

"Both, I guess." Naomi's nerve was gone. She had rehearsed for nothing. Veronica had a way of making her feel as if she were tumbling off her bike into the mud, even as an adult.

"She is a Wilma. I saw her harassing people on Facebook," Amani confirmed.

Naomi had been shocked. "I've never harassed anyone."

"Yep, harassment. You can't deny it. I follow her and have seen her going after… the ones even more desperate than the Wilmas."

"Deer hunters go where the deer are," Rika said, smiling smugly.

Naomi had felt hot. If only she could get a Seres from her bag to bring her heartbeat back to normal. "That's not true—"

"Going after poor women who don't have all that she does," Amani continued.

"All that I have?" Naomi was incredulous.

"Didn't you ever hear of picking on someone your own size?" Rika asked with a satisfied smirk.

Naomi could not help herself; her anger was moving her tongue on its own. "That wouldn't be you, then. If I had an ass the size of yours, Rika, I would kill myself."

The women gasped. That was crossing a line. While they had no problem picking on each other's physical attributes, there was an unwritten rule that those types of remarks remained behind each other's backs.

Naomi knew she had already lost the battle. She hated to let Brad down, but she was shaking and angry and there was no coming back from her faux pas. The women had glared at her as if she were a thief who had stolen the joy from their gathering.  She'd stood and walked to the door. Despite feeling their eyes boring into her back, she hadn't quickened her step. She wouldn't give them that satisfaction.

Someone's hand landed on her shoulder. She turned to see Veronica with a look of concern on her face. "Naomi, I know you and I have never been friends, but… I feel obligated to warn you—"

Naomi had felt her blood pressure rise. "You're right, we aren't friends, so I am not obligated to listen to you."

"Hurricane season is coming," Veronica spat in a hiss.

"What? Are you… are you mental? It sounds like you're cursing me or something."

"No, no, listen." Veronica had lowered her voice to a whisper. The women were still staring and Naomi was growing more and more uncomfortable with each passing minute. "Remember at the bay with Kevin? We were kids and we found that swatch of fabric? Kevin knew what it was, Sharon knew what it was. If you won't listen to me, maybe you'll talk to—"

"I can't talk to Sharon, remember, she wrapped her car around that tree."

Veronica's eyes had grown wide. "I know, I know. Believe me, that was for the best. Sharon—"

Naomi stopped Veronica's words with a vicious punch that landed on her frosted coral lips. Naomi had not hit anyone since that time at the bay that Veronica was referring to.

The mention of her friend's name and saying that her death was somehow a positive outcome had shaken her to the core. There was no way she could have prevented herself from swinging. Her rage was at its threshold. She feared that if Veronica had continued talking, she would have wrapped her hands around the woman's throat, squeezing until her palms nearly touched.

Veronica had cupped her mouth in shock. Nia was on her feet, rushing to Veronica's side.

Naomi was out the door before any of the women could say or do anything. As she was hurrying to her car, Veronica had called after her, "Go home and pay attention to that husband of yours. You need to keep an eye on him."

# CHAPTER NINE

*EMERGENCY PERSONNEL ARE NO LONGER ABLE TO HELP YOU. IF YOU HAVE NOT EVACUATED, PLEASE WRITE YOUR FIRST AND LAST NAME AND BIRTHDATE ON YOUR ARM IN PERMANENT MARKER.*

**EMERGENCY TEXT MESSAGES** continued to appear on their phones. Silence would have been preferable to the words of doom being transmitted. Brad, who had taken to pacing thirty minutes prior, announced, "I'm putting the tarp up."

"Now?" Naomi could see only water from their window. "It's too dangerous. The roof isn't even leaking."

"We need to protect it."

"That's not what a tarp is for." He wasn't listening, but was pulling on his galoshes and rain gear, which would do little against the rising flood water. "The rain stopped, but the water is still rising. Where are you going to put a ladder? Please, we can wait until tomorrow."

"I'm not having the stars fall on our heads while we sleep." He turned and smiled and his smile was so boyish that she remembered falling in love with him for the first time. Since then, the years had been a series of falling in and out of love.

She returned his smile. "My dad used to say that when I was little."

Brad nodded. "It's an island thing." He pointed to their ceiling. "Those stars are just nests for heavenly birds and the longer we keep those stars from falling, the longer we're safe from another storm."

She remembered her father saying the same thing when he adjusted their tarp during Hurricane Quincy. He had told her that it really didn't matter that they had the tarp without the bird; they all worked the same. When her grandmother died during cleanup, Naomi had felt guilty for pouting over a tarp.

Current day Naomi realized that she was nearly the same age her grandmother had been during Quincy. Her grandmother had seemed so… old. This realization raised her anxiety and quickened her heartbeat.

"Besides." Brad pointed across the street. "She's got hers up already."

Naomi couldn't argue that. The neighbor whose grass was always short and even—despite never seeing her mow—whose Christmas decorations rivaled the Macy's window, and whose barbecue always smelled like it was prepared by a Michelin chef, had a tarp securely fastened to the roof of her house. There was no explanation for how she managed to scurry up twelve feet of wet concrete without being noticed.

"She beat me again."

"I thought we were ignoring the neighbors?"

"*You.*" He chucked a finger under her chin as he headed to the garage. "*You* are ignoring the neighbors."

Having him touch her after days of seeming to avoid her bolstered Naomi's spirits. "Should I come hold the ladder?" she called, heading toward the garage to see him hoisting a ladder through a window.

"Can't get that automatic door open."

She frowned. "I think that's the universe telling you to wait."

"Even if I did get it open, the water would pour in here and soak your precious boxes."

The mention of her inventory shook some of the storm-related shock from her brain. She looked to her containers of Seres and silently counted them. "One's missing."

"Hmmm?" He was focused on finding flat earth to stand the ladder upon.

"A box, one of the boxes is missing."

"Maybe it's still in the car? Meaning, beneath the tree that smashed into the car."

Her heart picked up speed again. "Insurance won't cover the Seres, I guess." She could tell that he was no longer paying attention.

She went into the house to try to tally the number of bottles that had been in that box. She had a spreadsheet for inventory, but she didn't want to waste the battery on her laptop.

She looked out the back window to see if there was any activity at Veronica's house. It was dark, even though they were still an hour or so before sunset. Against the navy backdrop of the dark water and sky, she saw one of her containers.

After confirming that Brad was consumed with his tarp work at the front of the house, Naomi slipped on the boots Todd had given her, knowing they might not be tall enough to protect her from the flood, but the soles would help her maintain balance and protect her from the debris that lay hidden beneath the dark water.

Naomi struggled with the back door. The rain had caused it to swell and it stubbornly clung to the frame. Once she was able to wrench the door open, she stepped onto what was once their lanai.

The steel beams had collapsed and the screens had been blown away. The water was up to her hips, and her trek toward the container was impeded by downed tree limbs and blown-out shingles, shutters, and window frames that created submerged stumbling blocks. She did not want to fall into the filthy water and she tried to push the thought of live downed wires out of her mind.

She had moved the revolver from her pants to her shirt, using her bra strap as a makeshift holster and resting the nozzle against her breast. Brad had forced her to remove the bullets after she nearly shot him coming in the front door, but she still felt safer with the gun on her person.

She kept one eye on the plastic container that appeared to be caught on a pile of detritus. It was unusual to encounter alligators in the brackish water on the bay side, but it would not have been impossible for a toothy reptile to have been waylaid by the storm. Each step meant placing her foot into the unknown, yet she stubbornly pursued the container full of Seres. She prayed the majority of the inventory could be salvaged.

A dead raccoon floated past her and she felt herself tearing up, not for the dead mammal she had never met, but for the predicament she now found herself in. She could not retreat to the false comfort of financial support from FEMA and insurance. She had been down both paths before and they were dead ends. Finances had already put a strain on her marriage; she feared the damage from this storm would be the breaking point.

That thought breached the dam that held back her tears. After so many years, she allowed them to flow freely. Back in the house and in front of Brad, she would have to appear resilient. In the muck and potentially toxic water, she could allow any and all emotions to rise. She wanted to scream, but she was still close enough for Brad to hear. There was no need to endanger him by making him believe she needed to be rescued.

She looked back, seeing the tarp unfurl down the back of the house, waiting to be secured to the roof. She saw the image of a bird on the tarp, just like the one that had been given to her grandmother. She found it remarkable that that brand was still around and wondered when Brad had purchased it, as she was usually in charge of disaster supplies.

The box was nearly within reach when Naomi's foot came down on a slippery rock and her ankle twisted, bringing her to her knees. She swallowed water as she gasped in shock and pain.

"Why?" she choked, looking to the sky which was beginning to show a spectacle of stars as the sun set. She had forgotten that the universe presented the most glorious sunsets and starry nights following the most devastating storms. It was like a reward for withstanding the worst that nature could deliver.

The stars reminded her that Brad would finish installing his "star catcher" soon and look for her. She pulled herself up onto her good foot and tentatively placed the injured ankle on the muddy floor of the hurricane-crafted lake in her yard. The pain caused her to grimace, but she bit her lip and propelled forward, gaining on the plastic container that appeared even more devious now that it had caused her both physical and economic harm.

She leaned forward and grabbed the box by the handles, realizing that she now had to cover the terrain back to the house. She would be forced to be honest with Brad; there was no way to mask her wet clothing or the smell that was embedded in her skin and hair. *And a shower is still days away, maybe even a week or so,* she reminded herself, sinking into pity.

Once the container was freed from the jetson, it moved easily, floating atop the water. Naomi knew that boxes of Seres within would have provided additional weight. She paused to lift the lid and peer inside.

She prayed she would see her inventory intact, but her prayers were ignored. Instead, she saw an old book wrapped in yards of cellophane and a smaller box, locked with a padlock.

She looked back to the roof to see if Brad was finished.

The tarp was gone.

"Oh shit," she whispered. That was not a good sign. She imagined him, inside the house, storming with rage over some issue with the tarp and over her absence. She had to get back.

She pulled the container along with her, planning to examine it later. She bounced along tediously, floating more than walking to avoid putting too much weight on her ankle. It felt as if it took three times as long to return to the house as it did to retrieve the container and she cursed herself for her impulsivity. Losing a few boxes of Seres was not important. She had to remember that her perception was off, that her and Brad's safety were of primary importance.

"Brad?" she called as she carried the container through the back door. "I know I shouldn't go out; I just saw some of my stuff, what I thought was my box…"

There was no one in the living room. She checked the bedroom and the bathroom: no sign of Brad.

She went to the garage and peeked out the window Brad had used as an exit. The ladder was no longer there. She ran for the front door, fearing he had gotten disoriented in the storm, only to find the reality was worse than her fears.

Brad lay on their porch, wrapped in the tarp.

# CHAPTER TEN

*If time machines were real, the first thing I would tell my younger self would be to start with Seres early. Since I can't do that, I am going to tell all of you. Women need to help women. We can't thrive alone.*

**WITHOUT UNDERSTANDING WHY,** an old social media post that Naomi had crafted to entice customers replayed in her mind. If she truly had a time machine, she would only need to return to a few moments prior, to help Brad. He was unconscious and thankfully out of the range of the water for the time being. She couldn't determine the extent of his injuries, but he was breathing.

Naomi limped through the water in their front yard and onto the flooded street with her phone extended until she could find a bar. She tried calling 9-1-1.

Naomi started speaking before the dispatcher could begin her scripted dialogue. "I don't know what happened. It's my husband. He's not responding. I think he fell. Or maybe his heart."

The dispatcher sounded fatigued. "Ma'am, no one can come to help. There is a hurricane—"

"I am very aware!"

"Ma'am, please stay calm. Let me get some information from you and when it is safe to send emergency personnel—"

Naomi ended the call, wishing for the old, corded phones that provided the catharsis of being able to slam them down when hanging up. She needed help now, and she had no idea of how soon it would be before it was safe to venture out.

She went back to the porch and sank next to Brad. She repeated his name, over and over. It was as if she believed that saying his name would reprogram the algorithm of her life and he would be fine. She thought again of a time machine and how wonderful it would be to go back a few days and evacuate the island. They could be in a hotel right now, watching the storm on television from a safe distance. Lights would be on, food would be warm, and they would be together.

But time machines weren't real. What was real was that she was alone, in the dark, and responsible for caring for her husband when she did not know how. She managed to pull Brad inside the door and into the living room. She left him on the floor, still wrapped in the tarp, as she knew she lacked the strength to hoist him onto the couch.

If she started the generator, she would be able to turn on the lights and examine Brad. Simply having the lights on would feel like a major victory and provide a panacea for her nerves.

Using a flashlight, Naomi made her way to the garage. The generator was covered by an old blanket which she flung aside so she could wheel it to the outlet they had installed following Yara. She scanned the generator with her flashlight, mentally picturing Brad starting it up.

She pulled the cord and it sputtered in response. She pulled again, the effort matched with a chorus of choking sounds.

"No gas?" She was incredulous. The generator should have been the first item taken care of during storm prep. Brad had assured her that the tank was full. Then again, Brad had said several things that were not true in the past twenty-four hours.

Naomi searched the garage for a canister, hoping to find a full one since she knew that Brad had visited the gas station a few days prior.

She pushed through several plastic containers of Seres and saw a two-gallon canister tossed in the corner behind her inventory. It was open and on its side. She could tell it was empty without lifting it, but she lifted it anyway.

With all of their storm prep, how could this have happened? This neglect was dangerous and entirely unlike Brad.

As she stepped around her plastic containers, she noticed drops of liquid leading to the side garage door. Naomi had to struggle to open the door as the wind had contorted its frame, but once she did, she was nearly assaulted by the smell of gasoline. Had someone gotten in and dumped their fuel? She had thought she had seen movement around their home, but who would do this to them? Even Veronica would not assault them in this way; she was much more passive-aggressive in her attacks.

Naomi went back inside and headed to the living room to check on Brad. After making sure her husband was breathing easily, she turned her attention to the container she had rescued from the flood. With no generator, there was little she could do besides look at the old book. She was hoping for a distraction. Lifting the lid, she was met with a smell that she hadn't noticed when outside. It was the stale smell of antiques, the smell of flea markets and estate sales.

She pulled out the book, unwrapping it and placing it in the beam of her flashlight. The book was bound in leather, cracked in such a way that its age was evident, almost as if the cracks were the equivalent of the rings of a tree trunk. The cover was embossed with an ibis cutting into its heart with its beak while perched on a nest high above tumultuous water.

The pages were thin and worn and Naomi turned them carefully to avoid ripping them. There were words in some foreign language and sketches of a young girl, a pregnant woman, and an old woman. As she flipped through the book, there were additional sketches of women, always in groups of three and always in the same three stages of development. The pregnant woman strongly resembled the curvy goddess on the Seres bottle.

There was a page near the end that contained a series of numbers. Instinctively, Naomi pulled the map from her pocket to compare them. They weren't matches; they had similarities but the orders were scrambled. The map said 197993 and the book said 391979. The number 1979 caused her to pause.

*That was a big year,* she thought. That had been the year of Quincy; the old timers never let anyone forget that. "The storm of 1979," they would say, almost wistfully.

She looked at another number on the map, 1994512. *1994…* She remembered the emergency message asking them to write their names and birthdates on their arms.

She was looking at dates. 197993 was September 3, 1979, the exact date of Quincy. 1994512 was May 12, 1994, the same day her father died.

She peered at the mark on her house; there were no numbers next to it, just a mark. Todd's house had the same notation.

She was now desperate to open the smaller box. It might be paranoia, or it might be that the marks on the map were noting deaths and disappearances. More importantly, the numbers seemed connected to her.

Naomi quickly grabbed two wrenches from the garage and brought them back inside. She placed them midway on each side of the lock. Using all her strength, she pulled until the lock snapped. She had learned this trick from YouTube when she needed to rescue her clothing from the gym locker she had used once and then forgotten the combination months later when her membership ran out.

There were several items inside the small box. One was a half-heart necklace with part of a butterfly wing etched on it, along with the words "Lil Sis."

"Anna," Naomi whispered.

There was also a charm bracelet with a pink gemstone-clad ballerina that she recognized from the picture of Kevin's babysitter. Then Naomi saw something that made her stomach drop.

Her grandmother's strawberry pin cushion.

# CHAPTER ELEVEN



**THERE WAS A** shadow at Naomi's door. This time, she knew the shadow was not Brad as he was unconscious beside her.

This was not her imagination. Someone was trying to get in.

"Why aren't you here to help me?" she whispered to her husband. "I need you."

Naomi placed the lit flashlight on the floor and lowered herself onto her stomach. Her ankle still tender, she crawled into the dark bedroom and felt her way into her closet where she retrieved the bullets she had returned to the shoe box.

With shaking hands, she reloaded the chamber. She felt the pink duct tape and the inscription, *FOR HALEY,* and realized that this gun had helped more than a few people. And now it was meant to help her.

She sat with her back against the bed, muzzle pointed at the bedroom door. She cursed herself for not locking the front door behind her when she had pulled Brad inside, remembering that criminals took advantage of scavenging after storms. Though this was a bit early for them to know which houses were abandoned and left to pilfer.

She heard the front door creak open. This was followed by an audible gasp. The person breaking into the house must have seen Brad. The gasp sounded high and feminine and this made Naomi feel less afraid.

"I have a gun," Naomi called.

"Please don't shoot. I'm… I'm scared," a small voice answered.

Naomi pulled herself to her bedroom door and peeked out. A young girl stood in her living room, looking at Brad and at the contents of the container spilled alongside him. Naomi estimated the girl to be about thirteen years old. She was drenched from the storm and shivering.

"Who are you? How did you get here?" Naomi asked, lowering the gun, but keeping her hand on it, in case the girl was not alone.

The girl started to cry. "I ran. I ran here. I saw your flashlight through the window."

"Did your house flood or something?"

The girl shook her head, adding the movement to her already shaking body. "No. I had to leave; they're after me."

The girl seemed to notice the cover of the book which had fallen closed. "Are you?" She pointed at the ibis on the cover. "Oh my god, you're with them!"

The girl turned back toward the door, but Naomi called after her. "I'm not, I'm not with anyone. I found that book and am trying to figure it out." She softened her voice. "You're safe here."

This stopped the girl in her tracks. She turned slowly, pointing at Brad. "What about him?"

"Does he look dangerous?"

The girl appeared to consider this.

"I really don't know what's happening," Naomi continued, finding that her anxiety lessened as she attempted to calm the girl. "I'm trying to piece some confusing stuff together myself, but I promise, I won't hurt you." She gestured to the bedroom. "Come in here with me, we can hide in here. Whoever *they* are, they won't look for you in here."

The girl approached Naomi timidly. It was obvious that she did not entirely trust the situation but had run out of options.

ೞාౚ

**INSIDE THE DARK** room, Naomi asked softly, "What's your name?"

"Faith."

"Kind of ironic," Naomi muttered. "I'm Naomi."

"The men weren't far behind me," Faith explained. "What if they saw me come in here?"

"It's so dark—" Naomi started before remembering the unlocked front door. She cursed the Seres for not keeping her focused as promised. "Listen, I have to go lock that door you came in from. I promise I'll be right back."

"Please, no." Panic took over the girl's face and Naomi didn't blame her; she felt the same panic and was struggling to appear calm. She thought about Todd mentioning the old timers and wondered if her stoic father had felt fear beneath his controlled appearance.

"Here." Naomi took the Andy the Ant keychain from her pocket and handed it to the girl. "Hang on to this and squeeze it hard."

"What is this?" Faith asked. "It's not a weapon."

"No. It's a… it's a key chain with Andy the Ant on it. I know it's stupid to give it to you when you are too old for Andy and also in a room too dark to see him."

Naomi could almost hear the girl's smile when she replied, "I can see him, only he's not an ant. Ants don't survive hurricanes. He's a dolphin with a happy face and bright eyes."

Now it was Naomi's turn to smile. She decided to adopt Faith's strategy of imagining something formidable but found that her brain was stuck on Andy the Ant.

*Ants are ugly, but they're strong,* she reminded herself. *And they are industrious. What did my parents have against that park anyway?*

Naomi slipped the gun into her waistband before pulling herself to her feet, testing her ankle, then limping to the living room. What she saw in the dwindling light of the discarded flashlight caused her heart to catch in her throat.

The door was open and Brad was gone.

"My God—" she was interrupted by a man's voice coming from a darkened corner behind her.

"After I was so neighborly and gave you those boots, you went ahead and took something of mine."

She turned just in time to see Todd behind her, one of the wrenches she had used on the lock in his raised hand.

Pain like a lightning bolt shot through her. Then, the room went completely black.

# CHAPTER TWELVE

**THERE WERE NO** more sirens, no more messages. Naomi's world was soundless.

Her head was pounding. She opened her eyes a crack, but the pain was blinding. Though her sight was blurry, she could see she was no longer in her home. She was lying on a bed of straw like a bird in a nest. She wanted to touch her head, to feel if it was bleeding, but her hands were bound.

The revolver had slipped into her underwear, where it jabbed her hip. An uncomfortable feeling, but it had prevented the weapon from being discovered.

Sound re-entered her world first, followed by clearer sight. She heard chanting, toneless words that reminded her of the way her father had talked to the fire during Hurricane Quincy. Men's voices were saying unrecognizable words, followed by, "We give our hearts. Gladly, we give our hearts."

Naomi recognized the room she was in as belonging to the old firehouse. The large garage door to the front and the back door were open, allowing for a crosswind from Iago to fan the fire that had been built in the center of the room. There were gas tanks stockpiled mere feet from the fire; an absurd sight in a building that promoted fire safety.

Naomi counted seven men in her presence: Kevin, Todd, Brad, and four others. None of them looked at her; they must have believed she was still unconscious. She identified one of the men as being the deli clerk who regularly added an extra slice onto her cold cuts. Another man was tall, but she did not recognize him. The other two were police officers; she could not remember their names, but their fathers had been officers, as well.

Six of the men were chanting into the fire, circling the flames. Brad was unable to move. He had been tied to a pole in the center of the room, wrapped in the ibis tarp.

The chanting stopped and the men took a few deep breaths before stepping back from the fire. Naomi could see that the officers had their guns in their holsters. Todd and the deli clerk held machetes.

"Do we untie him?" one of the officers asked, pointing to Brad.

"Can't," Todd replied. "Thought we could trust him, being seventh generation. But I saw him. I've been watching him, both him and his wife. He was acting suspicious, like he might bolt. I even went to talk to him after he knocked her out with the benzos we gave him." Todd spat into the fire angrily. "He wimped out and didn't give her enough. I had to finish the job with a wrench, of all things."

"Bastard," the deli clerk sneered.

"And worse, I saw him on his roof. He was taking it down. He was trying to change things, the order of things."

It dawned on Naomi they were talking about the tarp. The one that looked like the tarp her father had given her grandmother, the one Brad was putting on their own home.

Todd pointed his machete at Brad. "We should have known when he refused to participate during Yara. What kind of seventh son shirks his responsibilities?" His face grew even angrier. "I gave. I had to give. It was his turn."

One of the cops motioned to Kevin. "And this one didn't help then, either. Sons of bitches have no respect for tradition, for the way things work. No wonder we've had so many storms; we're surrounded by non-believers."

"Then she's not really a sacrifice," the tall man said, and Naomi knew he was talking about her. "She wasn't given from the heart."

Deli clerk grunted. "Doesn't matter, we got three. The elders said as long as it was three, it would stop the storms."

A police officer agreed, "The Tylers gave, you gave." His finger moved from the deli clerk toward Naomi. "And for that one… it's still a good offering. Cold feet don't count. Her old man almost chickened out, too, back in the day. But Earl's love for his community outweighed that for his own mother."

Todd chimed in. "Then the bastard chickened out again, sending *her* away. She was in school for all those years. If there had been a storm—"

"Families only have to give one. Earl did his duty."

Todd nodded. "Earl did, but Brad didn't." Before anyone could stop him, he swung his machete, slicing open Brad's throat. Naomi stifled a cry, not wanting the men to know she was alert.

"There has to be seven of us," the deli clerk cried out. "What are you doing?"

"It's the sacrifices, more than us," Todd bellowed. "The sacrifices. You know, like *my wife?* None of you had any problem with getting rid of her. And this prick was fine with Claire being offered. Where did his faith go when it was his turn? Where is your faith now?"

Naomi's stomach dropped at the word *faith*. She slowly turned her head to take in the rest of the room. To her left sat Faith, with her hands bound. There was also a heavily pregnant woman lying prone who was either unconscious or dead.

"We have to hurry," the tall man urged. "We can still offer the sacrifices." He moved to Faith, pulled a barrette from her hair and dropped it into the open container that had made its way from Naomi's house to the fire station. He then crouched over the pregnant woman and wrestled with her wedding band to free it from her finger. The deli clerk turned away, hiding his face with his arm. Naomi assumed the woman was his "sacrifice."

The tall man stood over Naomi. She squeezed her eyes shut but could feel him looking her over. *Please don't let him find the gun,* she thought. She felt him crouch beside her and knew he was looking for a trophy to take from her. She wore no jewelry, no watch. He reached into her pants pocket, the hip opposite the gun, perhaps seeking a cell phone or key and came up with the baggie of Seres.

"What the hell is this?" he asked the other men.

"It's fine," Todd responded. "We just need a memento."

Naomi heard the sharp cracks of three tarps being unfurled and laid on the ground. When she peered between her half-open lids, she saw that each had the ibis insignia. The officers pulled the pregnant woman onto one. An officer said a few words in a language unfamiliar to Naomi while the other grasped a long weapon that looked like a curved ice pick, like the long, sharp beak of an ibis. The man raised the weapon and then drove it into the pregnant woman's heart.

Naomi bit down on her tongue to stifle a scream.

"She needs to be in the water," the deli clerk said, his voice catching as he swallowed tiny sobs. The officers rolled the tarp around the woman's body and began to carry her outside.

"Then, we say she disappeared. After taking a nap, right? That's what our elders claimed with the preggos," one of the officers said.

"Show some respect," the other spat back before they disappeared through the door.

Naomi inched closer to the fire. She determined to be resilient. Despite knowing that her father was not the hero she imagined, she would follow his advice. She would free herself of the ropes and then attack, using the gun. She might not be able to take all of them, but she would not surrender without a fight.

"With the elders, the sacrifices went willingly," Todd mused. "Drugs weren't necessary."

"It's kinder this way," the tall man said. He pulled some needles from his pocket. "We knock out the kid and do…" He seemed to struggle to find the words. "The sacrifice with her."

Naomi remembered Kevin's babysitter and how he had said she was found in *pieces*. She had to free herself and help Faith.

"Then, for the old lady, it's the gentlest of deaths. Looks just like a heart attack… *if* they find her."

Naomi could not help but think of her father and grandmother. Heart attacks did not run in her family, *crazy did*. Crazy existed in all the old families of the island. She inched closer to the flames, hoping to burn her ropes without setting herself on fire.

A shadow darkened the space around her and she realized that Kevin was right beside her.

She looked up, wanting him to have to face her before using whatever weapon he had on her. To her surprise, he brought his finger to his lips, signaling her to be quiet.

Todd, the deli clerk, and the tall man were focused on making preparations for Faith. Kevin pulled a carved steel folding knife from his pocket and sliced through Naomi's ropes. He whispered to her as he worked: "It was a relief, Sharon's death. She was having a girl. That meant I would have to spend every storm worrying that I would be asked… to give one of them, that one of them might fit and it would be on me. I couldn't live with that. And then, I didn't have to."

Naomi realized that this was a confession. She also realized that it drew attention to them.

"You say something?" Todd approached, anger in his eyes. "That bitch is awake? What did you say to her?"

"Only that I am ending this." Kevin shifted swiftly from his crouch to a pounce. He pushed his knife into Todd's abdomen, dragging it as the man sputtered, slashing and tearing until Todd's intestines peered through the wound.

"What the fuck?" The tall man's eyes were wide.

Naomi reached into her pants for the revolver just as the deli clerk raced at Kevin with his machete raised. She lined the deli clerk up in her site, cocked the hammer, and pulled the trigger. He fell back, hitting the floor with a loud thud, and Naomi was shocked that her aim was true since he had had been moving and she had been trembling with fear.

She swung on the tall man, bringing him to the floor with two shots. She had never even harmed a human before, with the exception of hitting Veronica. Now she had murdered two people. This was clearly self-defense, but that reassurance did little to staunch the bile that was rising in her throat.

Kevin ran to Faith, cutting her ropes. "They have to have heard the shots; they'll be back here in seconds."

"Run," Naomi ordered Faith as she pulled herself up onto her wobbly ankle. Her head rang from the sounds of the gun and from the large lump that stuck out from her forehead.

"No," the girl said, grabbing Todd's machete from the floor. Naomi saw that Brad's blood was still fresh on the blade. Faith slipped behind the back door, just in time for the officers to reappear. They both had their guns drawn and Naomi knew she wasn't fast enough to target them both.

Kevin charged the officer to the left, who fired, allowing Naomi to focus on the other officer, aiming for his throat as she feared he might be wearing a

Kevlar vest beneath his shirt. The bullet hit his face instead, and he fell back, convulsing.

Naomi turned to face the first officer, but his gun was already trained on her.

"Drop it," he ordered.

"You're not in charge here," Naomi growled, fueled by the rage she had worked so hard to temper during the past year.

"You want to play games, lady?" The officer laughed. "This'll be fun." He lowered the gun and shot at her hand. She dropped the revolver, which skidded toward the fire.

Her hand felt as if she had grabbed live electrical wires. Kevin lay bleeding out on the floor beside her as the officer kicked her gun into the fire. She saw the pink tape go up in flames.

"You've got nothing," the officer said. "It's been a long time since your daddy was here to help you, and now your husband… no rescue squad for you, no one to get you off this island and to safety." The officer lowered the gun, aiming at her knee.

Before he could shoot again, Faith leapt from behind the door, swiping the machete across the officer's lower back, creating a gash that heralded her strength despite her small stature. He stumbled forward, falling onto his stomach.

Naomi limped to the fire, seeing the gun with its smoldering handle and knowing she had no choice but to grab it. She pulled her good arm out of her hoodie and used it to protect her hand as she knocked the revolver free of the flames. The pink tape had nearly burned off, leaving blackened residue, yet the FOR HALEY etching was still visible. The gun had gone through a lot to get to her and she still had a need for it.

Wrapping the hoodie sleeve around the handle, she moved to the stabbed officer who was breathing shallowly. She balanced the gun in her non-dominant, but unwounded hand.

"This act of kindness is more about the woman I am than what you deserve," Naomi said before emptying a bullet into the back of his head. With a body count of four, she no longer had the luxury of labelling herself "non-violent." Her husband was gone and she was a killer. Hurricane Iago had smashed through more than their car and lanai; it had decimated her reality.

She grabbed Faith's hand and began to pull her from the station. "We have to go. We have to get back to my house or to somewhere safe and wait for…"

She was about to say *wait for help* but she now feared that any emergency personnel she contacted would be involved with this dastardly ceremony. She also feared being jailed for her participation in the deaths of these men. "We just have to go."

"Wait." Faith ran to the container and retrieved her barrette. She also grabbed the ballerina charm and "Anna" necklace.

She and Faith pushed their way through waist-high water in the direction of Naomi's house. She had more bullets at home and they could lock the doors and wait for sunrise. She would tend to her wounds and then they would get on the first ferry that was running and leave the island for good.

Naomi no longer feared the alligators and other hidden obstacles lurking beneath the dark water. She only wanted this night to end. She had to battle her ankle and throbbing hand and became exhausted quickly. She tried to quiet her panting, not wanting to alarm Faith.

Despite her young age, Faith was stronger than Naomi and she was uninjured. The girl threaded her arm across Naomi's back and carefully placed Naomi's arm with the injured hand over her shoulders. She moved slowly so that Naomi did not have to struggle and managed to drag her across the swampy terrain.

When they were finally in the area behind Naomi's house, Naomi heard a woman chanting. She remembered the book and the men at the station and tried to match the odd words. These phrases were decidedly different.

"Wait," Naomi said, but Faith continued to pull Naomi toward the beam of a flashlight. As they grew close, it became clear that it was Veronica holding the light.

"You poor thing," Veronica said, approaching to touch the bump on Naomi's head. "Did a star break free and fall on you?"

"My dad used to say that," Naomi mumbled.

Veronica nodded. "It's an island thing."

Those words moved Naomi to tears. She no longer cared if she appeared resilient. "Veronica, I can't fight you right now. I have nothing left."

"I don't want to fight you either." Veronica pulled Naomi close to her, embracing her. Naomi was shocked but the hug was just what she needed.

When Naomi's tears subsided, Veronica pulled away, asking, "Can I show you another island thing?"

When Naomi didn't answer, but didn't refuse, Veronica leaned down and sank her hands deep into the water. "The mud. It has healing properties. Let's put this on your head and that bloody hand of yours." An odd smile crept across the woman's face. "I'll still help you despite the fact that you have been ruining my life for my entire life."

"Me?"

"You attacked me."

"Once! And it was more like a slap than an actual hit."

"You knocked my tooth loose." From the corner of her eye, Naomi saw Faith stifle a giggle.

Feeling she had nothing to lose, Naomi allowed Veronica to apply the mud, admitting that it did help with the pain.

"Our grandmothers used the mud, our great-grandmothers, too. If you hadn't been so busy trying to run off this island all the time, you might have picked up tricks like this." Veronica produced a broader smile so that Naomi was able to see the gap in the back of her mouth that proved the missing tooth. "And if you hadn't been so busy fighting with me, I might have taught you something."

"I wish I had stayed off the island," Naomi admitted.

"I wish you had, too. I tried to warn you that you were in danger."

Naomi was stunned. "This island stuff. You knew about all of it. Even what happened tonight? You knew about… about the—"

"Sacrifices. I had no confirmation until now. It was an island legend but the disappearances pointed to it being true."

Veronica placed a hand on Faith's shoulder, as if bracing the girl for what she was about to say. "Long ago, when the island was completely isolated from the mainland, the natives would offer sacrifices to appease the storm gods. But that was so long ago. No one messed with that kind of thing for centuries. It wasn't until Hurricane Quincy that… people started it again."

"The rescue mission," Naomi breathed.

Veronica nodded. "They picked up where the elders left off. The rumor is that the… the ritual put the responsibility on the seventh-generation sons. That's how they interpreted it, at least."

Naomi groaned, "Brad."

"Yeah. I tried to warn you about him. He could be… he was more than intimidating, he was scary."

This surprised Naomi, as she had never seen her husband in that light. "You thought so?"

Veronica snorted. "Anyone else had hit me like that and I would have pressed charges. Not against *his* wife."

Naomi wove this information together. "Kevin… Kevin was part of it but he… he didn't want to be. He saved me back there."

"He was always a good friend to you."

"He was. I guess I didn't realize—" Naomi shook her head, trying to clear her thoughts. "I didn't realize that he had been helping me all along. And you had tried, too." She took a deep breath and looked at Faith before asking, "What happens now?"

Veronica smiled again, a haunting smile. "Don't worry about the fire station. Me and the girls will take care of that." She brushed her hands together as if the solution were that simple. "The gators can have them. There are always fatalities with every storm."

"More than three this time," Naomi mused sadly.

Veronica squeezed Naomi's shoulder. "Get yourself and this young one to someplace safe. We will take care of the rest. It's—"

"An island thing." Naomi finished for her.

# CHAPTER THIRTEEN

*Can you afford to not feel your best?*


**NAOMI READ THE** most recent notification on her social media before deleting all accounts.

She and Faith were packed and ready to board the ferry. It had been a week since Iago and they had spent the days discarding items from Naomi's past.

Naomi had wiped the gun clean of prints, remembering Aida's message and thinking about the "war wounds" the revolver carried. She had attached the ballerina charm on the still-functioning holder on the grip. Its gemstones shone brightly and she knew that the new recipient would recognize them.

She then tucked the gun into the bottom of one of the boxes of Seres. She was "donating" the gummies, leaving them on Veronica's door with a note of thanks.

Naomi was numb to most things now, no longer dependent on the Seres to quell her emotions. She didn't know if Veronica would put the hormone replacement to use, but she hoped the woman accepted the protection the gun offered; as a lifelong islander, she would need it.

The ferry reversed out of port, sounding its horn. Naomi and Faith stood on the deck, watching the island shrink into the distance. It was early morning; Naomi could clearly see the sun, but she could not feel it.

She could not feel anything at all.

# ACKNOWLEDGEMENTS

**Heather Daughrity:** I am always thankful when Heather Daughrity signs on to edit one of my novels… this time around, it is a full project. I always know I'm going to get feedback that will enhance my story. She always gives small lessons on certain grammatical errors I've made, which helps it all make sense. She's complimentary of areas she likes and parts she thinks are humorous in the story. It always lets me know I am on the right track with what I've written for my story. I feel that if my editor enjoys it, then I have something good on my hands. And when part of my story is off, she offers perfect suggestions that always align it and get it back on course. I appreciate her being concise and always thorough in what my story needs. I am forever grateful to Heather for how she helps make my stories better than they were before she's read them. I'm sure the other authors will echo my sentiments.

**Joshua Loyd Fox:** Eternally grateful for Joshua Lloyd Fox stepping in to help me with the formatting of *Chambered* to get it on its feet. This collection of stories is not even a Watertower Hill Publication (which he and Heather Daughrity own and operate). I am a writer, and words cannot express the respect and appreciation I have for Joshua, taking his free time to teach me how to format a novel correctly. Just know that I see and recognize what you do on a daily basis, not just for me, but for so many others. Everyone, please take a moment to look through and support Joshua and Heather (and the other authors they represent at Watertower Hill Publishing. www.watertowerhillpublishing.com.

**Cathy Helms:** A special thank you to Cathy Helms who is so encouraging to me with book cover design and always helpful and available when I have a question. I appreciate you, your time, and all the advice you've given me.

**Rikard Rodan:** I know I say it all the time, but words simply cannot express my appreciation for you and your Nucly site. I have learned practically everything I know in Photoshop from you and your online school. Thank you a million times over for sharing all the Photoshop magic with me. I was able to make the cover and the title inserts for each of these stories because of it. Thank you for helping me make my mark on the book cover industry.

**Kevin Fennington:** Thank you for the conversations and lessons on revolvers and gunplay, and also, for the internet link on writing with weapons, specifically for revolvers. That helped out a whole hell of a lot for us writers in this project.

**Silas James Rowland:** Thank you, brother, for taking my author picture and to Sebal Studio (Greenville, SC) for the location of the photo shoot.

**Kyle Toucher:** Thank you for your suggestions and use of the secondary tagline in this book. They were only mentioned in passing, but they worked perfectly for our collection, so thank you for the use of those.

**Jeff Vandyke:** Much appreciation to you for all the encouragement and for putting up with me talking about my writing so much.

**Shane Willimon:** Thank you for your help in giving Anna Cheong her correct nationality and last name. You are always a huge help when it comes to Asian history.

One last shout-out to all the individuals who helped me with the formatting of *Chambered*. Some of you have YouTube videos that I studied to get this collection looking beautiful. I'm listing all of you out here in alphabetical order: Lee Bagwell, Abbie Emmons, Patrick Delaney, Joshua Loyd Fox, Laurie Griffith Jones, T.A. Hernandez, Kristin McTiernan, A.J. Pruitt, Rachel Terry, and Jeff Vandyke.

# ABOUT THE AUTHORS

**Wofford Lee Jones** is a horror/thriller writer who loves coffee, a good book, and a great story. His love for horror grew from watching movies in the late seventies/early eighties. However, it was only in his twenties that he started reading horror.

He enjoys art, drawing/painting, watching live theatre and movies, traveling, reading, book cover design and book formatting, and supporting his fellow writers.

Nightly and on the weekends, he can be found with a hot cup of coffee, studiously banging out that next chilling tale. He always strives to keep it dark, disturbing, and a little bit creepy. Welcome to his darkness.

He lives in Greenville, South Carolina, with his wife Laurie. He is working on his fifth and sixth solo books, a collection of stories titled *Fatal Potions,* and a psychological thriller novel, *Becoming Ally Winter.* He is also teaming up with multi-genre author D.A. Schneider, writing a horror vacation-survival novel, *Horror on Vacation,* as well as adding offerings to a Halloween novella anthology, *All Hallows Feast,* hopefully due out this October 2026. Stay tuned; there is much more darkness coming down the pike.

Consider signing up for his monthly newsletter. It comes out on the third of every month, and a free flash fiction story comes out on the eighteenth of each month (a gift for his subscribers). For more information about the author, please see www.woffordleejones.com.

**D.A. Schneider** is an author of horror and mystery who lives in Indianapolis, Indiana.

After trying for some time to break into the comic book industry with his artwork, D.A. decided to focus on writing instead. A former NFL and entertainment columnist, D.A.'s most recent books include the cozy murder mystery *Death of a Scholar* (Holly Reynolds Mysteries Book 1), a modern-day Agatha Christie-esque murder mystery, *Opulence & Misery*, and the horror/crime novel *Salvation*.

D.A. signed with KGHH Publishing in May 2017, Editingle Indie House in 2022, and Distinguished Skeleton Press in 2025. He co-founded Poe Boy Publishing in 2020.

**N.J. Gallegos** is an Emergency Medicine Physician by day, horror author by night. She lives with her wife and their two cats, Cat Bane and Wally, is a member of the HWA, and is a co-host on the *Scream Kings Podcast*.

She has two novels: *The Broken Heart*, following a disgruntled housewife who receives a heart transplant from a serial killer with bloody results, and *The Fatal Mind*, a *Frankenstein*-meets-*Black-Mirror* medical horror thriller.

Other works include novellas *Just Desserts*, *Only You Can Prevent Forest Fires*, and *It's Me, Hi, I'm the Zombie, It's Me.*

She has stories in *Winding Road Stories Horror Anthology: All Roads Lead to Hell, Hellbound Books' Anthology of Splatterpunk, Jane Nightshade's Serial Encounters, Gore 2* and *Gore 3: A Halloween Anthology, Dark Mirrors: An Anthology of Horror, Bashing Skulls: A Charity Anthology of Queer Horror, Bad Moon on the Rise: An Anthology of Unsettling Horror*, multiple works with Alien Buddha Press, and drabbles in *Drabbledark II: An Anthology of Dark Drabbles, Medusa Tales Magazine*, and *Sirens Call Publications E-zine.*

In 2022, she won first place in Alien Buddha Press' Horror Showdown. Her novella, *Just Desserts*, won an American Legacy Book Award in the Psychological Horror category.

Follow her on Twitter @DrSpooky_ER,
Bluesky @drspookyER.bksy.social, and visit her website www.njgallegos.com.

**Marie Selene Matter** has human teeth and human fingernails, just like you. She was born, raised, and currently resides in Centralia, Pennsylvania. She lives with two dogs, which is strange because they were both cockatiels before she went into the Cave. This year, she awoke from a *The Hangover* (2009)-esque blackout holding a bachelor's degree in cryptozoology with her name on it. She had also aged nearly a decade, which was inconvenient.

Marie has been writing fiction since she learned how to write, with her first ever work being a cat-and-mouse thriller-comedy comic about an abominable snowman hunting down the child who accidentally made it.

Despite her long history of writing for fun, "Taken for a Ride" is the first thing she's ever published. She already has like, four other ideas she's really excited about, though. And they're all really fucking weird. Enjoy. Or don't, she's not your mom.

To justify his online search history, **Evan Bond** calls himself a thriller/suspense author. He enjoys combining his love of the outdoors with his obsession with all things horror. When he's not writing, he can usually be found hiking or camping and calling it "research" for his next novel.

Evan Bond lives in the Tampa area of the Sunshine State of Florida with his wife, Melissa and their two crazy boys, as well as the Dog of Mischief, Loki, and Lydia, the strange and unusual kitty.

If you're looking for more high-octane thrills like his story "Excaliber," then consider checking out his first Amazon best-selling book, *Echoes of the Past*, or the frightfully entertaining collection of horror stories, *Charred Remains*. You can find these titles, among others, on Amazon or on his website below.

www.EvanBondAuthor.com

Follow on Social Media@EvanBondAuthor on Instagram, Threads, and Facebook.

Please also consider joining his Patreon page to support the eldritch horror that is his mind!

www.Patreon.com/EvanBond

**Elaine Pascale**, AKA "The Godmother of Horror," is the author of *The Blood Lights; If Nothing Else, Eve, We've Enjoyed the Fruit; The Kitchen Witches; The Language of Crows;* and *The Solstice.* She has also had stories published in over two dozen magazines and anthologies. She is the editor of *Darkness Most Fowl* and the co-editor of *Dancing in the Shadows: A Tribute to Anne Rice.* She is an active member of the HWA and also a voice-over actress. Elaine enjoys chocolate, a robust full moon, reading spam emails, and paddleboarding (when no hurricanes are on the horizon).

Find out more here:
Website: elainepascale.com
Amazon Author Page: https://www.amazon.com/author/elainepascale
Facebook: elaine.pascale
Instagram: @doclaney
TikTok @elainepascale
YouTube: https://www.youtube.com/@elainepascale/videos
Newsletter: https://elainepascale.substack.com/

Dear Readers,

Thank you for taking the time to read our stories; it is greatly appreciated. If you enjoyed it, please consider leaving a quick review on Amazon, Goodreads, Instagram, Facebook, or any other social media platforms you use. Reviews and ratings are so important; they give a book more visibility, which means more people will be able to find it, read it, and enjoy it as you did. If you could do that for us, you have our deepest thanks.

Sincerely,

The writers of *Chambered*